I0672476

WILL WEISSER

ÆTHERIA'S DÆMON

This is a work of fiction. All of the characters, organizations, and events portrayed in this novel are either products of the author's imagination or are used fictitiously.

AETHERIA'S DAEMON

Published by The Metanautics Department

metanautics.net

ISBN: 978-0-9895749-2-1

Second Edition: October 2017

For Margaret

AETHERIA

WINDWARD CONTINENT

SERISTIM

VALLAM
×

×MARITEN

ALTONIM

×SOUKIM

ALTANIA×

BRESSIM
×

SAENTIS SEA

KALSTEN

200 MI.

WIND DIR.

LEEWARD CONTINENT

DESPERNZI

SAENTIS SEA

CAELINDRA

AZORASTAS×

AZORKAS

SOFIDRA

APERANDI MTNS.

CAELRIDOR

MEVENTI

KAELINTA

×VENTITURAS

PORLAN

PEMARLTA

×
PORLANIM

×SIDEL

SCHA

×
ORINDOR

I died long ago.

But mourn not
for though I faded
I was not gone.

The time has come
for the tale of my rebirth.

The tale ends with a dream fulfilled
setting the sky forever aglow.

How it begins?
Open your mind to me
and I'll show you.

1

Meli closed her eyes to concentrate, ignoring the buzzing crowd. She didn't need sight to sense the aether all around. Before her stood a pair of columns. She reached out with her mind to the space between them, linking herself and the aether there as one. Once the link was made, the aether would respond to her will. She willed it to become solid, and the aether coalesced. In moments a new object appeared where before there had been none, to remain real as long as she held it in her thoughts.

She began by depositing a frame along the ground, then built upward. In the span of a few breaths a trellis took shape, its lattice woven in intricate patterns, stretching far overhead to a platform supported by the columns. When the trellis was done, Meli paused, struggling to maintain a convocation so large and so new.

She had finished the easy part.

The crowd behind her quieted in anticipation. Meli knelt, examining a pile of yellow-brown dust she had gathered beforehand. The vegetist convocation would require shifting her focus from the immense to the miniscule. It began with a seed, a tiny loop of the aether feeding back on itself. She had to coax that first iota into commanding itself, had to give it self-awareness, then build its strength so it could be self-sustaining. She worked quietly for some moments, adding minute layers over the core, until she was left with a bug-sized lump sitting atop the dust pile. With one finger she pressed it down into the center of the pile, then stood back to watch.

The first vine emerged. The seedling found the trellis, encircled it, then sent off more shoots as it climbed. Meli had no control now. The plant would convoke whatever form it wished for itself, though she had buried some suggestions within the seed's structure. She bit her lip as the vines finished creeping and began to thicken. Close, now. She heard the bark crack and spun to face the crowd, executing a bow with held breath just as the flowers burst forth. A gasp of amazement came, followed by cheers. Meli smiled and nodded before turning back to admire the explosion of violet and gold blossoms for herself.

The magistrates and guests applauded and surrounded her, offering congratulations. Meli tried to thank each of them in turn, but the weight of the trellis convocation still tugged at her consciousness.

"If you don't mind," she said. "Please, stand back."

She relaxed her focus. The trellis lost its color and cracks formed across its surface. Pieces of it fell as clumps of dust through the now free-hanging vines. The rest blew away in a gust of wind, and the guests scurried to avoid the dust cloud's path.

Meli checked to be sure the vines were supporting themselves, then, sheepish from the faux pas of dirtying the others, headed off to the food tables beside the open-aer dance floor.

"The flowers are wonderful, Meli." Celestra drew up in her magistrate's robe, hair pulled back, smooth face caked with pale-blue powder. "Such a precocious talent. You're less than half a century, aren't you?"

Meli took a small bow of thanks. "Tomorrow is my thirtieth appearance-day."

"Tomorrow! Pardon me for not remembering." Celestra held out her hand and took a moment to convoke a cup in it, then bent and scooped ambrosia from a nearby pool. She was past two-hundred, but time had not diminished her thirst for the intoxicating beverage. "Vegetism is a difficult art. It's so nice to see a young one like you attempt it."

"I've always been drawn to plants." Meli gave a small sigh. "The way they grow and change. Not like us."

"Hmm?"

"I mean how our bodies always remain the same as when we first appear. It's just a bit…plain."

"I see." Celestra smiled and waved to someone across the dance floor. "Excuse me, so many guests. Please, enjoy yourself!"

"Yes," Meli said to Celestra's back as she departed.

Enjoy herself. That was why she had come, to be sure. Except that something had changed. Or rather, she was just noticing the change now. Even at its size, the trellis convocation shouldn't have been so difficult to maintain. But a strange sensation had settled in the back of her mind, and it had been interfering with her concentration.

But by then new arrivals were approaching, and Meli had no choice but to greet them. Crowds soon filled the party installation, gathering upon the square white platforms and the crisscrossing wireframe stairways. Mekkanisms within the supporting columns pumped ambrosia to the upper tiers, from which it cascaded down into the pools below, turning the park ground into a maze of shimmering walls. The vine Meli had planted continued to grow, and by the time the Magistrate's Ball reached its zenith, flowers encircled most of the platforms and stairways, lending the air a perfumed smell. While Meli strolled and mingled, drummers pounded an ever-quickening beat, and guests convoked long hammocks to lie inside or jump down from, landing in pools surrounded by the discarded clothes of bathing couples and threesomes and foursomes.

A strong arm gripped Meli's waist. Felarian pulled and whisked her about the dance floor, his square face holding her gaze.

"You look divine," he whispered after a few whirling strides. His tongue drew a familiar line from her ear down her neck. "Any plans for your appearance-day?"

"Just a small gathering." The words came out a half-shudder. "A few close friends."

"What about the night before?"

Meli closed her eyes and smiled, then shook her head. "I'm tired. From convoking the flowers. You understand." A good excuse, though not the truth.

He grunted acceptance, and soon their dance ended and Meli found another partner. She repeated the motions again and again as the daylight faded, turning down a number of similar advances.

The same dances, the same words, the same party, year after year after year.

The sky turned nearly black, and though the more adventuresome guests would continue on in darkness, Meli made to leave. The strange feeling in her head had intensified. On the way out, she stopped at the central platform where she had convoked the trellis, found a healthy flower the size of two fists, and gently pulled its stalk free. Tucking it into her gown to shield it from the wind, she headed home through Sofidra's winding, dust-strewn streets.

At home she made a quick check of her plants, ensuring none of the pots she had convoked recently had crumbled from her being across town. She found an empty one, placed the flower inside, then filled the bottom with dust from the window ledge. The Magistrates would cut down the vines when they let the party installation crumble in the morning, but Meli would not let such a beautiful life go to waste. Satisfied, she disrobed and dropped into a chair to rest.

Her ease was short-lived. Alone in her dark house, the odd sensation she had felt earlier had free rein with her thoughts. It had grown into a pressure behind her eyes, fuzzy, as if someone had convoked a soft cloth between her mind and her senses. An undercurrent of fear came with it, not of something particular, but a pure sort of dread, staining the edges of her consciousness.

The pressure expanded, and the room changed. Gray mist seeped around her, slipping over smooth walls. Meli looked down at her hands and saw folds of white, and in between—

A nibble on her left index finger roused her, and the apparition vanished. Meli pulled her hand back, frightening the small creature on her armrest. A shrole, one of the commune of furry animals which had taken up residence in her rafters.

"I'm sorry." She clicked her tongue and beckoned it closer. The tiny thing let her rub its chin, shutting its eyes tight, then shook playfully and skittered away.

She looked about the room again, assuring herself she was still in her home. A strange dream; it had come on suddenly, as if the feeling in her head had forced her mind into a deep slumber. Even now she could feel it growing again, making her drowsy.

Sleep.

She wasn't sure whether the thought was her own, but she had to obey. She stumbled to the far side of the room and fell into bed, her head swirling.

Sleep rolled over her like fog covering the sea.

When awareness struck next, she stood in a whirlpool of gray. Her surroundings whirled, indistinct—the bundle before her drew all her focus.

In her arms she held a person, impossibly small. Not a normally proportioned human, though—the head was chubby and round, limbs curled up adorably like an oblong ball. A perfect circle of face lay within white cloth, under a scalp covered in thin, delicate hairs. She somehow knew the person was male, just as she knew that he was hers, that he had come from her body in some fashion she didn't understand.

But none of that mattered; they were together now, she and that perfect, beautiful human being, and she would never let him go. She stood and drank in his image for what could have been a moment or a hundred years of impossible dream-time, marveling, watching his long-lashed eyes blink and his lips curl into a tiny smile.

The dream shifted, grew hazy. She was waking up. Terror gripped her as she realized what she was losing. She fought, but the vision slipped from her mind like silk through fingers. Everything faded, and she was back in her dark bedroom, blinking away her half-dream haze.

She sat up, looked at her empty hands, and screamed.

How the rest of the night passed Meli could not have said, but the dawn found her back in her chair, dust from crumbled tears staining her cheeks, gripping her sheets with one hand, mumbling softly.

That loss—deep, so deep and painful. But what had she lost? What had she seen? How did such a simple image have the power to tear so wide a hole in her heart?

She jumped at the sound of her front door opening.

"Meli?" A familiar voice called. More joined in a chorus, "Happy appearance-day!"

Panic. No, she couldn't see them, couldn't speak to anyone right now. She felt in the aether for the doorway to her bedroom and convoked a solid wall over it, sealing herself in.

A moment later a knock came. "Meli? Are you in there?" Ghil's voice. Meli imagined the woman, her bubbly face crowned by curls set high, standing outside her door bearing food and drink. She cringed and added more material to the wall.

"Meli?" Palai this time, her best friend for most of her living memory. "What are you doing? Is something wrong? Can I help?" Her friends knocked more, shouted, and finally held an extended whispered conversation before they left. Meli waited a while longer before letting the barrier crumble into a sizable heap of rubble-shaped dust. She felt confused and empty, twitchy yet exhausted. She needed to leave the chair, to move herself. If she left the room, perhaps something would start making sense.

Like a mekkanikal toy, she rose and convoked a simple brown robe, then set off to walk alone.

She headed leeward through the city, around the Palace of Pleasure and the central square, through the brightly colored older districts. A woman saw her and shouted, "Meli? It's your appearance-day, isn't it?" Meli brushed her aside, staring ahead with empty eyes, legs moving of their own accord.

She stopped when she ran out of land at Tunel's Span, a rounded, flat plateau of bedrock on the island's leeward coast, joined to the main thoroughfare by the Hardened Bridge. She stood for a while and stared back the way she had come at the great sculptures lining the main street. Ball-players liked to convoke temporary grandstands on the Span, since the wind would blow the dust out to sea. Today a group wearing suits covered with long orange streamers was having a friendly match, laughing and kicking hundreds of balls about. On any normal day, she would have joined them, and yet here she was, utterly destroyed, pining for what? A dream?

No, it had been more than a dream. She had held in her hands a tiny treasure, the seed of a new life. Yes, a seedling of a person.

A seedling of a person? It made no sense.

It didn't matter. He was her seedling. And she wanted him back.

The realization was powerful and terrible at once. There was something missing inside her, a void she had never known was there, now impossible to ignore. She had to find her seedling again. She had to make the dream real.

She headed home, turning the thought over in her head. A person who grew like a plant? And not just any person, *her* person, not just a random appearance chosen by the gods. There was something special about the connection she had felt, as if upon waking she had lost an extension of herself.

Her mind was working rapidly by the time she returned, and she barely noticed arriving in her room and sitting on the sofa. She recalled the strange feeling in her head before the dream. What had caused it? The gods? Was all of it some sort of message, a glimpse of something more important?

Skittering and muffled squeaks came from the rafters. Two of the shroles were play-fighting again, crisscrossing the small room as they chased each other. Only two had originally wandered in to live with her, but after some years of finding her home acceptable they had convoked three more. Meli had observed plants doing the same thing many times, intermixing with each other when they convoked their seeds—some sort of defensive adaptation, she presumed.

One of the larger shroles grabbed a passing little one and began to lick its head forcefully, paw pressed against wriggling belly. The small one chirped unhappiness, then settled in and cooed at the attention. Watching, Meli felt a small calm amidst her mental storm.

She had been lucky enough to see the big ones convoke their offspring in person; most animals would not trust people enough to let them watch. The two parents had sat facing each other, their eyes closed in concentration, and soon fingernail-size balls of fur appeared in their nest, drawn from the aether. Within moments the new creatures had arms and legs and tails, and mouths to cheep with. Little miracles they were, drawn from nothingness into something wonderful.

She looked again at her flowers on the wall, and back to the shroles. The idea struck her, clear as the morning daylight, and the force of it made her jump to her feet.

She had to make one for herself.

That was the message of the dream—she was going to do what no one had ever done, and create a new person from scratch. That was what had drawn her to learn vegetism and animatism in the first place. She had found her true purpose, the one she had possessed all her life without knowing it.

"I'll convoke him!" She ran to the window, sending the shroles hopping away in fright, and shouted into the dust-clogged alley, "I'm going to convoke my seedling!"

She turned back, head still buzzing. Over the course of several deep breaths, her smile curled downward into a frown.

"How in ten gods am I possibly going to do that?"

2

Ariden approached the gambling terrace with the Scythe in his coat and blood on his mind. Ahead of him lay his quarry, the man he had pursued across Aetheria and back for one hundred and fifty years. One thought had driven him all those long miles and long days: Kill the Scarred Man. Now, only a narrow walkway separated them.

Gambling tables and their patrons dotted the terrace, a flat-bottomed, transparent bowl jutting from the side of the Palace of Pleasure. Ariden paused at the threshold long enough to be noticed, then lifted the brim of his hat.

All eyes fell on him. A grizzled pair of regulars, too busy with their endless games of Go-Round to shave, jerked back in shock. To their right, a foursome of novices played. A man and two women in violet and orange gowns sat at the far end of the terrace.

The faces were whole, all of them. Impossible. Two informants had told Ariden to search the Palace. The other terraces were empty. Had he arrived too late? Had the Scarred Man already fled?

Ariden cleared his throat. "Which of you dregs is going to tell me where Torseti is?"

Silence. The gown-wearers rose to leave, and the man in the center cast Ariden a menacing glare. Duris he was called, a Venerable Magistrate of Sofidra. Ariden had faced him in cards once, and found him confident, hard to bluff. Perhaps a show of weakness would make him overplay his hand.

"Good sir." Ariden made an attempt at a formal Sofidran bow. "Might I request the pleasure of your conversation?"

"You mock me at your peril, impudent thug. We have nothing to discuss. Leave this place, now."

"You refuse to parley?" Ariden showed his empty hands. "Approach me as you would a friend, and you shall be rid of me sooner."

The look in Duris's gray eyes was not what Ariden would have called friendly. But the magistrate cut an unimposing figure, with his short stature and double chin. Like as not, Ariden had him trapped. He had two choices, now: escalate or capitulate. Ariden held his breath for long moments while his opponent calculated.

Duris nodded to his companions, and they shuffled out as he returned to his seat. Ariden held his hands open until they were safely gone. Then he convoked a simple chair and sat, kicking up his feet and placing his hat beside them on the magistrate's table.

"You're not supposed to be here," Duris said. "Not after what happened last time. The watch has orders to remove you."

"From what? This terrace?" Ariden asked. "Or the whole Palace?" He gestured to indicate the building supporting them, the tallest in Sofidra, a gray and cerulean thorn overlooking the central square. Statuary and bas-reliefs adorned every space not occupied by the terraces, which splayed out in a spiral up to its apex. Each terrace had been convoked by a leading citizen, and each was dedicated to some Sofidran specialty, most often food, sex, mind-altering substances, or some combination of the three. Duris, as it happened, liked to gamble, as did Ariden. Perhaps that made them kindred spirits.

"For Elaethim's sake, spare me," Duris said. "Your feigned ignorance is as tiresome as you are vile."

Or perhaps not.

"Harsh words," Ariden said. "And all because I wish to see Torseti? You must admit, given my…excluded status…this would be a perfect hiding place for him."

"I admit nothing. Even if I knew where he was, I would never give Torseti to you."

"You two must be close." Ariden fingered the brim of the hat lying before him on the table. "Tell me, from where did he get that scar on his face?"

Duris narrowed his eyes. He cupped one hand over the table and convoked a pile of square dice, then began to stack them. A nervous habit—he knew he was cornered. "He had it when he arrived in the city. The two of us never discussed it."

"I see." Ariden leaned back, his hands behind his head. "Such good friends you must be. And yet it is a strange subject never to broach, yes? Allow me to advance a theory: Though you may have known him a long time, he and I go back even longer."

Duris shook his head, wobbling his chins. "And just how do you know that? He told me you two have never met."

Ariden's breath came out a low growl. "Tell me this—if Torseti is not who I say, then why is he taking such pains to avoid me?"

"Because he's heard of you and the things you've done!" Duris slapped his pyramid of dice off the table. "Sofidra is an open city, for those who abide by our ways. We take pride in that. But since you arrived you've caused nothing but trouble. I was willing to dismiss you as a nuisance before, but now you are on a mission to harass, perhaps even murder, one of our citizens—and you have the gall to ask me for help."

"Murder? All I wish is to meet Torseti, sit with him just as we are now, and hash out our differences with a nice chat. You could bring the city watch along. Bring them all, in fact."

Someone screamed to their left. Ariden's palm found the Scythe in his pocket. On the next table a hand was impaled on the felt, the hilt of a dagger jutting from it. The man who had done the stabbing laughed good-naturedly along with several others, while the loser of the bet cursed and winced as he yanked the blade free from his flesh. Blood poured over the table, then quickly dried into red-tinged dust. In moments, the loser's wound closed, and he picked up fresh cards and a new drink and continued the game.

Duris's gaze clung to where Ariden's hand disappeared into his coat. No doubt he had heard stories of the sword, and what it could do.

"A nice chat, eh?" Duris said.

A silence settled between them. Duris eyed Ariden with contempt but little concern. He had no reason to fear, after all—Ariden had no friends in this city, not a soul to vouch for him or come to his aid if Duris decided to sic the watch on him. And now that the magistrate had seen his true intentions, any hope of wheedling Torseti's location out of him was lost.

Ariden had one advantage left, however: Duris had no idea how desperate he really was. Whether or not Torseti was the Scarred Man, Ariden had searched too many cities, followed too many false trails. Now he would chase this lead to its end, even if it killed him.

Ariden sighed and stood, affecting resignation. He let his chair crumble behind him and headed toward the edge of the terrace.

"You're a wise man, Duris. May I speak to you truthfully?"

"If you're capable of it."

Overhead, a large black eagle swooped in lazy circles. The wall encircling the terrace was likely meant to reach to mid-chest, but Ariden stood a head taller than most men and leaned over it easily. The whole of the Sofidran island lay beyond, a maze of low, tan roofs surrounded by courtyards with wide arches, always facing windward to sweep out the dust. Past the city, a neat line divided the white, fog-covered Saentis sea from the flat, empty gray vault of the sky. Directly below, citizens gathered in the morning light for the weekly festival, appearing no larger than beetles from such a great height.

"I wish to stay here," Ariden said. "Permanently. It's true, I've had a checkered past. I've done my share of grisly work. But the time comes when an old fighter must leave his wandering ways behind and seek a new life. My business with Torseti is my own, but with the watch's help I'm sure we can settle it peacefully." He swept his arm out over the square. "Once that is done, I would be free to enjoy the wonders you have to offer."

Down below, many in the crowd wore sweeping gowns and long suits in brilliant colors, their hair twisted up in elaborate styles. Sofidra was known as an artist's city, and hundreds of illustrators and sculptors would make use of the festival to show off their latest pieces. Others would play music, sing, dance, juggle, tell stories, recite poetry, act out plays, or engage in one of the dozens of other, more inscrutable performance arts, competing for the rare attentions of those who had come only to spectate.

Yes, the city of artists—city of lackwits, more like. Gaudy, preening, obsessed with petty squabbles and self-promotion. The whole place could crumble at once and Ariden would be happier for it.

Duris snorted suspiciously. "The incident last week—"

"—was a misunderstanding. Please, do not hold my history against me. You have not inquired into Torseti's, after all. I'm asking for your help in putting regrets aside, so that I can retire in harmony with the citizenry of Sofidra."

"My help?" Duris's eyes remained narrowed, but he leaned forward. "If you wish to be invited to parties, there are many who could serve better than me."

"But invitations matter little when there is so much that I don't understand. And what better source of city lore is there than you?" Ariden pointed to the giant eagle. It was hovering directly above them now, kept in place by large propellers embedded in each of its wings. "For example, what is that bird? How can it have those mekkanisms inside it? I've never seen anything like that before."

Duris squinted, then stood and joined him at the wall. Ariden gave an inward cluck of the tongue. It was the same with all who possessed ostentatious titles and few actual duties: Flatter them by asking a question of no importance, and watch them respond with enthusiasm.

"Ah," Duris said, nodding. "It is quite the rare specimen. One of a kind, I believe. Meli's creation. She's a fine woman, though a bit eccentric. For years she's been involved in some sort of project to grow a human-like plant. Perhaps—*aah!*"

With a lift and a shove, Ariden pitched Duris over the wall, holding him on the other side by a fistful of that stupid gown. The gamblers gasped and sprang to their feet, knocking chairs over. Duris screamed and struggled, waving his hands, his thin hair blowing in the breeze.

"Listen, you smug pile of mold." Ariden gave him a shake. The old hang-them-upside-down routine might have been well-worn, but Ariden found the element of panic it added gave better results than a simple blade to the throat. "I may not win any festival prizes, but there is one art I'm skilled in. So unless you'd like me to practice it on you, you'll tell me where Torseti is."

One of the citizens below spotted the magistrate hanging and pointed. Within moments, a sizable portion of the crowd was running and screaming.

"You wouldn't," Duris yelped. "The watch will kill you."

Ariden gritted his teeth. "They'll kill me now whether I drop you or not. I've already passed the point of no return. Would you care to join me?"

Duris glanced down. He might survive such a fall, if he were lucky enough to avoid smashing his head, but Ariden judged the odds at worse than even.

"He—he's here."

"Here? In this building?"

"Up…"

"Up *where?*"

Light stretched below within the transparent floor. A subtle change, but obvious once Ariden spotted it. Duris was convoking a clear platform underneath him, attached to the underside of the terrace.

"You're too stubborn for your own good," Ariden said. "Do not test me."

"You're the one who failed a test," someone called from behind him. "Of your own stupidity."

That voice belonged to Petran, captain of the city watch. He stood in the center of the terrace, flanked by two of his men, a hulking brute wearing an inauthentic rendition of a classical fighting tunic. His neck and head formed a continuous cylinder, and judging by his grin, he was greatly looking forward to slicing Ariden up in pieces no larger than the dice lying in dusty clumps about his feet.

"Nice of you to join us," Ariden said. "Have you come to eject me again?"

"Not this time." Petran reached for a blade tucked behind his back.

"Gentlemen, please!" Ariden used both hands to open his coat, dropping Duris in the process. Luckily, the magistrate managed to convoke a handhold on the outside of the wall, from which he swung back and forth, shouting in panic as he struggled to finish his platform below.

Ariden kept his hands wide, so Petran could see he had no weapons in his belt. "I pose no threat to you. Let's take this disagreement elsewhere, so as not to endanger these good citizens."

Petran paused and looked at the others. The few gamblers still present stepped away. The other watchmen stared back uncertainly.

"He has the sword in his coat!" Duris shouted from the other side of the wall. "Cut him down! All of you!"

Spoilsport.

Ariden stepped forward to the table as the watch pulled their armaments: a pair of short swords for the ones in back and a set of daggers set within Petran's fist. From what Ariden could see, the material of the blades might be well-convoked, but the designs were amateurish. All of it was wrong: their stances, their formation, everything.

"This is your warning," Ariden said. "Back off, don't risk your lives."

They came forward.

So be it, then. Ariden plucked his hat off the table, a simple motion from an old fighter, who stuck to his long-ingrained habits until the end.

Except he didn't wear a hat.

He flicked the weighted circle of felt at Petran, and released his control of the aether before it struck. The hat crumbled into a cloud of dust, covering Petran's face in the irritating particles. The watch captain screamed in rage and lunged, swinging his bladed knuckles in a wide arc at Ariden's head. Clumsy as he was, Petran's sheer mass was still potent enough to overcome almost any weapon held against him.

But not the Scythe.

Before the hat struck, Ariden was already clutching the weapon's hilt. Simple it appeared on the outside, no more than a leather-covered grip and cross-guard, but the inside held the ability to accelerate convocations, producing new material at a rate few Aetherians imagined possible. Ariden leapt, pointing the guard-side at Petran, and imagined a blade extending from it, sized for balance, curved for slicing, and wickedly sharp. Then he focused and made it real.

A cold arc of gray metal shot outward, and a layer of ice formed on the grip, burning Ariden's palm. He twisted as he leapt and swung the blade in mid-aer, slicing Petran from shoulder to hip before landing beside him.

A chill wind passed over the terrace. Petran gaped down at his chest. The wound was not life-threatening, but when the pain hit his eyes rolled up. He stumbled to his right and collapsed against the wall.

The two remaining watchmen were no real threat, but more would soon be charging up from below. Ariden dulled his blade and barreled between them, sending one away tumbling and bruised and the other leaping in fright. Back over the walkway he ran, and into the palace tower, dark and hollow with a circular stair running along its outer wall.

"Stop him!" Duris's shout came from behind, over the panicked screams of the festival crowd.

Up. Torseti was up, Duris had said, and only now was his meaning clear. Ariden hadn't seen anyone on the higher terraces, not unusual for a festival day, but he had forgotten the private apartments at the apex of the tower. He took the stairs three at a time, and within a circuit of the building, the stomping of booted feet came up from below. The rush of the chase had him now. There would be no clean way back down, but it didn't matter, as long as he found the Scarred Man. Vision red, he pumped his legs harder, letting the blade of the Scythe crumble in order to gain speed.

Find him. Find him and kill him and get her face out of your mind.

The stairs narrowed and Ariden entered a curved hallway. At the end of the last turn, a solid, heavy block stood in place of the door. Torseti had prepared well for his coming; the material went beyond the frame, extending from wall to wall. Ariden shook his head and turned away, toward the outer wall, then aimed the Scythe. Bracing the hilt against the opposite side of the hall, he closed his eyes, focused and loosed the blade.

With a crash and a plume of dust, a cylindrical ram punched a hole through the aether-stone exterior of the tower. Wind howled as aer rushed through the narrow opening. Crumbling the ram, Ariden kicked at the hole a few times to widen it, then crawled through into daylight.

The minuteness of the buildings below dizzied him, but the noise of boots on steps from behind brought him back to attention. Ariden stowed the hilt and leaned out to grasp a piece of statuary. Creating his own hand- and foot-holds would have been safer, but he had never had the knack of convoking quickly unless he was using the Scythe's unique power, so he climbed along the tower's decorations, finger strength his only protection from driving wind. Long steps brought him to the outer frame of a picture window on the far side of the tower. To get inside the frame would require swinging out over open aer, with the penalty for failure being death. He slapped his fingers on the cold wall and leapt.

The smooth window smacked his palms and nose. Ariden opened his eyes. The apartment before him was covered in pillows, the floor a bed, gilded silk draperies hanging from the ceiling. Two men and a woman sat up at the sound of his collision. There was no doubt which one of them was Torseti: hairy-chested, with a thick beard, and a deep scar across his face.

Across. Not down. Not the right scar.

Not the right man.

He could have smashed the window, beaten all of them senseless in his rage, demanded the location of the real Scarred Man. But they didn't know, had nothing to do with him. Most likely the Scarred Man had never set foot in this city. How many years of Ariden's century and a half of searching had been devoted to this false trail? He couldn't even recall. All he knew was that the deep ache in his soul remained.

"Take it easy, now—we have him trapped."

Duris stepped out onto the scaffold he had convoked below Ariden's exit hole, surrounded by four of the watch. They held their swords high, fearing the Scythe, but he had no way to launch an attack from the narrow ledge. Was death his only choice, then?

No. Not yet anyway—not while the Scarred Man still lived. The highest of the round terraces lay below and to his right. He swallowed and jumped, aiming for the hard, gray bridge connecting the terrace to the tower.

He felt the drop, then his vision flashed white when he landed, pain radiating up his legs into his spine. His view of the world spun. He sat up, rubbing his head. Something hard pressed on his back—a statue of Sailach, the goddess of luck. He must have rolled onto the terrace and come up against it.

There was a commotion above as the men jostled on their scaffold. Sailach was with him, indeed; there was no way they would reach him in time to stop his escape. If he ran downstairs, he could easily—

A crack ran underneath him, forking and twisting through the base of the statue. Ariden rose unsteadily as the floor shifted under his feet. The goddess's face came even with his, its winking face mocking him.

This was one of Duris's terraces, and Duris could release the convocation whenever he wished.

The floor quaked and ripped, sending up a plume of dust. Ariden jumped for the tower, but the terrace tipped, catapulting him outward.

Head over heels, stomach in his throat, he tumbled down toward the city. A glimpse of the festival crowd, a rush of wind and a buzzing noise. Dread gripped him, and he closed his eyes.

Something caught his wrist.

3

The pain in his shoulder was so sharp that Ariden thought his arm had come off. But instead he was floating, held in the claws of the giant black eagle he had pointed out to the magistrate. The bird's propellers growled, straining under his weight. The downdraft stung his eyes.

"Like to wait until the last moment, don't you?" he yelled.

"*By plain time, is introduce for the lateness apologize.*"

Ariden's jerk of surprise nearly pulled him from the thing's grip. He hadn't expected it to actually *answer* him.

"What are you?"

The eagle didn't reply, seemingly focused on keeping them aloft. The thing couldn't rise with him in tow, and was reduced to falling in a gentle arc away from the tower. Shouts came from behind them, then quickly faded in the wind. Gliding here in the open brought back unwelcome memories of the small skyships Ariden had ridden in the war. When he looked down, the streets floated by, small enough to resemble an artist's model but unsettlingly real nonetheless.

"Where are we going?"

"*Mistress in lady to see, for wanting Ariden of task.*" Its voice was a high-pitched, throaty wheeze.

"Lady? Who do you work for?"

"*All will in time.*"

"Put me down." His shoulder ached and the creature's claws dug into the flesh of his wrist. The eagle made a wide turn over the Bazaar, heading toward the windward point of the curved Sofidran island. Below, the narrow streets between the courtyards were empty, but they wouldn't stay that way for long. He needed to get out of the sky where he could be spotted and slip through the alleys until he reached the sea.

"Pox! Let me go!"

The eagle beat its wings furiously, but kept its grip. When they had glided low enough over a span of flat, white rooftops, Ariden wrenched his wrist loose.

The claw cut skin and scraped bone, but he was free. He hit the rooftop with a smack, rolled, then came upright, head swimming. This roof was different from the others, made of thick brown fibers, now splashed with red blood from his wrist. The eagle flipped its wings back and powered its propellers, coming to a stop in mid-aer, then glided down and landed beside him.

Ariden stepped back, and the eagle came forward, matching him.

"Whatever your purpose, I'm not coming with you. Go away."

It took another step, staring with its beady eyes. "*Same place for go, there is already.*"

Could it truly understand him, or was its speech some sort of trick? Whichever the case, he was not about to stand around discussing things further with some poxing buzzard; there was no time for games if he was going to escape the city. Sofidra was too small and insular to hide in for long. Word would spread through the citizenry like a storm. The windward point was not the best place for a quick escape, but the important thing now was to get out into the open sea. From there, it would be a long, difficult journey sailing alone to the coast, but at least he would have a chance—if he could lose the bird first.

He stepped back again, and his heel passed the edge of the roof. Below, a two-story drop into a narrow alley—not a terrible fall, but he had already taken too many this day. But the eagle could continue to harass him as long as he stayed on the rooftops, which meant his only other choice was to fight it off. Instinctively, he reached into his coat for the Scythe—mold, he must have dropped it during the fall from the tower. Convoking another would take too long. Could he take the thing bare-handed? He had never seen a bird so large before; with its feathers ruffled it was nearly the size of a man.

"*Run is not before speak and listen.*"

Ariden sidestepped, heading toward the south-windward corner, biding time until his wrist stopped throbbing. The bird followed him carefully, as if it were afraid of startling him. Perhaps the front of the building held an easier way down to the street, though he would have to worry about being spotted by passing festival-goers. He preferred not to be seen until he reached the Saentis, to leave no trail for the watch to follow, but he might have to trade secrecy for speed.

Keeping his eyes on his foe, Ariden backed up toward the corner. Before he reached it, the roof opened up and swallowed him.

He plummeted through branches. Stalks and tendrils scraped his body and face until he landed in a bed of tangled plant matter. A vine flicked out, curling over his hand, then another took his ankle. The vines tightened and increased in girth, forming balls around his limbs.

He struggled and yelled and yanked, rustling the leaves above. The eagle glided down after him on its propellers and observed his thrashing. He could have sworn it giggled as it hopped down a nearby staircase and out of sight.

Panic would do no good. He had to plan. He was in some sort of workshop. The ceiling was composed of the coiled branches of the tree that bound him, and the white walls were covered with flowers in riotous shades of vermilion, bright orange, light blue and green. Purple vines hung down over the windows, blocking the light and lending the room a pink hue. The smell of plant matter was overwhelming.

He waited long moments, breathing deeply, gathering his strength, and pulled at his bonds again, slowly this time, tensing his entire body. There was a faint cracking sound. Then the tree shifted, convoking more layers of wrapping around him. Ariden exhaled and hung. Who would want to bind him like this? He had made plenty of enemies in his time, but the name Duris had mentioned as the bird's owner hadn't sounded familiar. Thinking back, though, he had seen the eagle several times over the previous few days, lingering in the distance or perched on a rooftop. Someone had been watching him, someone who wanted him alive, so they could do with him as they wished.

In that case, he needed to free himself at any cost.

If strength was not enough, perhaps a convocation could help. A saw would cut through the tree, but he had no way to grip a blade except with his teeth. An engine could do the cutting for him, but he had no mekkanist's skills to build one. And he could not pry himself out by making new material, since no ordinary convocation could come into existence in already occupied space.

But the Scythe could. He would have to convoke a new hilt to replace the one he had lost, and some sort of frame to keep it braced while the blade extended. Not an easy plan, but if he could manage it, the Scythe would cut the tree apart more easily than it had smashed the wall in the Palace. Ariden closed his eyes, listening for the bird's return, and began to convoke a platform in the corner. His first attempt came out lopsided, so he crumbled it and started over, using a simple three-legged design this time. When he was satisfied, he moved on to the business of convoking the hilt itself. He had performed that task countless times, but it was still a painstaking process, made more difficult by having to command the aether at a distance, to say nothing of the fact that he was hanging in mid-aer with his limbs painfully splayed.

Again he failed at his first attempt, then redoubled his efforts. For the Scythe's power to work, he would have to visualize the complex inner layers of the its hilt precisely. Sweat beaded on his brow as he fought fatigue and his own nerves. He had been lucky thus far that no one had come to fetch him, but surely his time was running short, and one mistake now could cost him everything.

Slight currents formed in the aether as it responded to his demands, creating a breeze in the room. A vine hanging from the tree's canopy swayed and bumped into the frame. The vine curled and probed, and in front of Ariden's horrified eyes wrapped itself around the intruding frame and the half-finished hilt, then crushed them to pieces.

Wonderful.

Creaking footsteps came from the stairs. A moment later the eagle hopped back in, followed by a tall woman. She was the sort whose entrance into a crowded room would turn all eyes toward her, her figure a collection of long, rounded lines—hips, cheeks, eyebrows, dark hair hanging over her shoulders—all wrapped in a swirling green silk dress. She convoked a perch on the wall and the bird alighted on it, flapping clumsily in the enclosed space, then folded its wings into its body so that it resembled a matte-black oval with a bulbous head. The woman patted it lovingly, then turned to Ariden.

"So, here we are. Welcome to my studio."

"Happy to visit," he said dryly. "You act as if you know me."

"Only by reputation. My name is Meli. I asked Elsa to bring you here because I need your help."

He shook his head. "Let me go."

"I was hoping to discuss—"

"Out. Now." He punctuated the second word with a shake of his fists, sending a few leaves drifting to the floor.

She frowned and crossed her arms. "You really think that sort of talk will convince me to free you? Elsa told me you attacked the captain of the watch. By all rights I should go and fetch them right now. I'm not in the habit of letting crazed hooligans roam loose, you know."

Ariden closed his eyes and breathed through his nose. The anger of losing the Scarred Man still bubbled within him, but he had always managed to control it when he truly needed to. For a while, anyway.

"I'm not a hooligan. Petran came after my head. I had to act, or die."

"Why was he after you?"

Ariden did his best to shrug with his arms spread. "An overreaction. He *thought* he saw me threaten the life of a magistrate."

"And what did he see?"

"I was asking some questions. Forcefully, perhaps, in an awkward location. But I wasn't really going to drop him from that terrace."

She raised an eyebrow. "And you don't think that was a bit...excessive?"

"I was in a hurry. They banned me from the Palace of Pleasure last week, and the man I was looking for took advantage of that to hide there. I didn't want the watch coming to throw me out before I found him, so I was forced to do some...regrettable things."

"Really? *That's* your defense?"

"It's the truth." Ariden lolled his head back, making sure to show the exasperation on his face. "All I have to offer."

"And just who were you looking for?"

"That's my concern."

"And mine. I need the protection of a great fighter. But it turns out you're nothing more than a criminal. If you were my bodyguard, I would fear *you* more than what you were protecting me from."

Ariden breathed deeply again. This was all taking too long—he had to come up with something, break her out of this line of thought. If this conversation were a fight, he would be in a corner, taking shots from all sides. He needed a quick knockout, and those only came from unexpected angles. "How old are you, Meli?"

She wrinkled her nose, suspicious. "I'm forty-three."

"Forty-three. Practically newly appeared. You and your friends, you think you can judge the rest of the world from your pretty little island, but you know nothing of us. Me, I'll have counted six centuries soon. Don't believe it, eh? Do you even know what was happening in Aetheria six centuries ago?"

She narrowed her eyes and remained silent.

"The war to bring down the Second Empire. I appeared south of Despernzi, right in the Third Emperor's homeland. Before I even learned to talk, they put an axe in my hand and stuffed me in a skyship, to fly to distant fields of carnage. That was *my* introduction to the art of killing." He paused to let her picture a grisly scene. "Yes, I've taken many lives. I've probably killed more people than you've met. Does that make me a monster? Or a survivor? Who better to protect you than one who has stared so much death in the face?"

Fear appeared in her eyes, no longer hidden by feigned confidence. "I shouldn't have brought you here. I need a guide, not a hardened killer."

"Hardened I may be, but I'm past adding to my total for its own sake. That's why Petran is lucky to be alive—he enjoyed the idea of swinging a blade, but he didn't really understand what one could do. Otherwise, he would have thought harder about who he was picking a fight with. No, my lady, you need a killer, but one with sound judgment, who knows when to use his sword, and when not to. That is the secret to surviving six hundred years in Aetheria."

Meli placed one hand on her chin, her brow furrowed. Long moments went by as she stood and considered. A good sign. The obvious move for someone in her position would be to turn him in immediately; the fact that she hadn't meant she was looking for some excuse not to. What exactly was this errand of hers, anyway? What was she planning which made her so desperate for his help?

She sighed, nodded, and approached the tree. "Bresan," she said, rubbing its trunk. "I know he disturbed you, sweet one. But please, let him go. I must leave soon, as we discussed."

The tree rattled in seeming irritation, but moments later the vines holding Ariden uncoiled. He dropped to the floor and rubbed his sore arms. Meli stood over him, hand extended.

"My hope is that if all goes well, you won't have to kill or hurt anything," she said, helping him up. "I merely need your protection as I travel across the sea to the Automatia, home of the—where are you going?"

Ariden looked back from the entrance to the stairway. "Away from here. As fast as possible."

"You said you would help me."

"I said you needed my help, not that I would give it." He hurried down the steps.

"Wait!" She followed, the eagle hopping behind her. "Won't you least hear me out?"

"Of course not."

"You should be grateful!" Her voice echoed down behind him.

He stopped. He shouldn't have done it, should have been making fast for the sea, but that desperate voice had deepened his already-piqued curiosity. "Where are you going, again?"

"The Automatia. Have you heard of it?"

He had, though how many centuries ago he could not say. It was a school of sorts, or perhaps more an enclave of like-minded individuals, dedicated to practicing the esoteric convocational art of automatism. "Does it still exist?"

"I have reason to believe it does."

"And why do you need me?"

"You can navigate our ship. And I'll need your protection, of course. You know what's out there—monsters, raiders, savage tribes. Even the bravest of Sofidrans would not abandon their homes to make such a journey."

"Last I heard, the raiders were busy killing each other on the North-Windward Coast. And there are no monsters or tribesmen in the middle of the sea."

"Don't be a pedant. If I'm going to be protected, I want the best. That's you, isn't it?"

He waved away her flattery. "But why *now,* after you learned of my crime? If the watch comes here and finds you helping me, you'll face their wrath."

"I've been making preparations to leave for some time." She headed down the stairs, Elsa the Eagle cocking her head at him as they passed. "I would rather take this opportunity than let it go to waste."

"Still, you could have waited for another fighter to come. How long would it have taken? A century? Two? It's not as if the world will end tomorrow. Why is this Automatia so important to you?"

She stopped past him and hesitated, opening her mouth and closing it again. Then she took a breath and emboldened herself, her chin held high. "I want to learn how to convoke a new person. An offspring."

He laughed, thinking it a jest, but her face showed he had wounded her pride. What could she be talking about? Animals and plants could convoke more of themselves, sure, but only the gods convoked new humans.

"You're serious?"

"Thirteen years ago, I had a dream," she said. "I was standing in a gray haze, and when I looked down, a very small person was lying in my arms."

"Sounds unsettling."

"It wasn't. I'll never forget the feeling—that connection between us. I've tried everything I can think of to bring it back."

Ariden rubbed his brow, attempting to unravel his utter confusion. "You're speaking of a guardianship. Bringing a newly appeared person into your commune, teaching them the ways of the world. That is not uncommon."

She shook her head as if she had done so in the same way a thousand times before. "No, that's not what I want. I told you, the person in the dream was tiny, not like a normal human. I even knew somehow that he came from inside me, that he grew in my belly."

"In your belly? Really? How would he have gotten out?"

"I don't know," she said with annoyance. "I suppose there could be different—"

Three bangs sounded below them—someone rapping on the building's entrance.

"Hey," a muffled voice called. "Open this, now!"

"The watch," Ariden said.

Meli's eyes went wide. She motioned for Elsa to go upstairs, then pointed at Ariden. "Stay here."

He backed into the shadow of the stairwell, away from the windows, and began convoking the hilt of the Scythe, though if Meli changed her mind and told them where he was, he wouldn't have time to finish it. Depending on how many men were at the door, that would get interesting.

"Yes?" Meli said from out of sight. Grumbles came from the other side of the door in reply. "No, nothing. No, I haven't seen her today; what is this all about? Well, she does what she wants, I don't have much control over her. No, I work here. It belongs to my friend Karis. Well, fine, of course. I'll be happy to help. I hope you find him. Goodbye."

The grumbling retreated and the door closed. Meli reappeared at the stair, lines of worry creasing her face. "They know you're in the district. They're going to check the other houses before they do a full search. Elsa!" Elsa flapped her wings upstairs. "Go to Karis. Tell her we have to leave. It's an emergency—we need a ship as soon as possible."

"I'm leaving now, all right," Ariden said. "Just not with you."

Meli balled her fists. "You do realize I could have told them you were here?"

He paused to watch her fume; she certainly was easy to rile. "Listen, Meli. Your story is interesting, and I'm truly grateful for your help. But I cannot pledge you my service. I have my own concerns to attend to."

He moved to step past her, and she smacked the wall with her hand to block him. On the other side of her, a convoked bar extruded across the threshold, penning them in.

"Then we'll barter," she said. "I know there's something you want. Everyone in town says you've been asking after someone. You pretend to be a common vagabond, drifting through taverns and gambling halls, but you came to this city for a reason."

It was his turn to be riled. He shot her a mean glare. "I seek a man with a scar on his face, from here"—he ran his thumb from temple to mouth—"to here."

"The only scarred man I know is Torseti."

Ariden shook his head. "He wasn't the one."

"Why are you looking for this man?"

Her words were a blade, slowly opening a wound in his mind, but instead of blood only a vision of the Enchantress's face appeared. Behind it were layers of pain, hidden in memories he didn't like to recall.

"I have to kill him," Ariden said through clenched teeth.

"Why?"

"He took something from me."

"Something?" Her eyes narrowed as she parsed his words. "Or someone?"

"Enough." Ariden's hands shook. "I told you it is not your concern."

Noticing his reaction, she backed away, letting the barrier crumble. "Perhaps. But if I am going to help you find this man, then I'd be responsible for you killing him. Don't I deserve to know what he did?"

Always it was the same. Meli thought she knew the story already: a love lost, a man seeking revenge for murder. Better to let her believe what she wanted, even if it was only half the truth. Only finding the Scarred Man was important. Once Ariden put an end to him, he would finally be free to join the beautiful face from his memory in death.

"If I say he has good reason to die, you will have to take it on my word," Ariden said. "And what do you mean, help me?"

"I've been teaching myself the principles of convoking intelligent life for twenty years. Elsa represents the pinnacle of my achievements. It's impressive how she speaks, isn't it?"

Ariden unclenched his jaw, letting the last of his anger melt away. Perhaps it was worth hearing Meli out, if only for a few moments. "I'd be more impressed if she made any sense."

"Regardless, I think you'll find that small creatures can be quite useful for gathering information. I could design you a species of bird, or an insect, then convoke a large number and ask them to seek someone matching a certain description. If they were able to multiply and defend themselves, they could cover all of Aetheria in half a year. Unless you consider examining every person in the world one by one to be the superior method?"

She allowed herself a tiny smirk, pleased at her cleverness. Ariden had to admit it was a fair idea. All he had to do was deliver this so-very-clever girl to the automatists, then wait for her to work her tricks, and his long search might be at an end.

But what of the risks? She was a typical Sofidran, hopelessly naive—not the easiest type of traveler to protect, even if he didn't anticipate real trouble. And then there was her mental stability; that talk of the tiny-person-thing was truly bizarre. Certainly she was beautiful, and intelligent, perhaps remarkably so. But her charms were wasted on him; he had known no woman in such a way since he had lost the Enchantress so long ago.

Still, it was either join her, or continue on after the Scarred Man alone. Her offer, if real, was too tempting to ignore.

"When would I be paid?" he asked.

"As soon as I reach my destination. Then I'll begin work on a convocation for you."

Three more bangs came from downstairs. Meli jumped in fright. "Oh, no. I'll try to get rid of them again."

"Stop!" His hand caught her shoulder. "They're not here to talk. We must leave."

Banging again, louder this time. They were breaking the door in.

"You agree then?" she said. "You're going to help me?"

"Just go!"

He pulled her up the stairs. The watchmen's footsteps clattered as they ransacked the floor below. Hopefully they hadn't been smart enough to place sentries on the roof. Ariden reached the top floor, and Meli stopped and stared at her tree, as if the reality of her chosen path had just set in, putting her in a trance.

"I didn't think I'd be leaving right this moment," she said.

"No better time," Ariden took hold of the trunk. "Tell this thing to open a space in its branches."

When he reached the outside, the rooftops were bare, and no watchmen stood in the alley below. At the horizon to windward, gray fog swirled over the sea.

"It's clear." Ariden pulled Meli up and set her on the roof.

"The Automatia," she mumbled. "I'm going at last."

"Yes, yes, fine," he said. "Lead the way."

She swallowed and nodded, then convoked a simple board to the next roof, and together they headed off to the shore.

4

Meli led them outward to the sea, keeping to the rooftops where she and Ariden would remain hidden. It was a new experience for her, clambering up there like a felid, and not an altogether easy one in her formal day gown. That was a price she paid for letting Ariden dictate her timing. One of many.

As she stepped on each of the flat roofs, she imagined the person who might have convoked it. Most of them would be friends or acquaintances. Perhaps even now they were at home, listening to the clack of her shoes on their ceilings. What were the chances she would see any of their faces again? She would be barred from returning to Sofidra, she was sure, once the magistrates learned what she had done. But how long would they really enforce such a ban? Fifty years? One hundred? Would she even want to come back by then?

No, better not to think about it. If she stopped and considered all she was leaving behind, she might break down then and there. She had made a decision to pursue her dream, and now she had to focus on the task at hand.

She stayed close to the edges, walking along parapets, both to avoid making noise and because some of the rooftops would be made of paper. Where she found larger gaps between the buildings, she convoked platforms to avoid going down to the street, making sure not to let them crumble until Ariden had come over behind her. A high yellow dust cloud moved across the sky as daylight approached its zenith, but there was no sign of Elsa anywhere. Perhaps that meant the eagle had met Karis, and was waiting at the point they had chosen to set off from. Meli kept her gaze on the horizon, waiting for the curve of the island to bring the place in sight.

At last, she saw through the haze the top edge of the great circular stands. The Amphitheatre, so close now. She quickened her pace and convoked a stairway to the ground. The Amphitheatre was built into the black cliff side, the tiers of hardened seats sloping steeply to the bank of fog where stages were convoked on performance days. But this day, Meli noted with relief, the stage area contained a dock, with Elsa perched at one corner and Karis kneeling beside her, attending the skeleton of a ship.

Karis looked better prepared than Meli in her Mekkanist clothing, a baggy gray vest over a black undershirt, her pants covered with pockets. Her dark-skinned face was screwed up in concentration, her button nose twisted below her close-cropped hair.

Even after years of friendship, Meli sometimes had to remind herself not to let her gaze linger on Karis longer than necessary, since she knew smoothskins hated being stared at. She didn't mean offense, it was just that a true smoothskin was so rare, especially on Sofidra.

Smoothskin—an interesting word for people whose skin wasn't all that different from anyone else. It wasn't as though most people's skin was especially rough or callused, after all, though smoothskins' faces did possess a suppleness and vitality that others tended to lack. But the term was more of a shorthand for people who possessed a number of particular traits, among them a small stature, slender build, round head, and large eyes. In other words, Karis and those like her were…cute. Almost as though she were an intermediate between a normal person and the image of Meli's seedling from the dream.

Meli made the final hop onto the pier, and Karis ran up and embraced her. Her head rubbed the bottom of Meli's chin when they hugged, and her hair tickled.

"Is it ready?" Meli asked. "The watch will be here soon. Has Elsa explained what happened?"

"As best she could. This is perhaps not the way I would have preferred to leave." Karis cast a baleful glance at Ariden as he made his way down the slope. "But all that matters is that we're doing it. We're *doing it,* Meli! I'm sorry…there's still much to convoke. I'm trying to finish the engines now."

Meli let her get back to it, stepping away to admire the ship. Wherever the sea stretched in Aetheria, thick gray fog lay over it, so that the true sea level was eight feet or more below them, where the waves lapped at the island's bedrock out of sight. The ship, wide and flat and wedge-shaped, was built to ride on top of this fog using a series of massive pontoons, the construction of which was one of Karis's mekkanist skills. But Karis's greatest trick was the engine at the rear, its propeller spinning slowly, with another engine half-built nearby.

"What is this?" Ariden pointed at Karis. "Who are you?"

Karis scowled. "This is the ship which is going to take you off this island, and save your life in the process."

Ariden looked it over and sniffed. "I suppose it will suffice. But you didn't answer my other question."

"That's because I don't answer to you." Karis put the mekkanism she was convoking aside and approached, dwarfed by his over-six-foot frame. "And I don't need you questioning me while I salvage the plans you've sent into disarray. Understand?"

"Please, no bickering." Meli stepped between them and put up her hands.

Karis would not be so easily put off. Small though she was, she possessed an outsize spirit. "I'm only pointing out that he was supposed to come along as our protector, not get us chased out of the city."

"Your friend was the one who decided to take me along, after she found out what happened," Ariden said. "Perhaps you should direct your attitude at her."

"Please," Meli hissed. "Can we just—"

"Who do you think told her to involve you in the first place?" Karis said. "That means the burden of your foolishness falls on me."

"Karis." Meli touched her shoulder. "We'll settle it later, all right?"

Karis exhaled. "You're right, of course." She showed Ariden her back. "We have too much to do. While I'm working on the engine, you could finish the fore-deck, or convoke the rest of the gunwale."

"The gunwale?"

"The railing around the side. It has to be solid to keep the fog out. Since this oaf seems to know all about ships, perhaps he can assist you." She stalked off to the end of the pier.

Meli closed her eyes, both to focus on the convocation and to keep from looking at Ariden. She found herself somewhat annoyed at his needling of Karis, but keeping busy would help put the incident behind them. She sensed the aether near the ship, and it responded easily to her thought, layering itself over Karis's base. The material she had chosen, though light and strong, was simple enough, and she had little trouble circling the deck in a matter of—

"She's charming," Ariden whispered.

"You're one to talk."

"And you're breaking our deal, you know."

She opened her eyes and turned. "What? Why?"

"You bartered my services for your protection. You. That means one person, not two. If she comes along, I can't guarantee her safety."

"But she'll be right there on the ship! What difference does it make?"

"Because." He held up a finger, adopting that ugly, cock-eyed look men get when they're about to say something stupid. "This is one thing too many. First, instead of fleeing somewhere sensible like the Leeward Coast, you want us take a slow route into the wind to find the Automatia. And when I ask you why, you spout some nonsense about convoking humans in your belly."

"It's not nonsense. Even if you and the entire rest of the world doubts it, I know it isn't." Meli struggled to control her voice. "For Elaethim's sake, I've been having this same conversation for over a decade, and you think *you're* going to be the one to dissuade me? You can't understand what it was like. Have you ever had a part of yourself taken away? Have you missed something so dearly, the loss was like a gaping wound in your soul?"

He took a deep breath, as if readying a mocking retort, but thought better of it and chewed his tongue. Had her words touched something in him? His dark brown eyes narrowed, as if a deep sadness rested behind them, a wistful remembrance of long ago. Then the look faded to his usual calculating stare.

"If the ship floats, we should push away now, before the watch finds us. And before I have to spend another moment on this miserable island."

He turned, pulled up his coat and jumped the rail.

Eight days passed in quiet before Meli saw the birds.

She had been sitting on her lounge chair, staring at the gray line behind the ship where Sofidra had been. Above, a parasol blocked her view of the bright white sky, while below, fog curled around the ship's pontoons, parting momentarily before rejoining the endless gray carpet in their wake. At times they had passed through areas where the fog rippled or swirled instead of lying flat, but always the ship rode steadily, floating along on its wide bottom, its three engines humming without pause. Every day, the same empty fog, the same whir from the engines, the same wind in her face, its slight chill itching her nostrils. And the same clear sky—until that day.

She should have remembered what the sea was like. After all, she had crossed over it once on her way to Sofidra, as did all its citizens, since no one had ever appeared on the island itself. But she was only eight then, and her first true memories began soon after her arrival: the people in their costumes, the delicious food and the joyous music. Then the next two decades had blown past like dust, and the outside world faded into the realm of stories.

Not anymore. Now she, Ariden and Karis were headed due windward, right into the mouth of the Kalsten strait, though they might drift into the coast sometime before then. What would the land there look like? Would reality match her story-fed imaginings of Aetheria? She could almost see in her mind the great black-capped mountains on the continents where the Behemoth Walkers lived who could crush a woman under a single toe, or the wide dust plains, where the people rode tame caprans and kept their faces covered to block the storms.

And then of course there was the Automatia. Ariden had said that between the variances of wind and engine, there was no way to be sure how long it would take to reach it, which only made the waiting more difficult.

She trailed her fingers over the side, letting the fog's touch tickle them, and a fist-sized bird came into view beyond the edge of the parasol. Moments later another followed, then more, until the bright blue creatures whirled about in a flock above her.

"Look!" Meli called. "Does it mean we're near land?"

Elsa lifted her head and flapped her wings, and Karis roused from where she had been dozing on a nearby couch.

"*Little bits flapflap turn and flap, but no talking them,*" Elsa said, after listening for several moments.

"Don't they look like the ones you released a few years ago?" Karis asked as she sat up.

"Not exactly. But sometimes new ones can intermix with existing species."

"Bah!" Ariden uncurled himself from his pilot's seat and snorted. Since their journey began he had mainly stayed at the rear of the ship, his back to the wind, working the tiller and eschewing all conversation. "Looks like they've been intermixing a bit too much."

He gestured to the opposite horizon, where another flock of birds was ascending. Soon a great multitude of them filled a swath of sky to the ship's left.

"Why do you let those things loose, anyway?" Ariden continued to gripe. "Aren't there enough of them already?"

"Of course not," Meli said. "Just look around; couldn't this place use more color? And why are you complaining, anyway? They haven't done anything to you."

Ariden snorted and turned away, making himself busy with the tiller. So it was back to ignoring her, then—sitting there hunched over, his mop of black hair falling over the dark coat covering his wide chest and long legs. For the hundredth time, she wondered if she had done wrong by letting Karis talk her into contacting him.

With a sigh, she turned back to the fog, remembering that day again.

Meli hunched over the table and watched a bird unfold itself in her hand, stretching one teal wing and then another, until it gave a final shake of its purple-ruffled head and their eyes met.

"Welcome," Meli said.

The room partition slid open, and a clank and clatter followed that made the bird jump with a frightened *cheep*.

"It's all right," Meli said. "It's just Karis. This is her home." She put the bird down and went to help pick up the mekkanisms Karis had dropped near the entryway, a great jumble of interlocking gears.

"Thank you," Karis said. "Just put that one on the table." She struggled to carry the rest in her short, stick-like arms.

"What are they?" Meli said, sitting and cradling the bird again.

"Engine parts. Well not really an engine—a transmission. I had some ideas for a design on the way here." After dropping her load, Karis collapsed onto her swivel-chair, wiped her forehead and smiled at the bird. "I like them. They're pretty."

Meli stroked the bird's head and it cheeped. By the window, two more flapped in their black wire cage and cheeped replies. "Yes." She paused. "Very pretty."

Karis leaned forward. "Meli, what is it?" She wriggled her nose the same way she did when working on a difficult mekkanism. "You've been thinking about *him* again, haven't you?"

"No," Meli said, a bit too quickly. "I mean, not really. It's not worth discussing, anyway."

"You can discuss it with me."

Meli rolled her eyes. "I only discuss it with you."

She realized that might sound insulting, and regretted saying it. But it *was* remarkable how Karis had become such a fixture in her life, after they had met by chance at that party. Magistrate Duris had introduced them, knowing Meli would want to meet such an unusual foreigner. Meli had forgotten what they had discussed that evening, though it had not amounted to much—Karis had been rather quiet at first. She assumed the shy girl would move on, as most outsiders did, leaving Meli with no more than a small bit of pleasant distraction from her troubles.

But Karis did not leave the city. Meli ran into her again a few days later, this time wandering in the central square, and the two of them began a series of ever-more-frequent chats. Unlike her other friends, Karis took an interest in Meli's work, and her collaboration and support had been instrumental in keeping up Meli's spirits the last few years.

Except that at times like these, staring into Karis's expectant eyes, Meli wished she were a bit less insistent when it came to giving her support.

"All right." Meli coaxed her latest creation onto her finger and stepped over to the cage by the window. "Don't make fun, but I had the strangest thought the other day: what if instead of there being something wrong with me, there were something wrong with the world?"

Karis snorted. "There are many things wrong with the world."

"Just listen: have you ever thought about why the gods make us the way we are? I was thinking of the animals, and how they partner with each other to convoke their offspring. It made me wonder why the gods choose to convoke two genders of human. Why only two? Surely the world would have much more variety with three or four."

Karis's eyes narrowed as she tried to follow along. "And this is somehow related to your dream?"

Meli nodded. "I can't explain why, but I feel like there's a piece missing—something about this world that's not right. For example, I never quite accepted the old explanation that sexual intercourse is a gift from the gods, to help us live pleasurable lives. If that were the case, why do most people have a strong affinity for only one gender? Why wouldn't everyone just be happy with either?"

Karis stared for a moment, then stammered, as if she were having trouble voicing her thoughts.

"I'm sorry," Meli said, looking down. "I know I must sound completely insane."

"No, no," Karis finally managed. "You're not insane. You're just…an unconventional thinker. This is what I've been telling you, that you need to be around other people like yourself."

"Oh, Karis, not the Automatia again." Meli let a section of the cage crumble, then placed the new bird in to join the others.

Karis's face appeared on the opposite side of the cage, striped by the bars. "I'm serious this time. I have a way."

"It's too dangerous," Meli said. "Besides, how can you even be sure you know where it is?"

"Because the man I spoke to had been inside it—the one who told me it was at the mouth of the Kalsten Strait. He gave me the key to enter, even told me of the work they were doing to build an automaton man. And that was many years ago—who knows if they've succeeded by now?" Karis's big eyes brightened. "Just imagine studying at a philosophic center like the ones from thousands of years ago, before the coming of the Plague Bringer, cursed be his name. Yes, they're secretive, to prevent anyone from causing such calamities again, but once we find them I'm sure they'll be happy to have us. Wouldn't you like to show someone besides me your work, without fear that they'll laugh behind your back?"

Meli shook her head, repaired the cage and walked out to the balcony. Why couldn't Karis understand? Of course Meli would have loved to be in a place where wise people met to learn, and create new knowledge. Even if an automaton man held little interest for her—an automaton would crumble when its creator released the convocation—they were at least a step in the direction of convoking a real person. And it wasn't as if Meli had never considered leaving before. She heard what the other Sofidrans whispered behind her back. Opportunities came often; sea-ships docked in Sofidra, bringing wanderers or bands of pleasure seekers from the coast. She had even met the occasional free sky-man or woman who had avoided having their ship taken by raiders.

But ideas were one thing; actually leaving the only home she had ever known to go on some grand adventure was another. Could Karis really find the Automatia as easily as she claimed?

Meli sat on the outdoor sofa, her back to the house. Elsa, resting on the balcony rail, rose on her claws and stretched her great wings, blacking out half the sky, showing off the mekkanisms buried within them. She reached with her neck and poked her beak into Meli's shoulder.

"Hello, darling," Meli said, giving her a scratch.

"Someone new has come to Sofidra." Karis took a seat on the opposite end of the sofa. "A fighter. And a former mercenary, by his claim. Someone with experience protecting others. We can talk to him, convince him to take up the trade again."

Meli took that in for a moment, then shook her head again. "What makes you so sure he's the one to take us?"

"Because I'm ready to leave," Karis said. "And so are you. There's nothing for you here, Meli. You're scared, is all. We could just as easily go alone, but I'll settle for bringing him, if that's what you need to convince yourself you'll be safe."

Meli looked out over the dusky streets with her chin in her hand. "You don't really know anything about him."

"Not yet, but we can fix that. We'll watch him, find out more."

Elsa gave a squawk of contentment and began cleaning herself on the balcony wall. The talking eagle was surely her greatest triumph, and also her greatest failure—for upon her creation, Meli realized she had reached the limits of animatism. Like so many others before it, that long avenue of study and practice would not yield her seedling. Still, it was Karis who had convinced her that creating Elsa might be possible in the first place, and she had been right. Who was to say she couldn't be right again?

When Meli looked back again, Karis had scooted closer. She took Meli's hands in her own. "You'll find a way to convince him to help us. You have to. Don't you see? Our knowledge and skills, combined with his muscle."

She leaned in.

"He's perfect."

Perfect. Observing the dour figure perched at the rear of their ship, the word might have been laughable, if Meli weren't stuck with him. She had tried to make the best decision she could, rushed as she was under the circumstances. It may have been too early to pronounce herself right or wrong, but she was disappointed already in how unpleasant the man was. What more, she hadn't given enough thought to his desire to find and kill this man with the scarred face. She had seen it then only as leverage, as a way to get what she wanted, without considering how disgusting his obsession was. What did he expect to accomplish by killing someone? Was there any pursuit in life more useless, more self-destructive than revenge?

Across the lounge area, Karis saw Meli scowling at Ariden and came over. "Did he upset you?" Karis asked as she sat beside her. "I'll talk to him, if you want."

That was Karis, always looking out for her. Ironic, since Karis's small size made her seem so vulnerable. But Meli had to fight the urge to protect her, reminding herself that Karis was at least five times older than she was, and didn't like being doted upon.

"No," Meli said. "I'm just feeling a bit low. It's not his doing."

"Are you homesick?"

"A bit." Though she suspected Karis knew it was more than a bit. Strangely, she didn't miss the people of Sofidra that much, at least not yet. Most of her good friends had grown distant in the years since her obsession began. Meli had been reduced to attending parties out of obligation, or to find a gentleman caller to relieve the occasional boredom. Instead, she had been thinking mostly of her house and Karis's workshop, and how long they had taken to convoke. One did not need to hold the full structure of a large object in one's thoughts in order to keep it whole; the aether would retain whatever form it was given, as long as the material connected to it was still held in its convoker's consciousness. As time passed, the focus required lessened further, until all that was necessary was an unconscious awareness, as effortless as trailing a kite tied to the wrist. Still, it had taken years to shape her home to her liking, and once they had traveled a long enough distance from the city, her link to it had severed. All that work, gone forever.

"Do you think Bresan will remain standing, after your building crumbles?" Meli asked.

Karis nodded and smiled comfortingly. "She's a strong tree. And I'm sure your friends will protect her if someone tries to tear her down."

Tear her down? Meli stifled a grimace. From the moment she had told Bresan to release Ariden, she had known she would never be able to return home again, but she hadn't realized that the citizens might try and take out their anger on her tree. She had to think of something else.

"Karis, talk to me again about the Automatia."

"What about it?"

Meli sighed and looked out over the endless fog. "We're doing the right thing, aren't we? The Automatia is where we belong."

"All over Aetheria, stories are told of the Automatia and its secrets," Karis's high voice was steady and calm. "Centuries ago I made a solemn vow I would do whatever I could to reveal the powers of the aether. I can't wait to find out what I'll learn." She gripped Meli's arm with her thin fingers. "But most of all, I'm glad I get to go with you. I wouldn't have it any other way."

She moved in for a hug, and Meli held her close and smiled. Karis was right, of course; thank Elaethim she at least had someone with her who cared.

And yet, when she retired that evening to the cabin, she still held a lingering feeling that something was wrong.

Another day came. Then another. In his pilot's chair, Ariden would shift in his seat, look this way and that while frowning, but otherwise he made no reports. Eventually they saw more flocks of birds, larger than the previous ones and colored pure black and white, but no land came to interrupt the sheet of fog. When hunger struck they convoked simple meals, enough to sate themselves and no more, for none of them were accomplished savortists. They had fashioned two rectangular cabins on either side of the open-aer lounge at the center of the deck, and Meli practiced her vegetism there, planting flowers and vines to grow along the walls. Karis passed the time fashioning ever-more elaborate furniture inside the cabin she shared with Meli, while Elsa napped or circled the sky above.

On the morning of the eleventh day, Meli watched as Karis approached Ariden and cleared her throat.

He spoke without turning. "Yes?"

"I realize it's overdue, but I wanted to apologize for our harsh words on the dock," Karis said. "My nerves got the better of me."

"Don't worry about it, short one."

She crossed her arms. "Don't call me that. Just because I'm a smoothskin doesn't mean you can disrespect me."

He turned, wearing a grin. "Of course not. I apologize, as well."

Karis narrowed her eyes. "What are you smiling about?"

"Hmm?"

"You're glad because you found a way to annoy me. Is that it?"

He shrugged.

"You don't need to be playing mind games with me, you know. Meli and I are on your side. Besides which, I see right through you—

all you're accomplishing with your little snipes is to confirm what an immature fool you are."

Ariden gave her his typical belligerent stare for a moment, then threw his head back and laughed.

"What?" Karis gaped. "What is it now?"

"You're doing great! Don't you see? You're battling back, gaining the upper hand. I respect that in a fighter."

"But we're not in a fight!"

"Everything's a fight."

Karis continued to stare open-mouthed, and for a moment Meli thought she would lose her temper, but she only shook her head and chuckled.

"Amazing," she said. "You really do live up to your reputation. For better or worse."

"What is it, then?"

"What is what?"

"I respond to your apology by insulting you. But instead of leaving, you're still here, giving me these half-compliments. You must want something. Just come out and say it."

She scowled, then took a long breath. "Your sword. I want to see how it works."

"No."

"Why not?"

"It's a matter of principle," He leaned back with his hands behind his head. "The sword was designed by a very old man named Gariul, and I promised him I wouldn't tell anyone the details of his esoteric convocations. You seem like a smart girl; if I show you the inner-workings of the Scythe, you'll probably figure out how to copy it, and I don't want that. At least not until we know each other better."

"Without me, you'd be dust on the streets of Sofidra. You would think saving your life would entitle me to a little trust."

Ariden contemplated that a moment, then sat up and cracked his knuckles. "I'll make you a deal, then. Beat me in cards, and I'll let you see it."

Karis grinned. "You're on."

Ariden locked the tiller and they decamped to the open-aer lounge at mid-deck, entreating Meli to join them as the third player in a game of Go-Round. Not her ideal activity, but she made an effort to remember the rules for Karis's sake. They each convoked their decks, and Ariden dealt first. The hands came and went. Elsa fidgeted on her perch, watching the action.

"I win," Ariden said.

Meli tossed her cards down in disgust. Karis shuffled her hand and muttered.

"*Cards much fortune holding Ariden today. Meli makes happy is not.*"

"You're just lucky we're not playing for pain," Ariden said. "By now you both would have had to re-grow a finger."

"You're revolting," Meli said, dealing again. "Why would you do that to yourself? Why not just play a game that isn't competitive?"

"Because I want to have fun, not bore myself to death."

"Violence isn't fun," Karis put in. "It's stupid."

"Life is violent," Ariden said. "If you can face the pain of a card game with a clear head, you'll be better prepared when trouble strikes."

"Thinking like that is what got you in trouble in Sofidra," Meli said. "People should find better ways to resolve their differences."

"And yet, you still wanted my help." He showed his cards. "I win again. That's thirteen in a row."

Meli grumbled and thumbed through the cards on the table. "Imagine—if I spent as much time studying convocations as you have gambling, I'd be running the Automatia by now."

"It's just a mixture of luck and tenacity," Ariden said with a modest shrug.

"No, it's not." Karis said. "You're cheating."

Ariden snorted. "You're showing your ignorance, short-one. It's Go-Round, you're supposed to cheat."

"You're supposed to change the faces on *your* cards," Karis said. "Those two blue ones you're holding are mine." She narrowed her eyes and the red-backed paper crumbled, leaving only the blue covers sticking to Ariden's fingers.

"You sodden...wait," Meli said. "You told me you were banned from the Palace of Pleasure, didn't you? Is this why..."

Elsa tittered. "*Heeheehee! Ariden not get away it with, eh? Heheh.*"

"Oh, buzz off!" Ariden tossed his remaining cards at her. Elsa made a rude sound and flew away.

Karis stood. "The sword. Let's have it."

Ariden muttered a curse and stood, then held his palms out in front of him. "Look. Don't touch."

Meli leaned in over Karis's shoulder. She had learned from her friend that mekkanists often built complex machines piece by piece, assembling them later. But Ariden convoked the hilt all at once, the different materials layering over one another with practiced efficiency. All too soon it was over, and the completed grip hid its innards from view.

Karis whistled low. "Can I see it work?"

Ariden nodded and stood, holding the hilt horizontally away from them. "Don't blink."

The blade burst outward with concussive force, faster than the eye could track it. A chill went through the aer, raising prickles on Meli's skin.

"Incredible," Karis said, rubbing her arms. "How does it make the aether respond so quickly?"

"I have no idea," Ariden said. "Gariul showed me the finished product and told me to copy it. It took months of practice, convoking the hilt a hundred times a day before I could reliably make one."

"And he trusted *you* to keep it safe?"

"He wanted me to fetch his partner from a band of kidnappers. Quite a story attached to that little caper. A strange man, Gariul was. I don't know if it ever occurred to him I'd still be carrying the thing around two centuries later."

"Give it to me," Karis said. "I want to open it."

"Easy." Ariden pulled the hilt up out of her reach, letting the blade detach and crumble. "Swords should stay with those willing to use them. 'Violence is stupid,' remember? Unless you'd rather be your own bodyguard when we reach the shore." He headed to the rear again.

"If we ever do," Karis grumbled.

Ariden turned quickly, viewing them both with narrowed eyes. Then he gave a quick chuckle. A little too quick. Meli and Karis glanced at each other.

"What?" Meli said. "What is it?"

"Hmm? "

"That laugh," Karis said. "It sounded fake."

"What is this nonsense? I didn't sound like anything."

"Your eyes just shifted," Karis said.

"Quiet down, you."

"You're hiding something," Karis said. "When I said 'If we ever do,' it bothered you. Ariden, *what do you know*?"

"Look," Ariden said. "It's nothing serious. Sea voyages cannot be planned precisely. But you wanted to go to the Kalsten Strait, yes?

Which means we have to keep going this way." He pointed at the front of the ship. "I think."

"You think?" Meli stepped forward.

"It's these poxing winds!" Ariden spun and threw up his hands. "All right? They're changing, I can tell, but I can't see where or why. I've never seen anything like it before."

Karis and Meli exchanged another glance, then converged on him.

"And you were going to tell us this *when*?" Karis asked.

"Just be patient, will you? Like I said, no sea voyage is perfect. Sometimes the wind dies down, sometimes you lose your way. But I've always gotten somewhere."

"You have no idea where we are, do you?" Meli said. "We could have been going in circles all this time."

Ariden huffed, preparing a tirade, but a sight above stole his attention—a scattering of black specks in the sky.

"The birds," Ariden said. "That's why."

"That's the best you can do?" Meli said. "Blame the birds?"

"You saw how many there are. They're affecting the wind somehow. Didn't I warn you they were a menace?"

"You're the menace." Meli's neck began to pulse. "What good are you, anyway? I knew this would happen. I should never have brought you with—"

"Shush!" He held a finger to her face.

She batted it away. "Pox-ridden sleaze!"

"Sshhhh!" He waved his hands and walked to the bow. "What was that?"

Meli stilled. A sound was growing over the humming of the engines.

"Sounds like...screaming," Karis said.

"No," Ariden said. He looked up. High above, a black speck was growing, forming into an arrowhead shape. A ship, twice as long as their own, rotating as it dropped at incredible speed.

Ariden hefted his hilt and gave it a twirl.

"Raiders."

5

Ariden felt the strange clarity that comes with the transition between peace and battle. The raiders' ship descended, and his life teetered on a precipice, where only a gentle push might change him forever. It was a feeling he knew well, and though he never welcomed it, he accepted it without hesitation, for to step back from the cliff and fail to act would only endanger them more.

"I don't understand," Meli said. "It looks like they're trying to collide with us."

"That's because they are." Ariden jumped to the stern and yanked the tiller to starboard. "Karis! The engines!"

Karis looked away from the approaching ship. "What?"

"Make them faster!"

She nodded and joined him at the stern.

"What can I do?" Terror had crept into Meli's voice.

"Hold on tight."

Sleek gray panels covered the sides of the raider ship, coming together to a sharp point at its nose. White exhaust plumed behind the turbines at its rear, while their own engines hummed louder at Karis's urging. Ariden pressed his weight into the tiller. The attack craft drifted ever-so-slowly to the left. The closer it came, the faster it grew, until it seemed near enough to touch. Ariden closed his eyes.

A splintering crack, and a crash which knocked him off his feet. He opened his eyes. Parts of the port gunwale and one pontoon were gone. The ship was left bobbing in the wake of the collision. But they were still afloat. Ariden dashed to the damaged area and looked down into the fog. Most likely the raider's momentum had carried them all the way to the sea below, where they would now be reversing direction. An intentional side-swipe, to throw them off-guard—only sensible, given that a direct collision might have killed them all, and that the passengers were the only valuable things on board.

"Meli," Ariden said. "Fix this." The outline of the raider ship's rear hatch appeared below, hazy in the fog. Then it stopped and waited—not engaging, only worrying him, drawing his attention.

Drawing it away from what?

On the horizon, a second identical ship was coming at them horizontally, its engines low and silent. Perfect. If they stayed on their present course—

The deck rocked and a snapping sound came from beneath Ariden's feet. Meli, kneeling near the damaged gunwale, screamed as a black spade burst through the deck beside her. The spade retreated, and spherical, mekkanikal insects crawled through the hole it had left. The insects were covered with segmented legs topped with razor claws. They half-rolled and half-scuttled about the deck in random directions, tearing it apart as they went. Automatons, launched from the ship below. Strange—Ariden would have expected to see such things at the Automatia, but why would this band of raiders have them? Meli kicked one as it passed, sending it over the side, while Karis herded several away with a freshly convoked rake.

"Make a blockade." Ariden pointed to the roofs of the two cabins at mid-deck. "Get on high ground so they don't slice your ankles."

He turned back to the ship approaching from the side, ignoring the yelling and deck-splintering coming from behind. The face of the ship's pilot came into view in the cockpit window. Ariden knelt and rested the pommel of the Scythe on the gunwale. Everything depended on timing—early enough to build speed, late enough to keep the raiders from turning. He waited, one heartbeat, then two, until the ship was nearly too close, then he closed his eyes and imagined a large blade. Very large.

The thought became real and the sword grew up and out, shaped like an axe head, nearly the size of the approaching ship. The cold ripped past Ariden's face and he hid it in his collar. By then the sword was tipping forward, slowly at first, then gaining momentum. He held the grip but had no control over its immense weight. The pilot's eyes grew wide—and then the blade cleaved into his ship.

The crunch rang sweetly in Ariden's ears and vibrated through his palm. Not a direct hit, but the right quarter of the raider ship came apart, then sped away, propelled by its suddenly misaligned turbine. Ariden detached the blade from the hilt before it pulled him with it over the side, and it fell out of sight along with the ship's remains.

"One down."

A deep shiver went through him and the freezing hilt tumbled from his hand. The convocation's immense size had chilled the aer so much that gray aether-snow had condensed. Flakes drifted past his nose, evaporating as they fell. He turned to see how the others were managing, and in that moment the ship listed hard to stern.

Ariden skidded, then slid down the inclined plane of the deck and landed on the fore cabin wall, now at a diagonal with the fog. The Scythe tumbled by a moment later. He dove and caught it, his chest dangling over the slope leading down toward the engines. Or what was left of them—two were nearly destroyed, apparent victims of whatever had also burst the aft pontoons from below.

"Meli!" Karis called down from her perch on the roof of the aft cabin, separated from Ariden by the plant-strewn lounge area where they had been playing cards. "Climb up!"

Meli sat hunched at the stern gunwale with Elsa nearby, shoveling away automaton spyders that had fallen beside her. Karis closed her eyes, and bumps and ripples formed over the deck, extending in a weave-work pattern for Meli to climb back toward the bow. Meli saw them and tossed her shovel aside to grab the lowest hand-hold.

A black shape rose behind her.

Karis screamed. Ariden leapt. He slid down the deck, fog whirling around him as it mixed with the cold aer. Two raiders in black armor stood at the hatch of a rising ship, tall men with nearly identical close-cropped hair. Ariden landed against the stern gunwale with a thump, and one of the men jumped forward, seeing his opportunity to catch Ariden off balance. But Ariden didn't need balance to kill with the Scythe. He aimed the hilt at the raider's chest, envisioned a blade and—

—nothing. Convocations were not as effective in the cold, and extending the Scythe was more demanding than most convocations. The raider swung a mace. Ariden turned and dove away, showing his back to the enemy but keeping his head intact.

A lesser fighter might have hesitated after such a close miss, but the raider used the power of his swing to hurl himself forward, crushing Ariden with his heavier, armored body. Ariden turned on his side and got his hands on the man's elbow, keeping the mace-wielding arm pinned to the raider as he wormed his way out. Meli was yelling something at the edge of his hearing, competing with Elsa's panicked squawks. Had the other raider boarded as well? Ariden freed one arm, turned the Scythe's hilt over and smashed the pommel into his adversary's nose.

Blood sprayed onto Ariden's face, thick and salty, and the raider backed off and scrambled to his knees. Meli was still calling out in alarm, so Ariden rushed forward before he had fully risen, tackling and lifting the mace-wielding raider up and over the side of the gunwale, where he flipped head over heels into the sea below.

Ariden looked up into the surprised face of the other raider, who was still aboard his own vessel. Both of them heard the splash.

"Isky!" The other raider yelled downward. "Hold on! We're coming down!" He retreated into the descending ship.

"Ariden!" Meli screamed.

"What?!"

She pointed up to the bow, where a third ship had descended, with two raiders dangling from it, on their way to flank Karis. Again with the distraction tactics—the raiders might not be his match one on one, but they knew how to make the most of their numbers. That raised the question: If he chased after these new ones, would the other ship return? Ariden leaned back over the stern, searching for signs in the fog.

"Hurry up!" Meli yelled. "What's wrong with you?"

"Shut up!" Ariden turned and jumped for the handholds Karis had created for Meli to climb. A few easy leaps brought him to the side of the closest cabin. Karis would be waiting on top of it, but Ariden didn't have a clear view of where the raiders were. With Meli's rebuke still stinging his ears, he disregarded caution and heaved himself onto the roof, leaving himself open to the blade swinging at his neck.

Fortunately for him it was a clumsy strike, but from his awkward position he barely managed to roll away. His ear stung—had it been cut off? The raider pulled his axe back, stepped forward and raised it again. Cold wind swirled around Ariden, pulling bits of snow along with it. He held out the hilt of the Scythe to block, hoping this time it would form a blade.

The raider fell straight down into a newly crumbled hole in the cabin ceiling.

Ariden glanced at Karis, who was peeking at him from the top of the wall facing the lounge area. He had forgotten the cabin ceiling was hers.

"You're welcome," she said.

"Had him right where I wanted him."

A shape appeared behind her. A second raider descended on a rope and tossed a net over her face. She screamed.

"Mold!" Ariden scrambled up and jumped. The ship above rose, dragging along with it the rope, the raider and Karis, thrashing inside the net. Ariden's leap fell short and he slipped, tumbling over the side of the cabin and onto the deck.

He flipped over and spat blood from a bitten tongue. The dark mass of the raider ship retreated into the aether above, on the tail of the one which had attacked from below. The net swayed, and Karis retreated into the distance, her cries vanishing in the wind.

She was calling Meli's name.

6

Karis yelled until her throat went dry and began to hurt, then continued yelling through the pain. This couldn't be happening. They couldn't be taking her away. The raider above her had disappeared up into their skyship, leaving her dangling below in the rushing wind. She gripped the net so hard the rope cut her fingers, and only then did she think of convoking a knife to cut her way out. But it was useless, already they were so high. Soon her own tiny ship shrank to a dot, lost in the fog and dust-clouded sky.

Meli! She had to get back, had to get out and find her again. How could this have happened? No, it wasn't real. The journey had been going well until Ariden had revealed they were lost, and then everything had spiraled into a nightmare. Her heart pounded and panic wrapped its cold fingers around her body. The wind howled and the net shook, its rough cord scraping. Her tears drifted off and crumbled into the aether. She had to get hold of herself. *Breathe. There must be a way out—think of some way out.*

A shadow passed over her. They had come underneath a larger ship. Much larger. The sound of the engines was louder than she had imagined mekkanisms could be. Her heart sank; she must have risen to an incredible altitude if such a behemoth had been nearly invisible from the ocean surface. The smaller craft towing her banked and came up alongside it, and what she saw then stole her remaining breath.

The fleet stretched out over thousands of feet of sky, a network of cruisers and support craft and swift fighters, some cabled together and some free. They came in incredible variety, with as many designs as there were ships, but none were more impressive than the flagship, its giant propellers lining a wide top deck, with crew scuttling all over its surface. The raiders there were perturbed, yelling, shouting confused orders in every direction. Even after "her" ship moved into a hover and Karis's net was hung above them, the raiders appeared too busy to concern themselves with her. She struggled to right herself, working out the limbs held at awkward angles. If she cut herself free now, she might get through the fall to the deck below without a broken bone. But that would only drop her right into their midst. How would they react then? And what did they have planned for her now?

She found the answer soon enough, when a stretch of deck below her crumbled, its dust blowing out to leeward, and the net dropped slowly into the opened space. In a blink she was below deck, sheer walls rising around her. Someone convoked a new covering above her, plunging the hole into darkness, and as the convocation finished, the rope holding the net snapped, crashing it and her to the hard floor.

Pain rippled through her bones. She began to cry out, but bit her lip. She wouldn't let them break her, not that easily. She rolled to her knees, shaking off the remains of the dust from the net, and gasped hard until her knee and elbow stopped throbbing. Total blackness surrounded her; the walls, the floor, even her own hands were invisible. The flat, cold walls lay at arm's reach on either side. She was in a tiny chamber, cold, probably from the engine exhaust. She banged on one wall, and it made a solid sound. Purple and green fibers danced within her eyes, and she curled into the corner to fight her disorientation.

She sat there a long time, acclimating herself, breathing the darkness, shifting her sore back against the wall. She had to regain control, compose her thoughts.

What did she know about the raiders? They had formed after the fall of the Third Empire, around the time she herself had first appeared. Taking advantage of the chaos and the invention of skyships, they pillaged along the already-ravaged North-Leeward and Windward coasts, at least in the periods when they weren't fighting viciously amongst themselves. Since then, they had fallen and risen in prominence, showing surprising longevity for a group dedicated to such reckless behavior.

But that was the nature of boredom—the greatest threat in Aetheria, Karis had heard it called. Never much of a problem for her; after all, there was so much out there to learn, so many crafts to master. But not everyone had the aptitude for such pursuits, and many who did were unable to find like-minded mentors. Add in a dose of humanity's taste for malice, and it was little wonder the raiders could persist in getting their kicks out of finding daring, creative ways to hurt others.

Better. She felt calmer now. But she still had to think of a way out. Could she convoke a tool to help her escape? A drill? Cutting through the wall might be possible, but the cold and darkness would make it difficult to convoke anything mekkanikal. Besides, she wasn't sure she wanted the raiders discovering her skills. A useful prisoner would be less likely to be released, and someone had to do the work of keeping these skyships aloft. She compromised and focused on convoking a bed—at least if she was going to wait here, she should be comfortable—but the cold interfered with even that simple process, making it difficult to place the tiny aer bubbles necessary to make it soft.

When the bed was finally done she lay down, but the less she moved the more her anger grew. How could they do this to her? Animals. Monsters! She had to convince them to let her go, and do it soon, so she could return to Meli before the distance between them became too great.

The distance from Meli—oh, no.

The ship! Karis's connection to it had vanished as she ascended above the clouds. She had convoked too much of it herself, the entire hull and all the pontoons and most of the deck—all would be destroyed now, and Meli would be stranded...or drowned. *No!* Karis had to protect her, she was so young and innocent. It was all Karis's fault. Without her, Meli would never have taken this trip in the first place. She had to escape, had to make things right.

If only she hadn't let her guard down during the battle. She should never have taken her eye off the raiders, but everything had been moving so quickly. And what did she know about fighting, anyway? She despised everything about it, wanted nothing to do with any of this. She shouldn't have been here; she needed to get back. Back to Meli...

She turned the thoughts over again and again, and as the day passed lying in the darkness her heartbeat slowed and her eyes grew heavy. Memories came as she slipped closer to unconsciousness, a string of uncontrolled half-dreams.

She was standing at the side of the magistrate's ball, watching the crowds dance and make merry. Karis had already decided by then that coming to the island had been a mistake. She had no use for art or fashion, nor the quick-as-wind relationships the Sofidrans practiced. Those things were trivial, distractions from discovering the true potential of the aether, the purpose of her new life. Socializing was a way to gain influence or knowledge, not something to be pursued for its own sake—that only led to heartache and ruin. Or so she told herself, until that party.

Karis had been eyeing the motors on some moving sculptures, idly wondering if she could take them apart without anyone noticing, when Meli arrived.

"Pleased to meet you, Karis," she said, the skylights throwing white bands of highlights over her long hair.

Karis held her breath. "You are?"

"Of course. I've heard great things about your work. Mekkanisms fascinate me, though my plants and animals keep me busy enough."

Karis was so lost in the moment she couldn't recall what she said next, only Meli's smile and those wide brown eyes, always holding a hint of sadness, but so easy to get lost in.

"Well, we should try to plan a collaboration before you leave," she went on, not noticing Karis's stare. "If it's not too much of a burden on your time."

She flashed those teeth of hers, glimmering white behind full lips. That was all it took.

In barely any time at all, Karis was coming by her home every day, and adding rooms to her own newly convoked residence specifically to accommodate their joint projects. But even when she spent every spare moment with Meli, her new friend's bloom never faded. Instead they grew closer, talking the day away, laughing, working together in intense concentration, the time flying until weeks turned into years without notice.

"Plants need to grow like a person needs to draw or paint," Meli told Karis one day as she hung up new flowers. "That's what makes them so special. But they also don't know when to stop—if you let them, they'll crowd each other out until they begin to die. Over time, the ones that survive learn to craft their bodies with weapons and defenses. That's why the key to growing a beautiful garden is understanding the balance between their different strategies."

For a moment, Karis could only sit back and behold her. "It would be nice to know their secret," Karis replied at length. "I used to wonder if there was a way I could ever grow bigger."

"I think you're wonderful the way you are." Meli flashed another of those smiles. "Wonderfully special." The words were meaningless placation, but what mattered was the kindness behind their intent, her going out of her way to say them.

Yes, brilliant Meli. Selfless Meli.

"Oh, I forgot," Meli said, putting the flowers aside and letting her shears crumble. "Severain is coming over today. You know, he has friends who have asked about you. Some of them are handsome. I could set you up with one, just say the word."

Oblivious Meli.

Karis had wanted to go to the Automatia. She had her own plans, to discover great things, to show a light of knowledge on the world. But once she met Meli, Karis couldn't bring herself to leave without her.

Then for years Meli had vacillated, saying she wasn't ready. Well, maybe she *wasn't* ready, but so what? Karis had known what was best for her. Meli would come, and they would be together, happy at last, without the distractions of Sofidra.

Pure and utter selfishness. She had tricked her best friend, her only friend, and now look at what had happened. Oh, gods…she was sorry.

Karis drifted further into dream, but in her disturbed state images from the past intruded. The ground bubbling, burning their feet. An ear falling. With her last trace of lucidity she pushed them away and brought Meli back.

"But how can I approach him? We don't exactly run in the same circles."

Meli sat on the balcony, speaking in a petulant whisper. Karis had sat down away from her on the sofa, but as they talked she had inched herself closer. It was so hard to keep from touching her. The pull grew stronger every day.

"You'll find a way to speak to him, and to convince him to help us." She gave in partially to her urges and took Meli's hands, pretending to desire only her attention. "You have to. Don't you see? Our knowledge, combined with his muscle. It's perfect."

Meli's eyes fluttered. She had struck a chord, there. Meli valued her future offspring more than anything, and Karis knew it.

"Take this chance," Karis continued. "You speak and speak of this dream, but how would you feel if this was your opportunity and you wasted it? How long would you regret it?"

Meli stared back a long time, her eyes glassy with tears, and Karis wondered if she had gone too far. Then she slowly nodded. "You're right. I need to make a decision, once and for all. Just decide and go through with it, no matter what."

She stiffened and sat up, exhaling with a shudder, as if the fear rattled her as it left. "You're a good friend, Karis. It's getting dark, now. I'd better get home, I don't want to interfere with your rest."

The dream shifted then, moving from simple memory to events that never occurred. Instead of letting Meli rise as she had then, Karis laid a hand on her arm.

Meli looked down, confused. Karis pulled her closer, her whole body shaking. Then the dream words came out, the ones she could never bring herself to say.

Don't go, Meli. Please. Stay.

She reached for Meli's cheek and their lips met.

Something changed, a brush of aer moving through the room. Karis shot up in bed. A light came from behind a pile of dust where the wall used to be, and a slender man with bushy eyebrows stepped into the opening. The veins in Karis's neck throbbed, her heart slamming in her chest, but if the man had noticed anything amiss, his face didn't betray it.

"Uh, he thought you should know," the man said in a nasal drone. "They're having an assembly."

"What? Who?"

The man shrugged. "Everyone." He headed back the way he had come, leaving the wall open behind him.

She stood and rubbed her eyes, almost wondering if she were still dreaming. Letting the bed crumble to keep it from stealing her concentration, she followed him into the hallway.

Sturdy walls gave way to thin brown paneling, dimly lit by overhead tunnels leading to the deck above. Patches and repairs covered every surface inside the ship, convoked in haste and without a care for existing design. As Karis moved further, the smell changed from the sharp chill of engine exhaust to the rankness of human bodies. She passed a series of doors on either side, then came to a wide staircase leading up. Voices drifted into the hall from a large room at the top, where the man who had fetched her must have already gone. The assembly area. She lifted her chin and stomped in.

She had expected some sort of inquisition: the raider king sitting atop his throne, flanked by his loyal minions, trying to intimidate her by flaunting his power. Instead, the raiders—almost all male, of course—were gathered in a rough circle around the low-ceilinged room, broken into clumps whispering among themselves. At the center, two raiders in studded black jumpsuits stood slightly behind a third, a tall fellow with a long face and reddish-brown ponytail.

"We know they're waiting off Mariten right now, vulnerable," the tall raider yelled. "How long do you expect us to sit here with our hands on our dicks?"

The recipient of his fury was a raider reclining on a long plush sofa, who wiped a bit of the standing one's spittle from his nose and brushed it through his dirty blond hair. "It's bait, Hindal." He spoke calmly, as if he were discussing plans for dinner. "The Reviled have stopped raiding so they can focus on destroying us. They have some sort of deal going with the Maritenians. If we go in there full bore, they'll tear us to shreds."

The one called Hindal scowled and paced, giving Karis a better view of the reclining one and his seat, its cushion molded to fit his head and limbs. Karis didn't take much stock in the looks of men, but he was so handsome even she had to acknowledge it, pale of skin with a dimpled chin and scruffy sideburns.

"You know a lot about battle, don't you?" Hindal said. "What have you ever done in a raid, other than run away?"

The reclining one smiled. He had a way of speaking in his low voice that made the others lean in to listen. "If I hadn't run away, none of us would be here now."

"Here? What does being here get us? The longer the Reviled control the Mariten coast, the more their strength grows. If you won't strike, then I'll take my crew out alone. We'll hit them from behind, let them know they're not as safe as they think."

Some murmurs of appreciation went up from the crowd.

"You're right," the reclining one said. More murmuring, surprised this time. "If we split the fleet, they won't be as safe as they think. They'll be safer. And it won't be until after they smash you that they'll realize how badly they overestimated you. You fetid idiot."

Laughter spread across the room. Hindal narrowed his eyes. "You're as worthless as you are cowardly. I gave you one last chance to make good, and all you've done is poxed us with a disastrous raid."

The other raider shrugged, rumpling his sofa cushion. "Things went a little bad. No reason for us to head north instead of finishing the job."

"One ship, three passengers. A moldy little raft in the middle of nowhere, and your crew can't even pick them up without losing one of my strikers."

"It turns out they had some kind of strange weapon aboard. Which is exactly the sort of thing we're looking for."

"Exactly the sort of thing *you're* looking for."

"We need something new. Those deck-eating spyders are worse than useless." Annoyance crept onto the reclining one's face.

"We don't need tricks and gimmicks. All we should be doing is fighting the Reviled, not pulling small-time raids with nothing to show for it."

"Nothing? What about my spoils?"

"What spoils? A smoothskin? She's odd, I'll grant you, but what good is she?"

"Why don't you ask her?" The raider sat up and turned to Karis. With a loud brushing of limbs and fabric, the rest of the room joined him. "Hello there, sweets."

The sight of their collective eyeballs felt like moving from darkness into full daylight. Sweat beaded on her forehead. She wiped it away, clamped her jaw shut and glared.

"Welcome to our ship," the reclining one said. "I'm Roilan, but you can call me Roi. What's your name?"

"None of your business," Karis said. "When are you letting me go?"

Hindal snorted. "Oh yes, Roi. She'll be helpful, I can tell."

Roi held up his hand to quiet the chuckling crowd. "You don't want to be here. I understand completely. And if you won't help us fight, then there's no point in us keeping you here. But before I let you go, I need to ask you some questions. After I get the answers, you can leave."

Karis took a deep breath. He had a charming tongue, which meant she had to tread all the more carefully. "Ask whatever you like. If I feel like it, I'll answer."

"All right. First question: who was with you on that boat?"

"My friends."

"Wonderful. Friends make the best traveling companions, I find." Roi leaned over and slapped Hindal on the ass. Hindal snarled in reply. "So then, where exactly were you and your friends headed?"

"Nowhere," Karis said. "Out to sea for a cruise and then back to Sofidra."

"Interesting. Not terribly believable, but interesting. Next: why does one of your friends just happen to possess a sword which cuts through striker ships like they were made of paper?"

Karis kept her mouth closed. No need to discuss the sword—she didn't need to give this scum a reason to go after Meli.

Roi tapped his fingers on his seat. "Let's back up a bit. Your male companion—what's his name?"

"Ariden."

"Can't say I've heard of him. And your other friend, the woman? Who is she?"

Karis bared her teeth. "You don't get to know her name."

Some of the raiders laughed at the five-foot-tall smoothskin woman attempting to sound menacing.

"Fair enough," Roi said. "Though the crew said there were some plants growing on the deck. Did you convoke them?"

"No."

"Then I'd bet it was her, right?"

She must have blinked, or looked down momentarily, because he nodded and smiled. *Mold.*

"Ah, yes. It all makes sense, now. Ariden was the muscle, and she-who-shall-not-be-named handled the finer touches. And what was your little contribution?"

Karis stayed silent, and absolutely still.

"There were three engines on board. Nice ones, to hear the crew tell it. Did you make them?"

She cast her gaze about the assembled crowd. Most of them looked bored, but a few were staring at her and smiling.

"Just leave me alone and let me go."

Roi held up his finger. "I said, after you answer. Phaestal!"

The tall raider who had fetched her earlier pushed his way out of the crowd. "Yeah?"

"You observed the entire raid through your spyglass, didn't you?" Roi asked.

"Uh-huh."

"And what did you see our smoothskin acquaintance doing, just after they spotted us?"

Karis frowned. It was as she suspected—if they knew so much already, then all of this was no more than a charade for their amusement.

"Uhh…" Phaestal rubbed his chin and stared at the ceiling. "I saw her run to where the engines were."

"And then?"

"And then she made them more powerful. To try and outrun the striker."

"You don't know that!" Karis hissed.

"Sure I do," Phaestal said, nodding casually. "You added some accelerant to the rotation chamber to make it spin faster. I do it all the time during maintenance cycles."

Titters came from the surrounding group. Roi grinned. Karis felt a flush in her cheeks. It was clear where this was going, and she had no desire to stand here until the sky darkened while the raiders continued their inane laughter.

"All right," she said quietly. "I'm a mekkanist."

"Self-taught?"

"No." Not with engines like hers, they wouldn't believe it. "I've had several mentors. All of them masters."

"I appreciate your honesty," Roi said.

"Are we done here?" Hindal said. "Mekkanists aren't going to beat the Reviled for us. We need fighters."

"Just hold on," Roi said.

"She's probably a Reviled spy," Hindal continued. "Chuck her overboard and let's get back to business."

Karis's heart skipped a beat. Hindal's matter-of-fact tone left no doubt he would do what he said. She realized with some embarrassment that she was staring at Roi, waiting for him to save her.

Roi's grin widened. "She stands out a bit too much to be a spy." Relief. "Tell me, that sword Ariden was using—did you design it?"

A few whispers went up around her. Nervous, angry—the sword was something they feared. But what they feared, they would want to control. She had to appear cooperative if she wanted to escape, but the more she told them, the more incentive they would have to go back after Meli. No. She wouldn't let that happen, wouldn't lead them to her friend, even if they threatened her life.

"I have no idea how to make it." That was the truth, at least.

"Who does?"

"Someone else. A man."

"And where is this man?"

"I don't know. He's dead, most likely."

Hindal snorted.

"I believe her," Roi said. "But what about this…bird?"

She sensed danger coming. "What about it?"

"The crew said it was unusual. It had some sort of engines in its wings. Could you convoke one for us?"

"No. I don't know how."

"And what about your nameless friend? Could she make one?"

"No one convoked it," Karis said a bit too quickly. "We...found it."

"*Found* it? You mean you just happened upon a giant, wild bird, and it took a liking to you? Decided to hang around for a while?"

"Enough," Hindal said. "No more nonsense about birds. I'm leaving, Roi."

"The assembly?"

"The fleet. You can join us in battle, or not."

Roi looked annoyed again. "Phaestal," he said. "Take our nameless mekkanist back to her cell."

Phaestal moved toward her, but she stepped away. "My name is Karis, all right? I've answered all your questions, now let me go."

"I'd love to. But there is the small matter of the code."

"The code?"

"The raider code." Roi swung his feet to the floor and stood, his fine sofa crumbling beneath him. "No raider shall let an insult or injury go un-avenged. Anything taken from us must be returned. Your friend Ariden has cost us quite a bit; those strikers aren't easy to make. Not to mention his capture of poor Sirdu. You're going to stay here until your debt is repaid."

"But *you* attacked *us*!"

"Shut up!" Hindal yelled. He turned back to Roi. "You've failed. Answer me: are you coming with us or not?"

Roi frowned. "It's a stupid idea, leaving this opportunity out there. For all we know they're stranded, just waiting for us to pick them up."

"For Elaethim's sake, have some honor. Yes, or no?"

Roi took in a deep breath, exhaled, then put on a half smile. "If you fight, you have my support."

The surrounding raiders burst into clamor. They broke from their groups, yelling across the room, pushing every which way. Roi and Hindal continued to speak at the center, but Karis could no longer hear them.

"Come on." Phaestal grabbed her elbow.

"Don't touch me!" She tugged her arm away and headed out the nearest exit, back the way she had come. The meeting had gone about as poorly as she could have imagined, but she shouldn't have been surprised. She was unused to dealing with such savages, people who dedicated their lives to killing each other over nothing. Still, she had been unprepared for their leader's guile—a mistake she would not repeat again.

Phaestal caught up with her and stepped to her side. When the noise of the raiders had faded down the hall, he spoke again.

"I hope you're happy with yourself."

"Why? What did I do?"

"You didn't help Roi, didn't tell him anything useful, so he's not going to get his way."

"Good," she said. "Why would I ever want to help him?"

"Because," Phaestal said, leaning over and whispering in her ear. "Now we're going to war."

7

The next wave bore down. Ariden inched further up onto his piece of floating wreckage in order to avoid it. A poor choice—the collision flipped his chunk of wreckage over, and he remained under the waves while it took its time righting itself.

The ship hadn't lasted long. A few moments after Karis was pulled from sight, the first creaks and snapping began. The pontoons burst, dropping them into the sea below, smashing apart what little of the ship was not already crumbling. Ariden clutched the soaked wreckage and shivered. He needed to convoke something flat to ride the waves, but the deep fog was colder than aer, the sea colder than fog, and he was spending half his concentration on keeping himself upright. Nevertheless, he closed his eyes and called to the aether, feeling the thin wisps of aer and depositing them into a circular, upside-down canoe. The combination wreckage-canoe soon became top-heavy, and it flipped and pinned him under again. Sputtering, cursing the cold, Ariden caught the rim of the canoe and hauled himself inside.

He let the original wreckage crumble and flopped into the pile of wet dust that it made. Now was a poor time to rest, given that any large wave would surely capsize him, but the mere act of floating in something concave brought a simple relief from which he was unable to rouse himself. He breathed deep, and the fog flooded his lungs, making him cough. A pox on the stuff—it was thick, tickling his skin as it drifted by on the wind, and it bathed every direction in an all-consuming cover of white. It had been a very long time since he had last been stuck beneath it, but not nearly long enough.

A high-pitched yell came over the waves. Ariden sat up, dazed. The yell came again—Meli, it had to be. His body told him to ignore her, but something deeper—perhaps an instinct honed from rising to train early so many times back in Caeridor—compelled him to move anyway. He slowly convoked a wide, flat oar, stopping several times to recover the canoe when it tipped from the extra weight. The sea spun him and he dipped the oar to halt himself, then paddled toward where he thought the sound might have come from.

He crested one wave, then another, taking cold splashes in the face each time. Each stroke of the paddle pained his cold, stiff muscles. Was he even headed in the right direction? The yelling had stopped, and the fog and waves remained unbroken on all sides.

"Meli!" he called.

Moments later, Elsa buzzed through the fog and hovered above him.

"It is can help!" Her high-pitched voice was a thin warble above the ocean's roar. *"Ariden is trouble, come trouble."*

Ariden pointed at the useless oar.

Elsa bobbed acknowledgment, then tilted her underside at him and convoked a thick length of cable from the area near her feet. Ariden caught it, and it wriggled in his hands, distinctly alive. He swallowed in disgust as he secured it to the edge of the canoe. Elsa took off, engines straining, and the cable went taut. Ariden manned the oar again, and between his muscle and her guidance they crested enough waves to reveal Meli floating on a shell she had convoked around one of the former ship's cabins.

Her face was strained with fear, her fingernails digging into the roof, though she had been luckier in her landing spot than him; a length of decking around the cabin kept her upright and afloat. Ariden ran the canoe up onto it and hopped aboard.

"Thank the gods," he said. "I'm poxing freezing."

She pointed, eyes wild. "You!"

"Me!?"

"You let them take Karis!" She waved her finger up and behind her. "What are they going to do with her?"

"How should I know? They came from the north; perhaps they'll take her back there."

"North! Good gods, we have to go after her."

Some welcome this was. He pressed his back to the cabin and sat. "The wind will push us leeward."

"So what? You're just going to abandon her?"

"Don't twist my words. I intend to go after her, but if we want to change direction, we need a sail and we need a keel. How are we going to convoke something that heavy in this fog? Perhaps you should think for a moment, before you start yelling orders."

"You're the one who failed to protect her in the first place. Ariden, the world's greatest fighter!"

That one got to him. "I warned you, didn't I? I told you, if it came down to it, the deal was with you, not her. You have no one to blame but yourself."

"I knew it," Her voice dripped with loathing. "You never planned to help her. You might as well have wished for her to die, you puddle of slime." She shuffled to the far side of the cabin to seethe.

Ariden stood and spat in her direction, watched the saliva fly off into the wind, then kicked his canoe into the waves. He needed to convoke a proper hull for the junk he was floating on if he wanted any hope of drying off. He closed his eyes and reached out to the aether, but the moist aer attached itself to the wet deck sluggishly, as if it were as miserable as him.

"Find her, Elsa, please."

Elsa had landed on the cabin roof, and Meli rubbed her head as she spoke. "Help her in whatever way she needs. Stay as long as you need to. I'll send a signal so you can find me again."

Elsa nuzzled her hand, bowed, and took to the sky.

"What are you doing?" Ariden shouted. "We could have used that thing; we need a way to see over the fog."

"Stop being so selfish."

"Selfish? I'm trying to—"

A groaning noise within the cabin interrupted him.

Meli looked down, then at Ariden. "What was that?"

"Don't open it," he said, holding out his hand to form a weapon. "Wait for my signal."

Meli nodded. The groaning came again, followed by thumps as someone banged on the inside of the wall. Forming the Scythe in the cold would take too long, so Ariden convoked a basic spear the length of his forearm. He signaled to Meli, and the wall cracked, then collapsed into a cloud of dust as a man fell through it.

The man stumbled, waving his hands to ward off the sudden light, then looked up and saw Ariden ready to run him through. He squeaked and dropped into a quivering ball on the deck. When Ariden stuck the point of the spear into his ribs, he let out another high-pitched squeal.

"What are you doing?!" Meli yelled.

"I suppose I should kill him," Ariden said. "He did try to plant an axe in my face."

"I give up!" the raider shouted, arms cupped over his head.

"He's defenseless," Meli said.

"So what?" Ariden poked him again.

The raider screamed and scuttled back into the cabin. "Please, ma'am, don't let him kill me!"

"Ariden," Meli said. "Don't do it."

"He'll probably cut our throats the first chance he gets."

"I won't, I swear it!" The raider uncovered his face, revealing a pug nose and scruffy chin. The top half of his jumpsuit had torn in the fighting and he hadn't repaired it, leaving his substantial gut hanging over his waistline. "I'm sorry about the axe. I saw you were beating my friends and something came over me. No hard feelings, right? It was just a simple raid."

"A simple *raid?*" Ariden kicked him in the belly, and he rolled over and groaned.

"Stop!" Meli yelled.

"You stop. This man helped kidnap your friend, remember? You act like you prefer him to me."

"I don't prefer him, but what good does…oh…" She swayed and buckled as a large wave passed under them, then dropped to the cabin roof.

"What now?"

"My head has felt strange since the battle." She sat back up. "Just forget it."

"Strange how?" the raider asked.

"Shut up, you," Ariden said, readying another kick. "Are you sure you don't want me to get rid of him so we can concentrate on getting to shore?"

"No!" the raider yelled.

"I already told you, we're not going to shore," Meli said. "We're going after Karis and Elsa."

Ariden crossed his arms and frowned. The idea of heading north *was* appealing, especially if it meant taking out his anger on the raiders—just having this one nearby was enough to make his sword arm ache. But how realistic was tacking into the wind, on seas this rough, in a craft they had improvised themselves? No, they had to reach land first, by the quickest route possible, and then locate someone who could build them a better ship. Of course, depending on where they landed, finding someone like that might not be easy, either. But there was no use in bringing that up now.

"We don't have the means to assault the raiders as-is. Even if we could find them, they'd be thousands of feet in the aer."

"Then we'll bring them down." Meli closed her eyes and took several deep breaths. Her skin had grown pale. "Elsa will help us find them. And don't forget, we still have him." She pointed at the raider.

"He doesn't seem all that useful. But unless you want the wind deciding our course, then you'll have to find a way to convoke a keel."

"Then I will. After I lie down a bit." She hopped down from the cabin, landing unsteadily on the tilting deck, then curled up with her back to them.

The raider bit his lip and swallowed. "What about me?"

Ariden took a melodramatic turn toward him, letting the spear swing, which had the intended effect of sending the coward cringing away. "You're getting tied to the mast, after I convoke it," he said. "Then once the keel is done, maybe I'll toss you inside it. Could always use some more dead weight."

Ariden gradually constructed a new ship around the remains of the old one, and the day passed as slowly as it always did when he was engaged in miserable labor. The wind and waves were as chill as ever, his mind fatigued, and the enormity of the task ahead never seemed to diminish.

When night fell he had completed most of a new hull, but the greater part of the mast, sail and yard, the most basic of riggings, and a till-controlled rudder remained half-finished. Alone he worked, while Meli only muttered and moaned. By morning she lay at the gunwale, incapacitated, letting the tips of the waves splash her in the face.

"Oh, Elaethim…kill me."

Elaethim ignored her request, and Ariden did his best to as well. The rigging had come apart in the night, and for every knot and pulley he fixed, two more crumbled away.

It seemed that the only one of them who had slept the night through was the raider, who blinked awake suddenly, his hands twisting in their bonds behind him. He worked his jaw and yawned.

"What's wrong, my lady?" he asked.

Meli answered by rolling over, convulsing and spitting over the side.

"It's the motion of the waves," Ariden gritted his teeth as he stretched to grab a line. "In the war I saw many men become ill this way. Some were so bad we thought the plagues had returned."

"Yes, of course." The raider nodded stupidly. "I've seen it on the skyships, usually with the newer recruits."

"No one asked you, scum," Ariden said.

The raider frowned. "I told you, the name's Sirdu. And I'm only trying to help."

Meli rolled onto her back. "Then help me. What do you do for the new recruits that get this?"

"Drop them off on land," Sirdu said. "Unless they throw themselves overboard, first."

Meli groaned. Ariden rolled his eyes and returned to work, scraping out the clods of mud which had washed in overnight.

"Perhaps a story would take our mind off our troubles?" Sirdu said. "Have you ever heard 'Lastari's Tower?'"

"Innumerable times," Ariden muttered.

"It was the height of the classical age," Sirdu intoned, trying and failing to give his uninspiring voice some grandeur. "Before plants and animals covered the world, dust filled the aer and the sea, and the gods walked Aetheria and demanded that the people bend to their will."

He stared at the wet deck in front of him. A lumpy gray-black mass appeared there, undulating as he convoked shapes upon it, poor excuses for rocks and animals and gods.

"Such was the lot of Lastari, whose city Altania was besieged by The Great God Estinpar, who sought worship and tribute." A group of gray buildings appeared in the center of the rocks. "The Altanites refused, being a proud people of that age, and Estinpar removed himself, grumbling of his future revenge. Many years passed, and the people forgot the god and his demands, and returned to their daily lives of simple joys. Lastari in this time grew bored of her surroundings, and seeking new knowledge and adventure to leeward, left the city to explore the seaside, promising to return in a century or less to see her friends again.

"Long did Lastari walk, and many things did she learn. In those days, the philosophers had not yet joined together in their enclaves, and instead each man and women was likely to know one of the three esoteric convocations of legend, which they trusted others to use freely. Perhaps it was this learning, combined with her own innate genius, which led Lastari to deduce the existence of a fourth legendary convocation. Little is known about it now, of course, except that it was perhaps more powerful than any of the others, and Lastari had pledged upon her return to use it for the benefit of all Aetherians of high moral standing.

"But in the fiftieth year of her journey, Lastari felt a terrible sadness come over her heart, beckoning her home. Upon her return, she found her deepest fears had come true: Estinpar had returned, grown to a mile in height, and had crushed the entire city to dust under one of his massive boots."

Stretching against the ropes, Sirdu dropped his booted foot onto the tiny city, squishing wet dust over the deck.

"You had better be planning on cleaning that," Ariden said, returning to the tangled ropes.

"All her friends, gone in an instant!" Sirdu tried to comply with the command by kicking at the dust, but only succeeded in spreading it around further. "She swore to take the god's life then and there—impossible, you may say, but Lastari knew that the fourth legendary convocation, combined with her fury, had the ability to accomplish such a feat. Estinpar sensed this, and rather than stay and fight, he transformed into a bird and flew to his home in the sky."

Ariden tossed down the rope he had been convoking and breathed deeply. "Listen…Dirku?"

"Sirdu."

"Right. Shut up."

"But there's much more in the story…"

"I know the poxing story. And if you value your nose staying attached to your face, you won't keep telling me things I already know."

That quieted him for a while. Sirdu went back to sloshing his foot in the muck, while Ariden returned to his labor.

"An old tale can be made new by the right teller," Sirdu said, having finally worked up the courage. "Or so it's been said."

"Allow me, then," Ariden replied. "Classical age, city smashed, Lastari builds a tower higher than anyone has ever seen, it falls down, the end."

"Well, there's a lot more to it than that…" Sirdu mumbled. He strained uncomfortably against his bonds once more, sighed, then closed his eyes and tucked his chin to his chest.

Another day passed. Ariden convoked a sail and a rudder, his fingers dust-caked and sore and his eyelids made of bedrock. Sirdu continued to talk whenever he felt he could get away with it, perhaps because it was his only way to punish Ariden for keeping him tied up.

Meli mainly gurgled in anguish. Ariden could only imagine what being so ill was like. The closest he had come were the nerves before a life-or-death battle or an important fight, but from the noises Meli made, what she felt was far worse.

There was nothing to be done for it, though, besides pushing forward with convoking the ship. By nightfall, the mast and rigging were done, the sail ready to hang. Ariden collapsed, utterly exhausted. He was tired of the gray haze surrounding them, of the bone-chilling wetness that leaked into the ship no matter how tight the seams. His eyelids felt heavier than bedrock, and no sound would now keep him from a deep slumber.

How much time passed before the wind picked up, he did not know, but the sky was still dark when howling gusts intruded on his consciousness. The sea grew fierce, rocking the ship nearly onto its side with each swell. Meli's groans and shudders became ever more disturbing, and Ariden passed the long, cold night drifting between sleeping and waking nightmare.

When day broke, Sirdu was slumped against the mast, lines of wear across his stubbly face. Meli lay with her eyes open, quiet at last though her skin was a pale green. Ariden rose and teetered about the tilting deck, convoking a bucket to bail the dirty sea wash between dizzy spells.

More repairs followed. Then he picked up the sail and began to attach it to the yard. Meli stirred and spoke in a rasp.

"Ariden. Karis…we have to get her…we have to turn north."

The cloth slipped from his hand and he grunted in frustration. "Your devotion is inspiring."

"How many…" She gulped. "If we turned now, how many days until we reach the northern coast?"

"Could be a couple weeks, perhaps."

Meli made a sound Ariden hadn't heard since the war, from a man whose intestines had been lying in a pile before him at the time.

"We've been drifting leeward all this time." Sirdu leaned forward and winced as his wrists caught the mast. "We should keep heading that way. We're probably close to shore by now."

"Once again, your opinion was not requested," Ariden said. "But he is right, Meli."

She shook her head. "I won't leave her behind. We had a deal. You will sail this ship north if I request it."

"Indeed I will," Ariden said. "Eventually, with or without your help, I'll get this sail and keel in order. And then, we'll spend weeks charging over the waves and weaving through the wind, back and forth and back and forth, up and down—"

"Stop!" Meli shouted. "Enough." She buried her head beneath her arms.

"Right, then." With her continued silence as his assent, Ariden gave the ropes one final tug, and the sail billowed, pushing them leeward.

8

The next time Phaestal came to her cell, Karis was waiting for him, sitting on the bed cross-legged and facing away. He entered and stood there staring at the back of her head, breath whistling out his nostrils.

"Hello?"

She ignored him, and he turned and left without another word, closing up the wall behind him. Message delivered. Now to repeat the ritual for as many days as it took them to free her. She had lasted one night alone; she could wait however long it took. If these stupid boys wished to kill each other for sport, then they were free to do so, but she would never be party to their atrocities.

She lay in the darkness, convoking tiled patterns or simple projects to amuse herself. Waiting through the night before had been relatively easy; she was tired, and knew she would have had little more light outside her cell than in it. But the day would be a different matter. Now was when she would have to be stronger. She listened to the drone of the ship's engines, and time dragged at a slug's pace. She had no way of knowing how long it had been when the boredom truly began to assert itself. But boredom she could handle—it was the memories that boredom dragged to the surface that were the real trouble.

Because as much as she would have liked to forget, her current reality was all too familiar—that feeling of imprisonment, of being trapped by threats of violence. That was how she had lived every day at the beginning of her first life, as a member of the God's Chosen.

At least, that was what Sylas had called them. But in truth, he was the one doing the choosing, the unquestioned leader, the only mouthpiece of the word of Ba-el. To help spread that word, Sylas recruited his "little ones," found them and raised them, taught them to obey and to perform in his shows. Then as now, smoothskins were rare, and the sight of so many together, doing the things they did, brought in large crowds to stand and gawk. Some of the gawkers, out of boredom or curiosity, would stay afterward to hear Sylas's sermons, and thus become potential new disciples for his flock.

She remembered well one day in particular, when she stood behind Sylas, watching him. They had set up camp among the dusty remains of what had once been a great city, before the Lost Coast was Lost. The sky was at its brightest and the disciples had finished convoking and trimming the stage. Sylas sat in his simple chair, judging the final preparations, tapping his finger in anticipation. No matter how many shows they performed, there was always tension just before, brought by the knowledge that so many eyes would be upon them, and there were so many ways to get something wrong. Many years later, when she saw the troupes in competition to perform the biggest plays in Sofidra, her first thought had been to wonder why anyone would voluntarily subject themselves to that jangled, hairs-on-end feeling.

Karis approached and touched Sylas's shoulder. He whirled his head around, anger in his gray eyes. He was gangly, his body mostly limbs and his face mostly cheekbone, and he had an otherworldly aer about him, as if his mind straddled the realms of man and god. As a rule, little ones never spoke to Sylas, and though she could not remember the exact circumstances, it must have been a deep trepidation indeed which had caused her to break that taboo.

"I don't want to do the show this evening." She refused to meet his stare. "Can someone else take my place?"

She braced herself, but to her surprise his face softened. A friendly smile crossed his lips, one she had never seen before. "Karis. Beloved of the God. Pray tell, why do you ask this?"

She hesitated. She had prepared a dozen possible excuses, but something about his sudden calmness made her reveal the truth. "It doesn't feel right to me, the things we do."

"Not right? The sacred passion of Ba-el is not *right*?"

In her gut she knew she had made a mistake. She stammered, but before she could correct herself he snapped his fingers.

"Vikter!" A figure behind him turned. Sylas continued to hold Karis's gaze as he spoke. "Please accompany our little one this afternoon, and make sure she gives a good performance. And make sure she continues to do so, every day for the next six weeks."

"No." The word was no more than a squeak. Not Vikter. Anyone but him. A walking mound of muscle, topped with that glassy stare. She couldn't recall why, but the thought of him made her queasy to this day. Her memories grew hazy as he approached, but that terrible dread hung with her still. She didn't want to be in the show; why was he making her? Why? Why did the raiders keep her on this ship, when all she wanted was to leave? She held her ribs and shook her head, shuddering in the dark.

She was breathing heavily, unable to get enough aer. When would Phaestal return? Would he really wait until the next morning? Perhaps he would check on her again at midday. But had that time already passed? All she wanted was a little light and fresh aer, just to be taken out for a little while and—

Stop. What was she thinking? She hadn't wanted to acknowledge Phaestal's existence before, and now here she was, losing her grip, hoping for his next appearance. Could she really be considering going outside with him? No. They hadn't broken her that easily.

Strength renewed, she sat up tall and continued to wait.

The rest of the day and most of a night passed before she gave in.

The decision to capitulate was like having a weight removed from her chest. Once she had made it she realized it was not the boredom or the loneliness or the visions of her past which had made her confinement unbearable, but the uncertainty. Just how long would they be willing to leave her in the cell? A few days? A few weeks? Longer? And every day she would have to face whichever raider they sent to fetch her again, knowing that a simple word would free her to at least walk the ship and see the daylight.

She slept briefly, waking when wall behind her cracked and crumbled. She stood and faced it. It would do no good to dwell on how she had betrayed her principles. Meli needed her. It was better to leave the cell, to find opportunities to escape. If she had to appear cooperative in the meantime to have free run of the ship, then so be it.

Phaestal stepped over the knee-high pile of dust at the entrance and raised an eyebrow.

"Uh...so...are you gonna help me with my work?"

"If I come with you, do I have a choice?"

"I guess." He shrugged. "I don't know."

He headed back down the hallway, but this time left the wall open behind him. Karis sniffed. Even though it was dusty with the remains of the door, the smell of the aer from outside was intoxicating. She strode out after him.

Phaestal noticed her following and slowed. He turned right, into a section of hallway where the ceiling opened, so that they were walking through a narrow trench under the top deck. There he convoked a set of stairs, and Karis followed him up into the day.

Her mind buzzed, primed for input. The scene on the deck was calmer than it had been the day before, when the crew had been reacting to the botched raid. Now only a few were rushing to attend to some duty or another, while the rest stood around, socializing in small groups. The chattering lot wouldn't have looked out of place at a festival in Sofidra, if it weren't for their clothing: skintight jumpsuits were the rule, usually black. Accessories varied, although flight goggles were not uncommon, and hair tended to be tied back or kept short if not hidden under tight caps. As before, the raiders paid little attention to their prisoner. That might make it easier for her to slip through when the time came to escape.

Near the center of the deck, a raider had convoked piles of cakes for the others to eat. Phaestal picked up two as he passed.

"Want one?" he asked, raising his nasal voice over the wind.

"No."

"They help the work go by. Got a special ingredient."

"What special—" Karis drew back in shock. "You're *vipping*? Up here?"

"Nah," he said. "Just something with a little buzz. I don't go for the hard stuff; Roi doesn't like it. But if you're interested, I know some guys who could probably get you some."

Insanity. It had been a hundred years since someone had given her vipp at a gathering in Sidel, but she remembered well the dizziness and confusion, the irrational thoughts winging their way through her consciousness. If the raiders were taking it on the ship, where a misstep meant plummeting to one's death, then they were more obscenely reckless than she had imagined.

"If you didn't know, I'm basically in charge of keeping the ship running," Phaestal said, oblivious to her reaction. "It's hard enough on a normal day, but now Roi wants everything tuned up as high as it will go. We're going to need to replace the manual control systems, too. This bird isn't that maneuverable, but there's a chance we might need to give it some hard turns. You know—" He shot her a sidelong glance. "During the big battle."

Karis trailed her hand along a low rail which separated her from a dozen engine towers mounted to the starboard side of the ship. Between and beyond them lay nothing but aer. No chains bound her, no one was close enough to grab her if she jumped. Just one hop over the rail, and she would be free. But even if she had a parachute or some other method of slowing her fall, the raiders would only fly down and scoop her up again, perhaps trawling with a net if she tried to hide in the fog. No wonder they put hardly any effort into watching her; getting off the ship would not be nearly enough to escape, not this high up over the open sea.

Further along the rail, a group of raiders loitered next to another man who knelt near a detached engine chassis. A row of orange pipes lay on the ground beside him, and he reached back and inserted one into the machine. He repeated the motion and picked up another, but this one changed shape in his hand. By the time it was in front of him it had morphed into a three-foot length of flexible material in the shape of a penis. The nearby group exploded into laughter.

"Diseased mucklizards!" He tossed the thing over the railing. "Which one of you put that dick there?!"

"Pathetic," Karis muttered.

Phaestal looked back as he mounted a ladder to the engine level. "What's the problem?"

"The behavior here. Aren't you ashamed of it?"

"Why? It's a joke."

"I shouldn't expect you to understand." But she tried again anyway. "Haven't you ever wondered why there's no women here?"

"That's not true. We have some women. Like…" He contemplated. "Like Jaela. And uh…well, some others, for sure."

She shook her head and sighed, then followed him down to the engine-access catwalk encircling the ship. Though being leeward of the hull blocked some of the wind, the downwash of the propellers still flapped their clothes and rattled the thin grating that stood between them and a deadly fall to the sea below. Karis tried not to look down.

Phaestal shimmied along to an unused engine, then crumbled its outer casing. "You know, I never met a smoothskin before. But I've heard about you. They say you're quiet types. Like, you take things really seriously."

"They say?"

"Yeah."

"Well, why would you judge *me* based on what someone else said?"

He shrugged. "Just telling you what I heard. You want to take a look at this?"

She flashed him a sour look, then leaned in to view the engine's interior and nearly gasped. Karis had been studying engine design for over a century, but the really large ones could still steal her breath. The

Sofidrans saw mekkanisms as a means to an end, a way of making flying billboards to display their paintings and so on. But there was an undeniable beauty within the engines themselves, all those parts, so precise, moving at such incredible speed.

"It's a good design," she said. "Excellent, really." She leaned in further, rubbing the parts with her hands. "The main shaft is worn down."

He nodded. "There's not as much dust way up here, as long as we steer around the big storms, but it still gets in there eventually. You fix this one, and I'll check the next one over."

"Wait. You want me to repair *your* engine? Why would you trust me?"

Phaestal scratched his head. "Roi told me to. But even if you messed it up, one engine malfunction wouldn't be a big problem. The stability system could handle it."

"The stability system?"

"Yeah. It's the reason we can have this engine off right now without the ship lurching to one side. It keeps everything in sync; without it, we'd drop out of the sky like bedrock."

She made the mistake of looking down, then clutched the handrail as hard as she could. "But who convoked the stability system?"

"Roi did, of course."

Of course. *Welcome to our ship,* Roi had said. Indeed, the flagship was a product of many convocations from many raiders, its parts interlinked so that a loss of one wouldn't damage the integrity of the whole. But looked at another way, it was really Roilan's ship alone—because he kept the engines in sync, he was the only individual they could never get rid of.

Phaestal headed off to spin down another engine, leaving Karis unsupervised with the first. What was she supposed to do, now? She didn't want to help them, but if she broke the thing further or refused to do anything at all, then Phaestal could report her shirking to Roi, who might punish her with more confinement. Was that worth it, for such a simple task as bolstering the main shaft?

She sighed with distaste and convoked with as little effort as possible, stopping every few moments to turn the shaft and ensure it was symmetrical. Once it was restored, she backed away to admire the whole engine again. A nice one it was, indeed; the set of pipes for funneling fresh aer from the top struck her as particularly clever. For all she knew it might be the most advanced model in all the world; how surprising to find it in the hands of barbarians like the raiders. But they were the ones who had use for such engines, as horrible as those uses were. How sad that she hadn't lived in the time of the First Empire, or even back in the philosophic era, when mekkanikal and other convocational secrets were pursued by many, for the betterment of all.

"You done?" Phaestal called. "Once these are running at full power, we're gonna go to the landing strip and look at the skiffs." He stuck out his lip and stuffed his hands in the pockets of his flight suit as he walked away, his voice rueful. "Only have a few days left till we reach the coast."

Karis squared her shoulders and stomped after him to the next tower. "You can stop that now."

"Hmm?"

"Acting so put-upon. As if I'm supposed to feel sorry for you."

He glanced at her with a flat expression, then spoke back into the engine. "If Roi had his way, things would be different."

What a pile of mold. "Roi wants the other raiders dead. He said as much at that joke of an assembly."

"Yeah, well…the problem is there's a score to settle. The Reviled killed Roi and Hindal's mentor, a guy named Tiresius. Maybe Roi and Hindal don't always get along, but they can't just stand by and let the Reviled take over."

"The Reviled. Who names themselves that?"

"They didn't." Phaestal finished his inspection, convoked a new casing and motioned for her to follow him toward the bow. "Their real name is the Rebel Airfighters. But Roi started calling them the *Reviled* Airfighters one day, and…you know."

She shook her head. "Everything always comes back to Roi. Why do you let him tell you what to do? What makes him so special?"

"Because he has a plan. Hindal and his crew, they just like to fight. Doesn't matter who or why. But Roi wants the war over quickly, so we can get on to more important stuff. It's just that all the strongest fighters are loyal to Hindal, and he has the better ships. Roi never gets a chance to do things his way."

"And what is his way? What would you do if you wiped out the Reviled?"

Phaestal shrugged. "Anything we wanted, I guess. That's what raiding's all about."

Anything they wanted; like attacking her ship. The memory of Meli frozen in fear sent a rush of anger through her. "You'll just be a bigger gang of thugs, running loose, wrecking cities, putting people to the sword."

"So? Cities can be re-convoked. Sword wounds heal. Anyway, that's more like what the Reviled like to do. Maybe Hindal, too. But Roi's different. Like I said, he has plans, and he's gonna make them happen. You know, back when he was a new appearance, he ran with a local gang in Vaetan. They didn't have a purpose, just liked to go around causing problems for the fun of it. Then one day, they were fighting another gang, and a local official got caught in the middle. I guess the guy got tossed off a roof or something, because he was messed up pretty bad. Anyway, they ended up catching Roi and throwing him in a foundation."

"A foundation?"

"Yeah, like for a building. No aer, no light, nothing. For three years."

"Three years?!" She had spent one day in her cell, *one day*, and by the end her flesh was ready to crawl off her bones. But if Phaestal's story was true, how could Roi of all people have chosen to put her there? How could he visit that same horrible punishment on others? "That can't be. He's lying."

"I don't think so. He doesn't like to talk about it much; only told me once, when I was sort of down about stuff. I get the feeling that they forgot about him down there." Phaestal cleared his throat and straightened. "But just imagine the sort of man that could overcome something like that. How strong would he have to be? That's why I let him give me orders."

Good gods. A better question was: What would an experience like that have done to Roi's mind? But she chose not to voice it aloud, given Phaestal's devotion to the man. Better to view all of this as more motivation to find a way off the ship.

They worked for the rest of the morning as ships passed through the wide gray sky, returning from a scout or practicing maneuvers. Karis grew tired and hungry, and Phaestal must have as well, because he led her back up, then forward to the terraced wall of the command deck, where groups of raiders were congregating for a midday meal.

"What are those?" Karis pointed to a pile of plane-shaped wireframe scaffolds.

"Gliders," Phaestal said. "They're easy to make, so Roi wanted to see if we could use them to board the Reviled ships."

He wandered ahead to join the others. Karis lingered, keeping the gliders in the corner of her vision. Convoking her own ship to escape on would never work; she had never built a skyship from scratch, and even if she could figure out how to make one, she would need space to work, and time alone in the light. But the gliders were only a simple cage of solid aether, with cloth wings. If she studied one carefully, copied it, perhaps even attached a small engine for more distance…could it be that easy? She could wait until the raiders were even more distracted than usual, sometime when—

"And how's our smoothskin doing today?"

Roi approached from behind the command deck, trailed by two other male raiders and a woman Karis hadn't seen before. He took a moment to wave at some approaching pilots before turning back to her. "You like those gliders, eh?"

She jumped to attention as if pulled by a string. "What? No."

"They're just decoys, really," Roi said, sidling up to her. "The Reviled used something similar in the past. If they've scouted us, I want them to think we're copying their tactics. But I have something new planned." He turned back to the others and waved Phaestal over as well. "Come on, take a look."

He led the five of them to the edge of the landing strip which took up much of the ship's forward area. There, a half-circular contraption protruded from the deck. Phaestal got down on his hands and knees in front of it.

"A fling-gun?"

"Exactly," Roi said. "The Reviled have enough single-engine skiffs to overwhelm the flagship if I bring it in close. So we're going to convoke these guns all around the perimeter. I want one every fifteen feet—no, ten. Mounted on a swivel, with a sight for aiming. Can you do it, Phaestal?"

Phaestal furrowed his brow. "I don't know. How much time do we have?"

"Hindal says he'll have the fleet convened in three days. Then it's a short flight up to the coast." Roi clapped Phaestal on the shoulder and leaned close. "I know you can do it. I've seen you accomplish more in less time."

Phaestal looked down and blushed. "Maybe if Mylon and Karis help me."

"Ah," Roi said. "She's been cooperative, then? We appreciate your contributions to the cause, Karis."

She flashed him her most insincere smile. "I'd hardly enjoy having the Reviled destroy this ship with me on it."

"That's what they all say." Roi grinned. "But we'll make a raider of you yet."

He strode off toward the command deck, a few of the others in tow.

"All right, Mylon, get over here," Phaestal said to a short raider with a bald head and pug nose. "Everyone get a good look at this so we can copy it. We'll alternate convokers around the perimeter, so we don't lose any zones if someone has to leave the ship. We'll see how many we get done before dark."

Karis knelt as if to study the gun along with the others, but her mind only wandered back to Meli. Three days more of waiting, then each day after would take Karis north, further from where they had separated. Phaestal and Mylon headed off to eat before starting work, and Karis stole a glance back at the gliders. Raiders milled around nearby, with more attending the skiffs near the landing strip behind her. After having Roi sneak up her, she was more aware of them casting suspicious looks in her direction. No, she couldn't spend too much time studying the gliders yet; not until she could guarantee no one would notice.

She sighed and turned back to the fling gun. She had never seen one before, but was familiar with the concept. On one level, all engines worked the same way—convoke an accelerant and trap it in a circular chamber, usually with some sort of notched wheel to turn a shaft, and it would spin until it wore down or ran out of fresh aer. But fling-guns had no shaft; instead, their operator convoked balls of dense, hard material, dropped them into the chamber to gain speed, then depressed a lever to shoot them out the side. Assuming the thing didn't tear itself apart, the result was a weapon which could shoot small holes in a plane at moderate distances, especially if the wings were...

"...flimsy. Oh, no."

The gliders. Even if she were spotted taking off, with the wind at her back she might have had enough time to fly out of sight before they could scramble a ship. But now the raiders were mounting guns all over the deck that could shoot her down in moments.

And she was helping them do it.

Roi!

Had he set this up on purpose? Was that even possible? How did she get herself into this mess? Were they really going to force her into a battle thousands of feet in the aer? She sat cross legged, back slumped, and stared at the horizon. Nothing but emptiness there, pallid, forsaken of life and hope. She buried her head in her lap, covering up with her arms.

She should have told Meli how she felt, before the attack, before they had even left Sofidra. Why had she been so afraid? Because she knew Meli would say no, of course, and then their relationship would never be the same.

And that would have been for the best. If they had lost their friendship, she would have never taken Meli on this journey, and never put her in danger. Now Karis had to find some way back to help her, at a time when she couldn't even help herself.

"Are you all right?"

A hand pressed on Karis's shoulder. She flinched away.

"Relax. I just wanted to say hi."

The hand's owner stepped back and gave Karis space. It was the same woman who had been walking with Roi before. Her face was lean and small, though not as small as Karis's, and covered with freckles matching her bright red hair. "I'm Jaela. Sorry if I bothered you."

"It's all right." Karis coughed the sadness out of her voice. "Phaestal spoke of you."

"Fondly, I hope."

"No. I mean, no, it wasn't unkind. Actually, he didn't really say anything." She made a face at how she stumbled over the words.

Jaela's crooked teeth poked out of her smile. She was pretty; not the total, overwhelming beauty of Meli, but attractive enough in her own simple way. "Phaestal lives in his own world sometimes. You'll find that a lot around here."

"I suppose." Karis was wary of speaking behind his back. Jaela didn't seem like an ordinary raider, though perhaps being a woman accounted for much of that. What was she doing here, among these people? Had she been kidnapped like Karis, and somehow never escaped? No, she seemed too confident for that. There was something about her that made Karis feel as if she knew her well, despite them only speaking for a few—

"What is it?" Jaela asked.

Karis realized she was staring and looked away. "Nothing. I suppose I should be copying this gun. You heard what Roi said."

"Hmm. I'm no good at mekkanikal things. But if Phaestal believes in you, I'm sure you can do it."

"It's not a question of whether I can do it," Karis said crossly. "It's a simple system, I can duplicate it easily. But why would I want to? I don't like weapons. Why should I make something to help you people kill each other?"

"But they'll help us defend ourselves in the battle." Jaela knelt beside her.

"I don't want to be in a battle."

"You're scared?"

"Of *course* I'm scared." Karis's voice rose as she spit the words. "Why wouldn't I be? Why aren't you? How can you all be so casual about flying toward your deaths?"

Karis turned away, closed her eyes and breathed deeply. This wasn't like her, getting worked up so easily. She wasn't herself on board this ship. One more reason she needed to get away.

"I am scared," Jaela said. "A lot of the others are too, I think. But they love it. The fear makes them feel alive."

She touched the back of Karis's neck, sending a chill down her spine.

"Don't worry," Jaela said. "When the battle comes, I'll watch you. I may be no better off than you, but I'll try to keep you safe."

"You will? Why?"

When Karis looked back, Jaela was smiling again.

"Why wouldn't I? Well, I'll let you do your work now. Roi wanted me to keep an eye on you, but I don't think I really need to. If we're going to war together, we need to trust each other, right?"

Karis nodded and Jaela walked away, thigh muscles flexing in the tight black fabric of her suit. Karis checked, but none of the raiders were looking their way. The deck was clearer now, the pilots having gone back to their ships or below deck to relax, but some food still remained near the center of the ship.

Preferring solitude to sating her hunger, Karis got up and paced, as if looking for a good place to put a gun. She still didn't want to convoke one, but she couldn't sit and stew any longer, either, so she walked in a circle, thinking over Jaela's words.

She had circled half the deck when a high-pitched buzzing sounded over the side of the ship. Puzzled, she leaned over the edge.

Elsa floated a few feet below her. *"Karis is found not gone and take home Karis!"*

Karis yelped and popped her head up. A group of raiders laughed amongst themselves near the stern. Behind, one of them sat and convoked paper airplanes to toss into the wind.

She leaned back over the rail. "Elsa! What happened to Meli? Is she all right?"

Elsa buzzed harder, trying to remain stable in the turbulence from the ship's propellers. She convoked herself a perch on the side of the hull and grabbed it. *"Meli all right all. On raft with Ariden, sent so worried of Karis, sent Elsa rescue."*

Karis's tears welled. Meli was alive. And safe. The relief struck her so hard her head felt light. She nearly fell over the rail. "Go back to her, Elsa. She needs your protection. Go and tell her to meet me at the Automatia. Do you understand? The Automatia."

"No goes. Rescues Karis. Carry down escape now."

Karis straightened again. A tall raider in the laughing group had noticed her shifts in posture and was staring. "We can't. They'd see—" Oh gods, the fling-guns! "You have to stay out of sight. Whatever you do, don't let them see you."

"Still leave with Karis. Help and leave."

"We will." As she spoke, the tall raider tapped a friend and pointed in her direction. "Listen. There's going to be a battle soon. The whole fleet is headed to war. There will be plenty of distractions, confusion, chances to escape. I'll talk to you again when I can."

"Yes yes, confudistractions. Will see see soon Karis sees."

Karis knelt and convoked a swiveling base for a gun as the two raiders approached. The tall one held her gaze, but said nothing. She continued to toy with the swivel for a few heartbeats after they passed, then checked back over the side.

Elsa and her perch were gone. Relief washed over Karis again, and she sat down on the deck, dizzy. Everything had changed so quickly. Meli was alive, and well enough to send Elsa after her. Now there was no doubt that she had to escape the ship. If she could just get away, she could meet Meli at the Automatia, and all would be well.

The battle. It would be her best opportunity, but she would have to wait for it. What could she do in the meantime, to turn the odds in her favor? Sabotage the ship? If the flagship encountered a major problem just as the battle began, it would certainly put the raider's minds elsewhere. In her mind, the ship plummeted, torn to pieces by the Reviled, its crew crumbled to dust and scattered into the sea. All of them, even Jaela, that slightly crooked smile twisting in horror as she saw her own…

Karis bit her lip and opened her eyes. No, she wouldn't have that blood on her hands. Instead she would wait, and not run the risk of them finding out about Elsa or her plan. The battle would come soon enough, and she would use it to be free again.

She resumed convoking the gun.

9

The waves're coming in again," Sirdu mumbled. His face was pale and twisted from the discomfort of sitting against the mast for so long.

"Mold." Ariden dragged himself up. He had been dozing again, on the what? Eighth day? Ninth? Sirdu had said that raiders afflicted with sky-sickness sometimes felt better after a few days, but Meli showed no signs of improvement. Meanwhile, the chores and repairs on the ship never seemed to cease, and between each night Ariden spent choking on fog, one period of daily misery blended into the next.

"There's a story I'd like you to hear, Sir."

"I told you, no stories."

"Just one. About Rafin, the Hunter. Do you know the tale of him and the Anathematist?"

"I know the tale of Sirdu having a gag stuffed in his mouth."

Sirdu cleared his throat nervously, but continued speaking; the days at sea had lifted some fear from his tongue. "Feeling weary on his travels, Rafin had stopped in the town of Dire Hollow for a respite."

"Sirdu…"

"Please, sir? Just a short tale? I promise it will be worth it in the end."

Ariden grumbled and stood to pull tight a section of sail, ignoring the captive raider.

Sirdu smiled for the first time in days. "By this point, Rafin's fame had already spread to the region of Porlan in which he walked. Not wishing to be bothered with admirers, he made his way quietly to the common house to make merry with the townspeople before he slept.

"But there was no merriment to be found in Dire Hollow that eve. Instead of fine talk and libation, Rafin was greeted only by dour faces and angry mutters.

"'A fine way to treat a guest,' Rafin mumbled into his cup, loud enough for the town savortist, a smoothskin named Toddil, to overhear.

"Toddil leaned in close to whisper, 'Good sir, please do not take us as an inhospitable people. It is only poor news which sets our hearts so low: word has spread that an Anathematist has convoked a castle on the hillside over yonder, and is there practicing his dark craft. We fear the wrath of the gods will be brought upon us by his evil ways. The people you see here will soon attend a meeting in which we will decide whether to move our town elsewhere, or risk our lives fighting this villain.'

"Rafin quaffed deeply and considered this news. Of course, his time was fifteen hundred years after the death of the Plague Bringer, cursed be his name, but still there remained a few of those who practiced such anathemic arts, and they survived the collective wrath of Aetheria through the fear they inspired in more wholesome folk.

"'Where is this hill, and the castle upon it?' Rafin inquired of the barkeep.

"'Just beyond the winding path to windward,' Toddil answered, with a hint of surprise in his voice. 'Though I pray you only ask so that you may avoid it in your travels.'

"'Not so, good sir of small height,' Rafin said. 'For I am Rafin, Hunter of Beasts and Destroyer of Monsterkin, and your words have roused me to action. I will take on the task of ridding you of this menace.'"

With great effort, Ariden got the sail affixed to the cross-beam again. It would have been a simple task a week ago, but now every movement felt like a slog through mud.

"His identity so revealed, the townspeople jumped up and surrounded him, asking questions of his exploits and wishing to see Demargar, the god-enchanted, hardened sword of legend. Rafin answered them each in turn as evening fell, until he was forced to excuse himself. Though he did not wish to give offense to his admirers, he wished to conserve his strength, for it just so happened that to windward also lay the ghoulsbreath he had been tracking for nearly a half-year."

"Convenient," Ariden said, just to let Sirdu know the story wasn't awing him into silence.

"The next morning, the townspeople saw Rafin off instead of holding their planned meeting, and he made his way down the path. He arrived at the Anathematist's castle without incident, and proceeded to battle his way through its defenses. I will spare you the details, sir, although they really are quite exciting, if you'd care to—"

Ariden fixed Sirdu with an icy stare.

"—yes, well, Rafin soon found himself face to face with the villain in his innermost chamber. Rafin drew Demargar right away, fearing he would be struck by a plague, but before he could lunge, the Anathematist disappeared into thin aether!

"Keeping his wits, Rafin struck the space in front of him. To his surprise, Demargar cut through a hanging curtain, which had taken on the appearance of the room behind it! The Anathematist was revealed, and immediately dropped to his knees.

"'I yield, my friend. Please have mercy,' he begged.

"Rafin was not inclined to show mercy, but he also could not bring himself to slay a man who knelt so helpless before him. Instead, he tied up the Anathematist and dragged him back to the town to face justice.

"All was proceeding well, save for the ache in Rafin's shoulders, when halfway to their destination the Anathematist spoke again.

"'My friend, I have asked for your mercy and received it—but please, do not reverse your judgment, do not deliver me to the hands of people who will surely put me to death!'

"'Silence, you filth,' Rafin replied. 'You will face the fate you have laid out for yourself with your evil ways. It is not my place to interfere.'

"'But think of what they will do to me! Pierce my eyes, strip my flesh and pull me limb from limb! Though my work was anathema, I have never harmed another. Please—I vow to you now by all the gods, I will stop all my convocations on the human body. If you untie me now, I will disappear forever into the wilderness—no one must ever know!'

"Rafin's heart remained hard at first, but as he walked he dwelled more on what horrors the townspeople would inflict on this man. He thought, 'For how many years have I walked, ridding this world of monsters, so that the suffering of Aetheria might be decreased? Is it truly right of me to inflict pain on this man, no matter his crimes?'

"And so Rafin stopped and, after acquiring many more assurances of good behavior, untied the Anathematist and bid him to go his own way into the wilderness."

"How noble of him," Ariden said, yawning.

"Ah," Sirdu said. "But do you know what happened next?"

"I cannot imagine." Though he suspected he could.

"A short time later, the ghoulsbreath leapt onto the path unseen, and dealt Rafin a smashing blow. But before the beast could tear him apart, the Anathematist reappeared, and reaching into his satchel, doused it with a liquid convocation that had the power—to control its mind!"

"Enough." Rage swirled from deep within Ariden, from a place he did not delve into often. Images drenched in pain and hatred came up with it, a man with a scar across his face, a woman's sly smile.

"No, you see, it was a well-known ability of theirs. Just as plagues ravaged the body, so did some anathematists discover the power to change—"

"I said, quiet!" Ariden sat up and raised his hand as if to strike. Sirdu turned his face, unable to shield himself with his tied hands. Ariden growled and spit, then stalked away.

"Please, Sir. I know you hate me, but I only want to be free to move. To stretch my limbs, to do something!"

"I've seen what you raiders like to do."

"Sir, I am not an evil man! Yes, it's true, I talk too much; the other raiders said so as well. But I only joined them because I couldn't take the tedium of my home village anymore. The Skyhunters let me fly, explore…"

"…kidnap the crew of passing ships."

"Honestly, we don't even raid that much anymore. Most of the time we're fighting the Reviled. Would you prefer we let them control the entire Windward Coast? If you think we're bad, imagine them running half of Aetheria!"

"I couldn't give two piles of mold what they do. Last I saw, you were the ones attacking us, not them."

"It wasn't supposed to be this way." Sirdu looked at his feet. "We were re-grouping, see? We needed time to rebuild our resources, after we got trounced in our last battle. When a scout spotted your ship, we figured there wouldn't be much risk in finding out who you were. You looked lost, you see. Your engines were good, they said, but you seemed to be going in circles."

Pox. Ariden glanced over at Meli, but luckily she didn't stir.

"Listen, Sirdu. Truth be told, I hold no special animosity for raiders. I see the appeal of it: flying around, destroying things, making trouble. The problem is, I've always believed that if you pick a fight, you live with the consequences. Someday, perhaps not soon, but someday, your friends are going to find out that when they came at me, they convoked more than they could carry."

"Oh, yes, Sir. I agree completely. No one expected to find someone like you aboard that ship. You fought off the whole raid by yourself! I wish I could convince you to come back and join us. I'd be a hero."

Ariden's deathly stare told of his thoughts on that matter.

"Just please, *please* free me. I could help you. I'm used to doing menial tasks on the skyships, they don't bother me. A great man like you should be giving orders, not scuttling like a rat."

Above, the top starboard corner of the sail had come loose again. Ariden shifted on his feet, and brown muck squelched between his toes. Soreness had spread from his frozen fingers to his cold hands. Normally his body would never tire, never feel pain for longer than it took to heal. He sorely needed a respite, just one day for his body to recover.

"You swear to do as you're told?"

Sirdu nodded enthusiastically. "You won't regret it. Sailach will bless you for your generosity! You know, that reminds me of a story. Have you ever heard—"

"No more stories," Ariden said. "Or I'll stick the prow up your ass and use you for a masthead."

Sirdu nodded and shut his lips. Ariden let the binds crumble. Sirdu shook off the dust, brought his hands up to his eyes as if in disbelief, and rose. Grinning stupidly, he backed up five paces to the gunwale, sat down, then tumbled backward into the ocean.

"Hey!" Ariden ran to the side to see Sirdu swimming away, gliding easily through the waves until he disappeared in the fog.

"What happened?" Meli mumbled, rolling onto her side.

"He left." Ariden's mind could barely process the chain of events, as if the fog had penetrated his thoughts. "The little weasel left us. We're going after him. I won't take this."

"We can't go after him—we can't turn the ship." Meli sat up and groaned. "And anyway, why are you so angry? You never liked him to begin with. You should be happy he's gone."

She was right. She may have been as useful as a lump of dust on a daybed, but this time she was right. Ariden threw his head back and laughed. Something got into him then, and he kept on laughing, until Meli looked at him like he was mad, and he began to wonder the same himself.

"Pox it." He slammed into a seat, arms folded on his chest. "I'm past caring. Wake me up when we reach land."

"I need to stretch." Meli took a deep breath, then sat up on her knees. "I can't believe I'm saying it, but I feel a bit better. The waves aren't as high anymore." She stood, and took a few tentative steps. "Still a bit dizzy, though. I had better stay rested."

"Of course you will," Ariden muttered, and closed his eyes.

They drifted on. The sea remained calm through the day, and despite Ariden's skepticism Meli got up and began to walk the length of the craft, convoking small improvements as she went. She repaired the broken rudder, then sat cross-legged at mid-deck, replacing the sail's rigging with an elaborate system of pulleys which made Ariden slightly annoyed by how well it worked.

Somewhere behind them, large waves broke with booming crashes. In the silence that came after, Ariden noticed the cloth bunched in Meli's lap was shaking as she wept.

"What's wrong?"

She continued to cry for a while, and he assumed she hadn't heard him. Then she answered, her voice hoarse. "What's wrong is I don't know where we're going. It feels like we're stuck on this sea forever."

"The waves go in one direction. They'll push us to land eventually. Surely even you can see that."

"You're so rude." She sniffed. "You never cared about Karis, so of course you don't care where we end up. How do you think I feel, knowing she's in danger all this time, and barely having the strength to move?"

"If I knew you were going to launch another accusation, I wouldn't have asked." Ariden turned over as if to sleep. He kept his eyes shut, listening to the roar of the ocean, but instead heard Meli gasp and hurry away.

He opened one eye. "What is it now?"

"Ariden, look!"

She stood at the starboard gunwale, staring outward. Ariden creaked to his feet. Through the fog, a dark shape came toward them, riding a wave. Ariden held out his hand to convoke a weapon, though he could manage no more than a lopsided cudgel.

The shape condensed, and Sirdu appeared from the fog atop a small raft, paddling as fast as he could, face panicked.

"Help!" he shouted. "Sir! It's going to kill us all! You're the only one who can stop it."

Ariden and Meli exchanged glances, baffled. "What in ten gods are you doing?" Ariden asked.

"It almost got me." Sirdu bumped his raft against the ship, then flung himself up and over the side. "You must have seen it. It was huge!"

"What almost got you?" Meli asked.

As she spoke, Sirdu was already scuttling behind Ariden to hide. "A monster," he squeaked. "A great man-eating monster of the sea!"

10

Meli scanned the ocean, but saw no signs of monsters, nor of anything else besides the dark gray waves coated in silt.

"Where is this monster?"

Ariden scoffed. "There is none."

"I saw it!" Sirdu said, chins quivering. "You have to believe me."

Did she, now? The fear written on his face seemed real enough; just looking at him brought a touch of it to her as well. "We should listen to him, Ariden. Why else would he have come back?"

"He's insane. We had best chuck him back into the sea."

"No! Please!" Sirdu looked ready to collapse, torn as he was between needing Ariden's protection and fearing his wrath. "You have to fight it!"

"Fight what?" Ariden pushed away from him and pointed at the waves. "There's nothing out there."

Meli looked again at the sea, then to the cowering man at her feet. Ariden had been cavalier about the prospect of raider attacks as well, and look at where that had gotten them. Queasiness still lingered in the pit of her stomach, adding to her unease. "What did you see, Sirdu? Tell me."

"Vipretheon." Sirdu blinked, as if blinded by the glare of his sudden revelation. "Of course. Why didn't I see it before? The legends were all true—the screeching sound, the strange lights."

"What legends? What lights?"

"It's an old sea tale," Ariden said. "The imagination of bored sailors, nothing more. Animals avoid the sea. Likely they find it as cold and unpleasant as we do."

"But it was real!" Sirdu shouted. "I was paddling, trying to stay near the ship, yet out of sight. I'm sorry I broke my word, Sir. It was stupid of me, so very stupid. But you had made so many threats, I didn't know what would happen if you lost your temper, so I thought some distance might do me well. After some time, a wave pushed me away, and I was lost in the fog. Then I felt it. Something in the aer. I can't describe it exactly, but it made my hairs stand on end. And then came the sounds, those unholy squeals."

"What did it look like?" Meli asked.

Sirdu shook his head. "It was hidden in the fog. But it stomped right past me."

"You just told us you saw it," Ariden said. "You're a liar."

"I saw something! A shape. And a light, a sudden, bright light. It was Vipretheon, I'm sure of it. All the tales say the same, that Vipretheon glows brighter than the day before he tears ships apart."

Meli craned her neck reflexively. The fog surrounded them everywhere, pressing in. It could easily hide a creature of any size, well after it had gotten close enough to strike.

"Ridiculous," Ariden said. "You say it stomped past you—what could it have stomped on? We're in the middle of the sea."

"I only know what I heard."

"Ariden." Meli pleaded with her eyes for him to take Sirdu seriously.

"Spare me," Ariden said. "It's not as if we were planning on staying here. If you want to rejoin us, raider filth, make yourself useful and help her finish the rigging."

Sirdu nodded and backed away, scraping. "Yes, of course. With pleasure, sir."

Ariden showed them his back, looking out into the fog. Meli moved to the opposite side and tried to do the same, but soon a wave of dizziness overcame her and she sat, her face in her hands.

Even after all the stories she had heard of the plagues, she could not have imagined the misery of being ill. At least with a plague, death was reputed to come quickly, whereas she had been stuck in limbo, capable only of wishing for death or dreaming of a miracle to make herself well. When the waves had quieted and her illness began to slink away, the relief was sudden, shockingly powerful, but soon the guilt of letting Ariden take them to shore and abandoning Karis crept into its place. She felt awful about the decision still, but she at least had taken some comfort from the thought that they might reach the Leeward Coast soon, hopefully near a city where they could convince someone to help them go after her friend.

And then, this news of Vipretheon. A vicious monster stalking them, and Ariden refusing to take the idea seriously. Meli could have throttled him for his obstinacy, if she'd had any strength in her arms. As if this entire situation weren't his fault, as if he hadn't gotten them lost, then failed in his duty to protect them.

Night fell, and the sea remained calm, with no signs of impending doom. Gradually, her fears of the sea monster lessened in their immediacy. With some help from Sirdu, Meli convinced Ariden to convoke and keep his esoterica-infused sword at hand; a painstaking process in the fog, he complained. Meli passed into a sleep as restful as any since the raiders had attacked, and the next morning continued to assist Sirdu in repairing and expanding the ship.

After hearing so many of Ariden's complaints, she had expected a monumental task, but to her surprise it wasn't that difficult at all. Now that she possessed a clearer head, she quickly set up a new cabin so they could sit out of the wind. She put up a new mast, taller and stronger than the pathetic beam Ariden had erected, and stood with her chest puffed out, smiling for the first time in a week as the ship out-sped the waves. Ariden took notice and turned away in his nest, grumbling. Good. Now she would show him what being made to feel useless was like.

The next day, she told Sirdu to man the tiller to keep the ship from turning sideways over the waves, then paced the deck, looking for more potential improvements. There was much to be done; the craft was hardly as stable or fast as she knew it could be, but she was no shipwright, and without Karis to guide her she feared making changes to the hull. Instead, she spent her time repairing the sections which Ariden had left in obvious tatters, and passed the day away quickly with the effort of holding the strands of aether in her mind.

She was inspecting a leak when the ship lurched, nearly sending her face-first over the side. Somehow they had turned, and a wave had caught them cross-ways.

"Sirdu!" Ariden bumped his head on the door of the cabin as he leaned out. "What are you doing?"

"I'm sorry sir." Sirdu held up a periscope. "I was convoking this. A useful tool, when I finish it."

Ariden rubbed his head and grumbled. "Keep your eye on the sea."

"I think it's a good idea," Meli said, taking the periscope in hand. "It will help us see over the fog. Ariden, why don't you take a turn at the till for a change?"

Ariden snarled, but marched to the rear of the ship. "Out," he said to Sirdu, jerking his thumb over his shoulder. He plopped himself down, wrapped in his thick coat, watching them both with narrowed eyes. Meli did little to hide her amusement.

He was still there, sleeping with the tiller beneath his armpit, when Meli emerged the next morning and ate her simple meal. Sirdu had woken before her, and was perched near him on the rear railing, looking out with his scope.

"Any sign of land?" she asked.

"Oh, no, ma'am," he said. "But if there were, it'd be ahead of us. I'm watching for Vipretheon. I could hardly sleep all night, thinking of its jaws crushing my skull. Or worse."

Meli frowned and stared into the fog where the scope pointed, perched between annoyance and anxiety. There was no doubt that Sirdu had seen something out there, but after days of nothing but quiet seas she had grown tired of his worried chatter. He was a strange man, not at all what she had imagined a raider would be like. There was an earnest simplicity about him which made her believe him despite who he was, but was there truly something dangerous out on those waves, or was Sirdu simply letting his imagination get the best of him?

"Sirdu. What else can you tell me about Vipretheon?"

"Nothing I haven't already told, my lady. All I know is stories, though perhaps I sometimes get one monster-slaying tale confused for another. Those were always my favorites, you know, the stories of the hunters. Especially Rafin. Have you ever heard of the time he fought the Psytherin monster at Tenstone?"

She shook her head warily.

"Rafin was still a young man then, and he had not yet acquired Demargar on his quest. He wandered to Tenstone, and there met a woman whose partner had gone missing among the field of bare bedrock which overlooked the town. None of the other townspeople would join her search, for they all feared the Psytherin—and what a true beast it was! A creature which copied the forms of other animals, but only in parts. The head of a rat it had, along with hands of snakes with fanged fingertips. It walked upright like a man, but stood ten feet tall, and had a thick tail with razor spikes running along its length. One swipe from that tail, it was said, and the Psytherin would flay the flesh right from—"

"On second thought!" Meli shouted. "Perhaps that is a story for another time. I think we have enough trouble with monsters without involving another."

Sirdu nodded solemnly and returned to his watch. Meli checked the fog one more time, then began her daily routine around the ship. It would help, she thought, if she knew what she was looking for. In the stories, monsters were always hideous, but really a monster was just an animal; perhaps larger than most, and by definition one that sought to kill people, but at its core no different than the many animals she had convoked and released over the years. Of course, Meli would never intentionally create something to hurt people, but every animatist knew of that danger. Animals were useful because they could exist without a human to keep them in their thoughts, but being self-aware, they acted according to their own wills, and could never truly be controlled. Meli tried to shape her creations as best she could, but the growing process was unpredictable, and sometimes animals changed once in the wild, reaching enormous sizes like the Behemoth Walkers, or taking on new forms entirely.

Her old mentor had once told her that animals often took on aspects of their convoker's personalities. Were monsters then merely a reflection of Aetheria's flaws, the creations of animatists who were somehow...unsavory?

As if hearing her, Ariden rolled over and belched. He resembled a hunter somewhat himself, wandering Aetheria with his blade. Perhaps that was why she had put so much faith in him, before she found out he was nothing like the chivalrous, noble Rafin.

"Did you hear that?!" Sirdu yelled from the far end of the ship.

"What?"

"It was a booming sound. Like the ones I heard before. It's here!" Sirdu pressed his face back into the scope, cradling it in his shaking hands.

Ariden stirred from his resting place with a groan. "The waves crash in the distance. It's constantly booming, you idiot."

"This one was different, I'm sure of it."

"Ariden." Meli strode to the rear to look in the periscope. "Is your sword ready?"

"Don't listen to him." Ariden pulled his coat over his head. "He's always hearing things."

Meli shot him a sour look, but her check of the scope revealed nothing. Sirdu resumed his watch and stayed put for the rest of the day. Without his constant stream of stories and chatter, the only noise was the slosh of the waves rocking the boat, and so Meli passed the time listening to their slapping tale.

When the morning light woke her again, the waves no longer came.

At first, relief, even joy that she could stand upright without losing her balance, without feeling her insides shift in her belly. But the sail lay still as well, hanging limp from the mast. Ariden woke, saw it and cursed the gods loudly.

"It'll pick up," Sirdu said. "The wind always comes back."

"Not this time," Ariden said. "This voyage is cursed. The wind has been strange—that's why your crew found us in the first place."

"Perhaps it's something to do with the monster." Sirdu swiveled his head from side to side, searching for the threat.

"A pox on your monster. If the wind stays like this, we're stranded."

Meli left them to their bickering and picked up Sirdu's periscope. She had been meaning to look through it more often, but so vigilant had he been in searching for Vipretheon that she rarely managed to wrest it away from him. Extending it to its full height, she convoked a small platform at the front of the boat, stood atop it and pressed her eyes to the viewer.

Fog. Somewhat lighter-colored than that which hung directly over the waves, but ordinary fog nonetheless. What had she been expecting, anyway? She swiveled the scope back and forth, and a black shape moved across the viewer.

"Ah!" She jerked back. When she looked again, the shape was gone.

"What is it?" Sirdu asked. "Vipretheon?"

"No," Meli said. "I saw something big. Very big. I think it's land!"

"What?" Ariden ran so fast the boat threatened to capsize, and Sirdu came soon after. "What did you see?"

Meli moved aside to let him peer into the scope. "I can't find it again. The fog parted for just a moment, and I saw a sort of mountain. Black, like bedrock."

That was enough for Ariden. He stomped around the boat, gesticulating in full command mode. "All right, you slob, convoke a pair of oars. Big ones. We're rowing until our poxing arms fall off."

The way they worked then, an observer might have thought they were experienced sailors, hand-picked for a racing crew. Sirdu convoked a long bench while Meli made the oars, and Ariden set up a pair of locks to place them in. Sirdu and Ariden went to their positions and hauled while Meli took to the scope again, one hand on her thumping heart. Land. And so close she felt she could almost touch it.

"Now!" Ariden called, pulling back on his oar. "Again. Keep it regular. Meli, what do you see?"

"Nothing." Only wisps of denser, whiter fog floating by as the ship moved between them. Again and again the oars beat the waves, Ariden calling out the time until they found their rhythm, grunting in unison.

The wisps turned, forming spirals.

"I see something," Meli said. "The fog is changing."

"Getting darker, you mean?"

"No." It was swirling. A great billowing cloud, moving toward them. "Oh no!"

She dropped the scope and fell to the deck, but too late. A wave lifted them. The world became a blur of spinning deck and fog. The back of her head hit the bench, and purple spots spread over her vision. She blinked them away as Sirdu screamed.

Time seemed to stand still. The aer had a biting quality, almost alive. Her hair floated upward, hanging before her face.

Vipretheon.

Wind sliced through the ship, the fog parted and the monster emerged. It came with a roar, booms and a piercing screech. The thing was made of the fog itself, a great whirlwind of it, with snaking tendrils flowing from its body to the sea. Within the tendrils, streams of color writhed, changing form from liquid to solid and cycling through all manner of materials: stone, gel, crystal and others Meli had never seen, sliding and morphing into one another. Around them purple and blue flashes of light traced forking paths, each accompanied by a boom and a hiss.

The manifestation passed on their left, rocking the boat in its wake. Ariden rose with his blade extended, a large and nasty one, with spiked protrusions along its curving length.

"Ariden!" Meli shouted. "It's not an animal! It's something else! Put your sword away!"

Half her words were lost as Vipretheon let out another ear-shattering boom. It moved with tremendous speed and disappeared into the fog behind them, but flashes of light betrayed its position. Ariden followed it with his sword while Sirdu whimpered beside her.

"It's coming back!" Ariden yelled. "Come on, you!" He ran up to meet it, his hair pointing skyward. He gritted his teeth and tensed.

"No!" A tickling sensation ran through Meli's clothes and body, concentrating in her teeth. "Don't!"

A piercing screech cut the fog and a flash of light shot out. Sizzling, it struck the point of Ariden's sword, then singed his hair on its way to the tip of the mast. The solid aether there exploded, filling the aer with splinters, and a large chunk smashed Ariden on the back of the head.

Everything went white, then black.

11

Karis hauled on the cable, leaning against its tug. She scrabbled her feet on the deck, then convoked two footholds under her heels and pulled again, fingers aching under her thick gloves. Phaestal stood a few feet down the line, half-hidden by her narrowed eyes, performing a similar maneuver. His strength gave out and he let go with a yell. The cable jumped from Karis's grasp—for all her effort, she had barely been helping to pull it at all. It zipped away, running out through its pulley to lie slack on the deck beyond.

Phaestal sat watching it for a moment, catching his breath, then crumbled his gloves and dusted himself off. It was mid-morning, and most of the raiders were below, sleeping off what must have been a wild affair the previous evening. Their absence lent an eerie quiet to the main deck, aside from the ever-present drone of the engines and the occasional whistle of a heavy gust of crosswind. Most of the raiders avoided the open aer when they could, and it was easy to see why; the sky was too large and white out here, and even the great expanse of flat decking, crisscrossed by seams where different raiders had convoked it, was dwarfed by the magnitude of the fog below. Karis preferred it, though, once she had gotten used to the biting cold and to the need to shout most of her words. At least in the open she could keep her mind free of the memories which came bubbling to the surface whenever she was confined.

"Well, that was a waste of time," Phaestal said. "We'll have to convoke a winch."

"Oh, great poxing gods of old," Mylon yelled from behind them. "Another few fingers-length and I would have had it tied. Just splice another one on, will you?"

"The cable is strong the way it is," Phaestal said evenly. "If we splice it, it could snap. Anyway, we still have to pull it taut if the control system is going to work."

Mylon growled and wiped his mop of black hair away from his pinpoint black eyes. He cast his gaze about, seeking a target for his rage, and found Karis. "It's her fault, you know. I can't believe we traded Sirdu for her. His stories may have been mold, but at least he could lift more than a gnat."

"If she's a gnat, then what are you?" Jaela asked. She sat atop a hulking intake vent, watching as usual.

"A scorpion!" Mylon said, and stuck out his tongue.

"I don't think so," Jaela said without missing a beat. "Some people are frightened of scorpions, but no one cares about you. You could be a mud-roach, but you're not nearly good-looking enough."

Karis had to smile at that.

Mylon noticed her and sneered. "Sure, laugh. I'll be glad when the wind blows you off the ship, smoothie. You're worth as much as the dust on my boot."

"All right," Phaestal said. "Can we just get back to work? Otherwise we'll *all* be dust tomorrow."

Karis took a deep breath. She just had to withstand the stupidity for one more day. She pointed at a crowd of raiders at the far end of the deck. "If this rig is so important, then how come they're not helping?"

"They're fighters," Phaestal said. "They work when the battle starts."

An ear-splitting screech brought their attention to the command deck above them, and Roi leaning over its railing. He tossed away the whistle he had convoked, tapped one of the control levers and shook his head. Phaestal put his hands out and shrugged, and Roi motioned with his finger for them to approach.

"Oh no," Phaestal said. "Come on, Mylon. Let's just hope he doesn't have any more new ideas."

Halfway to the ladder Phaestal called over his shoulder, "Karis, do you know how to convoke a winch?"

"Obviously!" There was hardly any mekkanism simpler—all she would need was a handle, a spool and a ratchet to keep it from unwinding. She knelt near to where she had held the cable before and visualized the parts. Even for a basic device, decisions needed to be made, and careful planning realized, in order to make the pieces fit. The spool and handle would work best vertically, as a capstan, but she wouldn't need an engine or accelerant; hand-turning would suffice, provided the gear ratio—

"Have you ever seen Mariten?" Jaela's voice cut into her thoughts. "What?"

"Mariten. The city the Reviled are defending. It's beautiful."

Karis wiped away her first aborted attempt at a spool and sighed. "No. I've never even been to the Windward Continent. It was one of the things I was looking forward to when..." She coughed. Too easy to let her guard down, with her thoughts going so many places. "I should finish this."

She began again, feeling the minute tugs of the aether as it responded to her commands. She concentrated harder and became aware of the shape it formed, seeing the smooth edges of the spool in her mind.

"You know what's funny?" Jaela asked. "You've never been to the Windward Continent, but I've never been to the Leeward Continent. We're like opposites, yes?"

"I suppose." Karis frowned at a bump that had formed when she lost her concentration. No matter; it wouldn't stop the cable from coiling.

"You know, when I first came aboard here, I wanted to see the whole world, just for the sake of saying I had. These big skyships just seemed like...freedom. I mean really, what's the point of having them, if you never go anywhere interesting?"

"Many would ask the same question," Karis muttered. Getting the gears to line up below the handle would be the most taxing part of the convocation, and Jaela's chatter wasn't making it easier. But Karis felt somehow obliged to let her continue, lest she be rude to the one person on board who had displayed a tiny amount of decency.

"The Leeward Continent is so exotic, don't you think? Well, perhaps you don't, since you're from there. But there's just something about the way it goes on and on...I'd bet there are so many wonderful places beyond Aetheria. I've heard interesting things about Scha, to southleeward. Where is your accent from, anyway? The south?"

"My accent?" How in the gods was she supposed to know? Probably it was a mixture of several places, starting with the Lost Coast, but there was no reason to get into that. "It's from...Ventituras."

"You lived in Ventituras? Oh, I'd love to see those towers!"

The Trepolinai, she meant—two round pillars stretching to the sky, swirled in gold and silver. In Karis's mind's eye they were as clear and beautiful as when she first beheld them. "I used to see them every day, actually."

"You did? Did you ever see the Ventiturans vote at their assembly? Oh, I wish you could take me there."

A memory stirred in Karis, her mouth full of dust, clogging her nose and throat. She shivered. "I'd rather not return, to be honest."

"Oh. I see."

Jaela tucked her chin and sat quietly for a while, kicking her feet. Karis should have left it at that, but something about the forlorn girl made her speak again.

"If you really want to go that badly, just go. You don't need my help."

Jaela shook her head. "I don't think Roi is planning on taking the fleet to Ventituras anytime soon."

"Leave on your own, then." Then winch was almost complete now, despite the distractions. The spring on the ratchet was a little flimsy, but she wouldn't be needing it for long.

"Maybe I could have snuck away the last time we were at port, but not right before a battle," Jaela said. "The others would never allow it." She drummed her fingers on the intake vent. "I suppose we'll just see what happens after tomorrow."

As Karis went to fetch the cable end, she peeked at Jaela staring out into the sky. Interesting that Jaela was speaking as if she were trapped, even though she seemed to get along well enough with the others. Was it merely pre-battle jitters, or was there more to her previous idea that they had something in common?

Karis hooked the cable to the spool and looked around for someone to turn it, but the others were nowhere to be found. "Jaela," she said. "Come help me with this."

Jaela smiled and hopped down, and together they pulled. The pressure in Karis's back and ribs felt good as she wound up the line bit by bit. Nice to be able to finish the job by dint of her own muscles, and even nicer to do it without involving Mylon. Jaela grunted good-naturedly beside her, grasping the same handle since Karis had convoked only one. She leaned to the side and pressed shoulder to shoulder with Karis. An accident? As a smoothskin, Karis was used to noticing such touches where others didn't, and usually they meant nothing. Usually.

"Jaela," Karis said. "Can I ask you a question?"

"Hmm?"

"You seem different from the others." Jaela shot her a confused glance and Karis shook her head. "You know what I mean. You don't act like them, but for some reason they still treat you with respect. I understand that you're a raider and I'm not, but—"

"Oh, sweetie," Jaela said with a giggle. "You think they like me because I'm a Skyhunter? I'll give you a tip: If you want them to respect you, you just need to throw around a little attitude."

"I didn't think I'd been all that nice."

Jaela shook her head. "It's different, though. How can I explain? Even if you're not one of them, you can still treat them like you are, you know?"

She smiled that simple smile again. But simple she was not, even if Karis couldn't put her finger on what exactly was hiding beneath that veneer.

The winch jerked to a stop. Toward the bow, the cable had become hooked beyond the outer handrail. "Hold on." Karis set the pawl to stop the winch from unwinding. "I'll free it."

She walked face down against the breeze, then leaned out over the handrail to see. The cable had flopped out over the side and gotten stuck behind a loose board—a pox on her for not paying attention. A quick tug did not dislodge it, so she leaned over further to see what sort of tool she needed to convoke.

A black, feathered wing stretched out below the curve of the hull. "Karis?" Jaela called. "Do you need my help?"

"It's fine!" Karis yelled. Elsa had seen her by then, engaging her rotors to hover in closer. But Jaela was already on her way, so Karis put her hand behind her back to make a shooing motion. "I'll have it in a moment." She peeked back down to see if Elsa was still coming.

Jaela screamed, "Look out!"

The winch spun, clacking its ratchet, and the rope unfurled and whipped toward Karis. She dove, but clumsily; the rope tangled around her feet and she tumbled, flailing, smacking her forearm on hard rail.

She landed right-side up, but her feet weren't standing on anything, and she realized to her horror that she was on the outside of the ship, holding onto the railing. The wind picked up and her grip loosened. For a moment she felt the sickening rush of impending doom, before a pair of hands grabbed her armpits and hauled her up onto the deck.

"Are you all right?" Jaela said, dropping her in a heap next to the now-slack cable.

Karis sat up, her heart pounding. "I'm fine. Thank you." No, that wasn't good enough, was it? "Really, thank you. I mean it."

Awareness of the incident was spreading over the deck, and a few curious raiders were coming toward them. Karis straightened up, trying to calm herself, preparing for the unwanted attention.

Jaela leaned in and whispered, "I won't tell them about the bird, you know."

Karis's slowing heart leaped back into hammering thuds. She jerked to the railing and looked down, but Elsa was gone. When she slowly turned back again, Jaela wore a sly grin.

"Please…" Karis said.

"Don't worry," Jaela said. "It's just between us, all right?"

The others were drawing near. "Why?" Karis asked.

Jaela came in close again. "I want you to be able to continue your travels, when the time is right. That's what the bird's here for, isn't it?"

Phaestal arrived before Karis could answer, puffing with his face red. "For Pfel's sake, what's going on here? What is this?"

Mylon kicked at the cable. "This is what happens when you put the smoothskin in charge of something. She's trying to sabotage us."

Karis growled. She was in no mood after what had just happened. "If I was, you'd be the first one I'd drop in the sea, you stinking pustule!" She poked a finger into his sternum.

"H—hey." He brushed her hand away. "Just…lay off, will you?"

She stepped back, surprised at his reaction. Jaela flashed her a grin and nodded. *Even if you're not one of them, you can still treat them like you are.*

"And the rest of you!" she continued, casting her gaze over the crowd. "If you're not going to help fix the ship, then do yourselves a favor and mind your own poxing business! That's right, you too. Just keep walking. Off! Scram!"

"Comrades, please!" Roi held up his hands for silence. None came. The assembled raiders ate, drank and caroused unabated.

Roi turned his hands inward, and in a few moments a cymbal and mallet appeared between them. He smashed them together and the crowd settled down.

"On this the eve of our victory," he said, "I must take advantage of this gathering to tell you all something."

"Lick my ass!" came a shout from down the table. The raiders had cleared the walls from several living areas to make a cavernous dining hall in the belly of the flagship. Weak rays of evening light streamed in from holes in the deck above, and the gloom hid whoever had spoken from Karis's view.

"Shut up!" Isky, one of the two larger raiders who always seemed to be at Roi's side, slammed his fists on the table. "Show some respect!"

Murmuring and commotion broke out at the other end of the hall. There was a twinkle as a drink traveled across the table, followed by someone being tackled and more yells.

Roi stood up, ignoring the shouts. "I just wanted to say what an honor it is to be fighting alongside you all. No matter what happens tomorrow, remember: we stand together, and I would rather stand with you and die than live among outsiders. Fearless and always feared!"

The raiders yelled agreement, then broke into a chorus of "Death Swoops from Above." Karis struggled not to convoke a pair of earplugs; she had been on board the ship less than a week, but had heard enough of that song for a lifetime.

"'Stand with us and die'? What's that about?" Mylon mumbled to her right between gulps of food. "He's giving up already?"

"He's trying to motivate you, dummy," said Dikta, Roi's other bodyguard.

"All right, all right, you don't have to be a moldhead about it."

Karis rested her chin on her hand and took a disc-shaped loaf of pitbread from a nearby pile. The raiders seemed to prefer food in shapes that were easy to throw. She set it on its edge and spun it like a top.

"You should eat," Jaela said. "It's good luck on the eve of a battle."

Karis gave her a weak smile and took a bite. It was Jaela who had insisted she come to the dinner. She had been cautiously optimistic about it at first, until she had arrived and Jaela had waved her over to the seat she had saved, not only across from Mylon, but so close to Roi that Karis could see the individual hairs in his perfect eyebrows.

Several raiders shouted from the far end of the dining hall, "Story! Roi, tell a story!"

"Are there any drugs in this?" Karis murmured, holding up the bread.

"Which one?" Roi said. "How about the Altonim Peace Conference? Surely you've all heard that one?"

"None," Jaela said. "Roi says a raider's best weapon is their judgment."

"Again! Again!" The raiders shouted.

"All right." Roi held up a placating hand.

The raiders gave a small cheer, then settled in to listen. Roi cleared his throat and pushed his food away, making a big show of it. The smacking sound of Karis chewing her biscuit seemed suddenly conspicuous in the quiet.

"It took a long time to set up that conference," Roi began. "I did a lot of the legwork myself. The idea was that Altonim would be neutral territory; a shared base of operations for us and the raiders formerly known as the Deadly Alliance. Of course, the Magistrate of Altonim was quite helpful in the preparations, since the agreement would mean no more raids on his city."

"Get to the good part!" someone shouted.

Roi smiled. "But what he didn't count on was Tiresius. Now, Tiresius was a great man, a brilliant man, but he could be rather…hard to deal with at times. The way he looked at it, if you gave him something, it meant that he could ask for something else. And if you gave him that something, it just meant that he could ask for one thing more. During the negotiations, it got to the point where I would arrive in the city not knowing if the magistrate was going to welcome me with an embrace, or with an axe to the neck.

"So the way the conference is supposed to work, we have a day to finalize the negotiations, then a reception in the evening, followed by a formal agreement the following morning. We arrive with three ships, holding the rest of the fleet in reserve. Everything is going fine. No one is happy with what they got except for Tiresius, but that's the way he liked it.

"So we arrive at the reception, me, Tiresius, Hindal and a crew of five. Everything is decked out, Second Empire style." A diorama came into existence in front of Roi as he spoke, extending the width of the table. "Huge banners and buntings, all in Altonim Pink. Dresses with trains that cover the floor of the hall, a ten-piece band, the whole mountain decorated in flowers."

The raiders stilled even further as they studied Roi's creation. It was all there, the banners, the plants, tiny figures in dancing poses scattered about a ballroom inlaid with elaborate tile-work. He had to have planned the scene in advance, practiced convoking it numerous times—or so Karis hoped, anyway.

"Of course," he continued, "we don't much want to socialize with the Deadly Alliance, nor do we really know anyone from Altonim, so the party is a bit boring. But that's a small price to pay, eh? I figure we'll put up with this for one night and then go back to raiding. At least, that's what I figured until Tiresius steps up and makes a comment to me. Very casual, very off-hand. 'Roi, I'm going to fuck that girl before this is over.' And he winks and nods toward the woman he was just dancing with: the Magistrate's partner."

Roi raised his hands as if defending himself from some unheard criticism. "Now, I must say I did find this turn of events somewhat concerning. But what was I to do? Tell him no? This was Tiresius. I just had to hope he was joking. So I ignore it, time goes on, the crew and I eat and drink, tell some jokes. Hindal is being stuck up and no fun as usual.

"Then I notice something: Tiresius and the Magistrate's lover are gone. As in nowhere to be found. Mold! I maintain my composure, of course, but at the same time, I start looking for the exits, scoping the city guards and the Alliance—we don't have the numbers to fight them both at once. I tell Hindal to get the crew ready to leave if necessary, then I back off to the corner of the room near the band-stand, and that was when I heard it."

He paused and lowered his voice, and the raiders leaned in to hear. "A moan. Coming from behind a curtain to my left. Then another. Now, sometimes you may overhear things, and you know, logically, it can't be that loud in reality, but I'll tell you that to me it was as deafening as the roar of an engine. And they were getting louder, too. The Magistrate is on the dance floor, looking around as if he's searching for someone. I'm sweating so bad that if I had shaken my arms I could have covered our escape in a cloud of dust."

Jaela chuckled, then eyed Karis and grinned. Karis instinctively returned the smile. But why would Jaela look at her?

"I turn to the band, and tell them to start playing 'Twenty Round and Face Down'; a loud song, you know, the kind where everyone is supposed to dance. I tell them it's a special request from Tiresius, to help seal the peace. They start playing, but then the moaning gets louder. People are coming over to ask me to dance. I decline, as politely as possible, smiling while I'm sweating out an ocean. Then, out of nowhere, Hindal comes over and tells the band to stop playing."

"What?" someone shouted.

"That's what I said. He tells me he doesn't like the song, that it's not *appropriate* for the occasion and so forth. I'm yelling over him, shoving him away, which only makes him angrier. The band gets nervous. Some of them stop playing. And meanwhile, behind the curtain, things are getting intense. *Uh! Uh!*" He banged his palm on the table, rattling crystal platters. "So, I do the only thing I can: I shove one of the players out of the way and grab his slide-horn."

Roi convoked a slide-horn in his right hand, though it was too small, more of a prop than an instrument.

"*You* play the slide-horn?" a man down the table asked, obviously on cue.

"Not a note. But I give it a good raider try, blasting away at the thing. Hindal looks at me like I'm insane. I try to go with the band as best I can, except I'm not keeping time to the music; I'm following the sex, trying to cover up the yells. And let me tell you, she was really wailing by then. It sounded like—" He put the horn to his lips "—Ah! *Honk*! Ah! *Honk*!"

He tossed the horn over his shoulder and waited for the laughter to die down.

"By this time everyone in the room notices what I'm doing. The rest of the band stops, so I stand up and improvise a solo, as loud as possible, just playing anything to get attention while the noise behind the curtain dies off. And when I finish, everyone applauds, the whole place goes insane." He stood and took a bow before his imagined audience of revelers, then waited in silence for their equally imaginary applause to die down.

"So you pulled it off?" a raider asked after some moments.

"Yes. And no. See, there was one thing I hadn't considered. You know how after a really good fucking, your mind goes blank? Unless you're careful, convocations can crumble, especially recent ones.

"Well, let's just say the Magistrate's partner had taken care of the decorations that evening…personally."

Some of the raiders tittered.

Mylon leaned over to Dikta and whispered something.

"He's talking about the curtain," Dikta mumbled back with annoyance.

"Or rather, the lack of a curtain," Roi said. "Just the two of them, standing there before the entire party, nude. Tiresius still inside her."

He sat back into his plush chair and made a little flourish with his hand, and one of the curtains in the diorama crumbled, revealing two naked figures behind it. Whistles and a smattering of applause went up from the table.

"So what happened?" someone yelled. "How did you get out?"

"Well, the confusion helped, of course. I had a stiletto in my hand before the Magistrate could finish ordering the guards to execute us. I stabbed a couple of the band members and yelled, 'It's an Alliance ambush! Save the city!' That gave us some cover for the scramble. What I'll never know is how Hindal made it out, since he was holding off six or seven of them while Tiresius and I ran down the mountain. Good gods, Tiresius must have been cold that night.

"Of course, eventually they did figure out what was happening, and marshaled a force to come after us. But Tiresius had a safeguard in place. A ship, waiting high above the party grounds, loaded with hundreds of drop-balls about the width of this table. He signaled them, they dropped the ordnance, and moments later..."

Dozens of finger-wide balls dropped from the dark ceiling, smashing the diorama with startling force, until colored chunks and gray dust rested in a flower-like splay.

"...the whole place was rubble. The Magistrate died, the Deadly Alliance was severely crippled, and Altonim never tried to parlay with raiders ever again."

"And that," Roi said, flexing his fingers and placing them behind his head, "is the story of the *last* raider peace conference."

More shouts and clapping came, while Roi convoked a hand broom to clean the table. The daylight was almost gone, and the raiders returned to their shouts and songs in an effort to wring out the last of their enjoyment. Karis kept her mouth closed, but she could not keep it from curling into a frown. Only one night remained before her plan would come to fruition. If she failed, would she end up any better off than the Altonim Magistrate?

"Karis!" Roi said. "You don't seem impressed with my story. Can you do better?"

Half the table was looking her way. What was his game, now? Did he want to see if she would push back, like she had done to the raiders on the deck?

"It was a good story," Karis said. "But it's fake. I don't think it actually happened."

"Settle down!" a raider shouted.

"Yeah, smoothskin twerp!"

"Oh, it happened," Roi said, waving down the table. "Just ask Hindal. Of course, it's possible I embellished a few details, but that's all in the telling."

"I suppose it's convenient that you and Hindal are the only ones who know," Karis said, her glare unshaken. "That way no one can find out whether or not you planned to bombard the conference from the beginning."

The other raiders hissed and shouted her down. Roi locked eyes with her. She had expected anger, but he only smiled knowingly before turning to join another conversation.

After the meal, Karis filed back with the others through the halls. From the time she had begun cooperating with the raider's efforts, she had returned each night to find her cell upgraded, until finally she had been moved to a real cabin along the outer hull, with a small window at the far end, and no solid wall blocking her in.

That night, when she reached the outside of the door, she checked to see if anyone was looking, then continued into the interior of the ship.

The passages here were dim even in daylight, and now she was forced to navigate solely by touch. It was good practice, though, learning to follow her planned route: down the ladder, down again, two turns to the left and over a catwalk though the ship's hollow belly, then down through a hole into the crawlspace. She waited a few moments in the dark, listening to the rushing noise of the wind against the bottom of the hull, feeling the hum of the ship, but there were no louder thumps to suggest she had been followed.

Good. The next step was easy; she relaxed the bit of focus she had kept since the last time she had come, and a hole formed in the floor in front of her. Such a small thing at a large distance was hard not to let crumble, but she had to keep the hole she had cut out three days ago covered, in case a raider flying underneath noticed it. Even now the wind made a ghastly whistling noise as it blew past, reminding her she would have to plug it up again soon.

She crawled over and stared down at the ocean, stained black by the night. Fresh aer tickled her face. She could do it—convoke something to ride down in, and jump through this instant. But the failure of the engines she had worked on would be noticed, and she

couldn't risk having the raiders search for her, even in the dark—
especially since Elsa wouldn't know where to find her.

She sighed and convoked a new cap for the hole, shaping it to
look like just another patch placed by a hurried raider. She had
managed to speak to Elsa again after the morning commotion had
passed, and had relayed two simple instructions: wait for the battle to
begin, then head under the ship. She still wished that Elsa had not left
Meli's side in the first place, but now that the eagle was here, she had
to ensure that they both had the greatest chance of escaping safely.
When the time is right, Jaela had said. She could have turned Karis in,
revealed everything about the plan, but she hadn't. Karis would try not
to forget her after she left.

Karis shuffled back to the crawlspace entrance and hauled herself
up, pausing at each junction to listen for sentries. Tomorrow. So soon,
and yet it couldn't come fast enough. She had to stay positive, keep
telling herself it would be all right. Elsa would arrive, everything would
go well, and the new day would see her released.

12

Grass brushed Ariden's elbows. A breeze waved the stalks and ruffled his hair. He sat on a plain, rolling hills stretched before him. Squinting in the bright daylight, he did not see the figure to his left until she touched his neck.

"Welcome," she said. "I've been waiting for you."

How had he forgotten she was there? That perfect face and seductive red lips, and a voice that fell on the ears like a burst of sweetness on the center of the tongue.

"It's been how long, and all you can say is 'welcome'?"

He leaned in to kiss her, and she rapped him playfully on the back of the head. Or at least it looked playful; her hand felt like solid rock.

He rubbed his head, stunned and dizzy. "What was that for?"

"This is not a place for carnal acts, Ariden. You're in the realm of the gods, now."

"Yes, but—"

She smacked him again.

"Ow. This looks like the plains of Porlan. The place you died."

"The place where you let him kill me."

Her words cut him. "I'm trying to make it right. Trying to find the Scarred Man."

"You tried and failed. If you are here, then your life has ended."

The day had brightened further, and her features were bathed in white. He held his hand to his eyes. "If I can stay with you, then I am elated in death. Why is the light so bright, my love?"

"You are in the presence of the gods. And I have a name. Use it." She wound up and smacked him again.

"My love," he said, swaying, his head pounding. "When you hit me like that, it makes the ground seem to move up and down."

"Ariden, wake up," she said.

"What?"

"Ariden!" Meli's voice cut through the haze. "Wake up."

He groaned. The grass and the light were gone, replaced with the hard bottom of their miserable little boat, and the gray dreariness of the fog. The pain in his head remained, spread over the inside of his skull, though it stung not half as badly as the realization that the Enchantress had been only a dream.

"She was there," he moaned into his hands.

"Who?"

He ignored Meli and curled into a ball. She had been right there, so close. Why couldn't he truly have been dead?

"What's he doing?" Sirdu asked. So he was still alive as well—what a blessing.

"How should I know?" Meli said. "I thought he would crumble at any moment, the way he was moaning."

"Mold," Ariden mumbled. Small waves were rocking the boat sideways. The motion must have repeatedly knocked the back of his head into the gunwale as he slept. "You could have convoked me a pillow."

"How did you scare off Vipretheon?" Sirdu asked. "I didn't see a thing with my head between my legs."

Vipretheon. Ariden's hands reached for a weapon which wasn't there. He scrambled to his knees, but the pain in his head knocked him back again. Had he indeed scared the thing off? He couldn't remember fighting it, nor what it looked like.

"If it attacked me," he mumbled, "it must be dead."

"You didn't touch it," Meli said. "And I'm not sure it was ever alive. It was some sort of…moving convocation. After it had crippled the ship and almost killed us, it disappeared."

"I was worried it would come back," Sirdu said. "But I don't think it will, now."

"What makes you so sure?" Ariden asked.

"The aer feels…flatter," Sirdu said. "That strange sensation is gone. And anyway, it has been an entire day."

"A day!" Ariden shot up again and grimaced.

"The wind is still light," Meli said. "So we've been waiting and watching."

"Thank you for your attention," Ariden mumbled, rubbing his neck.

"Oh, well, pardon me, Sir. But we weren't watching you."

"Hmm?" Ariden spun around and looked up. "Oh, good gods."

Bedrock cliffs a hundred feet high loomed over them. Tendrils of mist crawled over the stony surface, with crevices stained yellow from moss between them.

"Why didn't you say something?" Ariden shook his head in a vain attempt to clear it and took stock of the ship. "Make another set of oars and locks, and let's get rowing. Daylight is fading."

"Are you sure you're all right?" Sirdu asked.

"No," Ariden said. "I feel like Estinpar crushed me under his boot, but if I can get off this poxing boat, I'll be right enough."

Sirdu did as instructed, and Meli took to the bow as they got underway. "The cliffs are sheer," she said. "And too wet to construct a platform. It's pointless to row to them if we can't climb."

True to her words, their landfall consisted of waves crashing against jagged rock. Ariden handed Sirdu his oar and stood to survey them.

"Convoke a spike up high and a rope leading down," he said.

Meli made the spike and the rope, a tattered thing which could only have come from a truly exhausted mind. Ariden wasn't sure he trusted it to hold his weight, and the waves were too unpredictable near the rocks to grasp it, anyway.

Meli tried and failed to convoke a platform lower on the cliff, but all her attempts were washed away by the pounding surf. Ariden paced the deck, gritting his teeth at the throbbing pain.

"Why did you have to send away that buzzard of yours?" he growled. "It could have carried a rope to the top."

"If you're not going to suggest something useful, then stuff it." Meli cast her gaze about. "Look down there; the rock extends down into the sea. Perhaps we could run the boat aground."

Ariden squinted into the fog and saw a vague shape. "Likely it's nothing," he grumbled, but nevertheless he sat at his oar again and hauled to turn them southward.

"A port, a port, a port of any sort, that's where I'd like to be," Sirdu sang. Ariden shoved the point of an oar into his belly. "Oof!"

Hundreds of tugs later, Meli pointed. "There. Do you see it?"

Night had fallen, but the dim glow from the horizon illuminated a shallow ramp leading up to a small alcove.

"That's impossible," Ariden said. "It's too perfect."

"Are you telling me you don't want to go in?"

He answered by laying in hard on his oar. They landed, and the scrape of solid aether on bedrock had never sounded so wonderful. Meli stepped down from the bow, and Ariden ditched his oar and hopped off before the boat drifted back into the sea.

"Wait for me!" Sirdu shouted.

They scrabbled upward until they had climbed far enough above the fog and waves to convoke handholds, then continued up into the alcove, which was deeper than it appeared at first glance. Meli threw herself to the floor and lay face up, laughing quietly.

"Ground," she whispered. "Sweet, beloved, solid ground."

Ariden could not disagree. He found a wall with his back and slid down to a sitting position, his boots and clothes sloshing on the damp floor. Sirdu stumbled past into the darkness of the tunnel beyond.

"How far does this go?" His voice echoed after tens of paces.

"Doesn't matter," Ariden said, closing his eyes. "I'm spending the night here."

Sirdu muttered nervously, but eventually returned and found a resting place which suited him. Within minutes his snores filled the alcove, with Meli wheezing in the brief silences between.

Ariden's veins throbbed behind his closed eyes. He tried to picture the Enchantress's face, but his imagination could not match the fidelity of dream. He drifted off, trying to return to that place, to find his way back to her, but each time he awoke again in failure.

How pathetic he felt, chasing after a dead woman in his mind. But the pain and weakness had sapped his will to maintain dignity. He slipped into dream again and again, forgetting each time that his surroundings were not real. He found himself fighting, rowing, arguing with Meli or Sirdu aboard ships that did not at all resemble the one they had carelessly let crumble into the surf. Finally, after a frustrating session in which Vipretheon, which had somehow taken the form of his old fighting trainer from Caeridor, beat him handily in wrestling, he opened his eyes to the gleam of a new day.

"Oh, gods have mercy!" Sirdu stretched and rubbed his belly. "Why didn't I convoke a bed?"

Ariden stood and rolled his spine to work out the kinks. When he had woken on the boat he had felt more dead than alive; now the balance had shifted, but only slightly. His muscles were still sore, and the throbbing in his head continued. It had been a long time since he had sustained an injury which took more than half a day to heal. Just what had Vipretheon done to him?

"Could anyone else use a bite?" Sirdu asked.

"By all means, convoke a feast," Ariden said, yawning. "Hopefully you'll still be eating while we pull away on our new ship."

"You should look back here, first." Meli stepped out from the rear of the alcove. Her change in appearance stunned Ariden into silence—a blush had replaced the sickly green on her cheeks, and she had changed her clothes, dropping her ragged gown in favor of a form-fitting hiking suit. Her eyes, previously glazed, sparkled with vitality. "There's a tunnel. It leads to a staircase."

"A *what?*" Ariden stalked past her. In the dim light at the rear of the cave, smooth black stairs wound upward, cut into the bedrock.

"This bodes ill," he said. "We'd best leave the way we came."

"Why? These could lead to the top of the cliff. They're exactly what we need."

"That's the problem. Life never gives you exactly what you need. But enemies do, if they wish to deceive you."

"You're purposely being obstinate." She walked past him and took the first few steps, staring up beyond the curve. "An enemy? These stairs must have been here for centuries at least, if not millennia."

She continued up the steps, out of sight. Behind Ariden, Sirdu shuffled his feet.

"And what of you?" Ariden growled. "I suppose you wish to go up as well?"

"Oh no, sir," he said. "I defer to your judgment. If you wish to stay, I'll help you convoke a new ship. After breakfast, of course."

"Come on," Meli called. "Don't you want to know what's up there?"

You will be, for one thing, and that's reason enough to stay away. Her newly zealous manner grated on him—"purposefully obstinate," indeed. But it wouldn't do to leave the woman who had promised to find the Scarred Man to wander to her death.

"Let it be known that I disapprove," Ariden called, stuffing his hands in his coat and stomping up.

After a right turn, the stairs ran a long stretch through darkness before winding back around toward the cliff-side. There, the wall opened to reveal a landing perched thirty feet above the fog, with another stair leading upward on the far side. To the north, the cliffs curved slightly to form a bay, ending at a point of crumbling bedrock. On the other side, the land gradually descended before disappearing into fog.

"It looks like the stairs just keep going up," Meli said. "They must go all the way to the top."

Ariden grunted. "The land slopes down to the south. If we sailed a few miles, we might find a beach."

"No *thank you*." She headed up the next flight and disappeared into the darkness again.

Ariden stayed, staring out at the gray ocean and sky. This was wrong; all wrong. First the wind, then the encounter with Vipretheon, of which he remembered only bits and pieces—a screeching sound, and strange lights traveling over the sea. What was the meaning of it? And now, this stair. Bedrock was the foundation of all the world, millions of miles of implacable hardness, with only a tiny portion of it cut by human hands. Why a cave mouth, at nearly the exact point where their ship had drifted to shore? Why the stairs leading away from the fog, just when they wanted to escape it the most?

Sirdu's heavy breathing crept up behind him. "Sir?" he panted. "You think there's something up there that could hurt us?"

"I have no idea what's up there. I only know I don't like it."

"But who would make a stair like this?"

"The ancients, it had to be. It's known they had some method of cutting through bedrock."

Sirdu gazed at his surroundings with newfound awe. "Then it must be empty, if it was made so long ago."

"Unless someone else has decided to use it in the meantime."

Ariden continued upward, not wanting to let Meli get too far ahead. As he climbed he convoked the hilt of the Scythe in his right hand, finding it came together easily now that they were out of the fog. The stairs went on much as before, smooth and angular, winding inward through rough-hewn corridors, then back out toward slit windows providing light and fresh aer. By the time he found Meli waiting on another balcony, he had finished the sword and tucked it into his coat.

She had convoked a railing and was leaning out to look down. They had climbed well above the level of the cliffs, which stretched out to the north and south below.

"We must be in some kind of thin mountain," she said. "Like a tower."

"A tower made of bedrock. Rather unusual, don't you think?"

"The ancients probably thought so, as well," Meli said. "Perhaps they honored this place by building a temple on top."

"Can't see much sense in climbing a mountain," Sirdu puffed. "Maybe there's another tunnel? We could have missed a side passage."

Meli looked down the stair, then back up, slight trepidation on her brow. Perhaps Ariden's warnings had finally sapped her confidence.

"We've come this far. Going back down is easy; we might as well see what's at the end."

"As long as it's not *our* end," Sirdu muttered.

They climbed further, until Ariden came to the foot of a stair with light shining down it from above.

"Wait. I'll take the lead." Pulling the Scythe from his coat, he side-stepped past Meli.

The stair wall spread, and he advanced upward into a shallow trench, carved into a tremendous bowl at the summit of the circular mountain. At the center of the bowl sat the remains of an altar: a slab of bedrock, held up by two others set at right angles, surrounded by rock sculptures of long-necked, long-limbed creatures with multiple heads. Or so they appeared to him—the works of the ancients were often as abstract as they were unsettling.

Around the perimeter of the bowl, high bedrock walls rose, and above them eight equidistant spires jutted upward, with white, wisp-like filaments woven across the empty space between, filtering the daylight. The threads formed polygonal patterns, repeating themselves in miniature copies within their boundaries. Here and there among the stacked layers, small nests of material were concentrated, and some of these shook with the movement of strangers walking atop them.

"What's up there?" Meli called. "What do you see?"

Ariden said nothing, ignorance and confusion holding his tongue. She climbed up herself with Sirdu at her heels.

"What is this place?" she said.

High above, a segment of the web parted, and a platform descended through the gap, suspended by two thick, braided strands. The platform drew closer, revealing a figure standing in its center, dressed in a sheer white robe with a white headscarf. He kept his eyes closed as he dropped, focusing on his connection to the web, letting the ropes crumble strand by strand in order to allow him to fall gradually. He alighted on the ground with perfect control, then stepped forward and opened a pair of green eyes, set in a handsome face marked by the barest trace of beard.

"Hello, Meli." His voice carried a hint of gravel, but was otherwise clear, strong and even.

Meli looked at Ariden in bewilderment, then back at the stranger. "You know my name?"

"I do," the man said. "And yours, Ariden."

Ariden squeezed the Scythe, his wariness melting into anger. "Have we met?"

"We have not. But I was told to prepare for your arrival." He bowed his head. "My name is Targael. I'm glad you have joined us at last."

"Told?" Meli said. "No one knew we were coming here."

"No man, perhaps. But I received my instructions from Naal herself."

"Naal?" Meli stared up at the web, understanding dawning in her eyes. "You're a priest. This is a cult center."

"Indeed."

A cult center? So the people Ariden saw moving above were all religious adherents, who came to this place to worship their god in solitude. But that did not explain anything. What were he and Meli doing here? How could a god have told the priest their names?

"It is our hope that you will stay with us, for the time being." Targael motioned to three more platforms of white webbing descending behind him. "I offer to make you comfortable, and to address the many questions you clearly contemplate. And so it is, I bid you welcome to the Sanctuary of the Inaali.

"May you fulfill the God's purpose in bringing you here."

13

Even after Karis had been given control of the door to her cell, Phaestal had continued to fetch her each day and escort her to work. But the morning of the battle, she lay in bed long past daybreak, listening to the commotion on the deck above, until it became apparent he wasn't going to arrive. She almost felt herself missing their little ritual as she made her way alone up to the deck. Clearly, being aboard this ship was warping her mind.

She stepped out into the light, her eyes adjusted and she gasped.

The fleet had convened.

So many ships, so magnificent, so deadly. Hindal's flagship, smaller than Roi's but covered with armor plates and crossbow ports, floated above and to starboard, and groups of raiders in hanging baskets traversed the thick cables anchoring them together. Whip-fast strikers filled the rest of the sky, wedge-shaped and jet black like the ones that had attacked her and Meli, spilling icy clouds of dust from their exhaust ports.

Raiders scurried around her as she wandered the deck. Some of them were new faces, Hindal's men, headed for a gathering spot near the runway. Hindal himself was there as well, judging by the size of the crowd. Phaestal stood off to one side, telling Mylon something about the aft engines. He acknowledged her approach with a nod.

"Do you think they're ready?" she asked.

"Are *you* ready?" Mylon leered at her with those beady eyes of his. She'd grown a special dislike for him as the days had passed, not that he was much different from the rest.

"Why wouldn't I be?"

He gave an ugly smile. "Battles bring surprises."

"Karis has done a lot of good work," Phaestal put in. "Maybe more than you."

"Well excuse me," Mylon said. "Didn't know you two were so friendly."

"We're not," Karis said, crossing her arms.

A call went out from the foredeck, and Phaestal and Mylon moved with the others to a great circle forming there. Karis stayed to the outside as usual, convoking a step-stool to see over their heads.

Roi stepped into the center, flanked by Isky and Dikta, and greeted Hindal with a press of foreheads. Hindal convoked a model of the Mariten coast on the deck, and Roi took to one knee to study it.

"Everything is well," Hindal said. "The scouts saw the entire Reviled fleet tied at anchor on the city walls yesterday."

"Did the Reviled see the scouts?"

"It's possible a few may have been spotted flying away."

"So we won't have the element of surprise," Roi said. "Sounds well, all right."

Hindal bristled. "They have no way of knowing how many ships we'll attack with, or when. But even if they guess correctly, all they've got for defense are lines of trebuchets on the walls—far too inaccurate to hit our skiffs and strikers."

"Right." Roi pointed to the map. "So we'll hold the flagships here, well out of range. But what if they've managed to scramble their fleet since you saw them?"

"Then we'll see it through the scopes. If my scouts fly red banners, it means attack as planned. Blue means the Reviled ships are no longer at the city. In that case we'll make a turn here, prevent them from flanking us, then strike the city over land."

"And what if they don't try to flank us? What if they come at us ship to ship?"

"Then the fun starts." Hindal grinned. "Unless your crew would rather be chased in circles all day?"

Some snickers went up from Hindal's portion of the crowd.

Roi stood and surveyed his raiders. "My friends! I consider myself the luckiest man in Aetheria, to count each of you as one of my allies."

Roi swept his eyes over the crowd, and his gaze lingered on Karis. At first she thought it was her imagination, but no; he had deliberately locked their eyes before turning away. Why her, over everyone there? Something about his look stirred a long-dormant memory, sending a chill down her spine.

"We stand here on the verge of a great moment in history," Roi continued. "You will be the ones spoken of in the great tales. Think of it: how many people did you know in your former lives who talked of days like this, who boasted, who postured, who pretended? And all of them—miserable. So afraid of death, they will never understand what it's like to truly live."

The crowd nodded and mumbled agreement.

"Anyone can *speak* of battle, of victory, but only you, the truly elite, get the chance to actually experience it. The time has come to show the Reviled who rules the sky. Tiresius's memory will not go unavenged. Fearless—"

"—*and always feared!*" hundreds of voices cried.

"Stations!" Hindal shouted.

The raiders broke off, heading to their smaller ships or back to the cables. Karis passed through the crowd, shaking off her lingering ill feeling from Roi's stare, searching for an out of the way place to think it over. Just nerves, perhaps. Roi had pointed to a place on the map a good deal off shore for them to wait, if the scouts flew a red banner. That would mean a longer journey with Elsa to escape to land, but was still far preferable to what would happen if the blue banner came and the plan changed. In that case, it sounded as if Roi and Hindal wanted to take the flagships directly into the fight, and her along with them. She exhaled nervously and ground her teeth. How much longer would it be, exactly? A day seemed too long a wait with nothing to do.

"Hey, what's that?" came a voice from behind her.

Three raiders strutted up the deck—Hindal's fighters, judging from their bearing. One of them, a tall, barrel-chested man with jet black hair tied back, had tossed the remark at a crouching raider she recognized as Cindlan, Roi's errand boy.

"It's a...parachute." Cindlan was a creasedskin, with wiry gray hair, a wrinkled face, and skin sagging over muscles bereft of vigor. More common than smoothskins, creasedskins were much less likely to be treated differently than anyone else, which had always seemed rather unfair to Karis.

"A what?!"

"You strap it to your back like this, see?"

The tall raider's companions laughed. He leaned over Cindlan and snarled. "Parachutes are for those who can defend themselves once they land in the sea. What are you going to do down there, eh?"

"Roi said that he'd come and—"

"Oh, mercy's sake!" The tall raider gave Cindlan a playful smack that sprawled him onto his chest. "We have to get off this ship, Mitz. It's all defeatist cowards and traitors." He wheeled away and caught Karis staring. "Like what you see, little one?"

She stiffened, but caught herself and chuckled contemptuously, then showed him her shoulder.

"Hey!" Two large strides brought him close. He loomed over her. "I'm talking to you. You like this?"

He crumbled the sleeve and chest of his jumpsuit, then flexed his muscles. His body blocked the wind, his musky scent taking its place. "I never had a smoothskin before. Love those little titties. Want to fuck me and my friends before the battle?"

A tingling numbness washed over her, the same one she had felt when Roi held her gaze. The man's size, his posture, those wide shoulder muscles and cold breath, they were all the same as Vikter's had been. A sick feeling welled in her throat.

She shook her head, stepped back, then broke into a run.

"What's her problem?" the raider said before his voice drifted into the wind.

She found an alcove on the other side of the command deck and nestled into it, covering her face. She felt dizzy and her body shook, as much with disappointment as with fear. She shouldn't have fled. All of that had happened a long time ago. This day was too important; she couldn't let some dog-headed fool turn her into a gibbering mess.

"Are you all right?" Jaela stood over her, appearing from nowhere. "I saw you running. What happened?"

Karis inhaled sharply and sat up. "I'm just nervous. About the battle."

"You can't pay attention to those guys," Jaela said. "They all think their dicks are a gift from Elaethim."

As if she needed to be told that. After three hundred years, did Jaela really think she was unused to men approaching her? "I know what they're like. He just reminded me of something, that's all. From long ago."

"What is it?" Jaela convoked a pair of stools and sat down, her face bright, ready to receive some juicy piece of gossip.

Karis took the stool next to her, but folded herself and turned away. "You'll excuse me, but I've said too much. It's not something I talk about."

"Why not? It might make you feel better."

"No." Karis closed her eyes. She breathed deeply, but the swirling feeling in her mind refused to leave.

Something touched her palm. Karis stifled a gasp—Jaela had joined their hands in her lap.

"Why can't you tell me?"

"I…" Karis licked her lips. "I just don't…" She looked into Jaela's eyes, and the words seemed to come out on their own accord. "I was thinking of my first commune. They found me at the height of the Turmoil of the Fall, when I appeared on the Lost Coast."

"The fall of the Third Empire?"

"Yes. Three centuries ago."

"What happened to them? Were they killed?"

"No. They weren't killed. And they weren't a real commune, either. They were a cult of madmen. The Lost Coast was a terrible place then. Feral gangs were everywhere. To me my commune was safety, order and the word of God. I didn't know better…" Her voice cracked.

"It's all right," Jaela said. "Just let it out."

Karis gritted her teeth. "I don't want to let it out. I don't want to think about it ever again. I shouldn't be here and I don't know why I'm telling you this!"

Jaela shrank away. Good. She would miss the girl, but their time together had to end eventually.

They sat there in silence a while longer until Jaela sniffed. Now *she* was upset? This was too much.

"I had a life, you know," Karis said. "I had a purpose before you all brought me here."

"I know," Jaela replied softly. "I know you're smarter than people here give you credit for …" She sniffed again. "I'm sorry if I'm bothering you. I guess I just wanted to talk a little. Woman to woman. There's so few of us here…"

She turned away and sniffed again. Karis took a deep breath. This ship, this whole situation was insane, and perhaps it infected each of them with their own unique brand of insanity. But Jaela deserved better. She had to say something, at least, to pay Jaela back for her kindness.

"Jaela, listen to me."

A wary glance.

"Whatever you do, don't trust Roi. He acts friendly, but he's manipulative. That's all I can tell you, I suppose. I wish I could help more, but you know I'm leaving soon."

"Can I come with you?"

Karis jerked back in surprise. "You—you want to?"

"What if the fleet gets destroyed?" Jaela wrung her hands and looked down. "But it would never work anyway. They'd come after me. Maybe you could disappear, but I'm a raider. They could find me wherever I went."

She was right. The raiders were too well-known in every city along the North-Windward Coast. People would notice newcomers, ask questions. They would leave a trail unless they went directly to...

"The Automatia," Karis mumbled. "We'd be safe there."

"The Automatia? You mean that school?"

Karis nodded. "I've wanted to go for two hundred years. I was on my way there with Meli when you all stopped me."

"Meli?"

"My friend. I helped her create Elsa—that bird you saw yesterday. For all I know, she's there already. If we go, we could find her, and escape this madness at the same time. And the raiders wouldn't be able to follow—it's said that getting into the Automatia without the key is impossible."

"And you know the key?" Jaela's face brightened with hope.

"Yes, of course." Karis closed her eyes, recalling the words the traveler had told her all those years ago: Pfel, Ord, Estinpar, Sailach. The names of four gods. No need to tell Jaela yet, though.

When Karis looked again, Jaela's smile was too broad for the dangers that lay ahead. The poor girl didn't understand how hard their escape would still be.

"We have more to do," Karis said. "I have a plan, but we shouldn't discuss it here. The longer we speak, the more we raise suspicions."

Jaela nodded. "I think I have a plan, too. We'll split apart for now. Find me before the battle starts."

She winked and left her stool before Karis could say more. Karis watched her leave, checked their surroundings, then headed off in the opposite direction.

The day grew to its brightest, and while most of the raiders busied themselves readying their ships, Karis wandered the perimeter of the deck. She had pictured her escape route many times, but now she had to reconfigure everything around the idea that Jaela would be coming with her. Oh, gods, did she really have to take on this responsibility, and at the last possible moment? And what about this alternate plan? It sounded like Jaela might have a ship ready, which would certainly be more convenient than having Elsa carry her down to the fog and improvising from there. But even if they had another means of escape, she couldn't just leave Elsa waiting below the flagship.

She watched the skiffs take off one by one, drifting into wedge formations above and below, until the twin flagships were surrounded by them in a great swarm. It wouldn't be long now. Karis mounted the ladder to the command deck to look out for Jaela, and found Roi standing on the bow side, peering through a telescope. The raiders around him were silent, with none of their usual singing and cracking jokes.

She didn't see Jaela anywhere abovedecks, so she leaned against the rail and watched the horizon. Clouds of brown dust pooled there, blow-off from the land, and as the flagship pulled closer she saw birds and filaments of airborne plants hanging within them. So close to the coast, now. The ship dropped lower, into the dirty aer. Karis chewed off bits of her fingernail and watched them grow back.

"Red banner! Red banner up! All ships out!"

Luck was with them—the flagships would hang back, out of the battle. The last few stragglers on the main deck ran to their skiffs, and Karis sighed in relief. With the flagship mostly empty, nothing could stop her from leaving once the skiffs headed away.

Jaela appeared atop the ladder, saw Karis and nodded knowingly. Behind her, a scout ship passed toward their stern, trailing its snake of red cloth. Before Karis could discreetly pull her aside, Jaela headed over to where the other raiders crowded around Roi. Annoying—how were they to discuss anything with her over there? Perhaps she knew more than Karis about how much time they had before the battle commenced. Karis grudgingly followed her toward the bow.

"...and reverse the forward engines," Roi was saying when she arrived. "Stay even with Hindal's ship."

"Karis." Phaestal stood to her right, holding a long telescope. "Want a look?"

She pressed her eye to it and bit her lip. After so much time, land. And not just any land—the ancient coastal city of Mariten, its white towers gleaming through the haze, protected from storms by their natural shield of high bedrock. As the scouts had promised, large ships were tethered all along the curved wall below.

"I don't see the trebuchets," Karis said. "Have they crumbled them?"

"Maybe they put them behind the walls," Phaestal said.

She turned the eyepiece, focusing deeper into the city. "I see something moving down there. Whatever it is, it must be huge."

"Something's wrong," Roi said.

Everyone on the command deck looked his way.

"Those aren't ships tied there." He dropped his telescope. "Look at how they're moving in the wind."

Phaestal snatched his scope back from Karis. She grunted angrily and leaned over the railing, as if the additional inches would help her view.

"You're right," Phaestal said. "They're bobbing. They're way too light. Just inflated balloons."

"But if those are balloons," Karis said, "where are the ships?"

Roi turned away from the city and looked up. He took a deep, resigned breath. "Where else would they be?"

Karis's stomach sank, like someone had dropped a plumb down her throat. Directly above them, the hulls of Reviled destroyers descended out of a manufactured cloud of fog.

"Get to the escape ship," Roi said, heading for the ladder. "They've got the drop on us."

He vaulted over the rail and slid down, and the other raiders hurried to follow. Karis hung back, stunned at the sight of the Reviled ships. A small, gray blob rolled off one, forming a sharp point as it fell. Then another. And another. A heartbeat later, and they had tripled in size into giant, heavy arrowheads.

Headed straight for her.

14

Ariden pulled his sword, and in a burst of cold the tip landed on Targael's neck. The priest lifted his chin slightly, but otherwise remained motionless.

"What are you doing?!" Meli had been struggling to grasp Targael's words when Ariden had moved quicker than she could see. The Inaali, the fabled cult of plague-killers, knowledge-keepers, and dispersers—she had not only found them, but they had been expecting her arrival.

"What does it look like?" Ariden said. "I'm going to interrogate him, then kill him."

"Stop. Put the sword down."

Targarel's eyes flitted from Meli to Ariden and back.

"How did you know our names?" snarled Ariden.

Targael swallowed, the bulge of his throat rolling over the point of the blade. "Naal spoke to me, through my mind. She predicted your coming, and said you were to be held in great favor. If you would please…"

"Ariden." Meli squeezed his shoulder. "Don't do anything rash. We need to find out what's happening."

Ariden pressed forward slightly, rocking Targael back on his heels. He spoke to Meli as if the priest weren't there. "The gods have gone unseen since time immemorial. If indeed one of them has spoken to this man, then he is involved with forces beyond my knowledge. Do you still wish to remain here?"

Meli nodded; she had to know. With a grunt, Ariden crumbled his blade.

Targael exhaled. "Your caution is understandable. For Naal to manifest herself to one of our adherents is rare indeed; my own experience was the first in living memory. But you have nothing to fear from our order. We believe only in harmony, and the expression of peaceful free will."

"Your order, eh?" Ariden said, looking up. "What is this place, exactly?"

"The Sanctuary is our home. A cloister, where we work to cleanse the world of the evils which plague it. But before we can do that, we must first root it from our own minds. If you wish to learn more, come with me and see for yourself."

He walked them over to the set of webbed platforms lying limp on the floor. He showed Meli hers first, giving a little bow; this message from their god seemed to have put her in their good graces.

"Step on the lift and grasp the line, here," Targael said. "We will do the rest."

Sirdu followed along next, eyes wide and shifting, still not looking entirely comfortable with what was happening. Ariden shuffled along behind, never letting the priest from his sight, hands held inside his coat.

Targeal stood upon his own pile of webbing and gave a signal, and the line above Meli began to pull. The edges of the platform went first, folding themselves into a sack around her, and then she rose, smoothly, not winched by automatist gears or pulled by hand. The fibers themselves acted as a sort of spring, convoked taut by unseen Inaali above, then allowed to slacken. An impressive feat of concentration, and a design which would have interested Karis immensely.

The thought made Meli's heart sink; how she wished Karis were here now. But wherever she was, Meli would find her. She had to find out what was happening, investigate the Inaali and these strange occurrences, but not for too long.

Meli rose into the first layer of web, and the black bedrock walls of the crater vanished in a sea of white. The platform came to a rest and its sides dropped, revealing the first level of the Sanctuary proper. White-robed adherents stood watching them, separated by wide spaces where only a few strands of web held together thicker platforms, arranged geometrically around the circle.

Targael stepped onto one of the platforms and motioned to a thick-set woman whose reddish-brown hair fell down over her eyes.

"Friends, this is my Secondary, Verestrai. She will take over for me, if my time comes to join the God."

Verestrai nodded and smiled.

"If your time comes?" Meli said. "You mean if you disperse?"

"That is not the term we use," Targael said. "But yes. The foremost goal of every living thing is to find the way to release ourselves from this world, and thus enter the next."

"If your goal is truly to die, it seems an easy one to accomplish," Ariden said.

"Not simply to die, no—to willingly give up our essence to the void. To some, this act comes easily when it is their time; our job is to minister to those who wish to pass on, but cannot do so in peace." Targael stepped off the edge of his platform, and a nest of fibers coiled themselves under his foot to catch him. "Come this way. Walking the web is not a difficult skill to master, but it can prove troublesome at first. We will prepare areas on higher levels of the Sanctuary where you may move more freely." A path formed to where Meli stood, trailing behind Targael as he walked.

Sirdu followed along with the others, looking down nervously with every step. "Can't say I understand living like this. At least on a skyship I'd have a solid deck underneath me."

"The strands force us to master fear, one of the forces that binds us to this world," Verestrai said, bringing up the rear behind him. "And they remind us of our shared bond. If an adherent who convoked one strand passes on, the others are woven so that the whole does not collapse."

"For once the raider and I are in agreement," Ariden said. "Walk faster so we can get off this thing."

"I don't quite understand," Meli said, doing her best to ignore Ariden. "You do all of this—come to this remote place, study for years—and all just to disperse?"

"To let go," Targael said. "It is true, there is much good we can accomplish in life, but Naal teaches that wherever life spreads, suffering inevitably follows. The plagues were the first true evidence of that, and the fight against them and against the Plague Bringer himself, cursed be his name, was the seminal event of our order. But even as the plagues passed into history, new crises arose. Never will we be able to eradicate them, except by turning inward and focusing on our own release."

"But if everyone followed you," Meli said, "then they would all die. How is that a solution?"

"What better solution is there than absolute peace?" They reached the circular wall of bedrock and turned, heading up a stair made of webbing attached to it. "All living beings possess a will, Meli. When you perform a convocation, you exercise that will, bringing matter into existence until your focus is once again relaxed. The first of the great wisdoms granted to our founders was that this same will binds our own bodies together. You are not aware of this, because it is a subconscious act, woven into the deepest core of your being. That is why learning to let go is so difficult for some, even though it is the ultimate act of salvation."

"Salvation?"

"Yes. We believe that once we have exhausted our capacity for worldly pleasures, we continue living only because we are in conflict with ourselves. Sometimes it is a fear of death, or being unable to let go of those who have died. But the longer we run from such worries, the more our suffering increases. Do you see the wisdom of these words?"

She nodded, more out of perceived obligation than agreement. Dispersal was common enough in Sofidra, though Meli had never witnessed it herself. It struck those who might have had a purpose once—to make art, acquire power, experience pleasure, and so on. But as they aged, that purpose seemed to fade, and gradually they became more idle, until one morning their commune or neighbors arose to find no more than a loose clump of dust in their place. Meli had never spent much time thinking about it; dispersal was something that happened to other people, perhaps even to herself one day after she had had her seedling, but not something to dwell on, and especially not something to spend one's time actively seeking, as the Inaali were doing.

They reached the second level, where a large number of adherents were spread about the interior in groups, sitting cross-legged or standing and talking.

"It's beautiful here," Meli said. "The way the daylight comes through the strands."

"Beautifully dull," Ariden said.

"Hey," Sirdu said, tugging his coat sleeve. "Look at that."

"Get off me." Ariden yanked his arm away.

"But look at all the naked people." Sirdu pointed at a group to their left.

Targael noticed their tarrying. "Some in our order consider clothing to be an unneeded material possession, and thus feel it should be banned. I am sympathetic to their views, but for the time being Verestrai and I have chosen to wear robes, so that our honored guests may feel more comfortable."

"Hold on," Sirdu said. "No material possessions? So you don't have anything? No food?"

"Nothing but the web beneath us. Of course, you are welcome to convoke your own food during your stay. But I also invite you to join us in our fast, if you wish. You may find it unpleasant at first, but once the initial urges pass you will enjoy the sense of purity it brings."

"But what if someone gets a massive hard-on?" Sirdu asked. "Ow!"

Ariden withdrew his hand from smacking the raider and folded his arms across his chest. "We've gone far enough. I have some questions I need answered."

"Perhaps a respite is in order, then." Targael stepped out onto the web and closed his eyes. Fibers spiraled and weaved up around him, forming a domed room. When it was done, he waved all of them save Verestrai through the door to a pair of simple benches, all made of the same white material. Meli rubbed one before she sat; it was slightly sticky, and though each individual strand was weak, woven together tightly they formed a mat large enough to bear her weight.

Ariden alone remained standing. "These trappings may impress the others, Targael, but you have not revealed your true prize. Where do you keep this god of yours hidden?"

"You misunderstand, my friend," Targael said. "Naal is not here with us. At least, not in body. When I first heard her, it was as a voice in my mind, sharp and clear as you speak to me now. That was over thirteen years ago, and she has communicated with us several times since."

"And she told you that I and Meli would come? And nothing else? Nothing about why?"

Targael shook his head.

"What about me?" Sirdu asked. "Did Naal talk about me?"

"I'm afraid not...ah?"

"Sirdu."

"Ah. You were not mentioned. Nevertheless, we welcome you as our honored guest, as well."

Ariden frowned. "Speaking without a body is quite a trick, even for a god."

"I understand your misgivings," Targael said. "But what more can I say? I am bound to speak the truth, no matter how hard it may be for you to accept. Long has it been since any god has been known to walk in Aetheria, and yet we are not the only ones who worship them still, believing that they remain to watch over us. Is it so hard to imagine that a god might speak to her adherents as such?"

Ariden ignored the question, instead looking about the tiny room with a snort. "Where are we? Where in Aetheria did the waves push us?"

"The ancients called it Pemarlta, though that name likely means little to you. The closest city to us is Caeridor, just across the bay to the north. Besides that, the island city of Kaelinta lies a hundred miles to leeward. I'm afraid there are few settlements nearby—our order purposefully chose a remote location for our Sanctuary, and through Naal's blessing it has remained so through the ages."

Ariden rubbed his chin, lost in thought.

"Is that it?" Meli asked. "Are you satisfied, now?"

"Hardly," Ariden said. "Do you forget the attack we sustained?" He loomed over Targael. "How do we know you did not send that thing after us?"

Targael looked up at him, face blank, eyes professing innocence. "I do not know of what you speak."

Ariden scoffed.

"There was…a disturbance," Meli explained. "At first we thought it was Vipretheon, the monster of legend, but having seen it I would hesitate to call it any sort of creature." She closed her eyes and saw it again, that shrieking sound, those tendrils of light. She shivered. "It does seem an odd coincidence, how our ship was disabled, and then we floated here…"

Targael nodded thoughtfully. "Vipretheon is an old tale, predating even our order. We certainly had no involvement in your encounter, but nevertheless I can ask the adherents if they know more. Of course, it is also possible that the God herself was responsible. Perhaps this was her way of bringing you to us. Despite any temporary harm, all of you seem to have come out all right. Perhaps her plan is working far better than you realize."

Ariden huffed and paced back and forth. "I did not volunteer for any plan. An attack on me is an attack, regardless of whether it comes from man or god." He pointed at Targael. "Then again, who is to say it was not a man? You could have been watching us from afar, eavesdropping with some secret convocational trick, and blaming this god of yours when pushed into a corner. Is that the case, simpleton? Are you a liar?"

Targael stared up at Ariden with perfect serenity, which only seemed to enrage the other man further. Ariden snorted and turned to leave.

"Where are you going?" Meli asked.

"I remain unsatisfied. I will see the rest of this place. By myself, this time. No guides." He swept off into the light, letting the webbed flap fall behind him.

"Sirdu," Meli said. "Follow him. Keep him out of trouble."

"What? How am I supposed to do that?"

"Just *do it*."

Sirdu rose, gave a hurried bow and shuffled off in Ariden's wake. Meli exhaled in frustration.

Targael cleared his throat and crossed his hands. "I don't believe he likes me."

"He doesn't really like anyone," Meli said, giving him a slight smile. They were alone now, and the lack of tension from Ariden's hostility made her words flow more easily. "I'm sorry for his behavior. We're all a bit overwhelmed, I'm sure, but at least I have the courtesy to accept your hospitality graciously. It's a pity our stay here must be short; I must leave soon to help my friend Karis."

"Karis? What happened to her?"

Meli sighed. "Another terrible incident, this one all Ariden's fault. In truth, if I'd had my choice I would not have had him accompany me here. Then again, I hadn't meant to come here at all…"

"That is a topic I wished to broach." Targael leaned forward. "Of course, the God already knows the true reason you have come. But for my own curiosity, I do wonder…where did you come from, Meli? How did you find yourself traveling the wider world with such companions, before these…incidents befell you?"

Meli sat up straight and took a deep breath. She had to proceed carefully. As friendly as Targael seemed, she had to remember that the Inaali were dispersers; they worshipped death. Would they still be so welcoming if they learned her purpose was to create life?

"I come from Sofidra," she said. "I left the island to seek wisdom. To learn secrets and convocations not available in the cloister of the city."

"Incredible. No wonder the God chose to bring you here. Meli, I must tell you that your arrival will inspire strong feelings among the adherents, as it has in me. Mostly I am awed by the God's power. I feel we have only slightly pulled back the veil on this mystery. But if you keep your mind open, we can solve it together. In the past, our order played a key role in defending Aetheria from the scourge of the plagues. Now, with the God herself interceding, my heart tells me we may be a part of something even greater."

His hand found the web beside him, and he plucked at it, twirling the strands in his fingers. An inconsequential action, but to Meli it spoke volumes. Targael was nervous; this was the first crack he had let show in his placid veneer. And there was something about his story which bothered her, as well. Thirteen years—he had said that Naal first spoke to him thirteen years before. Just around the time of her dream.

What could it mean? Was he indeed lying? Did he mean to harm her in some way? That was what Ariden would think. But more likely, to Targael her coming represented exactly what he had said—a momentous event, a gift from his god. And where did that leave her? She had her own desires, her own plans, to rescue Karis and eventually to have her seedling. She did not ask for the burden of being a savior.

Better not to commit to any course of action yet. She would rest, use what resources the Inaali had to further her causes, but not marry herself to theirs.

"That may be so," she said. "Perhaps our meeting is a form of blessing. In Sofidra, the Inaali are renowned as great curators of knowledge. It is said you keep a history of Aetheria more detailed than any other."

Targael nodded. "We have a calendar as well, with the weeks accurate to the First Empire's original chronology. Preserving the wisdom of the ancients is an important duty passed down by our founders. And if there is something in particular you wish to know, I could put your request out to the adherents. Our history is kept orally, in the form of chants conducted at nightfall. It is the preeminent ritual of our order, taking many years to learn properly."

He cleared his throat. "I should warn you, the chants are introduced to new adherents gradually at first; to an outsider, they may feel somewhat...intense."

"I see," Meli said. "Still, I would like to attend the next one. If it is allowed."

"For you? Anything." Targael smiled. "In fact, I must return to my duties, so that the chant can take place as planned. Excuse me."

Meli followed him back out onto the web. Ariden, Sirdu and Verestrai were nowhere to be seen. Around and above, gray shadows moved over the strands as the adherents began to congregate.

"Fin, please roll this up and carry it to the top," Targael said to a woman standing nearby. He bowed to Meli one last time. "I will see you there at dusk."

Fin knelt and began to pull the domed structure from the webbing of the platform with rough jerks of her hands. A simple knife would have saved her some effort, and Meli nearly offered to convoke her one before she caught herself. The Inaali's uncompromising minimalism was so bizarre, it was easy to forget. Why deny oneself things that were pleasurable, or useful, when they were so easy to obtain? The only inconvenience which might occur was a little dust, but that could be disposed of easily enough, provided one were clever about it. That was doubtlessly what Fin was doing now, carrying the used webbing to the top of the crater to be thrown into the wind before it was crumbled.

"So," Fin said between tugs. "You're the one."

"Hmm?" Meli said distractedly. For the first time she took real notice of Fin. The woman was short, nearly as short as Karis, and rail-thin, but her face was rough and lined, and one of her eyes was slate gray, drifting aimlessly in its socket.

"You're the one heralded by the God."

"Oh," Meli said. "Yes. Or at least, that's what they tell me."

She flashed a quick smile, but Fin did not see the humor, looking away and continuing her work with a sour expression. Perhaps Targael's revelation was not a good subject for jokes. *Your arrival has inspired strong feelings among the adherents*, he had said. But which feelings? Were some among the Inaali against her coming?

Once Fin pulled the last of the dome free, she rolled it into a tight bundle and hefted it onto her back, then made to leave.

"Wait," Meli said. "Aren't you going to show me around, or something?"

"I'm not," Fin said. "But you're welcome to show yourself. You made it this far—I'm sure the God will guide you."

"That's it, then?"

"That is not it," Fin called over her shoulder. "You still have the chant before you. You want the secrets of the Inaali, yes? Wait until nightfall, then go and take them, if you wish."

She smiled wryly and continued on her way.

15

A screaming whistle filled the aer. Karis had just reached the ladder when the first of the falling drops hit the aft deck. She had expected to feel something akin to when the raider striker had collided with her own ship, a bone jarring crack not quite strong enough to knock her over.

Instead, the shockwave appeared as an expanding ripple in the ship's surface and dusty atmosphere. When it reached her, it burst her eardrums and knocked her sideways off the command deck. She spun in mid-aer. Reviled ships passed by above, followed by the deck, then the ships again before she smashed into something hard.

She blacked out for a period. Then she rolled to her knees, head throbbing, and cried out in agony. Her wrist, ribs and knee were surely broken. The aer was filled with splinters and dust. Engine towers were falling and chunks of deck furniture flew by. Black spots appeared and the images before her doubled. Sounds grew louder as her hearing recovered—cracking, screaming, someone faintly calling out a name.

"Ka—s!"

"Jaela!" Was it Jaela? Who else would be screaming for her here? Clenching her jaw against the pain, she struggled to her feet.

Another weight struck the center of the command deck above her. The entire ship came apart, splitting lengthwise. Karis hit the deck, just avoiding being thrown overboard. She flipped on her back and slid down toward the gunwale.

Gliders went by on her right, piling up in a corner. Some of them might have still been intact. She pulled herself up again and tried to run, yelling at the pain in her leg and chest. She could only move in slow motion. Another sky-shattering crack, and the deck dropped below her again, this time tilting toward the stern and sending her tumbling into the tangled mass of gliders.

The thin, flexible sticks of the glider frames struck her like switches, and Karis cursed in ways she hadn't realized she knew. Through the pain she tore into the pile, searching for a glider that wasn't crushed. No time. Some of the raiders must still be alive for the flagship to hold up as well as it had, but it was losing altitude, and at any second it would crumble completely. Of the few surviving gliders, she picked one on which the wing material wasn't too torn, wrenched it away from the others, and crawled inside.

How in Ba-el's name did the thing work? The cockpit was nothing more than a small seat affixed to the frame, with a paper canopy in front—torn, of course. She hoisted the glider up on her shoulders and through the shearing pain carried it to the edge of the ship, sat in the seat and pushed forward.

The glider drifted out a few feet, then plummeted straight down.

It occurred to her she had no idea whether the glider could actually fly. Perhaps the raiders had given up on the designs before testing them, or Roi had arranged the entire setup just to fool her. She yanked and slammed on the controls, a stick and two pedals, with no effect. The glider remained level, plummeting like bedrock with a slow lateral spin. She grabbed at a lever above her head in panic, and the plane dropped nose down into a dive.

"Pox!"

The airframe rattled and wind roared past the canopy. Her stomach churned. The glider spun faster, and Karis instinctively slammed on the foot pedals. To her amazement, they were now working; pressing the left pedal slowed her spin to the right. She grabbed the stick and pulled back, and the glider began to level off.

Her relief didn't last—she had lost so much altitude that swirls and eddies had appeared in the fog below. She pulled back harder on the stick, and the glider rattled and made cracking sounds. The poxing thing was coming apart around her. She closed her eyes and tried to convoke with the fast-moving aer over the frame, shoring up the joints. All the while she pulled hard with both hands, stretching her muscles to their limit.

The glider leveled out and Karis opened her eyes, breathing heavily. Without the stress of turning the rattling ceased and suddenly she was flying, really flying, so serene and so, so free. This must be what the raiders lived for. She rubbed her wrist and knee—the bones had set but they still throbbed with pain. The city and the land were ahead of her. She could make it all the way there, she could escape, just—

A clump of dust broke off the canopy, smacking her in the face and blinding her. She spat it out and looked up in time to see the thin fabric of the wing beginning to crumble.

Mold, she had flown too far from whoever had convoked the glider, or else they were already dead. She began to convoke a new wing surface in mid-aer, but doing so would be a losing game; the entire glider was going to fall apart soon, and smacking into the sea from this height would likely kill her. Her heart thumped wildly as panic set in again. To go through everything she had done, only to die. There had to be something she could do, anything.

Just below and to her right, another ship was flying toward the coast on a parallel course. She pressed the stick sideways and worked the foot pedals, but over-steered and nearly sent herself into another dive. She tried to correct, cursing as she repaired the stick crumbling in her hands. The ship drew closer—one of the SkyHunter's skiffs. The pilot had seen her and approached, dropping his aer speed to match hers. A pair of surprised faces peered over the railing of their exposed deck.

"What's this?" the one on the left said, his voice nearly lost in the wind. "Should we kill her?"

"No!" she shouted. "I'm one of you! Help me!"

"Hey, I know her." The one on the right's shock of black hair flapped in the breeze. "It's Roi's smoothskin."

"The glider's crumbling! Pull me over!"

The black-haired raider leaned over and put out his hand, but fell short. Instinctively he convoked a long pole with a handle to extend his reach, but the glider hit a patch of turbulence and rocked Karis away, her hand grasping nothing.

"A grapple!" the raider shouted, almost too faint to hear. "Make a hook and line!"

She nodded and used her sliver of spare focus to convoke a grappling hook, willing the aether to respond as fast as she could, depositing it in long, curved tines. She began creating a length of rope attached to one end, drawing it out and looping it over her arm as she went. The frame around her cracked and fizzled—no time left, she had to make a throw. She gritted her teeth, attached the rope to her belt, then tossed the hook at the ship.

It caught. The rope yanked her out of the glider's cage in a painful splintering of solid aether. The wind rushed cold around her. She grasped the rope and hung on tight in the driving wind, keeping her eyes closed as she swung back and forth. Fear coursed through her, but she forced her eyes open.

The city spread out below her. The skiff had gained altitude as it approached the scene of the battle. Sky fighters of every shape and size filled the aer around them, cutting through clouds of dust where other ships had disintegrated. But her gaze was fixed on the city itself, the white towers and the giant shapes lumbering just beyond the walls. One of the shapes rested a pair of oversize, tentacle-like hands on the parapet, then raised up a simian face.

A Walking Behemoth. So huge, so yet graceful and majestic— what was it doing here? The Behemoth tracked her ship with its eyes as if it could see her staring from such a distance. It reached below the wall, pulled up a chunk of bedrock the size of a small dwelling, and heaved it overhand toward them.

She watched the rock arc through the sky, awestruck at the accuracy of the Behemoth's throw, until it occurred to her that the projectile could actually hit them. She opened her mouth to scream and the ship banked right, yanking the rope on her waist and stealing her breath.

She swung out into the path of the boulder, then the sideways momentum pulled her away. The rush of wind from the rock's passage brushed her face. The ship leveled out and she swung back underneath it, blood rushing from the drop, making her light-headed.

Her consciousness fluttered, catching bits and pieces as the ship ascended again. The aer was thick with ships and dust now, drenched in chaos. Several more Behemoths stood on the walls, hefting bedrock and tracking their targets. Two more rock missiles went out, toward SkyHunter ships. Why only them? She knew the Behemoths were more intelligent than most animals, but what would cause them to take up sides in a human conflict? Whatever the cause, their intervention was effective. The strikers and skiffs on "her" side were disorganized and confused, spending their time dodging rocks instead of mounting a unified offense against the Reviled ships or the city.

Pure madness, that's what it was. She had to stop dangling like a worm and convince the raiders up top to escape.

"Hey! Pull me up already!" The ship dipped, causing her stomach to roil. Far above and to the left, a lump of bedrock hit a striker, smashing it into hundreds of chunks which cascaded streams of dust behind them as they fell. Karis screamed again, not using words this time, just belting out whatever sound her small lungs would allow.

Two heads popped over the side of the ship above.

"Get me up!" Karis yelled in her most commanding tone. "Hurry!"

The ship dipped again, then turned hard to avoid a mid-aer collision with a passing skiff. The two men stumbled and their heads disappeared, but a moment later they popped back up. The first raider convoked a hooked pole to get hold of the rope, and then the two of them began to haul her in. She gripped the rope and waited as the two men pulled, grateful but annoyed at being so helpless. As soon as they brought her within range of the ship, she grasped the side and hauled herself in, then rolled onto the deck, trying in vain to catch her breath.

"First time I ever caught a passenger in the middle of a battle."

"Hindal's never going to believe this."

Karis rolled to her knees in the center of the cramped deck. The crew were Hindal's men, though not his best fighters, assigned to a relatively slow skiff with an open top. A third pilot stood at the fore, his back to her, while to her right sat a rack of bladed weapons, likely meant for a land assault on the city, but useless now.

"Wei, why the pox aren't we following the back-up plan?" the black-haired raider yelled. "We're not here to collect smoothskins."

"I was trying to flank, but everything's poxed up." The pilot cut his control stick right, and they all grabbed the railings. "Half the ships are gone."

"We lost that many?"

"Look out!" The pilot turned again, cutting away from the path of an incoming Reviled formation. Six ships, flying in a diamond pattern. Two of them broke off and moved to intercept the slow-moving skiff, ramming lances arrayed around their sides. "Hold on!"

Karis wrapped her arm around the railing and held her breath. The pilot banked hard, nearly putting them into a roll, then at the last moment gunned the engines and pulled up. The pair of Reviled ships flew past just below them.

"We're outmatched here," the black-haired raider said. "Where are our support ships?"

"I'm telling you, they're gone. All of them turned and left as soon as we engaged."

The pilot pointed at the horizon to the south. A set of black dots hung there, nearly invisible in the dust haze.

"It's Roi," the black-haired one said. "He betrayed us, the poxy coward. Left with his entire fleet."

"We're poxed," said the other, leaning down over the railing to observe the carnage. "They're going to pick us off here. The Reviled already closed the gap behind, there's no way out."

"There has to be a way out." Karis jumped to her feet.

"Shut up!" the raider yelled. "You and your friends are the reason we're trapped."

"Listen," she said. "Work together. We can fly low, under the flagships. We can still escape."

The black-haired raider turned, his eyes so filled with hate that Karis stepped back. "You poxing traitor! *True raiders don't run!*"

He slapped her, knocking her down into the gunwale. She stumbled, head spinning, pain sharp on her cheek. A pair of meaty hands closed on her throat.

"Roi's little pet!" The raider shook her neck, smacking the back of her head into the railing. Spittle flew from between his teeth. "My friends are dead!"

She wheezed and gurgled as the fingers compressed her windpipe. The world grew dark around the edges. Clouds of dust under the bright white sky. Weapons rattling in their rack. On the control panel, a line of levers. She chose a lever and reached out to the aether, convoking a lump of heavy material to weigh it down. The darkness grew and the raider drew back his fist to throw another punch.

"What are you doing?" The pilot grabbed the lever and tried to wrench it back up, but she had glued it in place. "Stop! I need to pull up!"

A black shape approached and struck them with a tremendous crash. The hands ripped away from her throat and she dropped to the deck.

She opened her eyes. The shape was gone, the wind blowing fast and fierce. The body of the formerly black-haired raider stood in front of her, headless. It wavered for a moment, then fell as it cracked and broke, the pieces decaying into brown chunks. The other raider had disappeared entirely, leaving only the pilot slumped unconscious against the controls. The Reviled striker that had rammed them receded fast into the distance, visible through the large divot it had made in the gunwale. Karis struggled to her feet, her perception surreal due to lack of breath, and grabbed the remaining railing as the nose of the ship dipped.

They were going down.

She clambered over what used to be the raiders in the middle of the deck and grasped at the controls. The pilot was still slumped over the panel, blocking her, so she shoved him off with all her weight. Unfortunately, she had uncovered an array of dials, levers and buttons which held no meaning for her. She tugged at the controls randomly, but the dive continued unabated. Just her luck, caught in a falling aircraft three times in one day. There had to be something, some way to survive.

You strap it to your back like this, see?

Cindlan's words rang in her ears. A parachute, of course. She could do it—she hadn't learned of such designs for a century, had never tested one, but it was still her best shot. The plane was pitching steeply now, and she had to scramble up to the tail on convoked handholds. She pressed her fingers to her closed eyes and began the convocation. It would have to be her fastest ever, even more so than the grapnel. *Focus, draw the aer in, give it form.* Silk cloth unspooled in front of her, piling onto the deck. One edge, then two. She held the side she was working on up into the stream of wind. It was taking too long; in moments she'd be smashed. *Ignore it, just finish, get the ropes in place, secure them in a bunch to the tail.* The plane was nearly vertical now, the wind howling. She fused the chute to the skiff, picked up the piled cloth and tossed it upward.

The plane rocked and jolted, and then the control panel at the nose rushed up toward her. She grabbed the railing and her neck cracked like a whip. The pilot rolled and fell out below her, hurtling toward the ocean.

Her neck throbbed with blinding pain, possibly broken, but she couldn't rest yet. With one arm still hooked through the railing, she shored up the body of the skiff in anticipation of it falling apart, adding a layer of aether over the hull and repairing as best she could the giant hole in the middle. The result wouldn't be aer or seaworthy, but it would at least provide a vaguely boat-shaped platform to rest in.

The remains of the skiff descended into the fog moments later, then bobbed and shook as it settled nose-down into the waves. Safe. *Safe!* Karis climbed through the gray mist, let the parachute crumble and slumped against a horizontal portion of deck. The battle continued above her, but she rolled over and ignored it, too exhausted and sore to care. She closed her eyes, letting the waves rock her, wallowing in the feeling of being alive and free.

The roar of engines above grew louder. Too loud. Propellers split the fog and the prow of an enormous cruiser descended over her.

She gasped and scuttled back to the rail, as though that would help if the raiders wanted her dead. But no, the cruiser carried SkyHunter markings, not Reviled. It had a curved hull and top-board propellers that enabled it to hover like a flagship, though it was fully enclosed and much smaller.

Halfway up the side, a porthole crumbled, and Roi stuck his head out of the opening. "Need a lift?" he yelled over the roar of the engines.

"What?" Karis shouted. "What are you doing here?"

"Looking for survivors," Roi replied. "I saw that little maneuver you pulled with the parachute. Very nice."

"Go away! I don't need your help."

"I wouldn't be so sure about that. The Reviled are going to sweep the oceans once they finish smashing Hindal's ships. If you're lucky, they'll just take you prisoner."

"And what do you call what you're doing?"

"Like I said, I'm offering you a ride. No catch this time. It's your choice: Come with me or wait here. But at least you know me. You really want to take your chances with the Reviled?"

She furrowed her brow. "Is Jaela alive?"

"Of course," Roi said. "She's here with me."

"All right," Karis said. "Convoke a ladder."

She clambered up the rungs as the ship lifted away. Inside, she convoked a simple seat and collapsed into it, rubbing her aching wrist. For some reason it had turned out worse than her knee or her ribs or her neck or any of the other hundreds of bumps she had received. Roi sat back in his command chair at the front of the ship, while the others aboard busied themselves helping to pilot or simply staring out the portholes. Most of Roi's inner circle was there: Phaestal, Mel, Isky and Dikta, and several others whose names she didn't know, as well as Jaela, who knelt near the front windows. She might have expected some sort of welcome from the other woman, but the mood inside the cabin was grim, the raider's faces strained as they watched the remainder of the battle play out.

Karis got up and wandered forward, peeking out each window as she went. Just as Roi had said, Hindal's ships were being routed, picked off one by one as they flew in circles. When she reached Roi's seat, she found him staring with the others, hands folded under his chin.

"Are you upset?" she asked mockingly. "This is all your doing, isn't it? You pulled out your ships at the last moment."

"I did what had to be done," he replied. "That doesn't mean I have to like it. Hindal wasn't exactly a friend, but he and I shared something—a bond you wouldn't understand. Now, if he's still alive, he'll be an enemy forever."

She snorted. "Sure. So where are you taking me now?"

"I told the remaining crews to rendezvous near Bressim. I'll check in there, make sure they wait for us to return. Then we're taking this ship off alone."

"Where to?"

"The Automatia."

She swiveled her head. "What? Why?"

"To see your friend, of course." He looked up at her and grinned. "Meli, I think her name was?"

Karis staggered. Jaela, crouching on a low stool on Roi's other side, stared back at Karis, her face impassive.

"You told him…you told him that?"

"Oh, she's told me many things. About you, your avian friend, and especially how you feel about me. What was the word? 'Manipulative?'" He clucked his tongue. "How *rude*. And to think I treated you as an honored guest."

Behind him, Jaela's lips were a curved dagger. Blood flooded into Karis's cheeks and forehead.

"But!" Roi raised a finger. "I'm willing to let the past be the past. The Automatia will be instrumental in our comeback, I'm sure of it. Times have changed, Karis—that's what Hindal couldn't see. Ship-to-ship fighting doesn't work anymore. We've killed too many, taken too many risks. There's not enough pilots left. Look at what the Reviled have done; sure, the bit with the inflatables was clever, but convincing the Behemoths to work with them—now that shows a true ability to adapt. And what do we have to counter them, hmm? We need new tactics, new knowledge. Something truly revolutionary. This school of automatists can give us that—and now, thanks to you, finding it is our new mission."

Karis turned away; she couldn't stand to look at him, at either of them. "Why did you take me out of the sea?"

"Because you can still be useful to me."

She spun back around to face him. "Useful to *you*?"

"Indeed. I've investigated the Automatia before. I know it's supposed to be at Kalsten's mouth. But there's still this matter of a key…"

"I'm not giving it to you."

"Why? Because you lost our game?" He pulled Jaela close and the two of them shared a quick but passionate kiss, framed in the light of the front picture window. Karis's stomach clenched. "You'll get over it, Karis. Like it or not, we both want the same thing. I have the ship, you have the will—if you want to see your friend anytime soon, you'll change your mind."

Karis opened her mouth, but could not speak. Instead she huffed, backed to the rear of the ship and hid her face in one of the portholes. The other raiders stared at her as she passed. How many had known of the trick? Everyone? How could she have been so stupid?

Blurry, bright fog streamed by outside. Karis nestled into her corner and convoked a thick dome around herself. She'd had enough; she would leave, tell them all to pox off and jump into the ocean, Reviled or no Reviled.

But she couldn't do that, could she? What if Meli was at the Automatia? She knew that was where Karis would have wanted her to go; Karis had even told Elsa as much. And she especially didn't like the idea of Roi finding Meli without her there. Even without the key, he might have the resources to get inside the school. It was Karis's responsibility to protect Meli, and the only way to do that was to remain close to Roi, on the ship.

But there had to be another way. Even if Meli wasn't there, she still wanted to go to the Automatia, but not like this, not with these people.

She sat alone, biting her nails, wrestling with the sickness in her gut. Roi was right. They had tricked her, they had won, but what difference did it really make?

The Automatia was all that mattered. Her dreams were there, of being the light, of solving the mysteries of the aether. And Meli could be there too. Meli who had put her faith in Karis. Meli who she had failed once already.

Karis held herself tight, fingers on thin arms. The ship's engines roared as it rose higher into the sky.

16

Dahl the adherent sat cross-legged at the center of the circle. His dark, defined muscles rippled as he breathed into his belly.

"Focus." His voice was so low Meli could almost feel it in the web beneath her. "Focus on a plane, then a line, then a point. Then remove the point. What remains? Another plane, invisible, a background upon which to project your thoughts. Collapse it now into its own line, another point, but leave no background, only emptiness—what happens when the point is removed?"

He opened his eyes to check on the others, caught Meli staring at him and grinned. Meli shut her eyes quickly. That made her shoulders tense, which she had already been told was wrong. She was supposed to be relaxing, wasn't she? Relax, and clear the mind. Where exactly on Dahl's nude body had she been staring, anyway?

"Patience." Dahl's bass rumble continued. "A difficult skill to master. All of us wish to meet our God, and yet unless we find patience, we cannot know peace, and without peace there is no salvation. It is one of the great truths of life that the greater our patience, the sooner we achieve our goals."

Meli took a deep breath, into her belly as she had been shown, then let it out slowly, listening to the hiss through her nose. A long day it had been, and unusual by any standard. To wake up in a cave by the ocean and end up here, among these strangest of strangers—well, lacking focus should have been understandable under the circumstances.

After her meeting with Targael she had wandered at first, taking in the sights of the sanctuary. Her favorite so far had been the Calendar Wall, where adherents painstakingly scratched marks into the bedrock with tools made of the hardest materials which could be convoked. One mark for each day, arranged in a concentric pattern which they said counted each of the 2,954 years of the order's history. An Aetherian year, they said, was not exactly 3 centemerans and 3 weeks totaling 330 days as commonly believed, but in fact was somewhere between 331 and 332. Meli could not follow how they derived their results, but the sheer scale of the thing was breathtaking;

if she stood close enough, the tiny ticks on shiny black seemed to stretch up and out to infinity.

Karis would have loved it.

The Inaali prayed frequently—before meals, after meals, at midday and seemingly whenever a group of them were together and the mood struck. Meli joined in one such session, and found it pleasant enough, though she did not know the words by heart as the others did. But it was soothing to hear their calm voices asking Naal as one for serenity, wisdom, and release from the physical world. If anyone in Sofidra prayed, and Meli was not sure it ever happened, they did so privately. Religion there was not so much disdained as it was ignored, discarded like the previous week's fashions. But now that Meli had participated in some of the Inaali's rituals, she wondered if the Sofidrans were missing something beneficial about the practice, even if she didn't join the Inaali in their wish to be released from their bodies.

She explored her way up to the highest level, where the chants were held. The eight spires which made up the outer walls of the mountaintop were no more than thin pillars there, and the wind tore through them as though it sought to scour the mountain from the land. The view of the open sky, the ocean and the mountains to leeward would have justified staying longer, but a cloud of dust moved in from the sea, forcing Meli down below, where the adherents were already putting up webbed walls between the giant columns of bedrock to block the infiltration.

Unlike her experience with Fin, most of the adherents smiled at Meli as she passed. But they also avoided addressing her directly, shying away discreetly if approached, as if they had suddenly remembered an important errand. Meli also became aware that they were staring from a distance, often catching groups of them looking away just as she turned her head. Was it simple curiosity, distrust, or something else? If she was going to learn anything useful from these people, she would need to ingratiate herself with them, but their wariness made her hesitant to explain about her dream, and the true reason she had set out on her journey.

By the time evening had approached, Meli felt the long day weighing on her legs and eyelids. A simmering frustration filled her at having learned so little—she, who could charm anyone in Sofidra were she motivated to put her mind to it. But the Inaali were not like the Sofidrans, and they seemed reticent to discuss any of their secrets with her outside of the chant. Targael had suggested this current meditation class to her, though she had been dubious as to its utility. Mostly, she had hoped that sitting in the circle with Dahl and the others would help pass the time, so that she could finally see this famed chant of theirs. Instead, it had only seemed to make the evening longer.

Perhaps Dahl was right; she did need to work on her patience.

"That is enough for today." Dahl exhaled and smiled, showing his teeth to each of them in turn. Handsome he may have been, but he had a certain smugness about him that Meli found distasteful. "Thank you all for accompanying me on my journey. I'm afraid we must forego our parting prayer this eve; the chant will commence soon."

The circle broke up, and the adherents chatted as they headed toward the nearest stair. Meli was following them at a distance, her hands folded, when a blood-curdling noise came from above them.

A human voice, it must have been, but it sounded more like an animal, one deeply in pain, keening low until its voice broke high as if in panic, then returning again to a thrumming depth. On and on it went, as Meli stared upward, open-mouthed.

Dahl, walking behind the others, noticed Meli's shock and stopped.

"Is that...the chant?" she asked.

"The opening rite." Dahl was unperturbed. He motioned for her to follow. "Come. We may be the last to arrive. I will escort you."

"But it sounds like someone is in pain."

"Performing the rite takes years of practice." Dahl gave a slight bow in reverence. How could he be so calm? Even at this distance, the noise was enough to make Meli want to pull out her hair. "Soon the main chant will commence. Will you join us?"

No! Meli wanted to say. But surely she was being foolish. It was only a man, only a sound. It could not hurt her. And yet every fiber of her being longed to escape from it. There was something about it that made her feel ill, almost like she had felt in the boat, but deeper, more subtle, as if the sound were taking her soul in hand and twisting it.

"I think..." She swallowed. "I think I will go another night. I'm tired. It's been a long day."

She did not wait for a response, but turned and headed down the stair, toward the lowest level of webbing. The Inaali slept communally in large fluffy pillows of webbing—their only physical comfort, as far as she could tell—but they had sectioned off rooms near the side of the crater for her, Ariden and Sirdu. She found all three empty, so she chose one, pulled the flap tight behind her, and nestled down into the dark interior.

The sound of the opening rite continued to reach her, muffled but perhaps the worse for it, since her imagination could fill in the gaps where the sound did not penetrate. After a seeming eternity, the screaming ended, replaced with a low hum. The chant proper. She could not hear the words, only slight changes in pitch and volume of the crowd as a whole, and though the sound itself was almost pleasant at the edge of her hearing, she still felt a lingering agitation as she tried and failed to drift off to sleep.

"It's just a noise," she mumbled to herself, convoking layers of cloth to wrap around her head. She lay awake in the darkness, wishing she could still her thoughts.

Two days later, Meli sat among a loose collection of adherents, practicing convocation of the webbing material—a slow process, as any kind of learning was in the beginning. The fibers themselves were simple—she had been able to copy them from nearly the first moment she tried—but the trick was in their placement, coiled like a spring, loosely bunched for softness or tightly woven for tougher jobs for which other Aetherians would have employed a more solid convocation.

"Excellent, Meli." Ferusch leaned over her and smiled, the hairs on her upper lip spreading. "You have true talent." She was a corpulent woman, ruddy with enough wrinkles to almost be a creasedskin, and a bulbous nose which covered half the hair underneath it. Ironically, she was one of the adherents who allowed herself to convoke shears and trim the top of her head, which meant she also accepted the benefits of the physical world enough to wear robes, much to Meli's relief.

"Thank you," Meli replied.

"You know, you never complimented *my* skill when I first arrived." Fin sat nearby, legs up on a webbed pedestal, convoking little balls of fiber and tossing them into a growing pile.

Ferusch cleared her throat. "You're still a newcomer as well, Fin. But perhaps if you spent less time searching for complements and more time focusing, your skills would bloom faster. Just look at what Meli has made; it's a…what is it?"

Meli looked down and blushed. Ferusch had told them to end the lesson by creating whatever object they liked, and she had chosen to make a sculpture of her seedling. But the webbing was a poor modeling material, and she was no artist; the curves of his cheeks had not come out exactly the way she saw them in her mind. "It's, uhm, a pillow."

"A pillow?" Ferusch scowled. "It's a rather bumpy, ugly one, isn't it?"

Meli hugged the bundle tight. "He's *not* ugly."

"You should listen to Ferusch. She's an expert on ugly bumps." Fin cackled and tossed another ball away. "She has a giant one right on her face."

Meli chuckled, then covered her mouth. Ferusch's nose had turned a bright red.

"The lesson is over, my kindred!" Ferusch turned and waved her hands to the others, who responded with puzzled stares. "Our junior adherent will have the honor of releasing the practice material into the wind." She looked back. "That means you, Fin."

"Obviously it means me." Fin stretched, then knelt and began tucking her discarded webbing in one arm.

"I'm the newest one, though," Meli said.

"You are our guest, not an adherent," Ferusch replied warmly. "We would not deign to assign you tasks until you have spoken your oath."

"I still want to help." Meli knelt beside Fin and flashed a smile. Ferusch grunted, but turned away and said no more.

Together they gathered the half-finished projects, and, arms full, headed for the upper level.

"Thank you," Fin said in a harsh, clipped tone, as if it pained her to use the words, though Meli still felt she meant them.

"It's no trouble," Meli said. "I've been meaning to get to know you better, actually. You seem different from the other adherents."

"I do?" Anger flashed on Fin's face. She glanced over, her dead eye continuing to stare in front of them.

"Yes, I mean..." Meli cleared her throat. That had come out all wrong; Fin must have thought she was referring to physical differences, but Meli had been thinking that Fin seemed more...real somehow. She had even considered sharing the secret of the dream with her first. "What I mean is, you're so forthright. Sometimes it seems like the others avoid saying what they mean."

"Ah." A slight relaxation. "Well, don't be too put off by them. People come to the Sanctuary from many places, but the order changes them. There's a pressure to adapt, to make themselves a part of the crowd."

Why did Fin alone seem immune to those forces, then? A question for another time. "Tell me…why do so many people come here? Is it to seek knowledge, as I did?"

Fin chuckled. She had a biting laugh, full of scorn, but infectious as well. "It is a bit of a mystery, isn't it, why anyone would live in this place? Some who arrive here are the newly appeared, who know no other life. Others come for enlightenment. Still others seek out the Inaali due to simple curiosity, and for whatever reason like it enough to stay. Then there are the true dispersal-seekers, the ones who are genuinely tired of living, but cannot let go."

They had climbed the final stair into the chanting area, now clear of dusty aer. Meli stood a moment, looking about with trepidation. The Inaali had held another chant the previous evening, and once again she had declined to participate. She was not looking forward to the coming evening's events.

"You're thinking about the chant, aren't you?" Fin headed for the leeward side. "I didn't like it at first, either."

"I don't know how you can stand it at all!" Meli said with a bit too much enthusiasm.

Fin chuckled again. "I had to force myself to go. But it is worth it; otherwise one cannot completely understand the Inaali." She stepped as near the side as she dared, framed against the mountainous landscape beyond, then set her bundle of webbing down and began to toss the pieces one by one over the edge. "The chants contain the history of Aetheria. And I mean everything: the coming and fading of the plagues, the Wars of the Cities, the origins of the First, Second and Third Empires, all in great detail."

"And you all can remember that?"

"History is stories. People may not remember facts, but they can remember stories, and inside those stories are knowledge, secrets…sometimes important ones." Fin tossed the last of her load into the aer and headed back the way she came.

"Why did you come here?" Meli asked, hastily preparing her own pile.

Fin spun, eyes narrowed, hands clenched. "What?"

"I only…" Meli stammered. It had been an innocent question. "You gave a list of reasons. But you never said which one was yours."

Fin eyed her cautiously. For a moment she seemed on the verge of explaining something, but then she thought better of it. "My reasons are my own," she snapped. "Do not speak of them again." She hurried away, long hair bouncing behind her, leaving Meli alone on the mountaintop.

Meli shook her head. That had certainly been unexpected. And she had certainly been too hasty in planning to open up to Fin. The woman was surely at least as odd as anyone else in the Sanctuary, though in a different manner.

Meli turned around and tossed away her refuse piece by piece, until she came to her seedling-figure, wrapped in its web-blanket. She paused and smiled at its face—it *was* a little ugly, but compared to her real seedling anything would be—then held it up to the wind to crumble it. A touch of melancholy filled her heart. How silly. It was just a floppy toy, a moment's diversion, and yet letting it go was more difficult than she anticipated. But she had to get rid of it—the Inaali frowned on any superfluous material being left on the web. She hesitated another moment. It would be all right. She could lose this one, as long as she made sure to convoke the real thing one day.

She relaxed her focus, and the doll flaked away, the brown dust flying out into the vast emptiness before her. Saddened, she bowed her head and headed back down.

She wandered for a bit, and came upon Ariden sitting on a rocky outcropping near the outer wall. He regarded her coolly, arms crossed, his face even more dour than usual, if such a thing were possible.

"Where is Sirdu?" she asked.

Ariden grunted. "Don't think I'm unaware of you telling him to follow me. You'll be pleased to know that having him on my tail the past few days has brought me no end of irritation."

Meli shrugged. She couldn't say it *dis*pleased her.

"In any case, he's been too hung up on all the nude women to properly attend his duties. Last I saw of him he was attending a 'meditation' session with a gaggle of them. That fool wouldn't know meditation if it came up and sank its teeth into his rear end."

She rolled her eyes and crossed her arms, mimicking his gesture. "So?"

"So what?"

"You said you were going off on your own to find out what was happening here. So what have you found?"

Ariden exhaled, long, slow, and full of discontent. "Nothing. I've questioned them with every method I know, save the unpleasant ones, but there is no grand conspiracy here. All I see is a genuine religious order. Most of its members are lackwits, true, but earnest lackwits. They study their convocations, chant their history and have a fetish for death. But as far as having a secret plan, or hiding something? No."

"You attended the chants, then? What did you think of them?"

"Pointless and boring." He picked his nose and spat.

Was she losing her mind, then? How could she be the only one so bothered by them? "So, you've changed your mind about Targael?"

"Not necessarily. I have found no evidence of malice, but it may still exist in places unexamined. I am just as ready to leave as I was when we arrived. Why are you staying here, anyway?"

She opened her mouth to answer, then realized she didn't quite know herself. Could the Inaali help her convoke a person, or not? It was too early to tell. "We've only been here two days."

"Two days gone is two days wasted. And if I'm going to waste my time, I'd rather do it somewhere I can play cards. I say we make for the city of Caeridor."

Meli sniffed. Bands of travelers from Caeridor were not uncommon in Sofidra, but she had quickly learned to avoid them. They tended to be bores, going on endlessly about fighting, making boasts and bets, and causing such a nuisance that the city watch had to follow them at all times. "You know, now that I think of it, Caeridor would suit you well."

"It was my home for many years, and will serve our purposes nicely. The whole society is based around its fighting arena—fight and win, or sponsor a great fighter, and all the power of the city is yours. With their resources at our command, any other destination in Aetheria should be within reach. Isn't that what you want? Or have you forgotten about your friend Karis?"

Meli frowned. If he was looking for a way to wound her, he had found it. But she wasn't going to let him boss her around.

"You will wait here until I am ready to leave, and not a moment sooner." She stomped off, or at least imitated a stomp as best she could on the spongy web.

He made a snort, or perhaps a snicker, behind her. She deserved it. There was no reason for her to suddenly get cross at him, except that she was disappointed in herself. Karis was waiting for her, needed her aid, and here she was taking meditation courses and praying. And worst of all was her avoidance of the chant, after all the talk of its importance; how utterly selfish.

Well, no more. When the time came that evening, she would get it over with and attend. With any luck, she would know enough by then to plan her next move, and show Ariden who was taking the initiative.

She spent the rest of the day in solitude, hardening herself, building up her nerve. That was a mistake, she realized, as soon as darkness began to fall and the howls of the opening rite began again. By building up the chant so much in her mind, she had made it into more than it needed to be. But it was too late now; she gathered herself together and left her room to join the others heading upward.

The higher she went, the louder that awful wail became, and soon it was only with great effort that she could bow her head and take a step forward. She got in line behind the robed adherents on the third level and grimaced. One more stair, and she came upon the Inaali in a great circle. The sound of the rite continued, louder than ever, reaching a climax. The hairs on Meli's arms and shoulders stood on end. Her heart pounded. She had to stop this, it was ridiculous. Was she going to let a sound stand between her and the knowledge she needed?

When she reached the circle, the man in the center performing the rite lowered his voice to a hum. The others near the rim hummed as well, slowly increasing their volume. Meli sighed with relief and stepped into place, watching and keeping quiet. The Inaali looked similar in the dim light, either naked or robed against the wind that howled through the gaps in the eight bedrock spires around them. She wished Ariden or Sirdu were there, if only so that she could see someone she knew, but they had not appeared. Soon the humming filled the space around her, penetrating her body with its vibrations, making her feel weak and out of control.

The line of adherents swayed back and forth, and Meli swayed with them, shoulder to shoulder. The humming became louder, separated into voices, some speaking fast and some slow, some mumbling and others so loud her ears hurt. Her head began to pound, echoing her heart, and blackness rolled in around the edges of her vision. She shook her head to ward it off, but the sound was inside her, forcing her consciousness into a deep well. Fear came with it, panic at losing control, and another sort, a dread both pure and familiar.

She had felt this sensation once before.

Her sight faded to a still blur. The sound was palpable now, thick like jelly. Meli fell to her knees and tried to scream, but whatever sound she made was not loud enough to pierce the din.

MELI.

The voice sliced like a spear through her mind. Deep, bold and powerful. She had to answer.

Yes.

HEED MY COMMAND, AND REALIZE YOUR DESIRE.

That voice. It was the voice of the world itself. Her vision was black, only the words existed. *My desire? You mean…*

YES. IF YOU OBEY, YOU SHALL BRING FORTH A CHILD.

She gasped for aer, but darkness filled her lungs. That word. *Child.* She knew what it meant instantly, as if the voice had impressed it in her mind. Was this real, or a dream? She struggled, searching for a way out and back to wakefulness.

THIS IS YOUR TASK. SEEK A MAN NAMED RAENDAL. YOU SHALL FIND HIM IN THIS PLACE.

A blur of wide spikes appeared—mountains, sliding by underneath her as if she were traveling at incredible speed. She did not recognize the landscape; nevertheless, she knew where to find the place she saw.

DO YOU UNDERSTAND?

Yes.

GO THERE AND TAKE THE SOURCE. BRING IT HERE.

The view slid again, shifting hundreds of miles to the south in moments. She saw a circular wall of mountains, a crater filled with twisting plants.

Why? she asked in her mind. *Why are you doing this?*

The crater dropped away into the darkness.

GIVE THE SOURCE TO THE DAEMON WHICH DWELLS THERE, AND HE WILL GRANT YOUR WISH.

But… Her thoughts were jumbled, her vision breaking up.

DO NOT DELAY. YOUR CHILD WISHES TO SEE YOU AGAIN.

Light streamed from above her. She was lying on her back. "But…"

Blurry shapes composed themselves. The faces of the Inaali. They crouched and stood around her, eyes wide. She had collapsed during the chanting. That voice, that dreadful voice still reverberated in her skull. What had it said last?

The Inaali supported her as she sat up, some calling her name or asking what was wrong. But their attention went beyond mere curiosity; they probed her skin with their fingers and stroked her hair, desperate to be close to her. She writhed and pushed them away.

A familiar face appeared in the back of the crowd. Targael.

"Meli! What happened? What did you see?"

"But what...what is..." The words came slow, congealed on her sluggish tongue.

"What is what?"

She lifted her head to the sky, letting the evening light pour into her eyes, and the question pounding in her mind found its way out her lips.

"What is the Daemon?!"

17

The raiders stayed in the aer over Bressim a few days, just long enough for Roi to meet with his captains and finalize the crew.

Karis stayed alone on the ship, stewing, and did not see the meetings. Instead, she passed the time by going over the previous week again and again, castigating herself for letting the raiders lull her into letting her guard down, for trusting Jaela, and especially for not attempting an escape before the battle. It came to the point where all she desired was some peace after the chaos, but her mind refused to leave her alone, recalling the incidents whenever she let it fall idle.

She spent most of the daylight staring out the window at the sky, waiting for Elsa. The eagle's continued absence first brought relief that the raiders would not be able to capture her, soon mixed with worry at the thought she might have been killed in the battle. At night, Karis went to sleep thinking of Meli and the Automatia, to remind herself why she was choosing to remain with Roi, and whichever elite band of raiders he had picked to accompany him.

Or at least, she had assumed he would pick an elite band. But when the raiders did embark, it seemed Roi had actually lost some of the crew he had intended to take with him. Karis had expected a change of vessel as well, for the escape cruiser was cramped and slow, and it was to her surprise when Roi climbed aboard and ordered them to leave while still on it. Though the raiders quickly began expanding and upgrading the cruiser as they flew, as the days went on the ship developed a rank smell from the bodies trapped close together, and it became clear that they would never match the speed which Karis knew their best ships could achieve. Roi kept his chin high, acting as though nothing were amiss, but his plan had clearly had a downside; by abandoning the battle, he had lost more than a little face among his loyal cohorts. Whatever he expected to get out of finding the Automatia, he would have to return with something significant to their cause, or perhaps not return at all.

Roi's bodyguards Isky and Dikta were aboard, of course—the twins, the others called them, though they were not twins but merely similar looking, nearly inseparable lovers. Jaela had remained as well—

having her nearby was nearly enough to make Karis ill—along with Mylon and Phaestal and the gray-haired Cindlan. Then there was a new addition, Paolem, a grim-faced man with a bald patch. His main skill set seemed to be grumbling and shirking whenever something needed to be done; Karis suspected he had come along only because none of the other crews wanted him.

Aer travel, even in a sub-standard ship, had its advantages. They reached the Kalsten strait in less than two days, and the first sight of the fog-footed bluffs at its narrow mouth made Karis's heart pound. The ship descended, approaching the shore, and the crew took to the portholes to search for signs of the Automatia.

Nothing. Not at the mouth of the strait, nor the lands immediately surrounding it. They searched on. Weeks slipped by while they combed up and down the coastline, north then south, leeward to windward and back again, finding only small towns and villages and endless miles of forest-covered mountains. Karis withdrew further, spending most of her time behind a partition at the stern, staring out a porthole, thinking daily that Meli would surely have reached the Automatia by now, assuming that she had figured out whatever they were missing and had known where to find it.

The crew grew sullen as well, Roi not the least among them. As the days went on he spoke less and less, sitting at the front window in the pilot's room, hands folded beneath his chin. Karis couldn't help but feel a twinge of joy seeing him so miserable, despite knowing that her hopes of entering the Automatia rested on their luck changing.

Then, one morning when the dust hung especially thick over the north leeward coast of the strait, Roi emerged from the pilot's room, wearing a wide smile.

"We're here," he shouted to the groggy crew. "Phaestal, cut the engines. We're putting her down in that clearing."

Karis rubbed her eyes and shook her head. "What's going on?"

"A change of plan," Roi said.

"We're giving up?" Paolem asked. "Going back?"

"Not at all. But it is time for a new approach. We'll land, stretch our legs, and I'll explain more. Unless you would all rather take another trip up the strait?"

The crew eagerly took up ready positions around the ship. Phaestal appeared from around a corner and pushed past Karis.

"Hey," she said. "Watch it."

"Huh?"

"You almost knocked me over, oaf."

He sniffed. "Well you were just standing there. Why don't you help?"

"Oh, pox off!" She headed to one of the portholes.

The ground below was coming up fast, a series of steep hills lined with eldertwist trees. It was the first time she had seen the land of the windward continent so closely. The ship made one final turn above a flat, grassy field nestled into a curve of the mountains. At the far end, the ridges came together into a narrow valley, forming a pathway to a small village.

They descended slowly for a few moments, then suddenly dropped, landing with an ear-splitting thud and a chorus of surprised voices. Cracking sounds came from below as pieces of the ship fell away from the impact.

"Idiots!" Karis shouted.

"A wonderful landing." Roi hopped out of his chair and headed toward a convenient tear in the damaged hull. "Let's see what's out there."

He clambered out and the others rose to follow. Karis shielded her eyes as she left, both from the daylight and from the clouds of dust kicked up by the ship.

"Line up, everyone." Roi paced across the field with his hands behind his back. "Crew meeting."

Karis joined the others in a row along the side of the ship.

"From now on," Roi continued, "we're no longer raiders."

Shocked faces and angry whispers.

"Why in the gods aren't we raiders?" Mylon said, his voice an indignant squeak.

"Please." Roi held out his hands for calm. "It's only a ruse; of course our hearts will remain true to the SkyHunters. But the legends make it clear that the Automatia only accepts students with pure motives. They believe by doing so they can ensure their convocations are only put to the uses *they* deem 'proper.' Therefore, we need to take on new identities. And to do that, we'll need practice."

He motioned to the village on their right, its conical rooftops just visible over the curve of the hill.

"From this point on, you are *in character*. No cheating, not even when you believe you're alone. Don't talk like a raider, don't dress like a raider, don't even think like a raider."

"But if we're not raiders," Cindlan said, raising his hand, "then who are we?"

"A good question. I am a holy prince from Azorkas, far to leeward. And you all are my retinue."

That provoked a good deal of hushed conversation among the crew.

"Sir?" Cindlan raised his hand again. "What's a retinue?"

"Hmm," Roi said. "Think of yourselves as my servants."

Karis scoffed. "Why would we want to serve you?"

"Because you like me so much." He smiled.

She crossed her arms and shook her head, but the others were already discussing how to approach their new roles.

"Don't you see, it's like a game," Cindlan explained to a skeptical Paolem. "We'll make up new names for ourselves and everything."

"Ah, better hold off on the names for now," Roi said. "We don't want to get confused too early. Let's start with some Azorkan clothes."

"Do you really think anyone here knows what Azorkans wear?" Karis asked.

"No." Roi said. "And neither does anyone at the Automatia; that's the whole point. So just make something up. Something frilly and leeward-looking should suffice."

Before Karis could protest further, the others began to crumble their jumpsuits and convoke new outfits piece by piece, critiquing each other as they went. Jaela walked to the front to catch Roi's eye, then dropped all her clothing in a flourish. He nodded approvingly as she began to construct an outfit out of silver lace ribbon, curling in layers over her pale skin.

Karis turned away in disgust, heading to the other side of the ship. *Something frilly and leeward-looking.* She had always favored simple, functional clothes. She could tell already this "Azorkan" idea was going to bring her no end of irritation.

She closed her eyes, searching for the space in her mind she would have to relax in order to crumble her top. After years of wearing the same outfit, the mind trained itself to push the convocation into the background, so that it actually took some effort to feel it again and let it go. She took a deep breath, searching, then found it. Her shirt flaked and fell away into fine dust. Karis wrapped her arms across her chest to prevent the wind from stinging her.

A cough. She looked behind to see Phaestal, standing alone beneath the ship's nose.

"What are you doing?!" She quickly convoked a cloth to pull over her shoulders.

"I uh…" Phaestal took a step back and fixed his gaze on the ship. "I saw you were upset. I wanted to see what was wrong."

"I know what you came to see. Go away."

"Hey, that isn't…" He hesitated, as if unsure of whether it was worth defending himself further.

She gritted her teeth and began to raise a solid black wall between them. "Just *leave*."

He frowned before the wall grew high enough to block his face, then she heard him move away. She waited for a few moments to make sure he had really gone, then sat with her head in her hands. What was wrong with her, anyway? Did it really matter what they did? Yes, having the raiders around set her on edge, especially Jaela, but she just had to hold on a little longer. Make it to the Automatia, find Meli and forget about these people forever.

Soon after, she marched with the raiders in a loose formation down the hill to the village. They seemed to have settled on bright shades of yellow and green as being emblematic of "Azorkan" fashion, and thereafter had set about outdoing each other in gaudiness. The tall, top-heavy twins looked particularly ridiculous in their matching shoulder ruffles. Roi, playing the part of the prince, wore a heavier coat than the rest, with red pleats down its side and an oversized hat which he said was a far leeward symbol of authority, a claim Karis didn't care enough about to challenge. The path before them was barren, its only plant life the groups of shrubs which rose between moss-covered chunks of bedrock. Nearer to the village, the scrub thinned out and was replaced by human-tended foliage, decorative vines and flowers which interwove in solid walls, filtering out some of the airborne dust. The crew turned a corner and entered a small town square.

The first thing which caught Karis' attention was the mekkanikal washing-wheel, a rotating line of buckets attached to a cable on pulleys, stretching down out of sight. They had to lead somehow to the ocean, since the buckets were coming up toward the village full of liquid, and dumping out one by one into a trench set up between the houses for the residents to wash out their dust. Nearby, a set of smooth red benches stood in a circle around the village's center, where more plants grew in a cluster, presumably for decoration, although whoever had planted them seemed to be having trouble keeping their growth under control.

"Hello there!" From the other side of the square, a man saw them and waved. He got up from his bench near where two women were sitting, playing some type of ball game with a group of fuzzy mountain shroles.

Roi waved at him, then looked back at the rest of the crew. "Remember, all of you: behave. Better to say nothing than to reveal ourselves."

He walked up to the man and bowed. "Greetings to you, Good Sir of this beautiful land. I am Roilan of the Royal Priesthood of Azorkas."

The man stopped in his tracks, mouth hanging open. "Azorkas! No!" He took another look at the crew, and for a moment Karis thought he might laugh them all out of town. But instead he spun and called to his companions. "Girls! You have to see this! These folks are from thousands of miles away."

The women arrived moments later, more similar looking than not, short with unkempt curls bouncing over pendulous breasts.

"This is Sixpel and Ladetha." He pointed and they smiled. "And I'm Vom. So pleased to meet you, your...?"

"My official title is 'Highness,'" Roi said, exactly as if he believed it. "But please, call me Roilan."

"Roilan!" Vom pulled Ladetha close and nuzzled her hair in excitement. "To think Zed would smile such fortune upon us! Bringing a visitor all this way to share our company and our bread."

Karis stifled a snort. Zed was the lead figure of the Six Endless Ones, a group of gods long forgotten on the leeward continent, except in stories told to the newly arrived. Never did she think she would meet someone who still worshiped him.

"Ah, not quite," Roilan said. "We're actually here searching for the legendary automatist school—oh, hello over there!"

He waved to several villagers who had emerged from houses across the square, and were staring in various states of curiosity and suspicion.

"Don't even try it, Wailiu!" Vom called. A tall woman across the way put her hands on her hips and grimaced. "I met them first, and I'm going to host them for supper."

"That may not be necessary," Roi said. "As I was saying, the Automatia—"

"Yes, yes, the Automatia. Listen, forget about what the others in the village say. Especially Wailiu. She thinks she runs this place, but I'm the best host here. We'll convoke a big tent, have a feast. You can sit right next to me and my ladies."

"Is it nearby?"

"Is what?"

"The Automatia."

"Oh, the Automatia. We'll discuss it this evening, yes? I know some good stories, but I'd love to know more about your home country. Do you drink ambrosia there?"

"Yes. I mean, I don't, but some in my retinue will."

"Retin...?"

"Never mind. I just need to..." Roi trailed off as Vom suddenly broke away toward an open area of the clearing.

"We'll put the tent right here, yes? And some tables here for food. Wailiu's husbands will perform some dances for you. Do any of your performers dance?"

"They're not performers," Roi said, following him. "I don't mean to press the issue, but we need information. We've heard that the Automatia is located on the strait; since you're from here, we were wondering—"

"Ah yes. Information. Only the pure-hearted pass through the mouth into the Automatia, isn't that what they say?"

"I've heard that."

"But what purifies the heart more than some drinking and dancing, eh? Why not stay with us a while? I'll tell you more about the Automatia, much more. And we have everything here, great company, great food, great drink. Just watch out for Wailiu after she's had a few."

Roi bit his lip and sighed. "I would like to ask around the rest of the village, as well."

"Of course, of course! Sixpel, start on some ambrosia for our guests. You remember the convocation, don't you? Which one of you convoked the ambrosia we had last week? You? Better let Ladetha do it, then."

Roi marched back to the crew, face somewhat drawn.

"Well?" Mylon asked. "What are we doing?"

"We're staying," Roi said. "I hope you're all in a festive mood."

The feast lasted well into the evening, until the raider crew and the villagers alike sat around, overstuffed and sleepy, as the white sky faded to gray. Mylon and Cindlan sat at the end of a long table, looking bored. Perhaps they missed their compatriots in the fleet—feasting among strangers was interesting up to a point, but Karis knew that not being able to tell raider tales and sing raider songs was grating to them. Cindlan in particular tended to stay near Mylon when not running an errand for Roi, perhaps because the others wouldn't tolerate his presence. Karis had overheard Isky saying Cindlan had only appeared twelve years ago, which explained his tendency to ask irritating questions on every topic imaginable. He had stopped bothering Karis with them quickly after she had stonewalled him as part of her general policy of ignoring them all, though in truth she found him less personally objectionable than the others.

But if she could tolerate Cindlan, whom did she *dislike* the most, aside from Roi and Jaela and Mylon? Isky and Dikta were an obvious choice. The two of them were sitting on a cushion in Roi's general vicinity, but in the specific vicinity of each other as they snuggled close, Dikta's head tucked into Isky's neck. The two men were built like fighters, even more so than Ariden had been, tall with large, tight layers of muscle. Perhaps they had been part of a striker crew before Roi had made them guards. Their new assignment suited their temperament, though—quiet, ruthless, but not bloodthirsty. Karis had the feeling that the pair would never go out their way to harm her for the sake of it, but neither would they pass up the opportunity if presented with one.

Karis focused back on Roi, lying in a nest of overstuffed pillows at the seat of honor, head back with his eyes closed, mumbling some story or another to Vom. But if he were in a stupor, it would only be due to exhaustion, not drink, since as far as she could tell he had not touched the ambrosia. *Roi says a raider's best weapon is their judgment,* Jaela had said. But what was he worried about in this place? Perhaps he did not trust Karis, with good reason, or the townspeople, who continued to drift in and out of the party as it drew to a close. But with Isky and Dikta sitting just to his right, such guardedness was hardly called for.

Not that she was planning to do anything to him, anyway—if she were going to take a rash action, it would be to run away. During the long, slow periods of the trip—and there had been many—the sheer absurdity of staying with the people who had kidnapped her and held her against her will struck her hardest. If she wanted, she could leave the village now, head up over the mountains and never see any of the raiders again. She didn't really *need* them to get to the Automatia, after all. She would make it there eventually, if she was determined. Whether it took her a year, ten, or fifty, she could do it. But what would happen then if she did find the school, and Roi was already there? To her, and to Meli?

A man ducked into the tent area and wandered past the dozing raiders. His black hair was long and shaggy, and he stared about the interior with eyes wide, drinking in the sights as fiercely as Vom drank ambrosia.

"Vel! Over here!" Vom yelled. He turned and spoke to Roi. "That's Vel, our new appearance. Wandered in from the mountains six weeks ago—don't think he's much older than that."

"Charmed," Roi said, as the man shuffled toward them, smiling.

"We call him Velocher—'fast hands.' The first thing he did when he came here was sneak up and try to and steal some rolls from our luncheon. Didn't realize we could convoke as many more as we wanted, you see. Vel, go ahead and eat some food from the table, there. Food. Foo-ood. Good boy, there you go. He'll learn to speak in a few years, I think."

Vel headed toward the heaping piles of sauced noodles. He stopped as he passed by Karis, head swiveling as if it were attached to a crank. His mouth fell open for a moment, then he smiled, leaned down, and touched her hair. The wide-eyed, dumb look on his face when he entered had been replaced with one of awe, or sorrow.

He opened his mouth again, his tongue moving up and down as it felt for words that wouldn't come. The tips of his fingers brushed Karis's ear and she pulled away in disgust, slapping his hand. He drew back, startled, then hung his shoulders and hurried off.

"Vel! What are you doing? Don't touch smoothskins without their permission, Vel, it's rude! So sorry about that…"

Karis looked about the tent—some of the dozing raiders had awakened and their eyes were on her. Suddenly uncomfortable, she stood up, straightened her new baggy overcoat and marched outside.

The night aer was cool and calm, the valley sheltering them from the wind. Karis frowned and headed into the square to put some distance between her and the party. There was a small set of ancient ruins nearby, Vom had told them proudly. She crossed behind the houses and walked out along a row of creeping vines until she found them. Two sets of bedrock pillars, standing out in the open, clearly shaped by intelligent hands though their original meaning was lost. She walked up closer and a black shape jumped out from behind one of the pillars and hissed.

Karis leapt back, hands up. The shape crept out into the open, where the fading light fell on it. One of the shroles from earlier—a larger kind than she was used to, three feet long, covered in light brown fur with beady black eyes. She approached again and the animal ducked back behind the pillar, then poked its head out to see if she was still there. A game. She followed it, walking around the side of the ruin. To her surprise, it popped up on top of a pillar behind her, chittering with laughter, then hopped off and scampered away again.

She stared for a moment, puzzled, before she realized there was more than one shrole. A third shrole appeared with two smaller cubs riding on its back, and Karis knelt to try and motion them closer. The group kept their distance until she left the ruins, then followed her through an alley back to the town. They must have been a single mixing colony, just like the one Meli had kept in her house.

Meli. A sudden grief overcame her, and she stared at her feet as she walked. How she longed to see Meli again, to embrace her, to finally tell her how she really felt and apologize for putting her in danger. Of all the past follies she had dwelt on in the darkness of the raider ship, the mistake of hiding her feelings from Meli stung the most. She should have said something, after a day, a year, any time before it was too late. Even if she knew what the answer would have been, even if the revelation would have put a gulf between them and doomed their friendship. How pathetic that even after three hundred years, her heart was still so prone to foolishness that she would trade that risk for another, larger gamble, and lose.

The noise of footsteps on packed dust sounded from down the alley. The shroles scampered away and Karis pressed herself up against the wall out of instinct. The noise grew louder, and Paolem passed by, muttering, pulling on his hair as he stomped up the path.

Odd. She waited a few moments, then walked to the mouth of the alley and peered out. Paolem stood at a door not far away and knocked. Karis convoked a low wall to hide behind, mimicking as best she could the hard red material the villagers favored for their houses.

The door slid open, and Paolem and the building's unseen occupant spoke in hushed tones. Soon Paolem began to whisper excitedly, then the door closed and he walked away, smiling. Karis ducked down behind the wall as he passed. What in Aetheria was he doing? Whatever it was, Roi must have put him up to it. But what was Roi's plan, and why was he keeping it a secret from her?

Nighttime proper had fallen now, the pale glow from the sky barely enough with which to navigate. She slipped down the alley and back toward the tent, her vision of the future as dark as her view of the path.

Karis woke before first light. She rolled out of bed in the cabin she had hastily convoked, stretched, and crumbled open the door.

The washing-wheel creaked as it turned, dumping ocean into the trough nearby, but the rest of the village was silent. The aer felt slightly wet and the night had left a thin coating of dust over every surface, which the townspeople would most likely wash away using the wheel's delivery. It would be their first and only chore of the day.

The flap of Vom's elaborate party tent opened, and Roi stepped out, his hair sticking up from wearing his over-sized royal hat. He sniffed, rubbed his eyes and yawned, then noticed Karis.

"Oh, hello," he said.

She nodded.

"Quite a bash last night. I don't think I've ever told so many stories in my life, especially not about life in 'Azorkas.'"

"You'd better have plenty more, if you plan on staying. I assume Vom has already planned another 'welcome party.'"

Roi chuckled. "He'll be disappointed. I've learned all I can here, and I don't think any of the crew will mind spending one less moment in this gods-forsaken place."

"What did you find out?" She crossed her arms.

"Not much," Roi admitted. "Vom keeps repeating that line about Kalsten's mouth, as do the others."

"But we checked the mouth of the strait. Many times."

"Indeed. Quite a mystery, isn't it?"

Karis raised an eyebrow. "What are you getting at? You think I know the answer?"

"If you don't, perhaps you should have been thinking harder before now."

She grunted. "You have a theory, don't you?"

Roi nodded. "We're looking for the mouth of Kalsten, yes? But we're assuming Kalsten refers to the strait itself. The locals call this whole area Kalsten, both here and on the southern side. So perhaps we're not looking for the mouth of the strait, but rather some other type of mouth. Now, what could that possibly mean?"

Some other type of mouth? What was he— "Oh! A cave."

"I knew I was talking to the right person."

Karis shook her head. Everyone knew caves were miserable places—wet, mold-infested, and most of all bathed in eternal darkness. Legend had it horrible creatures lurked in them, beasts who had never seen daylight, whose bodies and souls had merged into the surrounding black.

The Automatia, down in a cave. It was a ludicrous idea, and yet, perhaps that was the point. If their goal was to stay hidden, what better way than place themselves where no one would ever look?

"Even if it's true," she said, "where would this cave be?"

"Well, I certainly don't know, and neither does anyone else here, unless they're far better liars than me." Roi paced back and forth, speaking to the ground. "All of which leaves me a bit stuck. My plan had been to politely excuse ourselves, then go on to the next village, and the next. Keep searching, keep asking the locals for clues. Except…"

She smiled. "…except none of them may know, either."

He held up his hand to quiet her. "I know, I know. This is where you ask, 'How many miles of coastline along the strait?' And I say, 'Five hundred or so,' and you say, 'How many villages are there, here and on the leeward side?' And I cut to the chase and ask 'Just what are you implying?', and you grin that wicked little grin of yours and ask me, 'How long do you expect the crew to play along with this? They only follow you because they believe in you, but once they lose faith they'll leave.' And then I hang my head in shame at having my failure laid bare, and you walk away feeling oh-so-superior. Is that right?"

Karis's smile had vanished. She narrowed her eyes.

"Except that none of that gets us any closer to the Automatia, or to your friend. So why don't you try offering some ideas instead of taking so much glee in this situation?"

Oh, no. Not that easily, he wouldn't.

"You need me," she said. "Maybe more than I need you."

"You're a valuable addition to the crew."

"The crew is completely useless."

He shrugged.

"And another thing." She pulled at her collar. "I want to re-convoke my old clothes."

"Now, Karis, if you want to play the game, you need to follow the rules."

"If Meli is there, they'll see that she already knows me. How are you going to explain that, if we all traveled here from Azorkas? But if I came from someplace nearer, and you just happened to pick me up on your way…"

Roi rubbed his dimpled chin. "You do have a point. Very well, a special uniform exemption has been granted. Now, have you got anything for me, or not?"

She held her hands behind her back and paced a circle. The Automatia in a cave. No, it would never work. No matter how advanced their convocations, they would still need light to see by. An idea came and she scratched in the dust with her toe, then wiped it away. Still, there was something there, a notion to be teased out. She paced, turning the problem over in her mind for some time. Then she looked up at the sky.

"I've got it."

She stepped back and convoked a set of poles, followed by a flat, thick canopy, forming a smaller version of the tent beside them, just wide enough to bathe them both in shadow. "If the Automatia is located in a cavern, there's no reason for them to make the entrance easy to find. They would probably keep it camouflaged, to hide their comings and goings from…"

"Uncivilized folk?" Roi offered.

"Right. But how could they run a school underground like that in the first place? Everything would be completely dark, unless they had shafts to let in light from above."

She pointed up, and a set of holes crumbled in the canopy ceiling. The ground below turned a lighter shade of brown. "I can see the sky through these because the cover is thin. But as the cave went deeper into the bedrock, the shafts would have to be longer, which would filter out the light."

"So it doesn't work," Roi said. "The shafts can't be too wide for security, but if they're narrow they wouldn't be able to see."

"Unless." Karis closed her eyes and focused, feeling the aer drifting by the tops of the holes. She convoked it into crystal, and soon ovals of the smooth, transparent substance sent pinpoints of light onto the dusty ground.

Roi held his hand under one of the bright points, watching it dance over his skin.

"That's how they do it," Karis finished. "And that's how we'll find it. In order to work, the lenses need to be smooth, which means they'll also reflect light from above."

"Ah. So we attach a lens of our own to the ship, hook up a mirror to direct it, then sweep the light across the ground and look for flashes. When we see them, we'll know the Automatia is below." He smiled and smacked his fist into his palm. "You're a wonderful investment, Karis. It's just too bad you're not as smart as you think."

"Why is that?"

"You shouldn't have just come out and told me what to do. Now what's stopping me from leaving you behind?"

"You!" Her pulse thumped in her neck.

He laughed. "A jest. I'll need your help again, after all. You don't think that's all the Automatia has in store for us, do you? They're sure to have some sort of traps set up, the kind only you can figure out how to disable."

Karis let out a deep breath and unclenched her fists. Pieces of the canopy fell around her, crumbled when she had lost focus in her anger.

Roi winked, then turned and walked back inside the tent to gather the others. Karis could only stand and watch him go, shaking her head in disbelief.

18

Eight spires of bedrock ringed the top of the Inaali sanctuary. Why eight, Meli did not know. Perhaps the ancients favored that number and held it sacred, as the First Emperor was said to have done with the number ten. Then again, perhaps the pillars were older than the ancients, and perhaps it was the gods or mere chance which chose their form.

Meli had never been one for numbers. Once or twice she had wondered if it was significant that she'd had the dream of her seedling in her thirtieth year, three of the Emperor's tens, but mostly she spent her time concerned with living things, whose wants and workings were fluid and gradual, not easily captured in the hard certainty of the numerical. Meli had heard tales in Sofidra of women and men who dabbled in number theory, seeking the unalterable truths of ratios and tangents. Such people sometimes descended into madness, it was said, for within the simplicity of their theorems they uncovered endless new patterns, and spent their remaining days lost in uncanny sequences of numbers which had been convoked into the structure of the universe by some primordial mind.

In much the same way, the spire upon which Meli sat that morning, weeks after her vision during the chant looked from afar like nothing more than a simple leg of bedrock. Rough at the base, it tapered to a smooth tip high above the interior of the mountaintop. But inside, the ancients had carved a winding stair leading to a parapet at the top, accessible from a fold in the rock near where the Inaali held their chants. If she stayed longer at the Sanctuary, she would doubtlessly find many more such secrets, both in its structure and among its occupants. That fact made her strangely uneasy, perhaps because she had grown weary of the unexplained and the unknown. She would have preferred to have all the paths before her illuminated and straight, rather than making sharp turns in the darkness, as did the long stairway that had brought her to her current resting place.

Then again, the view at the top was quite lovely.

At this point, Meli would take any form of solace she could get. It had been only a few days since she had fully recovered from her ordeal during the chant—before then, she had walked about half-awake, her thoughts wracked by strange images and ideas, as if the vision had done some grave injury to the structure of her mind. Targael, to his credit, had been nothing but supportive during her period of confusion, showing the utmost patience as he spoke her through the experience again and again, even though it took an eternity for her to be able to recall their conversations, and for his words to begin making sense.

She had told him everything while still in her stupor. What the words of the vision meant for her—about her dream, and her true reason for leaving Sofidra. Targael had been understanding of her deception, perhaps more than she deserved, and he took responsibility for any suffering that resulted from her inadequate preparation for receiving the God's word. As for the others, their attitude was more perplexing. Where before they had viewed her with mildly veiled suspicion, now some of them stared openly in adoration, sometimes falling to their knees or approaching with held breath, asking for a blessing or words of wisdom from the God, as if she had any to give.

Was it a god that had spoken to her that evening? It was hard to imagine it could have been anything else, but she did not feel particularly blessed. She did not think of herself as a chosen one; she was no pilgrim on a fated journey, just a lost soul searching for her missing friend, and her experience in the chant did not change that. If anything, the long and terrible recovery period had made her think of Karis even more, and the horrors she might be suffering at the hands of the raiders.

A sound from behind snapped Meli to attention: footsteps, heralding Targael's approach onto the parapet.

"How does the morning find you, my lady?"

Confused. Confused and despondent in too many ways to count. "Fine, thank you."

Targael walked to the edge, showing her his back. He leaned out over the bedrock wall and sighed. "Our world. I know in my heart it is a vice to be rejected, and yet from such a vantage one cannot help but be amazed by its beauty."

"When I come here, I like to imagine I can see all of Aetheria," Meli said. "That perhaps if I looked hard enough, I might find Karis, and know where she had been taken."

She rose, letting her chair crumble, and joined him at the low wall. Together they squinted at the vast expanse of ridged lowlands and craggy mountains beyond. Green and orange foliage covered the hills which rippled away to the right, two species of trees arrayed in zigzagging lines, leaves flapping in the breeze like banners in a battle of old, fighting for control of the land so slowly that no human would ever follow their progress. Rugged and wild, all of it, and full of danger—the thought of having to cross it made Meli's throat tighten. Once, her plan to have Ariden accompany her had allayed such fears. And now? She had come a long way, both in distance and in self-understanding, but experience had also taught her that she wasn't ready to brave the wilderness alone just yet. Ariden had proven himself inadequate when he lost Karis to the raiders, but he was the best she had, unfortunately.

"The adherents have finished their research," Targael said. "We told and re-told the remaining stories last evening. Are you ready to hear what they found?"

Perhaps she was, and perhaps not. But the time had come for her to leave this place, and Targael's news was the only thing she had been waiting for.

Targael cleared his throat. "Of the sacred words the God spoke to you, 'Seek a man named Raendal' were the ones we had the most success deciphering. Based on your description, we believe the name refers to an old hermit who lives high in the Aperandi mountains to the north."

Meli closed her eyes, remembering. "Yes. That must have been what I saw. What else do you know about this man?"

"Tales of him go back to the days of the empires, if not before. Most stories paint him as rather eccentric and unfriendly, and the times when he meddled in others' affairs ended poorly for all involved. Then, many centuries ago, he removed himself from society entirely. He is said to be a master of many esoteric convocations, but he guards his knowledge jealously. Perhaps he felt his withdrawal to the mountains would help him better conceal the secret which the God instructed you to find."

"You mean the Source?" Meli asked.

"Yes. The nature of what the God called 'The Source' is a matter of some debate amongst the adherents. It is not a name Aetherians have used in our history. Our only clue comes in the form of the phrasing: 'Take the Source. Bring it here.'" He spoke the words with reverence. "For you to be able to take the Source from Raendal, it must be able to survive outside of his influence."

"Could it be a living thing, then? That I'm meant to remove from his possession?"

"Possibly. But we think it unlikely that the God would condone such an activity, unless the being in question wished to escape."

Meli drifted back to the memory, probing around its edges. She had repeated the words of the vision to Targael as faithfully as she could, but there was more he did not know. The voice had imprinted itself deep within her mind, and had left feelings behind where it had touched. Some of them were sharp. Ugly.

"No." She took a deep breath and pulled herself back into the now. "The voice said 'take,' not 'rescue.' That is what it meant."

"Then unless the Source refers to a piece of bedrock, we are left with only one solution: perhaps it is not a thing at all, but knowledge. A convocation, lost for many years, which you are meant to learn."

"But I cannot take knowledge from Raendal, unless he wishes to teach it."

"Yes, and no. It may be that the Source is a convocation which has hardened."

Meli nodded. That would fit—it was well known that after a convocation had existed for many centuries, its internal structure began to set into place. If it survived intact long enough, like the Sofidran Amphitheatre, it might not crumble at all, even when released for an indefinite time.

"And what of this place I am meant to bring the Source to?" she asked. "The giant crater filled with plants?"

Targael shook his head. "History is silent on it. But there are rumors, stories the newer adherents have brought with them from their former lives. They say there exists a place to north-leeward like the one you describe. The crater itself, like all bedrock, is as old as the world, but what lies within it seems to be of more recent origin, at least within the last century. The area surrounding it is remote, but those few who live nearby call it the Lost Jungle, and do not think its coming to be a good omen. They have told of ill feelings striking those who pass by."

"Ill feelings?"

"Indeed. Such fables are typical of isolated mountain folk, who often indulge in superstition. But in this case, it is clear from the God's words that the Lost Jungle is a location of some importance, though for what purpose I do not know. As for this Daemon of yours, I'm afraid I can say even less. No one amongst us has heard such a name before."

This Daemon of mine? As if she had made the thing up. She turned away and faced the ocean, its whiteness visible between the spires on the far side of the mountain. "And what of my other request?"

When she looked back, Targael's normally benign face held a sour expression. It was the same one he had worn days ago, when she asked him if the order knew of any convocations which would help her create her seedling.

Targael composed himself and said, "That, I have not passed on to the others."

Her annoyance gave way to anger. She would not be cowed by his disapproval anymore, nor be made ashamed by the people who claimed to hold her in such high regard. "You swore to help me in any way you could."

"And I shall. But I will not pursue such a question on your behalf, and risk the destruction of this order." Targael's fingers twitched, and he searched in vain for piece of webbing to dig them into, settling for worrying the hem of his robe. "For thousands of years we have taken a vow to help all life find the peace of letting go. If the adherents learned that you, a savior blessed by the God, wished to convoke new human life, it would cause a great schism. The Inaali cannot function if our guiding principles are undermined."

"But it was *your* god who told me I would have an offspring."

"You are welcome to your interpretation of the God's words. I will not assume to know her mind. And until I see this offspring myself, I will not risk the sanctity of our three thousand year tradition."

He let out a long, slow breath, and turned away. She saw him then for what he truly was—a coward. For all his espousal of the Inaali beliefs, Targael was too invested in the future of the order to ever disperse himself. Perhaps he told himself that he was what was needed for the greater good, so that other people might reach their potential. Men who live by lies have to find a comforting one to tell themselves, after all.

"This matter is not worth driving a wedge between us," Targael said, his composure regained. "Even if I did put your question to the adherents, the esoteric secrets we hold are not of the form you animatists practice."

"Meaning?"

"How to explain…you understand the difference between the aer and the aether, yes?"

"Yes." Though the terms were sometimes used interchangeably, it was common knowledge that aer truly referred to what she felt and breathed, while the aether was the force underlying it, omnipresent, indivisible.

"Then you know the aether is what listens to our requests, and acts on them. Some of the requests, such as for basic materials, are intuitive, coming easily even to the newly appeared. But there is more that the aether can be made to accomplish—much more. It is little different from instructing a human, in a way. If I knew how to say 'forward,' 'back,' 'left,' and 'right,' I might command you to walk here or there, fetching me objects. And if I grew used to commanding you in such a way, I might not realize you had the ability to move in other ways as well, if only I knew the word for 'jump.' Do you understand?"

Meli nodded. Commanding the aether was a bit like speaking, only in the language of the mind rather than in Aetherian. "To perform an animatism, I must know how to ask the aether the right question."

"Yes. And discovering a new question, or what we would call an esoteric convocation, is truly difficult, unless one has an example to show how it is asked. That is why our order holds certain convocations as secrets, while others we feel are best forgotten. The ones we keep have a simplistic character; at a basic level, they do not nest within themselves, and cannot be used to build complex creations, like the ones favored by the automatists you were seeking to visit. Their arts would not be welcome here, nor would an animatist's, for yours are the most dangerous of all—simple convocations which grow in complexity on their own. How do you think the plagues began, anyway?"

She crossed her arms. "I do not create plagues."

"Of course not. Convocations which warp the human body are anathema, at least in modern times. But the basic precept of our order remains the same: relief of suffering through simplicity.

"Do not forget that it was we who stood up against the Plague Bringer, cursed be his name, we who brought order back to the world when it was on the verge of falling into chaos. Those of us living two and a half millennia after the last plague was extinguished cannot know our true fortune. The tales speak of flesh rent asunder by plagues spread through aer, people screaming, begging for someone to kill them while they lived on for years, writhing in great open fields."

He noticed the look on her face and frowned. "I apologize. I know that you are not party to such atrocities. But still the warning must be given."

"You scold me as if I were newly appeared."

Targael sighed. "I don't know what to do with you. Your situation is unique, Meli. Never before has an outsider received the word of the God. Change is coming, and none of us can know where it may lead. But the God has spoken, and you will have our support when you undertake your mission. We do not have much to give, but what we have is yours."

Meli gave a little snort. How gracious of him. When she undertook her mission? What made him so certain that she would? But it wasn't just Targael's haughtiness which bothered her; a hint of melancholy had crept in when she learned the Inaali had no knowledge which could help her convoke her seedling. Her *child*. She hadn't expected them to, not really, but oftentimes she found traces of hope twinkling in dark crevices, after she thought she had stamped them out.

"I do not wish to be abrupt, but morning prayers will begin in a few moments. Will you join me back in the Sanctuary?"

"A word first, if I might." Ariden had moved up the stairway like a specter, his approach unheard.

"You are free to speak your mind, though your timing is inopportune." Targael had drawn himself to his modest height, and lost the familiar tone he kept with Meli. "I am needed below. The adherents should not be made to wait."

"That's fine," Ariden said. "Because I'm speaking to her, not you."

"I'm sure whatever you have to say can be——"

Ariden pointed down the stair. "Get lost."

Targael examined Ariden, Meli and the stairway in turn. "Very well." He nodded at Meli. "My lady."

Ariden watched him go, then sauntered to the parapet and sat on top of it. He looked down, then convoked a small lump of heavy, solid aether and chucked it over the side. Moments passed as he watched it pass out of sight. "Long fall."

Meli tucked her hands in her sleeves and hugged her fur gown close. The spire, which she had thought of in the last days as her own private sanctuary, was feeling less private by the moment.

"Well?" she asked.

"'Well' yourself. I am ready to leave this place. You were the one who told me you would make a decision by today."

"It is still early in the morning." And she certainly hadn't had time to think through what Targael had told her. Then again, would the remainder of the day be enough? Or the next? "I'm surprised you aren't taking this opportunity to tell me what to do."

He considered that a while, sniffing and leaning back precariously, his hands behind his head. Speaking with him was so different from Targael; Ariden displayed no uptight formality, but he could be more infuriating in his own way.

"I voiced my misgivings about this situation before," he said. "And I am disinclined to change them now. Speaking as your protector, my best advice would be to run from this place and its godly visitations, and to never comply with their wishes."

"I expected nothing else."

"There is more. Throughout this venture there have been signs of danger, though I mistakenly ignored them at first. Prior to your vision, I was concerned with the feeling that we were being watched, or even manipulated. Think back to when you first began to plan this journey. Who did you tell? Could anyone you know have an interest in guiding our movements?"

Meli shook her head. "No one but Karis knew of my plans. If there is some force at work here, it is from no acquaintance of mine. It must come from a place beyond our reckoning."

"In that we agree. And there is your trouble. We have suspicions and doubts, but little hard information. Who knows, perhaps there is a small chance this voice in your head really is trustworthy."

She nearly chuckled at that. "Trustworthy? No. The voice spoke the truth to me, I could feel that; during our encounter it was as if we had one mind. But there were other things behind its words that remained hidden. It is difficult to explain. Remember what you told me at the bottom of the stair? That life never gives you exactly what you need? For years I needed my seedling more than anything, and now this vision has told me exactly how to get him. How could I possibly trust that?"

"Mmm."

"You know what else does not sit well with me? Naal is a goddess. A woman. In the old stories, she was a beautiful deity, kind-hearted, helping people. That voice, though—it felt neither male nor female.

And there was something about the way it commanded me." When she closed her eyes, the echoes of it rang in her head still. Louder than any noise, the words injected into every fiber of her being. She shivered. "I felt it had made its offer not for my benefit, but because my desires coincided in some way with its plans. But what those plans are, it was careful to keep in shadow."

"Why not bring this up to Targael?"

"I did. He said he has spent a century understanding the workings of Naal, and that the old stories cannot be taken literally. 'The miracle of the voice's predictions coming true is proof enough.'" She affected Targael's even cadence, which raised a smile from Ariden. "You know, I first heard those old tales when I was newly appeared, the same as everyone else. I remember I always liked Naal, over all the other gods." She frowned. "But I did not like that voice."

"Then your choice is clear: Ignore the god and continue on as planned."

"No. It is not." She wrung her hands, choosing to stare at her feet rather than look out over the landscape's vast possibilities. "I may not like the way the voice spoke, but I cannot simply dismiss its message. Not for something this important."

She heard nothing but the wind between them for a few moments until he spoke again.

"I understand."

"Well of course you—" She spun. "Wait. You do?"

He was no longer leaning back, but hunched as if deep in thought. "I had similar doubts about your ability to find the Scarred Man. And yet I concluded I had no choice but to take you at your word. When one's life is driven by a singular purpose, after a certain point no method for achieving it entails too large a risk."

Meli studied his face, searching for more hints to his thoughts, but found only the same hard expression with its faint etching of pain. *Who was this Scarred Man, and why does he rule your actions to this day?* The question would receive no answer, so she let it go unasked.

"I am not yet at that point," she said. "Not while Karis remains a hostage. Saving her is our first priority, regardless of what else happens."

"Then it is time for me to broach my reason for coming up here. I seek a modification of our terms." He paused to let the words sink in, studying their effect. "I will help rescue Karis, as I agreed. But once that is done, you will deliver on your promise to find the Scarred Man, and we will part ways. You are free then to decide whether you wish to continue to the Automatia or chase this Raendal, but I will have no role in either."

"You agreed—"

"That was then. Events have changed us. It is only fair that our deal changes as well."

She took a deep breath, letting the implications wash over her. Once the initial jarring had passed, she had to admit his words held truth. Theirs was a venture that had started badly and gotten worse, and so far neither of them had come out satisfied. Better to set themselves on a path with a clear goal, and then part cleanly. She would wait until then, with Karis by her side, to determine what to do about the voice and its demands.

Looking at Ariden now though, his square jaw set resolutely below his dark eyes, Meli still felt a pang of regret thinking of their eventual separation. Perhaps it was only her familiarity with him that she found comforting, among so many strange people. But she also wondered if there might be something better in him, a hidden core of tenderness beneath his cold shell. Or was he truly a lost cause, stuck in a hopeless cycle of violence which could end only in his death?

"What will we do with Sirdu?" she asked, as if he were some sort of pet.

"I suppose we should allow him to come along," Ariden answered, echoing her sentiment. "Come. I'm sure our robed friends will want to be let in on your decision."

He led the way down the narrow stair. Meli passed into the darkness, trailing her fingers along the spiral of cold, smooth bedrock, counting the steps past one hundred until they emerged through the rock fold onto the top layer of the web. Targael and a group of adherents stood in a circular prayer formation there, close enough that Targael could monitor their exit from the spire. He excused himself from the others as they approached.

"We're leaving," Ariden told him. "To Caeridor."

"Today?" Targael looked at Meli.

She nodded. "How long will the journey take?"

"The fastest route would be across the bay of Pemarlta. By boat, it would be—"

Ariden and Meli looked at each other, then both of them shouted at once, "No!"

"Very well," Targael said, somewhat taken aback. "You will have to travel by land, then. A journey of several hundred miles at least, over a much greater span of time."

"We'll walk fast," Ariden said. "Unless, of course, one among you knows how to build a skyship?"

Targael cleared his throat. "For an Inaali to build a mekkanikal device would be strictly—"

"Right, right." Ariden leaned in close and whispered to Meli, "Was worth a try."

"I'm afraid that none of us may accompany you, either—our place is here, in the Sanctuary. But we will record these events in our history, and pray daily for your safe return."

"A worthwhile enterprise, to be sure," Ariden said. "That's it then, eh?" He motioned to Meli to follow. "Let's find Sirdu and be off."

"Actually," Meli said, "I want to go back to the spire, first. If it's all right, I'd like to take in the view one more time."

Ariden grunted his assent and headed away. She watched him go, then nodded solemnly to Targael before he reentered the circle of devotees. Meli checked quickly to confirm Fin was not among them. She had wanted to speak to the woman in the days since her recovery, feeling that there was something left unsaid between them, but Fin had avoided her completely. That in itself only made her more curious; Meli would have liked to know what about her experience had made Fin so fearful or angry. But she could not force the strange adherent to see her, so she would have to settle for the experience as being another of life's many mysteries.

She felt a tinge of guilt as she marched up the bedrock stairs once again. The Inaali had shown her so much kindness; she could only imagine their horror if they knew what she was about to do within their own Sanctuary. When she reached the top, she wasted no time, stepping forward to run her hands over the top of the parapet. Focusing, she closed her eyes and recalled the convocation she had mentally prepared over the preceding days.

Tens of small lumps of black matter appeared in front of her, sheltered from the wind first by her hands, then by a cloth tent she convoked over them. The crucial moment of the animatism passed, and the insects became self-sustaining, beginning to move on their own. Wings sprouted from their backs and they hopped up, adjusting the length of their bodies to their preference, suiting themselves to their chosen task. Meli leaned down and smiled at them.

"Go," she said. "Go out to sea. Spread out and find Karis and Elsa. Tell them we're going to Caeridor. Caeridor, my little ones. Bring them to meet us there."

The bugs hopped and buzzed, delighted at the prospect of being themselves. She let the tent crumble and one by one they took wing, lofting easily in the wind. Some of them wouldn't listen to her instruction, and would go off and do whatever else they wished. But hopefully enough would heed her call, would multiply and spread out wide enough to find the images of Karis and Elsa she had implanted in their minds.

But whether they did or not, the task was done. She swept up her fur and headed down the stairs again. In her mind's eye, Karis's innocent face appeared over the darkness. The first step would be to reach Caeridor. Perhaps by the time they arrived, the insects would have done their work, and news of Karis's whereabouts would await. But if not, she still had the key to Ariden's obsession, and she would use it to ensure he acquired a ship. She would do whatever it took, muster all her powers, in order to rescue her friend.

And if Elsa hadn't found Karis by that time, then she would do it herself.

19

"Karis, we've got a problem here!"

Karis groaned, rolled out of her seat by the porthole, and squinted into the light coming from the hatch above. Her mind had been wandering as she sat and watched the endless seacoast of the strait slowly pass below her. Far too slowly.

"What is it *now*?"

"It's, uhm…" Cindlan brushed his gray hair out of his eyes and shrugged apologetically. "It's not me. Mylon says the controls are broken."

"Again?" She sighed and mounted the ladder up to the hatch. The wind was strong; even with the ship at a near-hover, she still had to shield her face when she emerged onto the flat top deck. She shouted through her sleeve, "What did you do?"

"Nothing. Look—" Mylon jiggled the control lever back and forth. "It won't work anymore."

"Mold." Staying crouched, Karis examined the cables leading away from Mylon's seat, to the array of mirrors and gears surrounding the huge lens pointed at the ground below. She found a gear that had come out of alignment, so she knocked it away with a hammer, then convoked a replacement.

A black object sliding by to her left drew her attention—sharp-peaked mountains dotting the cliff side to leeward, lined up like sawteeth. Most of the rest of the land in this area was flat, which Karis had reasoned would be more likely to contain the boreholes the Automatia required. But it was just one vast flatland among many, and every square mile of it needed to be swept by their comparatively small circle of light. The result had been weeks of watching and waiting, while the crew grew increasingly uneasy with each passing day, Karis not the least among them.

"Don't push it so hard," she said to Mylon on her way back to the hatch. "You're snapping it around."

"It's hard to control, all right? Why don't you try convoking something that isn't so fragile, huh?"

"Why don't you try picking your nose with an axe head?" Karis lowered herself down into the ship. "Imbecile," she muttered, just before she stepped onto Phaestal's face.

"Hey!"

"Sorry." She dropped the rest of the way to the floor. "What were you going up there for, anyway?"

"I saw the light wasn't moving," he said, rubbing his nose.

Jaela appeared from around a corner. She shot Karis an awkward glance, then turned to Phaestal and smiled. "Hey, the twins and I are going to play some Karrom, want to join?"

"He's busy," Karis said. "He's supposed to be piloting the ship."

"Fine, then," Jaela said curtly. She pushed past them, toward Paolem who lay slumped in the corner toward the rear of the ship. "Pao, you in?"

Paolem opened one eye, frowned, and turned over, pulling a hood down over his eyes. The normally sullen raider had been animated for a few days after they left the village, but his enthusiasm had quickly faded. Now he napped for most of the daylight, rarely eating, whether out of boredom or some grudge against the rest of the crew Karis didn't know, nor did she care to ask.

An itch in Karis's mind made her turn. Phaestal was still standing there, staring in his typically dumb way.

"*Yes?*"

"I guess I just wanted to ask you, before I go back to moving the ship; are you sure we're in the right place?"

"Of course I'm not sure. That's why we're searching, remember?"

"Right." Phaestal scratched the back of his head. "But so far we've been sticking pretty close to the coastline. What if the Automatia is further inland?"

Karis shook her head. "I was told I could find the academy by boat. That means there must be some kind of landmark showing its location, visible from the ocean." But was she really certain her information was correct? Her source had seemed trustworthy, but that was so long ago.

"I don't get it," Phaestal said. "Why did you and what's-her-name want to come all this way if you didn't really know where the Automatia was?"

Karis flushed. "Mind your own poxing business, and keep heading up the coast. We're going to find it soon."

"Look who thinks she's in charge," Jaela called from the Karrom table at the rear of the ship. "You really took my moldy line about pretending to be a raider seriously, didn't you?"

Karis opened her mouth, then closed it again. She could deal with the others' taunts, but Jaela had a way of shutting her mind down. "I thought of this idea, so unless you know a better way to find the Automatia—"

"Your idea's a pile of mold." Jaela stood up and came forward, hands on her hips. "And who cares if you do find the Automatia? Your friend probably won't be there; she doesn't want you slobbering all over her."

Karis's hand was slapping Jaela's face before she realized what she was doing. The larger girl yelped and stumbled back, clutching her cheek. Karis looked down at her hand in disbelief. Jaela came forward, eyes wide with fury and fists raised. Karis shrank back, arms in front of her face, bracing for the strike.

"Woah, hey," Phaestal said.

Karis looked up. Phaestal had stepped in between them and held Jaela by the wrists. She struggled for a moment, teeth clenched, then pulled away.

"You're taking *her* side?" she snapped.

"Both of you, stop it." Roi stepped out from the pilot's room.

Jaela ran up and embraced Roi, rubbing her red cheek onto his chest. "*You* have to stop listening to *her*."

"I know you're all tired," Roi said. "But now is when working together is most crucial. I remember Tiresius used to say, 'Anyone can form a crew when times are easy, but that's not when you need one.'"

"This plan is just too slow," Phaestal said. "Even staying within a mile of the shore, there's too much land to cover. If it's going to take us years to find this place, we might as well just admit the Reviled won."

"We could split up, then." Karis said. "Convoke multiple ships, use multiple lenses."

"Next idea." Roi glared at Karis. She understood what that meant—*I need the crew where I can see them.*

"There's nothing else," Karis said. "I know I'm right, I know they're down there somewhere. We can't just—"

"Hey, we see something!" Cindlan called from above them.

Their gazes shot to the hatch. Dikta and Isky jumped up from their table. Even Paolem stirred from his resting spot.

"A reflection?" Roi asked, one hand on the ladder. "You saw a light?"

"Yeah, a bunch of them! Just to leeward-south!"

Phaestal was already hurrying back to the pilot's room. Within moments, the ship began to descend, and Karis grasped a bar overheard in preparation for one of his bumpy landings. Her heart pounded as she leaned close to a porthole. The Automatia. After so long, had they finally found it?

The ship banked and dropped further, and soon the vegetation below them came into focus. Long, thin trees, driving upward to points like a bed of spikes. How were they going to land in this? As if on cue, the ship lurched, knocking several of the trunks over as it slid fifty feet across the forest.

"Phaestal!" she yelled.

A crunch and a crack, and then a thump. Karis opened her eyes. They were on the ground. Phaestal emerged from the pilot's room, looking a bit shaken.

"What were you doing?!"

"Not my fault," he said gruffly. "That thing on top messes with the aer flow."

"Never mind that," Roi called from behind. "Just move."

They filed out of the ship, Roi in the lead, with the twins trailing close behind.

"You're sure it was this way?" he called.

"Yeah," Cindlan said. "Up ahead."

Karis lingered behind the rest, taking in the surroundings. The ground was covered with low, spiny plants, forming a carpet which would have cut her feet if she hadn't been wearing boots. The trunks of the white, spindly trees filled her view in all directions.

She walked slowly, searching for a sign of anything human-made or otherwise unusual, and passed by tree trunks on either side, left, right, left. She rubbed her palm across a close one and it came back with sticky sap on her fingers. The forest was quiet, almost eerie. Deserted.

"There's nothing here," Roi said, returning from a nearby clearing. "No holes in the ground."

"I saw something," Cindlan said. The others glared at him, and he twisted his wrinkled face in indignation. "I know I did!"

They continued to search a while longer, peering behind every tree and every bedrock outcropping, before Roi signaled them to head back.

"Ridiculous," Paolem muttered. "Cindlan probably fell asleep and dreamed it all up."

"I think you have him confused with yourself," Karis said.

"This is a waste of time. Following a smoothskin into the woods!"

Karis opened her mouth to respond, looked up and stopped short. The brown and gray of the ship formed a broken outline behind the lines of trees. As she watched, the outline rose slightly, then fell again with a crash.

"Why is the ship moving?"

The others saw it too and halted. Isky and Dikta pulled swords from their belts, while forming spears in their opposite hands.

"Stay back," Dikta said. He and Isky finished their weapons in silence, and after a quick nod to ensure they were ready, the two of them pressed forward.

Karis leaned left and right, trying to get a better look at the ship. There was something beside it, pressing up against it, rocking it back and forth.

The twins disappeared into the trees, and for a few moments Karis heard only her heart thumping. Then Isky's laughter drifted through the forest. Karis exchanged a glance with Roi, then ran to investigate.

The beast next to the ship was squat and flat-footed, with a head resembling a battering ram. It was huge, twice the height of a human, and its back was covered in a heavy plate polished to a high sheen— the perfect material to reflect a bright light. It seemed unconcerned with the rest of the crew gathering around it, focused as it was on nuzzling the side of the ship, perhaps as a show of affection.

"Hey, stop it," Phaestal called.

With great cracks and thumps, more of the beasts emerged from the forest, traveling in a rough formation to windward. The herd's numbers were hidden by the trees, but from what Karis could see, the one currently in the process of tipping over the ship was approximately medium-sized.

"Get off of there, you!" Dikta convoked a ball of rock in his free hand, then chucked it at the beast. The creature barked in annoyance, but soon wandered off to rejoin the others.

"Was that a good idea?" Karis asked. "What if it had charged us?"

"At least something would have *happened*," Mylon said. The others muttered agreement.

They watched as the greater part of the herd moved past them. Swift despite their bulk, they disappeared soon enough, with one last honking bark in the distance to announce their departure. One by one, the crew stuffed their hands in their clothes or kicked the spiny plants below them. A gloom had descended; no one seemed to want to be the first to get back on that cramped, musty ship.

"Well," Roi said. "Nothing to do now but keep looking. Whose turn is it to work the lens?"

"Don't think it's going to be anyone's for a while," Phaestal answered. "Looks like the whole mount broke during the landing."

"What?" Karis pushed past him to see.

"Good. Might as well just crumble it, anyway." Paolem walked up and pointed at Roi's chest. "Enough of this. We should fly back to Bressim and rejoin the fleet. Take the fight back to the Reviled where it belongs."

"You must be joking." Roi batted his finger away. "Don't you remember what happened last time?"

"Why don't we go raiding here, then?" Mylon said. "Start with that village we went to. Hang that fool Vom up by his balls and play Karrom with his head."

"Amusing as that would be," Roi said, "it would not further our cause."

"So what would *further* us?" Paolem stomped away, waving his hands to punctuate his words. Karis had never seen him so animated. "The Automatia? It probably doesn't even exist."

"That's ridiculous," Roi said.

"What's so ridiculous about it, eh? Just because you heard some stories that could be from a hundred years ago, that means that they're all still there? Who knows what they've been doing in the meantime? Maybe they convoked themselves a plague and all dropped dead."

"They don't convoke plagues," Karis protested. "They're automatists, not anathematists."

Mylon cocked his head. "There's a difference?"

"I say we put it to a vote." Paolem turned to the crowd, holding his arms open dramatically.

"A vote?" Roi chuckled, but a trace of nervousness lay in his voice. "What is this, Ventituras?"

"Everyone who wants to fly back to Bressim, raise your hand!" Paolem's own hand shot up as he spoke.

The crew exchanged glances, weighing each other's intentions. Mylon's hand was the next to rise, followed soon by Isky's and Dikta's.

Roi grinned, nodding at Phaestal, Jaela, Cindlan, and Karis in turn. "Looks like we win."

Paolem pointed at Karis. "She's no raider. She doesn't get a vote."

"I say she does," Roi responded.

"Maybe we should vote on whether she gets a vote," Cindlan offered.

Roi rubbed his eyes and groaned. "Or how about this: All of you shut up, repair that lens and then get back to our search. That's an order."

More grumbling. Karis had never seen the raiders like this, especially Roi. They had reached a turning point; she could feel the tension coming from Roi as he lost control. And with all the effort as she had put into finding the Automatia thus far, she was finding it strangely disconcerting.

"I'm changing my vote," Jaela said.

Their gazes flew to her.

Roi's mouth fell open. "You're *what?*"

"We had a plan." Jaela pointed at Karis. "You said you wanted me to find out where she was going. But you never said you were going to *take* her there. Don't you see? She's not trying to lead us to the Automatia; she's taking us in circles, wasting our time until she can find a way to get her revenge on you."

"That's not true!" Karis yelled.

"Roi?" Cindlan said meekly. "I'm changing my vote, too."

Roi rolled his eyes. "Of course."

"I really did want to see the Automatia, I swear it," Cindlan continued, gaining confidence as Paolem came and stood beside him. "But you know, eventually the Reviled are going to figure out the fleet is at Bressim. Unless we go back, we're not gonna have any raiders left to fight with."

Roi sighed. "And what about you, Phaestal? Would you like to complete the betrayal?"

Phaestal looked at his feet and slowly shook his head.

"It doesn't matter," Paolem said. "We win the vote, so we're going to Bressim." He stalked back to the ship, making his pronouncement real by way of action. Like dust caught in a river, the others moved to follow.

Karis watched them go. So that was it, then. Back to Bressim. It wouldn't be so bad. Someone there would know how to build skyships; if she could convince them to help her somehow, she could return to this place eventually, without worrying about the raiders.

Roi stood still beside her, fuming. "Well?"

"Well what?"

"Explain why I should take you with us."

Her stomach dropped. He wouldn't. Yes, he would. Just leave her here, alone in the forest with those creatures and Ba-el knew what else around. But what could she say? She had no leverage anymore. For all she knew she wasn't even close to finding the Automatia after all. Suppose her theory of the light shafts was wrong somehow; the school could be right under her nose and she wouldn't...

"Under my nose," she whispered. "Wait!"

The crew stopped and turned.

"The mouth of the Automatia. The mouth. What's in a mouth?"

"My cock, if I'm lucky," Mylon shouted, before resuming his march.

"Teeth," Karis said. "Sawteeth. The sawtooth mountains."

The others stopped again, their faces ranging from consideration to confusion.

Paolem grew red. "Oh, come on!"

Roi held up his hand. "Just hear her out, will you?"

"Of course." Karis's hands were shaking. "It's so clear. Why would the Automatia be in some miserable, dank cave? The greatest, most advanced school in Aetheria; of course they'd be using some convocation to hide themselves."

"What convocation?" Phaestal said.

"I don't know," Karis said. "But I know it's connected to that mountain range over there. The shape was so distinct, it's right on the coastline—it all fits."

The others muttered and nodded. Paolem's expression began to sink. "Hey, what's going on? We were on our way to Bressim. We're going back there, right?"

"Are we?" Roi said. "Perhaps we should have another vote." He examined the others one by one.

"I think we should at least look into it," Phaestal said.

"What do we have to lose?" Cindlan added. "It's not far."

"And you two?" Roi crossed his arms and stared at the twins.

Isky and Dikta gave each other the same knowing glance they exchanged a hundred times a day, then both of them shrugged at once.

"That's five," Roi said.

Paolem's dismay grew further as his head swiveled through the group. "Please—sawtooth mountains—this is insane!"

"Now, now. I wouldn't want to subvert the will of democracy." Roi bounded up into the ship. "Phaestal, join me in the pilot's room. Mylon, repair any damage from the landing and inspect the ship. Isky and Dikta, help clean up the dust when Karis crumbles the lens."

Karis didn't move, still stunned by the force of her realization, as Paolem and Jaela slunk inside and the other raiders scrambled into their positions. Roi poked his head out of the doorway once more and shot her a wink and a grin.

"Come along, Karis," he said. "We don't want to be late for school, do we?"

20

The Inaali stood arm in arm in a great circle, faces raised to the sky, voices rising and falling in the final verse of their goodbye hymn.

A few more sour notes added to a long, excruciating cacophony. Ariden had met and heard of plenty of religious types in his travels—the Devout of Elaethim, various plant venerators, the mystic charlatans, worshipers of the Old Gods, even the truly fringe groups like the plague cults. For the most part, he could tolerate them—from a distance. But having to actually sit through these gods-forsaken rituals for days on end was nearly more than he could bear. He possessed a wandering soul, or so it was called, but it was more than that—just as Sirdu had claimed on the boat, he needed to *do* something, flex his muscles and effect some change. One more day here and he was liable to chop down their entire web with the Scythe, taking them all with it.

"Finally," he whispered to Sirdu, as the Inaali descended into a low hum.

"Huh?!" Sirdu started in his seat as he woke, looked around quickly and rubbed his eyes. "What?"

Ariden grunted and turned his attention back to Targael. The high priest approached Meli, touched his forehead to hers and whispered while she closed her eyes. When they separated, he walked past Ariden and gave a nod.

"What?" Ariden said. "No words of encouragement for me?"

Targael smiled without seeming pleased. "It was merely a blessing for safe travel. I would be happy to bestow it on you as well, if you wish."

"I'll pass. But tell your god I said thanks, anyway."

As a group, they made their way down a level in the web. They reached a small bedrock landing, and Targael called for them to stop. The Inaali gathered around in a circle again.

Oh please; not another prayer.

"Here we are," Targael said.

"Here we are where?"

"The exit." Targael gestured toward a section of the wall. The rock there had a slight green tint to it, but looked otherwise ordinary.

Ariden looked to Meli, then back to Targael. "This is a wall."

"We must not put our faith in material things, Ariden."

Meli strode up to the green rock and laid her hands on it. She furrowed her brow, sniffed, and tapped it with her fingers.

"I understand." She drew back a few steps, then charged forward at speed, shoulder first. In a heartbeat she was gone, lost to sight within the solid material.

Sirdu gasped. Ariden narrowed his eyes and glanced suspiciously at the circle of Inaali, who stood with their heads bowed, though Targael wore a slight grin.

"Well?" Ariden said to Sirdu.

"Please," Sirdu said, eyebrows high. "After you."

Ariden nodded. He approached the wall as Meli had. Was there any trick to what she had done? Was he about to make a fool of himself by smashing into solid rock? He tapped it once, then again, harder. Yes, there was some give there. The substance was not an illusion; it was solid to a casual touch, even a strong one. But there was some esoterica woven into it, which made it sensitive to speed. If he struck it fast enough, it parted away from him as if frightened.

He drew back and lunged forward into the wall. A moment passed where the green muck washed over him, sliding past his face and into his nose, and then he emerged into darkness and ran elbows-first into a someone's chest.

Meli yelped, staggering away from the impact. "Watch it!"

"I can't see anything," Ariden said, still dazed. "What is this material?"

"It's something special; an esoteric convocation, but a simple one. I was feeling its structure when you hit me. I think Targael meant for me to learn to duplicate it; he left this barrier up on purpose, as a parting gift."

Ariden heard sloshing behind him and moved out of the way for Sirdu to come through. A thump came from beside him as the rotund man dropped to his knees, followed by coughing and sputtering.

"All the gods great and small!" Sirdu yelped.

Ariden snorted and laid his bare hand on the wall, already returning to its prior shape. Feel its structure, Meli had said, but beneath his fingers he felt only rippling chaos. Perhaps with a clear mind and patience he could have learned to convoke it, but such delicate training had never appealed to him compared to practicing the movements of a fight.

"Finish your study quickly," he spoke into the surrounding blackness. "We should be off while the daylight is full."

"Hmph." Meli's footsteps clacked away down what sounded like a hall. "You are my protector, not my master. If you wish me to do something, you can ask politely."

"Listen here: my commands are for your own good. We're going out into the wilderness now, and there you'll find plenty of ways there to die. If you wish otherwise, then what I say goes, no questioning."

"I seem to recall I questioned you once, when you were in the midst of losing Karis."

"Again with that? I've told you before—"

"By all means, instruct me, *sir*." Her words echoed down the hall. "But unless my life is in danger, please do me the favor not speaking to me until we reach Caeridor." Her feet clacked away again. "Enjoy your walk alone."

"I'm not alone!" Ariden called. "I have Sirdu!"

He reached out to pat Sirdu on the back, swung his hand through the empty aer and nearly lost his balance. The raider must have slipped by him and gone ahead with Meli. Grumbling, shoving his hands inside his coat, he marched down the bedrock hall after them.

Ariden stepped through the thick vegetation covering the foothills below the Inaali's mountain. Up ahead, Meli had mounted the next ridge in her green tunic, supported on her walking stick, while Sirdu scrambled up beside her on all fours, grabbing chunks of loose bedrock with his bare hands. From what Ariden could see, she didn't appear pleased with the terrain, perhaps not a good sign this early in the journey. She did not stop, however, possibly because climbing the steeper slopes meant that Sirdu had to shut up for at least a little while.

The land had been much the same since they had emerged from a small, moss-covered opening in the base of the mountainside. Flaptrees, their spiraling branches covered with man-sized leaves, filled the valleys between each rocky ridge, while smaller, more wind-resistant plant life populated their tops. Footfalls in the lowlands could be treacherous, with seemingly solid swaths of moss and bush grass giving way to deep pits of slimy ooze underneath. For a long while they had convoked an elevated pathway across the gaps to speed their progress, but they had abandoned that strategy as the ridges grew steeper and further apart.

Ariden crested the ridge himself and, spotting Sirdu and Meli making their way down the other side, convoked a small whistle and blew it. When they looked up at him, he pointed to leeward-south. "That way!"

"I thought we were following the coast," Meli yelled.

"It's too rocky," Ariden replied. "We'll have further to walk, but we'll save time by not climbing over these crags."

Meli looked doubtful, but the pair of them made their way diagonally downward into the valley. Ariden understood her skepticism. Too much time on well-traveled roads had made him forget the mountainous terrain which covered the majority of Aetheria. Hopefully, what they had encountered so far would not be a portent of the rest of their trip.

By luck, they stumbled upon a valley which some recent warfare among the plant-life had left blighted, leaving only a dense carpet of packed dust under their feet, with tiny worms wriggling and burrowing within to avoid their footsteps. Soon, Ariden's long strides caught him up with the others.

"And so it was that Henrik came to Lafedine, where two sides of a city were split by a giant chasm," Sirdu intoned ahead of him. "Lafedine is long gone today, of course, but back then it was a mighty place indeed, filled with many great warriors, and always at strife, for the two sides were constantly at war. No one remembered what had started the conflict—some said t'was a blood feud, others a competition over a stolen lover, but by Henrik's time the battle had become something of a tradition; once a year at the turning of the tide, the populace convoked bridges over the chasm and set about battling until the sky grew dark.

"Now, Henrik was not the First Emperor yet, but he had great plans for Lafedine as the linchpin of his control over the Leeward Continent. And so when he arrived and observed the situation, he set to work right away to unite the city, by convoking enough rock to fill the entire inside of the chasm. At first, the city folk laughed at the absurdity of such a feat, and went to their beds filled with bemusement—but their mirth turned to anger when they woke up and saw Henrik standing atop the newly flat plain of Lafedine, smiling in his ever-friendly way.

"The citizens arranged themselves in rows, convoking armaments, for their laws stated that whenever a clear path existed between the two cities, both sides were required to do everything possible to maim and kill their enemies. 'But good ladies and fellows, I only mean to bring you together,' Henrik implored them. 'Each year your efforts are wasted in meaningless conflict. United and given direction, your city could be a force for peace and justice throughout the world.'

"But the citizens did not listen, and seeing his plans to build his empire under threat, Henrik signaled to his band of followers to blow their horns, and issued a proclamation: 'I have decided upon a course of action. I shall make my residence here, on this former chasm, and turn the space between the cities into my base of operations. All of you shall be welcome into my home, though the doors on the windward side shall only be open on odd days, and the leeward side on even days, and all guests shall be required to vacate by dawn's light, so that no citizen shall ever be forced to make merry with his or her enemy.'

"The citizens grumbled, arguing that the path between them was still open, and the leeward side complaining loudly of the windward citizens being granted first access to Henrik's party. But before you could blink, Henrik convoked a mighty set of walls to serve as the battlements of his new castle, blocking the cities from one another's view, and he explained that since the wind was an aspect of Elaethim, he could not slight the greatest of the gods by turning his back on it at the foremost. And so Henrik's gatherings commenced, and the time passed more joyously than before, for no one could throw a great feast as Henrik could, or his loyal lieutenants in the times when he traveled to further scout his future realm."

Sirdu saw Ariden coming abreast and cleared his throat. "Excuse me, Sir. Have you heard this one before?"

Ariden scowled, then shrugged. "Perhaps. It has been a long while, in any case. I suppose the First Emperor ends up solving the problem?"

"Indeed, Sir. You see, he closed the castle to rest for ten days, then announced a masquerade ball to coincide with the tide turning."

"I see. He invited both sides, and afterward revealed that they had celebrated in peace with their own worst enemies."

"You have heard it, then?"

Ariden shoved his hands in his coat and sighed. "Or some similar legend, of equally doubtful veracity."

"Oh? But the story is true. There were many who witnessed Henrik's feats of diplomacy."

Ariden looked up ahead, where Meli's feet and stick kicked up small clouds of dust around her lithe body.

"What happened to Lafedine?" he said.

"Destroyed. By the Second Emperor, so they say."

"I don't believe it. More likely they resumed fighting once the Emperor left, and slew each other until no one remained. Those prone to war do not give themselves over so easily to peace."

Sirdu frowned, and Ariden hunched his shoulders and walked on silently. Meli glared at him as he passed. He braced for a snipe, but ultimately she chose to ignore him, at least for that moment.

"We always took him for granted, I suppose," Sirdu said that evening as they prepared their cabins to sleep.

Ariden paced the perimeter of the rocky outcropping he had chosen for a campsite—it had good visibility all around, not that it did them much good at night. Would it be worth the trouble to convoke a set of walls or other battlements for protection? The day's walk had been completely free of animal sightings, monstrous or otherwise, and the really nasty specimens might be able to break through such barriers anyway.

"What was his name?" Meli asked Sirdu. "And where did he learn all his stories?"

"Gysia," Sirdu said, taking a final bite of his meal. "None of us really knew where he got them from. He used to tell tales of foreign lands where the people were odd shapes and colors, and of races of creatures which couldn't truly be called people, but couldn't rightly be called animals either. And of course, tales of monsters great and small. When I was newly appeared, I assumed he had traveled the world for hundreds of years, but later I found out he had spent his whole life in the village, just like the rest of us."

Ariden convoked a simple chair, sat back and breathed deeply. The endless repetition of the day's walk had exhausted his mind, but turning in before Meli might cause her to accuse him of shirking his duties. Above, the sky stretched out charcoal-gray, nearly uniform in its blankness except for a slight glow near the horizon.

"He sounds like an interesting man," Meli said. "What happened to him?"

"He dispersed. Didn't tell anyone beforehand. Someone went to visit him one morning and he was gone. I guess he'd told all the stories he had to tell. By the time I heard, his house had already fallen apart, and his remains were nowhere to be found. Taken off by the wind, they said."

"And he was the only source of information you had about the outside world, for what, thirty years?"

"About thirty," Sirdu said. "The little villages don't keep track of time so exactly. We did have news sometimes; travelers would come from nearby towns, bringing rumors. But it was just, you know, life. Day after day, the same thing, the same situations. And no one ever went longer than a hundred years without dispersing. It wasn't until I left and explored the world that I realized living beyond a century was even possible.

"I think it just grows too much for them, you know? Life was perfect there, but it was too perfect. People can't take it. When Gysia dispersed, it changed something for me. I decided I was going to live those adventures in the stories. Really live what was left of my life."

Meli sighed. "Well, we're both living our adventure now."

"Indeed." Sirdu convoked a small pile of rocks and began kicking them down the slope one by one. "But this walking is so slow. I'd rather be in a skyship! Going where we want, doing what we want."

"You can't just do whatever you want," Meli said, a touch of anger in her voice. "You raiders...honestly, I don't know how you live with yourselves, hurting people like that."

Sirdu frowned. "Yes, well. It's complicated, isn't it?"

"No, it's not. I would never hurt someone else on purpose. Why would you want to do that?"

"You have to understand the raider mind," Sirdu said. "It's something I've been thinking about a lot, since I met you. The raiders are outcasts, you see? There are probably as many reasons as there are people, but almost none of them have a place in regular society. Eventually, when you get enough of them together, they start thinking of everyone else as foreign. Maybe even not human. That's why they don't think twice about attacking cities just because they can."

"It still doesn't make sense to me. Even if you think us different, we weren't bothering you out there on our ship."

"I know, I know." Sirdu stared at the last rock sitting by his feet, then let it crumble to dust. "It's a powerful thing, feeling like you finally belong somewhere. And when people feel powerful…well, I can't explain more than that. I am sorry, though."

Meli stood up and stretched. "We all have regrets, don't we?" She glanced at Ariden, then retired inside her cabin.

More days and nights followed, as did the hills and valleys beneath their feet. Each path was different, yet the same, and as the time passed they retreated to inner spaces to escape the mindless trudge. Sirdu's stories petered out, and conversations became less frequent. When they happened upon the first river of their journey, Ariden was surprised to find it was the first time he had spoken that day.

"This is as good a place to cross as any," Ariden said. "If we can convoke a strong bridge. Something with an arch."

"I can do it," Sirdu said, puffing up behind him. "It would be like building the hull of a skyship."

Ariden knelt and examined the material flowing languidly between the grassy banks. It resembled the liquid of the sea, except crystal-clear, its surface broken by the occasional bubble stirring from its depths. Rivers were common enough creatures, usually encountered a few times during any extended land journey, but predicting their path or their disposition toward humans was tricky—most of them didn't seem to mind being bridged, but how to tell the good from the bad before one was halfway across?

Meli came up from behind. "I'll start convoking on the far side and meet you in the center, Sirdu. It won't take long."

"Just be careful," Ariden said. "It's aware of our presence."

"I know that. Don't treat me like a fool."

Ariden turned his back and stepped away, clamping his jaw shut to avoid another squabble. Now he remembered the other reason he had stopped speaking.

When the bridge was finished he led the way across, keeping an eye on the brook below. It burbled and whirled a bit as they passed, but otherwise took no action. Ariden had Sirdu help him attach some ropes, then they hauled the bridge across end-over-end to avoid its dust touching the liquid before going on their way.

They struck out over the steep hills again, holding onto thick tree trunks for support, until the terrain grew rocky and they were forced to convoke hand-holds and stairs to avoid slipping on the moss-covered surfaces. On one such mountain, black cylinders of bedrock jutted from the face, pointing out in odd directions, sometimes snapped off as if it were the site of some terrible battle which had scarred the land. Over the course of a day, they scaled a jagged, sheer cliff, only to find themselves staring at the base of a brush-covered mountain come nightfall.

"I thought you said we were avoiding the steep parts," Meli grumbled.

"No choice," Ariden said. "The valleys won't take us all the way to Caeridor. Eventually we have to cross these ranges, and not all of them have a pass."

"Do you think we're getting close?" Sirdu asked between breaths.

"Not even remotely. I don't recognize this terrain. More likely we're still south of the bay of Pemarlta."

Sirdu groaned.

The next day they headed down the mountain's plant-covered leeward face, bunching together in a branching gully. Toward the bottom, Meli slipped on some loose soil and dropped down several feet on her behind.

"Are you sure that the people in Caeridor will help us rescue Karis?" she asked, dusting herself off.

"If I can convince anyone to help us, it will be them. They don't call it 'The City of Fighters' for nothing."

"It's true," Sirdu said. "There are some raiders who used to fight in the arena. Tough men. None of them ever mentioned you, though."

Ariden shot him a look. "I haven't been there in nearly three hundred years, you dolt. But I was the greatest champion the city had ever seen."

"If you were so popular, why did you leave?" Meli asked snidely.

Why? That was far too long ago for him to recall, though there were small glimmers in his memory. "Let's just say that politics was never my strong suit."

"Uh huh."

Ariden headed uphill, showing her his back. "But it hardly matters. Once the people there find out who I am, we'll acquire a sponsor and get a good match, perhaps even with the champion. After I win it, the city will be at my beck and call."

"Well, I don't know about you," Sirdu said, pushing his way through branches, "but when I get to Caeridor, the first thing I'm going to do is to crumble these boots, kick back in a common house and enjoy the company of some fine women. No offense meant, my lady."

"None taken," Meli said, just before the leaves in front of her parted to reveal a tall creature.

The animal turned, balancing on its long legs like a man on stilts, orienting its long neck so they were face to face. Human face to human face—the thing had a flat, doe-eyed, but distinctly man-like visage on the end of its black and white striped body.

Meli yelped and stepped back. Ariden reached into his coat. The creature stayed still, blinked once, and hummed: a low sound, wary, not malicious. Meli composed herself, her curiosity overcoming her shock, and held out the back of her hand while Ariden and Sirdu watched in silence. The creature sniffed it twice.

"You are quite interesting," she said. "Just where did you come from?"

The thing whisked its head to the side fast enough to startle her again. It looked out above the foliage, narrowed its eyes, then bounded off, bursting through the grass with so much force that Meli lost her balance and landed a few feet down the slope.

Ariden ran up and examined the pathway of bent grass, but the creature was already long gone.

"Looks like something spooked it," he said. "We should move on."

Meli rose quickly. "You have your sword, don't you? You're keeping it ready?"

"Of course I do. Now, stop questioning me and *move it.*"

Meli's face turned sour, but her fear overcame her indignation and she hurried away. Ariden took one last look around the hill before following.

They exchanged no more words that day, even as they sat across from each other near the peak of another mountain, breaking for a meal. Ariden chewed and watched Meli as she stared blankly at a bed of wildflowers. Whatever had scared the tall creature had not followed them, or else its skill at concealment lay beyond his powers of perception. Still, the encounter stuck in his mind for another reason. No matter what he did, how seriously he took the threats around them, Meli seemed determined to condemn him at every opportunity.

He shouldn't have been bothered by it, shouldn't have given her more thought than necessary to keep her alive. But he did. Why?

After their time spent together, he sensed a certain willfulness in Meli's spirit. He couldn't quite understand yet what he saw in her, but he did find that quality attractive, even beyond the obvious charms of her looks.

No matter, though. All he wanted now was some peace, to end their constant tangles. Yes, he had been harsh to her at times. But what did she expect from him, anyway? He was an old man, who had agreed to protect her so that he could find a way to die. Was there any hope of reconciliation, then? Or would he find himself locked in this irritating cycle of jabs and snipes until fate split them apart?

They resumed their climb, and with a few careful convocations of ladders and footholds, and one giant heave, Ariden threw his body up onto the peak of the mountain. In a few breaths his body returned to full strength, and he sat up and looked out at the view the others were already seeing.

Horrifyingly endless. Mountain ridges stretching out forever, from horizon to horizon, covered in identical swaths of green and brown trees. They had come so far, but seemed to have traveled nowhere.

He looked at the others, measuring their disheartened faces, then headed down the dusty slope.

"Come on," he said. "Still plenty of daylight left."

"How about we rest a while?" Sirdu said. "One of you should tell a story or two. Change things up."

Meli shouldered past him and stepped down into Ariden's footprints. "The sooner we go, the sooner we get there."

Sirdu stood on his toes and shouted, "Ariden! How about a quick game of Karrom?"

"Eat infected boils, Sirdu."

Sirdu made a grumbling noise. "I don't have to take these insults, you know! I have half a mind to set off on my own."

He stood there a while longer, until a sound came over the wind, a high whistle like a distant animal's wail. They all stood still, waiting until the sound faded, then disappeared.

"Hey!" Sirdu yelled, hurrying down the slope. "Slow down, would you?"

21

Karis was walking up to the sawtooth peak when Mylon's excited call came from above.

"There's another one up here! That's three!"

Below, the raider ship floated, anchored to the mountainside where it became too steep for trees to grow. Below that and beyond, the land stretched out in dizzying fashion to the gray horizon, where a distant dust storm threw yellow streaks over the next ridge of mountains. Dismissing her caution, Karis hurried up the switchbacks of the convoked stairway, taking the steps two at a time to catch up with the others.

At the top of the peak, Mylon stood beside Phaestal, who was kneeling to examine a knee-high statue of the goddess Alysiema.

Karis doubled over for a moment to catch her breath, then asked, "Is there anything different about it?"

"No," Phaestal said. "It's just like the others. What does it mean?"

"I don't know." Karis examined the statue, resting her weight on one of the many arms splayed upward around its head. The female face seemed to look up at her, its irises flat metallic disks on white spheres embedded in its sockets. It was smirking. "Maybe it's some sort of map?"

"A strange map." Roi was standing off to one side, admiring the view of the fog-covered strait. "Three peaks, three identical statues. What could they be telling us?"

"Maybe the fourth peak has the answer."

"Maybe the fourth peak has a pile of mold in the shape of Elaethim." Paolem trudged over the top of the steps, sweat beading on his bald scalp. His skin was as pale as the fog. "This is ridiculous. Trudging up and down these peaks three times, for what? Because someone put some statues here?"

"This isn't just any statue," Roi said peevishly. "Alysiema is the Automatia's patron deity."

"Yeah well, how come they put it in the middle of nowhere?" Paolem gestured to the expansive landscape.

"Why did you come up here, anyway?" Karis asked. "Just stay in the ship next time."

Paolem pointed at Roi. "He said I had to!"

Roi made a brushing motion. "And now you have to go back. Help prepare the ship for takeoff."

"But I just got here!"

"You're late. We're going to the fourth peak. Might as well see this pile of mold for ourselves, eh?"

Paolem stomped away, muttering. Karis took one more look at the statue before she followed him. It was baffling, no doubt, and yet just seeing it made a familiar thrill rise in her chest. That feeling of being close to discovery. It was the same as learning a new convocation, finding clues, working through the problems until suddenly daylight bloomed. She had devoted her second life to the pursuit of that feeling. In a way, it had been her first love.

She took her seat inside the ship, waiting for the flight to the fourth peak. The memory of the first time she had felt this way came to mind. Over three hundred years ago, but still fresh as a windswept glade in her recollection. That was a smoothskin trait—most people forgot the details of their past after fifty or a hundred years, but for better or worse she could still picture the faces of the other members of Sylas's commune on the road out of Caelindra.

They had walked together, carrying nothing but the ragged clothes they wore, for Sylas preferred to convoke a new stage and props at each stop. And they made many stops, because according to Sylas, the people of Caelindra had turned away from the righteous path, and badly needed to be brought the word of Ba-eal.

Translated, that meant that the cult had been expelled from the big cities as the residents finally began to clean up the aftermath of the Third Empire's fall. Someone, or more likely several someones, had made threats which Sylas's meager army of fifteen or so non-smoothskin devotees could not defend him against. Karis hadn't known all this at the time, but she had sensed a change in the way the commune was behaving. It came from Sylas—he was moodier now, more prone to sudden rages and long bouts of depression. That attitude filtered down to his lieutenants through his increasingly harsh orders, and then on to the smoothskins, whom the lieutenants used as convenient targets for letting out aggression.

Leeward and leeward-south of Caelindra, the land was covered in deep layers of yellow-red dust, with only small, spiny plant life pushing up in tight bunches. The people there matched the land: rugged, independent free thinkers, less likely than the city folk to cast out a stranger, but also less likely to convert to followers of Ba-ael. The commune and their troupe of smoothskin performers moved from settlement to settlement with little to show for their efforts, until one day they came upon a particular semicircle of domes and spired castles spread around the flat, packed dust of the roadway.

It was their custom to make camp in the open in the center of a town, but this town's center was occupied by a large white communal dome, with two residents standing by the doorway who were not keen on letting them inside. Instead, the troupe gathered around in front, the smoothskins lounging in groups of two or three while the adults knelt and prayed, until a group of local officials arrived for a "talk." Karis was not privy to their words, but they seemed to be engaged in some sort of negotiation, which Sylas demanded be moved to a private location away from the troupe. He tapped some of his top lieutenants—including Vikter—and headed off with them, leaving the rest of the commune to fend for themselves.

A strange tingle passed over Karis the moment they passed out of sight. Did the others feel it as well? It was one of the very few times she could ever remember not being directly under Sylas's or Vikter's eyes. She wandered the camp for a while, but no one else seemed to be reacting as she was, so she settled down to listen in on her friends Maezlim and Della.

"I hope we get some good dizz tonight. Maybe if the locals turn out for the show." Maezlim was tall, and his voice was almost as low as a normal man's—only his thin frame and delicate features made him a smoothskin. "I know Sylas has been snorting a ton of it every night. It's not fair."

"I just want some food." Della had her back turned, and was messing with something in the dust. Karis peered closer and saw a black shape squirming. "This is all slime, this place. It's dirty, too."

"You're dirty," Maezlim said.

Della turned and stuck out her tongue at him, then grinned. Her upper lip seemed to be caught in a perpetual sneer, so that even her smiles came out crooked. "Hey, Karis, you performing in the show tonight?"

"They haven't told me." A sour feeling pulsed in the back of Karis's mind.

"Probably she won't," Maezlim said. "Lucky. It's because you're Sylas's favorite."

"I am not."

"I heard he was going to partner you off with Vikter, come the wet season."

Karis drew back. "You *did?*"

"Karis, look." Della held up the black object she had been poking—a large beetle, missing one wing and one leg, wriggling in pain.

"Ugh." Karis turned her head. "Stop that. Get it away from me."

A local woman walked by and shot a disapproving look at the three dust-caked smoothskins squatting in the square. Maezlim noticed her and spat.

"Dumb mucklicker. Hey you, I'll bite your tits off!"

"Sylas wouldn't like you saying that," Karis cautioned.

"So what?" Maezlim sat back and crossed his arms. "No one around here is going to see the truth of Ba-eal anyway."

"I wish I could find a felid around here," Della said, tossing the dead bug into the dust. "I once took apart a felid in Ordsneck. It screamed *so* loud."

"Stop it, I said! Don't talk about that."

"What's your *proooblem?*" Della said, drawing out the last word into the empty space below her sneer.

"Vikter not giving her enough dick, I'm guessing." Maezlim said. They both chuckled.

Karis stood, her fists shaking, and stomped away from the group, their talk and laughter fading behind her.

She wiped her eyes, stinging them with dust, and turned down an alley, avoiding the gazes of onlookers. Her and Vikter, joined in holy union? No, it had to be a lie. They were just teasing her, like they always did. By showing a reaction, she had ensured they would prod her on the subject forever.

These are my friends. She didn't understand exactly what that was supposed to mean, though. Who else could be her friend? Sylas told them often how those who hadn't turned to Ba-ael couldn't be trusted. But something just wasn't sitting right with her lately.

As she left the center of town the houses grew further apart and larger, some set up on stilts or shaped like pyramids. The structures people could build when they stayed in one place for years at a time amazed her, though she knew Sylas would disapprove of such sentiments. She continued to wander the back-streets, head down, not paying attention to where she was going, until she stepped into a front yard where a woman sat, tending a small tree adorned with hanging reflective panels.

"Hello," the woman said. "Are you new here?"

"I…" Just like that, it was happening. She was actually speaking to an outsider. It took a moment for the shock to wear off and words to form. "I'm here with the Commune of Ba-eal. We're going to put on a play in his honor this evening. Will you come see us?"

The woman looked slightly downcast. She glanced briefly at the door of her home. "I'm not sure. I'll ask my partner if he's interested. My name is Yan. What's yours?"

"Karis."

"Would you like to help me with my project? It's going to be beautiful once it's finished."

Karis cocked her head. A project? The woman was sitting and building…something. But for what? "Help you how?"

"You can convoke some chimes for me. They'll crumble when you leave, of course, but we can make some lovely music together in the meantime."

"I can't." Karis shuffled her feet in the dust. "I don't know how."

"You don't know how to convoke a chime?" Yan asked. "A flat square? How old are you?"

"Thirty-eight."

Yan pursed her lips and nodded. Her gaze fell over the scraps of cloth that passed for Karis's clothing. "Someone made these for you?"

"Yes. Sylas says that we must be clothed in the presence of outsiders."

"I see. Well, Karis, if you'd like to learn some basic convocations, I'd be happy to teach you."

Karis gulped. This had gone way over the line. If Sylas found out about this talk, he would have Vikter administer an appropriate punishment. But there was something about Yan's smile, the way it put a crease beside her kind eyes, that made her feel even stranger than she had before on this strange day. And there was a part of her that liked this new feeling, that wanted more of it.

"I have to go back now," Karis said. "Sylas may return soon."

"All right."

"But I'll see you again. Tomorrow, maybe." Karis turned and jogged away, not waiting for a response, the image of Yan's understanding smile still in her mind.

It remained there, just as fresh in the present day, as the raider crew tossed ropes at their dock below the fourth peak. Karis sighed. No more time for remembrance; everyone was busy again, convoking another stairway, making wagers on what they would find. The wind was stronger now, and the raiders placed two railings up each side of their steps. The cold of them burned on Karis's palms as she headed up to the peak.

She crested the last rock wall and found Roi and Phaestal standing silently over a small statue in the same pose as the others, facing—as always—northward away from the strait. Karis sighed, not trying to hide her disappointment, then knelt and began a perfunctory examination.

"Any ideas, Phaestal?" Roi asked, leaning against a rock he had convoked near the edge.

"Maybe it's not what we think," Phaestal said. "Someone could have put these here as a joke. Or to throw us off the trail of the real Automatia."

"That's ridiculous," Karis said. "There's someone nearby holding this convocation together, or they'd crumble in an instant."

"Not if they'd hardened," Phaestal said. "Or maybe whoever made them has some kind of secret method for convoking at a distance."

"No. They're around here somewhere. These statues are clues. It's a puzzle."

"Then you had better find a way to solve it," Roi said. "I left the others down in the ship this time—I don't want talk spreading around the crew that we don't have a clue how to proceed." He stared hard at Karis. "I'll tell them now that you're working on it. But you had better come up with something soon, if you want to see your friend again."

He motioned to Phaestal, and the two of them headed back down. Karis huffed and sat back on her haunches. Eventually they began to ache, and she dropped down on her behind. A puzzle? No, it was more like a cruel joke. She turned around and leaned back on the statue, too frustrated to bother convoking a chair, and closed her eyes. Yan's words came back to her, the ones from all those years ago.

"Don't give up, Karis. Relax your mind and feel the aether."

It was her third time sneaking away from the group. And the second time when Sylas and Vikter were supposed to have been watching. She had always assumed they would notice her leaving, had never realized before how easy it was to slip away. But she still knew the danger she faced, felt it tugging at her insides along with the self-loathing and doubt over her betrayal.

She gave Yan a half-hearted smile and closed her eyes to concentrate, trying to feel the shape of the rectangular chime in the breeze.

"Good," Yan said. "You're doing it. Keep focusing on the innermost structure. The tightness of the material. You have to think of both dimensions at once, the inner and outer spaces. Hold it up in the breeze…the aer flowing over it will help, as long as it's not blowing too strong.

Karis opened her eyes and beheld her creation: a lopsided, pale gray square. Beautiful, to her anyway. She smiled. "I don't think it will make good music."

Yan laughed. "That will come in time. You'll be able to convoke material that folds and bends, or snaps in two when struck. Heavy and light objects, different colors…it will just take practice. And some guidance. Here, I'll show you something else. Something fun." She convoked a small table, followed by a spintop sitting on a thin dish, both pale gray.

"I've seen tops before," Karis said.

"Just watch." Yan closed her eyes, lost in concentration, then picked up the top and set it in mid-aer over the dish. It floated and bobbed, then began to spin, picking up speed until its motion gave off a whirring noise.

"By the love of Ba-eal," Karis said with wonder, forgetting that she was taking the God's name in vain. "How do you do it?"

"The aether has hidden powers which can be unlocked with the right convocation," Yan said. "There are many of them to be learned. This one is called levitism. It's said the ancients used to raise entire cities this way."

Karis stared, rapt, as the top continued gaining speed with its spin. There was something incredible in that simple object, a feeling that there was so much more to the world than what she had already seen, and a long while passed while she reveled in it.

Too long. She checked the color of the sky and frowned. She would have to get back to Sylas, soon.

"I wanted to say thank you," she said. "For helping me. I won't be able to come back; my commune is leaving today."

Yan got the look in her eyes Karis had seen before, tinged with hidden sadness. Perhaps not so hidden, this time. "I wanted to ask you about that. Why don't you stay with us for a while when they leave?"

Karis shook her head vigorously. "That cannot happen. They are my commune. I'm not even supposed to be here with you now."

"But you seem to be enjoying yourself. Why let them control you?"

"Ba-ael is above all. Below him is man, then woman." She had heard the words so many times they came easily. "Then smoothskins, then..."

"Oh, Karis." Yan shook her head. "You must leave them."

Karis began to sweat. Her feet mashed the ground, as if they wanted to pull her back to the campsite. "You don't understand. You don't—"

Yan knelt and took her hands. They stared into each other's eyes. "Karis. Karis, listen to me. I need you to calm down. I want to show you something."

She opened Karis's palm and blew a gentle breath onto it. A hard, thin piece of solid aether formed there, a hexagonal shaft with a sharp point on one end.

"Your dignity is yours," Yan said. "Whether you're a woman or a smoothskin or both does not matter. You always have another option." She took the stiletto and held it up between Karis's eyes. "If you put this under a sleeping man's chin and shove it upward as hard as you can, he won't bother you anymore. Do you understand?"

Karis raised her hand to touch the thing. Its tip pricked her finger, and it was as if the pain jolted her from a dream. Her arm jerked and she slapped it away. "No! I love my commune! Don't say those things."

She turned and walked away, her body shaking.

"Karis, wait!"

She looked back.

"I'm sorry. Please don't go like this. Let's say goodbye on a good note."

Karis sniffed and shuffled forward. The memory was still fresh, though clouded with tears. Yan was smiling again, her arms open, and they had embraced for the first and last time. Karis held on to that image of Yan's face. She preferred to remember her that way, not to think about what had happened next.

Karis picked her head up and blinked; she had fallen half-asleep on top of the mountain. Glumly, she convoked some sand and drew patterns on the ground with the toe of her boot. To have come so far, only to get stuck like this—what a disappointment. Even the statue looked sad, its eyes cast down toward the ground.

Hold on. The eyes were looking...*down*?

Karis swiveled and checked again. The statue had the same flat metallic irises as the statues on the other peaks. But hadn't the eyes of the last statue pointed up? She pressed inside the sockets with her fingers, trying to move the eyeball. Nothing—it was firmly fixed in place. But now her mind was racing, her heart pumping with excitement. She peered closely at the hairs-width gap between eyeball and face. What was inside there? Was the entire thing hollow?

An idea occurred to her and she shifted her focus to her hand, convoking a simple wand with a hard gray tip infused with the esoteric convocation. It had been a while since she had practiced levitism, and though suspending an object in the aer could be tricky, imbuing the wand's tip with the basic property of exerting force over a distance was simple enough. Holding her breath, she held the tip of the wand on the statue's forehead and traced it in a circle.

With a click, the eyes slid up and to the right.

The wand turned to dust in Karis's hands. She jumped up, wiped herself off, and ran as fast she dared down the stairs to the ship.

"It's interesting, all right," Roi said. "But I still don't see the use of it."

Behind him the entire crew stood assembled. Skeptical though many of them were, the sight of her bursting into the ship, practically apoplectic with excitement, had roused them to climb the mountain again.

"It's a lock." Karis rotated the eyes in a circle for them to see. "There are ten different positions, and the eyes of each statue have to be looking in the right directions for it to open."

"How can you be sure?"

"I'm sure. The locking mechanism would have to rely on automatism. Inside the statue is a convocation which senses the way the eyes are pointed. If the lock is solved, then it triggers something to open a door."

"What door?" Paolem yelled. He was shivering, and had convoked a heavy blanket he was sharing with Jaela.

"What does it matter?" Karis asked. "It could be in the ground somewhere. Or perhaps the Automatia is in the sky, and the statues trigger a ship or a ladder or something."

"That'd be some ladder," Phaestal said.

Roi looked out to windward, where the black bedrock of the next peak was visible a half-mile distant. "You say there's a door. Earlier, you spoke of a key."

"Pfel, Ord, Estinpar, Sailach," Karis recited.

"So how do the two fit together?"

"I don't know," Karis said. "There must be some connection. The names of gods...eyes...gods' eyes?"

Roi shook his head and turned to Phaestal. "And you're sure you can tell nothing from the inside?"

"Nuh-uh. See for yourself." Phaestal pointed to the hole he had chiseled in the back of the statue's head. "It's the strangest thing; the convocation they're using is scrambled somehow. I've never seen anything like it; it's like they have some kind of coded layer over it, so no one can see how it works."

"Then we're stuck," Roi said. "We have a lock we can't decipher, and a key that won't fit."

"There's another way," Karis said. "We'll try every possible combination of positions until we find one that works."

Roi rubbed his chin and grinned. "Ah. Yes."

The crew muttered and grumbled to each other.

"No," Mylon said. "No way."

"What?" Roi said.

"You're about to tell us we need to stand on these peaks for the next decade, spinning those eyes around until the door to the Automatia opens."

"Not us," Karis said. "Phaestal is going to build a machine to do it."

"Me?"

"You know a bit about automatism, don't you? Enough to make four machines that spin at the correct rates?"

Phaestal scratched his chin. "I might be able to. If Roi helps me. Coordinating the spinners would be a lot like controlling the engines on the ship."

"How long is building this machine going to take?" Paolem moaned.

"As long as it takes," Roi said. "Now get to work. We'll need a bridge between the peaks, so we can walk. There's no way we'll ever get this done if we have to take the ship."

In the end, it took them well over a day. Convoking the bridge and its attendant handrails, trusses, and so on was a concerted effort in itself, given the height and the wind. The internals of the automatist mechanism should have been the easier task, but nevertheless prompted many arguments between Phaestal and Roi, while the rest of the crew looked on and offered unhelpful advice. Karis could only sit and stew, wishing she knew more about automatism, as the morning wore into evening again and each "last" fix ended up creating more problems.

Finally, the mekkanism was switched on. It was an impressive device, four man-sized boxes connected by hoses and populated by whirring gears and accelerant, with four knee-high levitist manipulators pointing out to each statue's face. Karis watched the closest one at the windward peak, set to revolve its levitist wand the fastest. Even so, it clicked along unhurriedly, both to ensure the actuator did not slip, and to give the raiders time to notice any change around them when the correct combination was found.

Phaestal collapsed back into his padded seat, breathing a sigh of relief. Karis stayed still, not daring to take her eyes off the statue. The device clicked on. The light in the sky was beginning to fade. Could this really be it? She longed to see the Automatia at last, and be among people other than the raiders. And what about Meli? Could she really be there as well, safe and happy? Would either of them really be safe as long as Roi was around?

Beginnings and endings…

She remembered the road. Dust clogged and miserable. Miserable because the commune had left the town after the three days that Sylas had agreed upon. Three days, three shows, no new converts, and Sylas in a particularly black mood. And miserable for Karis, because she was leaving Yan. Again and again the kind woman's words echoed inside Karis's mind, sending her stomach into knots. She felt empty, confused, alone.

There was a noise ahead and the smoothskin troupe around her halted. Six figures emerged from behind a hillock—no, not a real hillock, just something convoked to look like a pile of dust. The figure in front wore a white tunic with a two-handed sword strapped to his waist. The others were men and women and—

Karis's heart jumped. Yan was among them.

"How is this?" Sylas asked in his gravelly baritone from the front of the procession. "Have you all come to hear the teachings of Baael?"

"No," the strange man in front said. "We don't plan to keep you from your travels. But we do ask that you leave something behind."

Sylas nodded and said calmly, "I see."

Karis shuddered. She had learned not to trust that tone.

"The trouble is, we have nothing, good sir." Sylas motioned at his flock, clad in their filthy rags. "Only our faith."

"We want the smoothskin," the man said. "Leave her here with us, then go on your way." He looked back toward Yan. "Which one was it?"

Karis gasped and folded into the crowd, ducking her face. The other smoothskins bunched together, fearing they would be taken.

Just go away, please. Don't tell them I spoke to you. Don't say my name.

"I don't see her," Yan called. "Her name was Karis."

No! No no no nonononono.

"Ah," Sylas said. "Karis. Yes."

Just go. Please, run. They'll punish me but you have to run.

"I'm afraid I cannot help you," Sylas continued. "You see, all these smoothskins are a part of my commune. I depend on them as I depend on my left hand."

From her hiding place among the others, Karis saw the lead townsperson motion to the others. He drew his sword and came forward. He had made it three steps when Vikter stepped in front of him.

"Stand aside." The man pushed forward with the sword, thrusting the point through Vikter's chest. Vikter stood still as bedrock, his body too full of dizz to feel any pain. The man's face shifted to incomprehension, then horror, as Vikter slapped the sword away with one hand and struck with the other, sending the man reeling to the ground.

The other townspeople spread out, drawing weapons of their own. Sylas held his hands wide, his face to the sky, mumbling prayers. The troupe was shouting now, panicking, pressing in around Karis. All around came a great rumble, the dust shaking at their feet. Karis should have shut her eyes. She didn't want to see what happened next. Why didn't she close them?

A puddle of liquid seeped from the ground beneath the fallen man, sizzling wherever it touched. He screamed and tried to jump away, but his clothes and boots were already melting, his hair and scalp coming apart. As he struggled, he splashed more of the ooze onto his companions. The others ran, but by then everywhere they stepped was mud, bubbling and smoking, leaving skin sloughing from flesh. Sylas began to laugh and Karis doubled over, holding her mouth and nose against the smell.

Vikter and the other lieutenants did the rest, swinging fists and swords until any interlopers who had escaped the melting field lay prone or crumbled around them.

Sylas dropped his hands and surveyed the writhing garden of casualties. He pointed at Vikter and yelled, "Stop!"

Vikter looked up. His hands were bloody, the knuckles covered in ochre from the face he was punching.

Yan's face.

"Take the living ones and hang them up on bedrock." Sylas's words were claws raking her ears. "Cut off their left hands and impale the wrists, so that they heal over the rock." He spun, and for a moment he caught Karis's eye before he spoke again.

The two of them held each other's gaze for what seemed like an eternity, Karis alone among the crowd.

"Let them remain here forever, as a warning to those who seek to crumble the sacred union of Ba-eal."

As much as Karis remembered about her past, she could never remember what she saw next.

A series of ringing crashes woke Karis to attention. Phaestal, back in his "Azorkan" costume again, noticed it as well and jumped up.

"What's wrong with it now?" he yelled.

The statue had stopped clacking. Phaestal opened up the mekkanism and Karis peered over his shoulder. Gears lay inside, mangled and bent, covered in dust. Phaestal cursed and headed across the bridge to check the remaining boxes.

Soon they confirmed that the crash had traveled through the boxes like falling dominoes, wrecking all the others as well. Even the normally serene Phaestal looked distraught.

"Rebuild it," Roi said.

Phaestal sighed, but sat down and began to convoke. Karis watched with a frown, the long day and the painful memories having soured her mood.

"Just how long is this going to take?" Paolem moaned. "You'll never finish this before dark. I'm going back to the ship."

"You'll stay here," Roi growled.

"He's right," Mylon said. "This thing is trashed. You think you can just convoke a few parts and it'll be done?"

"Well you haven't been much of a help, have you?" Phaestal put in.

Karis closed her eyes and convoked stoppers for her ears to keep out their bickering. This was just a setback. A minor one, in the grand scheme of things, but a blow to the crew's sagging confidence.

And what of her own confidence? She couldn't deny something about this didn't feel right. What would Meli have done, if she had found this place? Karis had told her everything she knew about the mouth and the key, and if anyone in Aetheria was smart enough to open the door, Meli could have done it. But Meli also didn't know anything about automatism. If she had found the statues and unlocked them, it wasn't using a device similar to theirs.

Pfel, Ord, Estinpar, Sailach. Just nonsense, a list of gods long vanished from the world. Well, not quite vanished. One or more of them still convoked new humans out in the wilderness, though exactly which ones did so depended upon who one asked. She wondered sometimes whether the old gods were really the same ones still creating people today, or if those beings had died, remaining only in legends, and in the prayers of the cults.

Of course, to some who were charlatans, the gods were just names, a way to convince others to give them power. Just like how the First Emperor had used them to...

She opened her eyes. No, it couldn't be that simple. Could it?

"...and I'm tired of him and his belching all the time!" Mylon waved his finger angrily at Cindlan.

"Stop!" Karis shouted, jumping to her feet. "I understand now. It's days. Don't you see? Ten days of the week. Ten positions of the eyes!"

The others blinked in confusion, as if she were losing her mind. But this was the answer, she could feel it. The key was just numbers, the names an easy way to remember them. Karis pushed the others away and knelt in front of Alysiema's face. A vertical mark lay on the upper eyelid, representing her make-up. Or so Karis had thought. She grabbed the manipulator wand.

"Pfel," she said. "Pfelsday. The fourth day of the week." She clicked the eyes up to notch at the top, then four to the right. "Then comes Ordsday. Three."

She jumped up and ran down the bridge to the next peak, heedless of the others. Her skin prickled and her breath wheezed loudly in her ears as she covered the distance faster than she would have thought possible. By the time the crew arrived, she had already clicked the eyes into the third position.

"Estinsday, eight." Another run.

She swallowed and waited at the last statue for the raiders to gather around, her hand shaking so hard she could hardly hold the wand. "Sailsday, six." *Click, click, click.*

She stepped back. Nothing. No sound or motion. So she had been wrong again. Or perhaps she had been counting the wrong way, or had set the dials in reverse order?

"Look!" someone shouted.

Karis turned slowly, as if in a dream. The others pointed and whispered. Something was happening out in the strait, above the fog. The aer was moving, shimmering. A crack appeared in space, then another, as if reality itself were breaking open. Then the aer shifted again, and became slightly opaque. A shining, transparent canopy stood in the center of the fog, visible now that its light-bending convocation had been disabled. The canopy was unimaginably huge, surrounding a building set on a piled platform amidst the waves.

Karis ran to the bridge and gripped the handrail, not knowing whether to laugh or cry. The Automatia, automatist academy on the Kalsten strait. Not on the strait. *In* the strait. It had been there the whole time, right in front of them. Right under their noses.

"Sweet gods," Mylon said beside her. The Automatia building was a set of stacked cubes, slightly offset, each one many-layered with holes cut through them at regular intervals.

"I found it," Roi said. "You laughed at me, Hindal, called me a fool. But look at me now."

They all stood and stared, taking in the majesty of it.

"Hey," Cindlan said. "What's that?"

"What's what?" Karis said.

"Those little dots. They're coming out of the canopy."

Karis squinted. Tens of specks were flying in a loose formation directly toward them. Each one was no more than a few feet wide, and they drifted side to side as they flew, similar to the way Elsa did on her propellers. As they came closer, spinning circular blades appeared on their sides.

"They're sentries," Karis said. "Automaton flying guards."

"What are they doing?" Cindlan asked.

Roi narrowed his eyes and puffed out a breath.

"They're coming to kill us."

22

By the time Karis pulled her eyes away from the approaching automatons, the crew had already broken ranks and were scrambling back to the ship.

"Stop!" she yelled. "Don't run!"

No one listened, so she convoked a heavy bar across the narrow stair. Paolem, leading the charge, ran into it stomach-first. The others stared back at her in horror.

"Karis..." Roi murmured beside her.

"If you run to the ship, they'll think you came to fight. Stay still and act like a friend."

"She's insane."

"Or suicidal."

Paolem ducked under the bar. The others continued to argue, save for Phaestal, who looked Karis in the eye as he came back up the stairway.

"Are you sure?"

Karis nodded. At Roi's urging, one by one the other raiders joined her next to the statue. The sentries were close now, at least thirty of them, blades shining, moving at a speed which would give any swordsman pause. Despite her assurances, Karis gripped the bridge side rail and gulped. Of course she wasn't *sure* the sentries weren't hostile—only that it didn't make sense for the Automatia to kill any potential visitors on sight. But she felt exposed up on the bridge, and the drop off the side of the mountain made her dizzy to contemplate. What would she do if she was wrong?

Die, most certainly.

The sentries changed formation, spreading out laterally to surround the raiders, then hovered, propellers whirring, the angles of their bodies pitching up and back in response to the rising and falling wind. They were observing, looking for weapons or other signs of hostility, just as she had said. Either that, or arguing silently among themselves as to the best way to kill everyone.

One of the sentries, a gray oval except for the silver blades on its spine and sides, floated down below the others.

"INTEND WHAT."

The intonation was flat, and slightly menacing. No one moved or spoke.

"SPEAK INTEND WHAT."

Roi cleared his throat. "We came to enter the Automatia."

"AUTOMATIA INTEND WHAT."

"To learn. To find the secrets of the aether."

The sentry rose a bit, then dipped as if it wanted one last look at them.

"PROCEED ALL IN TO MAKE WELL."

The crew looked at each other, no one wanting to be the first to move. The sentries remained in formation.

"I think it's telling us we can go in," Karis said.

"Uh, excuse me?" Roi said. "Would you mind if we took our ship?"

"SHIP."

"Yes. It's docked just below us, you see. It would be the fastest way across the strait—"

"PROCEED ALL IN TO MAKE WELL."

"Right." Roi motioned them all down the stairs. "Go on, but not too fast."

They boarded the ship and flew between the peaks toward the blocky structure in the center of the strait, with engines as idle as possible while still remaining aloft. The sentries continued to circle around, overhead and below them.

"Fantastic, aren't they?" Roi mused, standing beside a porthole. "What do you think the others would say if I brought a thousand of these back to Bressim?"

"Assuming they'll be willing to teach you how to make one," Karis said.

"That reminds me. All of you, remember your characters! Make one last check of your clothes. This is it, people; don't drop your cover for a moment. And that includes you, Karis."

"What?"

"You heard me. Even if your friend isn't there, things will not go well for you if we're exposed. So if you'd like to stay at the Automatia, keep your mouth shut and defer any questions to me. That goes for the rest of you as well. The fewer people talking, the fewer stories we need to get straight."

"They're guiding us in," Mylon said from the pilot's room. "There's a landing pad there, down by the fog."

Roi straightened his coat and his freshly-convoked feather hat. "Smile, everyone. Let's make a good impression on our hosts."

He headed off to help Mylon and Phaestal land the ship—carefully—on the rectangular pad sticking out from the bottom of the main structure. Karis's heart skipped a beat when the ship *thunked* down—this was it. It was real, now. The door opened and she stepped out onto a grate, the fog of the strait swirling just below her feet. A door crumbled in the wall before them, the dust falling through the floor, but the interior was hidden by the glare outside. Holding her breath, Karis walked through.

They entered a storage bay, filled with small aircraft in various states of completion. The grated floor continued inside the building, where the walls were silver and polished to a high gloss, inlaid with a pattern of lines which formed an intricate relief pattern, zigzagging around the perimeter of the room and coming together in paths leading to the exits. In front of one of those exits, two women and a man stood shoulder to shoulder, all wearing the bright green robes of the automatists. A dozen or so others stood around the perimeter in less formal groups: curious apprentices, she guessed. But Meli was not among them. Karis bit her lip. In all the rush and excitement, she hadn't thought about what it would mean if her friend had never arrived. But no, she shouldn't give up hope, there would be plenty more people inside.

The man, sporting a balding pate of gray hair and intermediate in height to the women he stood between, said, "Welcome to the Automatia. My name is Bergan."

He opened his mouth to continue but the tall woman to his left cut him off. "That is, you are welcome only if you are true of heart and pure of mind." She might have resembled Meli with her tall stature, touch-of-brown skin and long black hair, had it not been for her pointed features: a sharp nose, slanted eyebrows, eyes untrusting slits. "Otherwise, you should plan to leave as soon as possible."

Roi shifted his gaze back and forth between the two of them, then smiled and raised his hands. "I assure you we are quite pure in mind and intention. My name is Roizilan, Holy Prince of Azorkas, and this is my retinue."

The roomful of automatists buzzed. Karis felt herself flush. The lie seemed far too obvious now that she was actually here, standing before these people. She braced herself to be escorted out.

Roi continued, "Though much of my commune in Azorkas is kept busy with their rule, I have chosen to spend my life in pursuit of knowledge. And so when I had learned all I could in my home country, I decided to undertake the long and difficult mission to join the famed automatist school of legend."

"We've been watching you," the tall woman said. She was watching them still, scanning the row of raiders-cum-actors as she spoke. "Your method for opening the gate showed some ingenuity."

"Thank you, Miss...?"

"I am Corrindal, and this is Yilia." She motioned to the shorter woman. "And despite your demonstration of skill, I feel compelled to say that the normal procedure for admittance is to be sponsored by an honored member."

Yilia cleared her throat. Her face was plainer than that of her companion, spotted red with her hair pulled back in a tail. "Technically speaking, those who open the gate are eligible to become students, regardless of whether they have a sponsor or not."

"*Eligible* being the key word."

Karis shifted her weight from side to side. In the back of her mind she had always counted on Meli being here to vouch for her. Had she been a fool? They had been a long way from the strait when they last saw each other. She had Ariden to navigate, but he had already gotten lost once...

"If I may," Roi said. "I understand your doubts. We are strangers from a faraway land, and the world is a dangerous place. But we had no way to meet any of your honored former students in Azorkas."

"The world is indeed dangerous," Corrindal said. "Why, just recently we received word of a major raider battle near Mariten; one band apparently suffered heavy losses, scattering them along the coast." She stared at Roi, her eyebrow raised just a hair.

"Disgusting," Roi said. "Luckily our route across the sea did not take us near such a place."

"Ah, well, you need not worry about such things now," Corrindal said with a smile. "We are quite well-defended here, as you have seen. Since the time of the Plague Bringer, cursed be his name, it has been our policy to protect our knowledge from those who would use it for undesirable ends. Hence the sentries...and other safeguards."

"Like our encodings," Yilia said. Corrindal shot her an angry look.

"Ah," Roi said. "The protection that was placed on the statues, to keep us from seeing how they worked."

Corrindal nodded. "You will find a similar puzzle placed over each of our mekkanisms, the answers to which will only be revealed once you show exceptional strength of character over a long period of time. While you act as our apprentices, you will not be free to come and go from this place as you wish; the skills of the Automatia stay within our walls, unless we decree to let them out."

"That is only fair," Roi said. "Am I to assume then that we are being allowed in? On a provisional basis, at least?"

The three automatist leaders glanced at each other briefly. Bergan nodded. Corrindal gave a bemused snort.

"Very well," she said. "We shall proceed with the initiation. Come this way; we have much to discuss."

Roi motioned to the others and headed after them, a smile plastered across his face. Karis followed into the hallway, along the sculpted lines in the floor. The building was mostly hollow, and built like a giant puzzle box, its polished blocks interlocking together, reflecting the light from hallways open to the aer at both ends. They passed smaller side rooms; some had people inside, and Karis slowed down to check if any of them were Meli.

Something hard banged into Karis's ankle and she yelped. It was a little silver box on wheels, with brushes poking out from its underbelly. It had been following behind her, sweeping up the dust left by her boots, but when it saw her it seemed more alarmed than she had been, spinning around and retreating down the hall. For the first time, Karis noticed just how clean the hall was. Dust was so ubiquitous in Aetheria that practically every surface collected a thin coating of the stuff. Only its sudden absence inside the Automatia had made her realize she had barely taken notice of it before.

Up ahead, Roi was still pontificating on life in Azorkas, fully absorbed in his role now.

"…where everyone is so entrenched in their traditions. Do you know that my countrymen have banned any sort of dancing which originates from the outside world? And all foreign food and drink is prohibited as well."

"The Automatia is also a place that adheres strongly to tradition," Corrindal said. "It is only because our beloved founders wished it so that we keep the gate key open; it was my desire to crumble those statues decades ago." She led them onto a wide, square section of floor inscribed with an image of the god Alysiema. Once Karis had caught up and they were all assembled, the floor rose into the aer without any visible command, lifted from underneath by some sort of silent engine.

They went up through a hole in the ceiling, passing several floors until they reached a wide area filled with evenly placed columns, full of apprentices sitting on ad-hoc pieces of furniture. Except for a corner occupied by rows of small cube-shaped rooms, this level was open on all sides to the strait. Outside, the building's cloaking canopy appeared slightly blurry in the fading light of evening. As Karis walked in, heads poked up from tables and sofas, staring at the curiously dressed onlookers, but she saw no familiar faces.

"This is the main area where apprentices sleep. You are free to claim as much space as you wish, as long as you leave the central walkway open, of course. Are you and your...retinue...ready to retire now?"

"Oh, I think there's time for a quick evening meal. And I'd love to find out when we can begin our instruction in automatism."

"You may begin tomorrow morning, if you wish," Yilia said.

"*But,*" Corrindal put in, "you must first convince the individual mentors you are worthy of their training."

"In any case," Began said, "the common room is back in this direction, if you wish to eat with the others."

The whole group turned and followed Bergan back to the lift. Corrindal happened to brush by Karis.

"Excuse me," Karis whispered, tugging her sleeve.

The larger woman whirled and Karis shrunk back, not wanting to draw the raiders' attention.

"Sorry," she said in a low voice. "But I was wondering if someone else had arrived here recently. A woman named Meli."

"Meli? Is she from Azorkas as well?"

"No. I mean, I'm not from there. I met Roi...zilan when they stopped in Sofidra. Meli is an old friend of mine. She was supposed to be on her way here."

Yilia shook her head. "I'm sorry, but no. We have no apprentices named Meli."

She left Karis standing there, mouthing the word, "But..." as if she was in a position to object. Roi saw her gaping as the lift rose again. He stood still, eyeing her with a flat expression, and soon the entire group was out of sight.

What had just happened? It shouldn't have been such a shock that Meli hadn't arrived yet, should it? Karis had come by skyship, and last she heard Meli was in a boat, not even floating over the fog. But after all the time they had spent before the battle and in Bressim, and combing up and down the coast, it had seemed reasonable, even probable, that Meli would show up first. But was that realistic? Or was it simply something she had wanted to believe, so that she could avoid thinking of the alternative?

Suddenly tired, Karis slumped into a corner and convoked a set of flat walls with a hard cot inside. No windows, just small slits for aer, so that the darkness enveloped her and she could pretend it was night.

Meli would still come. She had to. Even if she couldn't decipher the lock at first, she would never stop trying to enter the Automatia. If, that is, she were still alive—

Shut up!

Calm down. Karis hadn't led her best friend to her death. Meli was still out there, somewhere. She should leave right away, go and look for her. Or was that too rash? No, it would be better to wait a while. Meli could come to her tomorrow. Or in a week. A centemeran? A year?

The question had no answer, so she lay there, staring at the black ceiling. Here she was in the Automatia, the place she had dreamed of seeing for two hundred years, but instead of being filled with awe and wonder, she felt only lost and alone.

She thought back, far back to after she had left Sylas's commune and made her way southward, trekking by herself through endless wilderness.

Danger. Desperation. What had she been thinking? Would they follow her? Find her? And what would they do when they did?

After several weeks, she stopped checking over her shoulder. They weren't coming for her, and she was alone. She continued on, mile after mile, with no food and only whatever rest she could manage on the cold ground. All she knew was that she had to get away, had to cover some distance, but she was seeking nothing. There was no meaning to her life, no purpose. Looking back, it was surprising she hadn't simply dispersed, but something had kept her going, some will to live too primitive and stupid to know better.

The weeks turned into years, and still she walked. Probably she had wandered in circles many times before she came upon a frontier town. The sight of civilized people stunned her. Too shocked to be frightened, she wandered among the citizens and found them friendly enough. Most of them had probably thought she was newly appeared, until after many weeks she recovered her ability to speak. People began to approach her then, offering her things, asking her questions, but always there were those who stared, who treated her strangely for being a smoothskin. And so she drifted on to different settlements, slowly learning manners and how to mimic basic convocations, until in her fifty-eighth year she came upon the Great City of Ventituras, on the shores of the Meventi Lake.

There, she found wonders undreamed of, endless castles and mansions, parks and plazas, all the trappings of a metropolis untouched by the wars to the north. And more importantly, she found Halela and Lepri and Parthenia. Her new commune.

It was strange how it had happened. One day she was nothing more than a vagrant on the city streets, passing her time watching passersby under the shadows of the Trepolinai towers. Halela happened upon her, saw her sitting there and stopped and smiled and invited her to supper. Karis couldn't explain why, but somehow she knew; this one was different, there was no ulterior motive, no disgusting plans for her. This one she could trust.

The feeling only grew stronger when she met Lepri and Parthenia at their hillside estate. She was drawn to them as if under the influence of levitism, and soon she was seeing the three every day, and then living in a newly convoked wing of the house. Their commune was always looking for projects, and teaching Karis was one that they all enjoyed. She developed an insatiable hunger for new knowledge—not only about convocations, philosophy, and history, but about how to love, how to believe that others would want to spend time with her, not for *what* she was but because she was herself.

The years flew by. Halela and Lepri slept together most nights, with Parthenia joining them less frequently, and though they did not expect her to share in that part of their relationship, Karis would sometimes sneak into their chambers after they had fallen asleep and curl up beside them, feeling the rising and falling of their chests, secure in their arms.

If only she had known what was ahead, she would have tried to savor those nights more.

The changes had likely been coming a long time, but she had only noticed them that year. As the wet season passed into dry, Hal, Lepri and Parthenia began to go outside less. They slept later, ate little, spent the evenings at home talking quietly or more often just sitting in each other's company, dozing in their chairs. Karis would sit with them sometimes, squirming impatiently, making failed suggestions that they go out and visit the theater or the plazas. She was starting to notice women out in the city, tall, beautiful women, and certain thoughts were returning which she had kept out for decades. Sometimes on their ever-more-infrequent walks she would tell Parthenia about her feelings, and the older woman would smile and nod in her comforting, yet frustrating, way.

"If I met someone, and I fell in love, would I have to leave the commune?" Karis asked her one day.

"Perhaps." The trees had shed their flowers that week in the park, and Parthenia looked down at the red petals cascading around her sandals. "Sometimes it's better not to try and plan such things."

"But I don't want to leave all of you."

Parthenia nodded again. "You will see. Time will take its course."

Time? What did time have to do with anything? Yes, the world changed with time, the ground became wetter and drier and plants grew and cities rose and fell, but that did not affect her love for her commune. That was forever.

The day bloomed bright on Ventituras the next morning. Karis sat up in bed, sniffed and wrinkled her nose. A stale smell hung in the aer.

"Hal? Lepri?" She sat still and waited for an answer. The two of them were early risers, and often liked to surprise her with breakfast while the sky was still gray. But this morning the house lay silent. A dark, crooked line appeared in the wall across the room, and she rubbed her eyes to make sure she was seeing straight. She was; the line was still there in the wall, where it had not been yesterday.

A crack.

She got up and examined it. The crack ran all the way from the base moulding to the ceiling, and when she touched it the edges flaked away on her fingers. A cold sweat broke on her skin as she left her room and entered the courtyard. More cracks ran along the archways leading to the rest of the house. Karis broke into a run, her heart thumping.

"Parthenia!"

A chunk fell out of the wall to her left, dislodged by her footsteps. The entire house was turning gray as it crumbled. Karis closed her eyes to the stinging tears, navigating by memory, until she found the parlor where the others had rested the previous evening.

They were sitting there in their chairs, exactly as they had been when she last saw them, faces serene and eyes closed. Karis took a step forward and gasped. A piece of Parthenia's shoulder was missing, her dress torn. Bits of Lepri's wide lips, gone. She approached in a trance and touched a divot on Halela's ear. It fell to the ground, and half her face followed it. Karis sank to her knees, her tears dropping to dark circles on the dusty floor.

The ceiling fell, drowning her in her destroyed home, mixed with her commune's crumbled bodies. The dust enveloped her, choking, filling her mouth and nose and ears.

Karis opened her eyes in the dark of the Automatia, body shaking. There was no dust here, only clear aer and cold walls. *Calm down.* She lay there a long while, listening to the sound of her breath. Then the true wave of sadness rushed over her, thick and gut-wrenching. She rolled over, burying her head in her arms, and whispered to herself again and again.

"I miss you."

Stillness in the dark. She had no idea how much time had passed, and she was reminded of when the raiders had first taken her prisoner. She had been frightened then, but the dark could bring comfort as well. She held her hand in front of her face, but saw nothing, as if her body was no longer physical, her sense of touch only an illusion. Was this what dispersing was like? Floating in black, no body, just awareness? Many people believed they knew what came after death, and for most of her second life she had searched for answers to that question, and others.

The pursuit of knowledge. That ultimate goal, the one that had saved her after that horrible morning.

She didn't know how many days had passed after her commune dispersed, didn't remember how she had arrived at the deserted shoreline as night fell. She was sure she wanted to die, but once again something inside her was holding on, preventing her from leaving. Fear. To disperse, one had to truly let go, but her fear bound her inexorably to the pain of her existence.

She stepped forward, cold tendrils of fog seeping over her ankles, onto her freshly convoked platform. Her last walk, away from Ventituras, over the great inland Meventi lake. Foot by foot she continued, convoking more of the straight, narrow bridge in front of her as she went. Its surface squished under her toes, for it had to be light enough to float yet rigid enough to bear her weight. Before long the line of the shore retreated behind her, and she could feel the insistent tug of maintaining the platform on her subconscious. Maintaining a convocation when stressed or asleep was easy if it had existed long enough, but this bridge was too new, and too large. She would keep going, keep walking at a steady pace, until finally, when she was miles from land and utterly exhausted, the bridge would break and she would collapse into the lake and die.

Night turned to day and back to night, and still she walked. All she saw in the day was the sky and fog, and at night only the black line of the horizon. Each step was pain, rippling up her legs, through her core and into her mind where the link to the bridge grew ever more tenuous. But no matter how fatigued she became, the link would not break. She walked and walked as the days blurred together, her thoughts a hazy mess of every memory she'd ever had, but still her mind would not relax, would not let go.

Alone in the darkness, shambling, having forgotten who she was or what she was doing there, her existence was only the thin horizon in the distance. She didn't know anymore if she was truly alive; perhaps she had crossed over long ago, and was trapped in a waking death.

Overhead, in the black of the sky, she saw the first light.

It was deep purple, long and rippling, brighter in the center than around the edges. Her mouth fell open and she stopped walking. The lack of motion in her legs felt strange, but the light was stranger. Light in the nighttime, up in the sky—how could it be? What did it mean? Soon another light joined the first, this one bright green, then another, then another. Twisting, dancing together. It was the gods, it had to be—but what were they trying to tell her? The light-show increased in brightness and fury, bathing the fog and the platform and herself in its multi-hued glow. Karis dropped to her knees, tears streaming from her face. The lights. Gods, by all that was holy, those lights. They were beautiful, more beautiful than anything could be or deserved to be.

And then, as quickly as they had come, they were gone.

She sat and waited for what felt like an eternity, but the lights never returned. She should have missed them, should have felt empty and alone in their absence, but somehow the sight of them had charged her, filled her with a sense of wonder and purpose. The bridge collapsed then, and she dropped through the fog into the waves. But not to die. She was no longer exhausted, she had the strength of a thousand women, and as she rowed back to shore she marveled at her newfound sense of awareness.

She wanted now to find out everything about those lights, how they came to be, and who created them. She wanted to *be* them, to fill the world with beauty as they had.

She had been given a new life. A second life. And she wasn't going to waste it.

Karis sat up in her room at the Automatia and wiped the tears from her eyes. *I'm not going to waste it.* It had been a long time since she had made that promise to herself. She had tried to find the lights again, had traveled all over the Leeward Continent and beyond, branching out into new areas of knowledge, searching for anyone who was willing to teach her. The Automatia had always been a part of her plans, a stepping-stone to the knowledge she sought. After two hundred years, she wouldn't let her grief for Meli keep her from taking advantage of it.

Of course, Meli might still come, might still be all right somehow. But in the meantime, Karis would see what these automatists could teach her. If the legends were true, they held far greater secrets than their mekkanisms and encodings. If she stayed in their good graces and studied diligently, worked her way up their ranks and earned the trust of their leaders, they might share that ancient knowledge with her.

I'll be the light. I'm not going to waste it.

Rising, she crumbled the wall before her and went out to resume her new life.

23

Ariden lost count of the days. His long strides became shorter, and together with the others he stumbled along with barely a rest or a stray word, from the first strands of daylight until the sky's pale glow faded. The repetition brought a clear-headed awareness of his surroundings, from the small dimples and ripples in the rocks to the minute swaying of the leaves and grass. In time he saw the small animals which had surrounded them from the beginning but gone unnoticed, slithering and scurrying and flying creatures of all kinds, which sensed his gaze for a moment before they darted into the underbrush. Then there were the larger, rarer beasts, sometimes in herds and sometimes alone, visible on bare hillsides, raising their heads to the passing travelers. They had not seen the specimen with the long neck and human face again, though Ariden kept an eye on the horizon for whatever had been hunting it.

That was the true challenge: balancing the monotony of travel with always being alert. He recalled his mercenary days, before his search for the Scarred Man, and his first time guarding a caravan, though the details were faded and gray. Another far-off land and different traveling companions, two other swordsmen guarding a well-regarded savortist and her commune. The meals had been good, as promised, but that wasn't why he was there; the job had been its own reward. He was a fighter for hire, it was what he did, and with the Scythe at his side he had been in high demand. But he had never protected anyone on the road before, and as the weeks passed he made the mistake of believing the peaceable surroundings meant they were safe.

The monsters had attacked the caravan six to a side, as tens more streamed down into the valley behind to join the ambush. Slavering beasts with large snouts and spiked tails, the largest one snapped the wagon nearly in two with a single bite. So much for the glorious tales of the monster hunters. Yes, the old stories told of glory, but they left out the harsh lessons of the Scythe sliding across a throat, the fountaining blood, the crack of blade on bone jarring his hands, and the screams of the victims he failed to protect.

Would the caravan's fate have been different if the Ariden of today had been guarding them? Meli would likely say no, that he lacked the wariness she desired. And yet, there were some among the mercenaries of those times who stood too vigilant for too long, fearing for their life every day for years on end. Often they acquired a touch of madness from it, unable to sit still and seeing threats where there were none, or assaulting sworn comrades over the smallest slights. Ariden had seen a similar illness occur after the war, though those memories were dimmer still. Perhaps that was why he had adopted the seemingly apathetic attitude which Meli took issue with; it was the only way to stay sane after six centuries of life in combat.

One day they trudged down off a scrub-lined hillside and found themselves on a wide dust plain, flat as though a god had stamped it down. Here and there under the endless sky rose small hills of broken crust, the ground bubbling underneath with black muck, but otherwise the area was empty, shunned by the local animals and plants other than moss. Perhaps they should have taken that as an ill omen, but after so many miles of mountainous terrain they gladly marched on. Sirdu, who had days before miraculously grown tired of hearing himself speak, began to sing songs. Not raider songs, but traveling songs, with a strong beat and lyrics of discovery and triumph. To his shock, Ariden found himself stamping along in time, lost in the tunes until Meli suddenly laughed.

"What is it?" Ariden asked her.

She covered her grin with her hand. "You were singing."

"Was I? Is that so hard to believe?"

"No. It's just that…you were awful!"

She chuckled. Ariden shut his mouth as a bolt of anger ran through him, though only briefly, until he reminded himself that he cared not about her assessments. Still, the incident left him in a slightly dark mood for the remainder of the day.

That was, until the dust storm hit, and he remembered what it was to have real problems again.

Ariden lay in bed, listening to the tap of pebbles hitting the walls, the swish of fine particles swirling over the plain, and the wind howling over all. What little light came through the storm could only enter through the tiny aer holes in the ceiling of his hastily-assembled cabin, and Ariden feared making them larger would let in more dust.

Trapped again, a slave to boredom. If he were an artist, he would likely welcome the isolation—imagine the works he could produce with a mind so unoccupied. If he were a mekkanist he could invent contraptions to amuse himself, or if he were an animatist he could design ever more pesky creatures to run out and overrun the world, as Meli was probably doing now. But he was a fighter, and with no one around to fight his sanity dripped away each day he remained imprisoned.

Someone rapped on the far side of the wall. Ariden sat up and grimaced, not at the prospect of having company, but at the mess which would surely blow in as soon as he opened a hole.

Sure enough, the heavily robed figure brought a hail of dust with him when he entered, which settled in a pile in the corner. The guest removed his hood, and Sirdu's face emerged from its folds.

"What brings you?"

Sirdu shook off more of the brown powder and pulled off his ragged cloak. He examined it for a moment, deciding if it was worth keeping, then shrugged and let it crumble into the dustpile. He spoke with shoulders shrugged and chin down, making himself appear as small as his portly midsection would allow. "Entertainment. You said you didn't want to play Karrom before, but I figured you might have changed your mind, given our present situation."

"It's not my game. I prefer cards."

Sirdu smiled, perhaps pleasantly surprised that Ariden's response had not simply been to eject him bodily from the cabin. "We'll go one for one, then?"

Ariden sat up and stretched. "Very well. Your game first, then mine."

Sirdu convoked a table, followed by a Karrom board and his stick and puck.

"What are your rules?" Ariden asked, judging the placement of bumpers and walls. He was not terrible at the game, if memory served. A bit out of practice, perhaps, but he could give most of Aetheria a good match.

"No maximum stick length. First to three, bank scores don't count, no double-taps."

"And oldest goes first," Ariden finished. He took his first shot, and the game continued back and forth. A massacre. Sirdu scored three times in a row, not even letting Ariden bank one shot out of his home area.

Ariden gritted his teeth, then took a deep breath and pushed the board away. "Well done," he said, convoking a colored play-mat for Hidehigh.

Sirdu gave a little nodding bow. "It helps to think ahead when you place the puck. I've been doing that more lately...thinking of the future."

Ariden frowned. "Now I see."

"What?"

"The real reason you're here." He convoked five cards for his opening hand. "What is it you want from me?"

"Don't get the wrong idea; I only wish to help you. I'm grateful that you decided to bring me to Caeridor. Otherwise I would have been stuck with the Inaali forever."

"That was Meli's idea." Ariden nodded at Sirdu to begin, then examined the opening play. Four Behemoths and a blue scorpion—an interesting strategy, but manageable. They each convoked a set of dice, then shook them inside cups and rolled them out at the same time to determine Ariden's allowed moves. The results were not encouraging.

"I have a proposition for you." Sirdu said. "I'd be honored to stay in your service once we reach Caeridor. As sort of a...secondary. Like the Emperors had."

Ariden snorted. "I'm no Emperor. And I thought you were a raider."

"Perhaps not anymore. A man of your skills doesn't come along often. I want to apprentice under you, to learn some of your techniques. In exchange, I'll fight by your side if the going gets rough. I may have a fear of monsters, but against other men I can handle myself. I almost got the drop on you during that raid, remember?"

Ariden grunted. "You deal first."

Sirdu placed down two mountains and a seashore, then they both rolled the dice again. "I didn't mean to diminish you, sir. It was a lucky chance, was all. Besides, you were the one who saved us from Vipretheon."

"Vipretheon." Ariden wished again he could remember what had happened, or anything about the beast. "Meli didn't seem impressed by my performance."

"Well, I say just facing that monster and surviving is a tale for the ages. It must be a sign."

Ariden frowned as he convoked new cards to play. Sirdu's luck with the dice had taken all his easy wins, but perhaps with a few well-timed moves he could muddle his way through. "If you wish to assist me in battle, then go ahead. I've endured your company this long. Is that all you came here to say?"

Sirdu played a card instead of answering, a red capran. Ariden grimaced—exactly what he didn't want to see.

"I suppose now that we're officially allies," Sirdu said after a few more hands, "I wouldn't mind knowing a little more about your plans. How long are you planning to fight in Caeridor?"

Ariden fixed Sirdu with a mean glare. "Whatever we say stays within this cabin?"

Sirdu nodded.

"In that case, *ally*, I will tell you that the life of an arena fighter, even a successful one, is not easy. Much will depend on my ability to find worthy opponents who are willing to face me. In the past I could have relied on my connections in the city, but how many will remain after three hundred years? And then there is the matter of the ship. Even if I manage to win us one, we will still need a pilot, unless we take the time to duplicate it and learn to fly ourselves."

Ariden made several plays, knocking out Sirdu's cards where he could and preventing others from attacking.

"Perhaps I will be useful to you, then. I may not be a mekkanist or a skyship designer, but I know a bit about constructing and piloting. And then…" Sirdu looked down.

"…and then, we will fly to Karis. And the raiders."

"Which means your goal will be to kill my friends." Sirdu played a blue eagle over his Behemoth, then rolled. The dice disallowed all red cards, sending Ariden's defenses into disarray.

Ariden leaned back and arranged his hand, buying time to think of both an appropriate response to Sirdu's statement and a new card strategy. He made his play, then said, "That's something they've had coming for some time now. There's only so much raiding one can do before one poxes over the wrong person."

"Ariden, *please*. Find another way. A peaceful way."

"How can I find a peaceful way to steal a girl from a group of flying thugs? If Karis is still with them, they will fight for her, and I will have no choice but to repay them in kind."

"Some of them deserve that fate, it's true. Especially Hindal's men. But trust me, some are not what they seem, and you won't be able to tell the good from the bad. Let me speak to them before you do anything. Somehow I'll get Karis back without so much bloodshed."

Ariden tightened his lips. Sirdu's begging was stealing his focus from the game, and he was facing a once-in-a-lifetime run of bad luck with the dice. The smart thing for Sirdu to do would be to let him win, putting him in a good mood so that he might acquiesce, but on the next play the former raider pressed his advantage, saw right through Ariden's final bluff and took the rest of his cards.

Ariden sighed and tossed the used cards into the pile of dust in the corner. An intelligent man would have let him win. But Ariden didn't respect intelligence half as much as he respected boldness, and he rather liked this new, audacious Sirdu better than the old one.

"The raiders still owe me a debt," Ariden said. "And I will see it paid. But we have a long way to go before we reach them. If you can think of a plan in the meantime which can satisfy us both, I'll consider it."

His made it clear through his tone that he would give no more ground that day. Sirdu nodded in recognition, then set up the Karrom board again.

Midway through the fourth day, the storm abated as quickly as it had come. When the noise died the three of them stepped out into a world completely unlike the one they had last seen. Rolling dunes stretched out in all directions, twenty feet high or more. After a quick check of the wind they set off to north-leeward, letting their cabins crumble behind them to join the drifts. The dry season was well underway, which was likely what had precipitated the storm, and the loose sides of the dunes often collapsed under their feet, sending them skidding down with every third or fourth step. By the time they had crested the first ten, the yellowish brown substance was caked all over them, covering their faces and irritating their eyes and throat.

They stumbled on. Ariden squinted through his headscarf at the way ahead, but only the clouds of dust on the horizon filled his view, and a thousand steps became the same as one. The ache of tired muscles, not felt since his time on the boat, made their appearance again. He coughed up a lungful of dust and lifted his face covering to spit, but sputtered as a fresh helping of dust floated into his nose. His companions did not fare much better; Sirdu complained loudly whenever he could get a breath of fresh aer. Meli, though her suffering could not have been any less, was holding her sounds to soft groans. Even when she slipped on the far side of a dune, bringing great sheets of dust cascading down with her as she cartwheeled, she only grunted at the bottom, accepted Ariden's hand to pull her up, and continued on her way with shoulders hunched.

Days into their march a buzzing noise sounded overhead. They stopped and turned, waiting in silence as the noise grew louder: a propeller cutting through the aer. Sirdu pointed and Ariden looked, then waved his arms and shouted and jumped.

The skyship passed by to windward, so close that Ariden was sure he could see the head of its pilot in the cockpit. They all yelled as loud as they could, but the craft did not change course, nor make any other motion to acknowledge them. In a few moments it was gone, and the blowing clouds of dust filled the sky again.

Meli broke their prolonged, shocked silence. "Did it come from Caeridor?"

"I don't know." The words caught in Ariden's scratchy throat. "But we're getting somewhere. We may not even be halfway to the city yet, but wherever we are is closer to people than we were before. Let's just hope the first ones we meet aren't a band of slavers."

"What?" Meli said. "Slavers? I thought they only existed after the Empire's fall."

Ariden shrugged and walked on. "Some things in this world last far longer than they should."

The dunes soon began to lessen in height, and after another day of travel on flat ground they left the plain and entered a forest.

For a long while, Ariden had trouble keeping his eyes ahead and his mouth closed. Thick brown trees towered overhead, their trunks cylindrical columns which branched out only at the top, where rays of light filtered through. The ground between the trees was mostly clear, except for the tangled mass of roots crisscrossing the landscape, with tufts of yellow moss growing between them. The aer tasted fresh, and with the only movement being the swaying leaves far overhead, the place was eerily quiet—and disquieting. Without underbrush to hide in, no small animals scurried about, which made Ariden wonder if larger, more menacing ones had taken up residence in their stead. Nevertheless, he pushed forward with Sirdu close behind him, brandishing an axe in his new role as Meli's second bodyguard.

Half a day had gone by when the ground split open around them, and they stood before a chasm of moss-covered bedrock. The people of Lafedine came to Ariden's mind as they crossed the gulf by hanging a bridge along a thrown length of rope, but soon they came upon another great cleft, and then another. Soon the gorges were abutted by long shelves of overhanging rock, in maze-like, stair-stepping formations. The three maintained a more or less straight path at first by convoking staircases, but as the changes in height grew gargantuan they were forced to turn back more than once to seek easier routes.

"Any stories about these rocks, Sirdu?" asked Ariden. Of late the raider had been more quiet than usual.

"Oh, no, sir. Never heard of anything like these before." He paused in his climb and sighed. "I suppose you were right, my lady," he said to Meli. "I'll have some new stories to tell when this is all over."

He crested a bluff, turned around and stopped short. The stretch of land before them was covered with endless rows of low trees covered with gray spines, each one leaning over at the same angle, their trunks bent as if bowing in respect.

"Fascinating," Meli said.

"What does it mean?" Sirdu asked. "It almost looks like they're pointing us away. Warning us."

"They're pointing to windward," Ariden said. "The affairs of plants are their own. Do not let your superstitions get the better of you."

Despite his words, dark thoughts clouded Ariden's mind that night at camp. They rested on the highest bluff they could find, and the evening light cast a ghostly glow on the tops of distant trees. The view was beautiful, but there was something off-putting about the place, as if it had swallowed them whole and might never deign to release them. He made one more sweep of the perimeter before turning in, and caught Meli's eye as she was entering her cabin. She acknowledged him cordially, nodding with a slight smile, and he nodded back before she stepped inside. Something had changed between them since they had left the dunes. It was a subtle difference—a look of understanding when one of them was stuck or hurt, a helping hand or convocation to get past a tricky obstacle. And now that elusive smile. He could not pretend to know her thoughts, but he felt that if he dwelt on them too long they might disappear, like a scared mouse discovered on a table.

They continued northward the next morning, and the rock shelves grew wider and taller, until Ariden was made to feel like an insect, lost in a world whose scale beggared contemplation. Now planning the best route through the rock maze became even more important, lest half a day be wasted constructing a staircase up to a ledge that led nowhere.

He took them down into a canyon, past one switchback after another, in the hopes that a passage existed up the other side. At the bottom, he found what he was looking for, along with another thing he was not. Over the next ledge and past a gap lay a span of flat ground stretching off the distance, with thick trees like those they had already traveled through. Under the gap, a river flowed, wide and fast, roaring white over black rocks.

They stood and stared a while before Meli spoke.

"I suppose we could head back." She looked up as she said it. Sirdu followed her gaze and groaned.

Arden knelt, feeling for his instinct. The river looked angry. Something about the way the liquid swirled in the center disturbed him, as did the fact that it had chosen to flow uphill along this portion of its route.

"We could span it with another arch," Meli said. "A tall one."

Ariden looked back to the top of the canyon as she and Sirdu had. Such a long way. And over how great a distance had this river chosen to flow? Rivers had been known to span half a continent at times; would attempting to go around this one be an exercise in folly?

"What is the word?" he asked. "Do you wish to cross?"

Meli looked over at Sirdu, who made a small bow.

"If my lady wishes to go, I will stand by her side."

Meli nodded at him, then again at Ariden.

"Then we'll cross," Ariden said. "But not here. We'll find a better spot."

They headed downstream, climbing up a rock face studded with jutting horizontal columns, filling the gaps between them with solid convocations. The rock under Ariden's fingers began to feel wet from a mist drifting in from above, and once, then twice his feet slipped below him. He climbed another level, pumping his hands on his tired thighs, then turned the corner and saw the falls.

Or perhaps this stretch of river would be better termed a jump, as the river-creature was pulling its liquid body up and over one of the overhanging rocks to continue on its path above them. Ariden waited for Meli and then Sirdu to climb up, then put his finger to his lips and motioned for them to follow him beneath the overhang.

They stepped carefully, quietly, their backs to a jagged bedrock wall. The river slid by steadily, unperturbed. Light cascaded through the liquid sheet, sending rippling patterns over their bodies. Ariden looked back and saw the glow dancing over Meli's features, her delicate cheeks and nose crisscrossed with light, her eyes sparkling. He realized he must have been smiling at her when he saw her smile back.

Not looking, she stepped into a pile of loose stones, sending a few tumbling over the edge.

Meli's face went white. Ariden froze. A lump formed in his throat as he listened. Meli breathed hard, her shoulders rising and falling, while Sirdu looked left and right as if they were surrounded.

They *were* surrounded.

Ariden pulled the Scythe from inside his coat. He stood and waited, hackles up, the roar of the falls ringing in his ears. Nothing. His heartbeat quieting, he dropped his hands to his side and turned to leave their hiding-place behind the waterfall.

The rumble began far below them, traveling upward at obscene speed until the entire rockface vibrated. Meli put her hands to her ears and screamed. The falls twisted and coalesced, forming a massive body supported on two pillar-like legs, with tendrils spilling in every direction. Two black eyes swirled into being, and the liquid creature turned and saw them.

Tendrils whipped toward them. Ariden pushed Meli behind him and heard her back slap against the rock as the Scythe's blade came forth. He sliced up with one hand, cutting off the tendrils and freezing the thing where he struck. It roared, a terrible sound reverberating in his belly. Two more of the thing's arms rose up to strike him from opposite directions. Ariden grew his blade and took them out, and three more tendrils sprang up in their place. He stepped back, stumbled. Too many, he couldn't stop them all. He sliced again, and before he could bring the sword around, the creature grew a monstrous arm and raised it to impale him.

Sirdu's axe came down and hacked off the limb, sending the end of it splashing to Ariden's feet. With a roar Sirdu swung again, and again, pressing back the way they had come.

"Get across!" he yelled. "I'll distract it!"

His words quaked with fear, and panic jerked his movements. But Sirdu committed himself to the fight and attacked again, teeth clenched, aiming at the thing's body, increasing the length of his axe handle as he went. With each strike the river creature dodged, and

Sirdu stepped further away from Ariden and Meli, forcing it to chase him.

But the monster was too lithe, too cunning. It waited for him to over-commit, then struck, engulfing one of his arms in its own and tearing it off at the shoulder.

Meli screamed again. Sirdu staggered back and looked at his stump as it dumped a torrent of bright red blood into the chasm below. Then he began to scream as well.

"Meli," Ariden said, pushing her away from the monster. "Rope. Now!"

Sirdu sank to his knees and the river lunged again, engulfing his head in one clean bite. A flash of gray-brown coursed over him, and his body became a statue, skin and clothes falling off in wet clumps.

By then Ariden had crumbled his blade and was running, pulling Meli behind him. Tall trees were visible in the gap at the far side of the falls. He took the end of a rope from her.

"Something sharp!"

She convoked the grapnel quickly, scrabbling over wet rock while completing the rope at the same time. Ariden swung it overhead once, tossed it at the closest trunk, grabbed Meli by the waist and jumped.

They fell straight down, Meli holding him fast with all her limbs. The rope pulled taut and they swung forward. The river came up behind them, swiping down with a watery claw. Ariden twisted, pulling his legs away from the blow, and came up out of range past the tree trunk, swiveled and landed feet-first against it. The monster lurched forward and fell, unable to reach its full height so far from the riverbed. Instead it oozed along the ground, enveloping the bottom of their tree, hissing and foaming.

The rope cut into Ariden's hands as he braced against the trunk to hold Meli's weight. "The next one," he said between gritted teeth.

Meli began to convoke a bridge—nothing stable, just an assemblage of flat planks spanning the gap to the nearest tree. The trunk that was supporting them rattled and then lurched to one side as the river sloshed beneath them. Ariden dropped them both onto her platform, stumbling as it swayed under his feet. Their tree-trunk was leaning over, and the rigid bridge was already coming apart from the strain.

He held his breath and dashed across, holding Meli's arm in case she fell. A few pulse-pounding strides took them to the next tree, where Meli had already convoked a small platform to stand on. Ariden pressed his chest against the trunk and watched as the tree they had come from fell with a crash that echoed through the empty forest.

The river sloshed angrily and came forward again, spreading itself thin over the ground.

"No more close trees," Meli said.

She was right—he didn't know how far the river could stray from its bed, but they would never build another bridge before it ate through the trunk below them.

"Convoke a dam."

She nodded and closed her eyes, pressing her cheek to the trunk. Below them, a long semicircular wall appeared around the river, growing taller by the moment. Ariden contributed what he could by convoking a thin slide down from the edge of the platform, plummeting steeply at first and then gradually leveling out. After waiting far too long for the slide to have at least better-than-even odds of bearing his weight, he tugged Meli's sleeve and jumped.

A few moments of the ground coming up, and then he was hurtling off the end of the ramp he hadn't bothered to finish. He landed in a crouch on the root-covered ground and spun to check on the dam, worried that any break in Meli's concentration would destroy it. On the other side of the wall, the monster roared and seethed. Bits of its body splashed over the top, landing harmlessly in drops near Ariden's boots.

Meli scooted down a moment later, and Ariden caught her in his arms when she plummeted off the slide. He put her down and they watched for a moment as the river raged and the tree they had been standing in began to fall.

"The dam won't hold for long," she said.

"Then run."

With no more words, they sprinted away through the trees.

At its most fundamental level, a fight was about predicting reactions.

Yes, in most ordinary scraps, more factors would come into play—technique, toughness, desire, luck, and so on, but once the field was cleared of novices and cravens, and two warriors of more or less equal strength stood to face each other, invariably the victory would go to whoever could best read his opponent. The best strategy was worthless if negated before it began, and a mediocre strike could be a knockout if placed in the path of an oncoming adversary.

Ariden had learned to read the signs of a fight long ago, the feints and baits and switches. In a one-on-one match, few such moves could catch him unaware. But the same did not apply to life in general. People, as long as they were not engaged in the act of attempting to connect a hard object with his face, could still surprise him. No matter how many of his fellow humans he met or how many terrible events he witnessed, he was still shocked by their poor judgment or their deep insight, the depths of their cowardice or their bursts of unexpected courage.

Meli was no exception. When Karis had been kidnapped, Meli had gone into an emotional panic, casting blame, rashly sending her pet bird away, never to be seen again. That was not so long ago, and though Sirdu was hardly Karis, Ariden would have expected her to react similarly to the river's attack and the raider's death. But instead Meli's only action since they had stopped fleeing was to sit and stare, her back flat against a rock, her knees hugged tight to her chest.

They made camp where their intuition had told them further running would not make them safer, in a hollow with rock walls shielding them from the wind. Meli stared at the trees, then night fell and she stared instead at the darkness. Ariden lay nearby, out in the open, watching her from the corner of his eye. Why had she not spoken or moved? Was her mind broken? Had this latest catastrophe finally cracked her?

"It's my appearance-day, you know."

Her voice rang out clear in the still aer, startling him. The night had grown so dark he could barely see the outline of her lips as she spoke.

"At least, it could be. I thought I had kept track of the time, until the Inaali corrected me. Now I am not sure exactly what day it is."

"Well," Ariden said, "good wishes, anyway."

"If I were home in Sofidra, my friends would be throwing a party for me." Her voice was sad, but not upset. "I miss them, and the city. I'm homesick, Ariden. I have been since I left, but it's only in the quiet times that I truly feel it."

Ariden nodded. "The Great Dread, we used to call it. I've seen it strike men on their first voyages abroad, men who could snap limbs like twigs, who stood as tall and wide as these trees. But take them away from the place they had known all their lives, and in weeks they would be reduced to tears, blubbering on the deck of a ship as if mortally wounded. Oftentimes they would never recover, unless they turned back and abandoned their journey."

Meli gave a rueful chuckle. "It's stupid, you know. For the last thirteen years I did nothing but fret about how useless Sofidra was to me, how the people did nothing but gossip and try to impress each other. And yet here I am, acting like this really is the day of my appearance, as if I'm helpless without them."

"It was your home."

"But I wasn't happy there. Only...accustomed." She sighed. "Most people in Aetheria are happy. Why wouldn't they be? Look at the blessings the gods have given us. A beautiful world, the aether to command, and as much time to enjoy it as we wish. Why could I never simply accept their gifts for what they were? I'm nothing more than an over-dramatic fool."

"You're wrong. You have a real purpose, something that matters to you." Remorse pulled at his throat, and his voice became strained. "Do not belittle that. You have no idea how lucky you are. No idea..."

Her silhouette turned. "Ariden?"

He had already said too much. He should have left it at that, but something inside tugged at him to finish. Perhaps the day's events had affected him more than he cared to admit.

"I had been a mercenary for fifty years when I met the Enchantress." He paused, waiting to see if Meli understood who he was referring to. She remained silent.

"I had come to Porlan in response to her call for aid. A strange place it was back then, where rival clans battled for control of its vast fields, though not always with swords and arrows.

"When I arrived, I found her inside a vast palace, surrounded by high, sheer walls. She received me in a room adorned with great hanging tapestries in shades of ruby and emerald, and a great feast spread out before her. She was beautiful from the first, her long brown hair pulled back tight to her scalp, her skin powdered, her lips dyed bright blue. But I remained on my guard. I had been lured into the hands of enemies with offers of employment before, only to have attempts made on my life, and something about this exquisite clan leader and her overgrown house did not sit well with me. Nevertheless, seeing no obvious dangers, I resolved to sit at her table and hear her out.

"The mission was an assassination, she said, of a warlord who controlled the lands adjacent to hers. I told her I did not normally take on such tasks, as I found them distasteful. But she assured me he deserved to die, and listed his many crimes. Among them was that old capital offense, anathematism, by which he had acquired a long scar bisecting his face."

"The Scarred Man," Meli said.

"Indeed. At the time I knew that scars form when flesh is rent and kept apart for a long period, rather than being allowed to heal. She was the first to inform me that an anathematist convocation which infiltrates the flesh can leave marks as well, as the old plagues often did.

"Like most, I had assumed all the anathematists were dead, and I was shocked by her accusations. But I told her I would investigate this man on my own, and if his crimes matched her words, then I would do what needed to be done.

"She smiled at me then, and passed me a cup of ambrosia. A toast, to seal our agreement. I drank it without a passing thought, never expecting she was sealing my future, as well."

He paused. The old memories burned as they rose to the surface. "A moment after the liquid passed my throat I felt a rushing sensation, as if my mind was uncovering a new world around me. The room seemed to grow brighter and my vision blurry, and when my eyes focused again they found her face. Her gorgeous face…her lips, her eyes, her everything. She was the most sublime thing I had ever seen. And it was not only her beauty I admired; I loved her with every fiber of my being, wanted desperately to join with her, to merge our souls together. Confused, ignorant of what was happening, I confessed my love right there at the table. She nodded in a knowing way and led me into her bed chamber.

"Our union was rapturous, and sealed further my conviction that I would live for this woman, and give my life for her if she so desired. And these feelings did not diminish—the next morning, I felt them as strongly as before. Even speaking these words a century and a half later fills me with longing nearly impossible to bear."

"But you didn't love her," Meli whispered. "She was an anathematist; it was the drink."

"Of course. I realized that well before I left her palace on my mission. But that was of no consequence. The way the convocation operated, it did not matter what I knew to be true. I needed her as a man needs aer and blood flowing through him, and when she told me to go kill the Scarred Man, it became my life's mission to do so.

"I journeyed to the Scarred Man's castle, crisscrossing the land to avoid his allies, and waited outside for my opening. I desperately wanted to attack at once, to paint his halls red with blood so that I could return to my love sooner, but I could not risk his becoming alarmed and escaping. And so I hid until the castle was relatively empty, and slipped inside just before dawn.

"I found him sitting on a throne, enjoying a morning meal, and approached with Scythe in hand. He laughed when he saw me. Perhaps he recognized the convocation she had used, or perhaps I was not the first she had set against him in such a manner. But before I could inquire how he wished to die, he told me that my journey was fruitless. He had already sent a band of soldiers, hand-picked for loyalty and fierceness, against the Enchantress's palace to destroy her once and for all.

"I only half-believed him, but I could not take the chance that he told the truth. Vowing to return and finish my mission, I fled as fast as I could back to the palace."

A pressure had built in Ariden's lungs as he spoke. He hung his head and breathed hard, wheezing through his nose. Meli waited patiently for him to continue, unmoving, silent.

"When I arrived, the walls had already crumbled. My world crumbled with them. I knelt there in that pile of dust and begged the gods for death. But it did not come. For days and days I wept and screamed for them to take me away so I could join her, but if they heard me, they chose not to listen."

He blinked and wiped his nose. The pain was as bad now as it had been that day. Worse, even, for back then he had been ignorant of how many years would pass with no resolution.

"But she tricked you," Meli said. "Manipulated and used you. By killing her, he set you free."

"He did not." Ariden breathed deeply until his voice composed. "Even after her death, her order still stood. Kill the Scarred Man, she said. Only another word from her could remove that burden; with her gone, my only choice was to hunt him down before I too could pass.

"I went after him then, but he had already fled. And so began my quest, crisscrossing Aetheria with a singular goal. Decades passed, then a century, and by that time I no longer knew if my quarry was still alive, or if my quest was doomed to continue without end."

Images flashed before him, of a thousand meaningless trips, investigations and interrogations. All the while, that horrible tension gnawing at his core, the same one he felt now. So many years wasted in pursuit of a false goal. The journey changed him. Once he had laughed and took joy in things, treasured his friends and took pity on enemies. But no more.

"The quest has consumed my entire being. And yet it has been so long that I can no longer remember exactly how it began. Even now as I tell it, I am forced to imagine details for the story to make sense. And the worst part is...."

He choked, swallowed and began again. "I can no longer remember her name. All of this effort, all this pain to honor a memory I no longer keep."

"Ariden." Meli's body shifted as if she wanted to lay a hand on him, but in the darkness the distance between them was impossible to measure. "You must let it go. It's a lie."

"It doesn't matter. Even if it is a lie, it's real to *me*. Do you understand? Can you possibly understand that?"

He drooped his head, the spilled words stinging.

Meli said nothing. For a long time, the two of them sat together in the night.

"Meli?" he mumbled, wondering if she was asleep.

"Yes?"

"I am sorry. About today. What happened to Sirdu."

"It's all right," she said. "There are things I wish had gone differently. Things I would have stopped, if I could do them over. But the time came to make a choice, and whether or not I did my best, there's no way to go back. That's what happened with Karis, wasn't it?"

"Yes."

"You know, sometimes in life you think you're ready, you think you're in control of everything, but then something terrible happens, and you realize it was just a trick your mind was playing, that you deceived yourself into thinking you were safe so that you could go on and do what you needed to do."

Ariden nodded, though she couldn't see it.

"Still though, we go on. I used to think leaving Sofidra forever would be the end of the world. But even after losing everything—my home, my friends—I'm still here. Life does go on." Her clothes rustled as she curled up on her side.

"For those who have something to live for," Ariden said. "The others disperse, I suppose."

"Well, I suppose I should be happy you're so driven, then," Meli said, yawning. "If you went and dispersed right now, I'd be in deep mold out in the wilderness by myself."

She lapsed into silence, and soon was snoozing quietly. Ariden stayed awake a while longer, staring at the distant horizon.

"Don't worry," he mumbled into the night.

24

What a strange feeling, to see so many people, after so much isolation.

And what people they were, appearing in a great crowd all at once as if convoked, heading toward Caeridor along the same wide thoroughfare as Meli and Ariden, singing songs and banging drums, colorful streamers woven into their disheveled hair. At first, Meli could hardly grasp what was happening around her. She stared at the passersby and they stared back, sometimes muttering in a strange dialect of Aetherian. They felt less like humans and more like a dream, a long-forgotten memory of life not spent trudging endlessly through empty wilderness.

Meli's feet hurt, that much was real. The pain reminded her of Sirdu, and his promise to crumble his boots when he reached the city. If he reached the city...

She felt guilty at how many days it had been since she last thought of him. She was almost jealous of Ariden, the way he had been able to put aside his feelings over Sirdu's death so easily, or else to keep his grief well hidden. For weeks after the incident with the river, Meli had habitually imagined herself in Sirdu's place, feeling the fear and pain as he was about to die, to the point where she had spent many nights unable to sleep.

Meli had never reacted well to death; she had always avoided Sofidran funerals, which, while lavish, were so ephemeral—once over, the mourned faded into the memories of the mourners, and rarely did they remain there long. Death meant nothing left behind, that was the way of things, and Meli had never met anyone who seemed quite as bothered about it as she was. Karis had come the closest, speaking in quiet moments of wanting to leave behind a legacy of discovery, to "become a part of the workings of the world" as she put it. But for Meli, something simpler would have sufficed. She would have liked to build a cairn in Sirdu's memory, but they hadn't been able to find enough loose bedrock near the campsite, and so she resolved instead to one day tell to her child the story of Sirdu's incredible act of self-sacrifice, in the hopes that he might pass it along to others.

Yes, Sirdu would have liked that.

Time was melting away by the time they left the forest and climbed into the mountains again. They walked for so long that each new feature of the landscape blended together, and any progress they made toward their goal seemed immaterial, for it lay so impossibly distant that to even contemplate reaching it was folly.

Meli wasn't sure, but she thought perhaps half a year had passed before the mountains began to flatten and they saw small frontier villages hugging the sides of distant hills. Day by day, the settlements grew larger, until the paths between them became a true road again, the volume of foot traffic capable of beating down any plants attempting to colonize the dust. They passed multi-leveled castles of massive size, meant for housing or worship or just decoration, and a wide swath of convoked rolling hills, upon which a group of enthusiasts was practicing some sport involving rolling around on wheeled contraptions.

Then the crowd had descended upon them, and Ariden had told her they were close. Just like that, close—as if the word held any meaning after a journey of so many miles.

A surge of people to her left knocked a man into her, and she stumbled forward into Ariden. Someone was leading a large animal close by, forcing the crowd to part, and others were shouting and throwing liquid-filled bladders in its direction. The people around them became suddenly more boisterous, and Meli had the uneasy feeling of losing control of her own movements. Ariden felt it too; he took her by the wrist and pulled her ahead, shouldering his way through. Somewhere in their journey she had lost the instinct to shrink away from his touch. His hand was calloused but strong, and he guided her firmly until they were away from the densest part of the throng, then nodded before letting her go.

She returned the nod. Such simple understandings had often been the way of things between them, ever since their conversation the night after Sirdu had died. They had not spoken of the Scarred Man or other such topics since, but their other talk had flowed more freely; Ariden in particular conversed more, checking on her progress, even making jokes and smiling occasionally. Very occasionally.

They came up to a low hill, the heads of the crowd visible below like a field of multi-colored bushes. In the distance, half-obscured by a haze of dust, was a mile-wide slab of brownish-gray aether-stone, adjacent to the sea and surrounded by a foggy moat.

"Caeridor?" she asked.

"Indeed."

Meli sighed. It had taken them so long to arrive—far too long. She would have liked nothing more than to stop and rest a while, but for Karis's sake they needed to procure a ship as soon as possible.

In the plain below, the crowd split into tented encampments. In the aisles between were pens where caprans, waist-high animals with scruffy white coats and curved horns, congregated in great numbers. In some of the pens the caprans rested, while others held circular tracks for racing, or small pits where the animals grappled their heads together as men and women looked on and shouted.

Meli and Ariden navigated a path through the camps, blending in well enough with the motley assemblage. Halfway through the wide plain surrounding the city, they passed a giant stage, with streaming banners and large circular horns to amplify the performers' voices. A man at the center bellowed unrecognizably, pumping his fist in the aer with each sentence, and the crowd responded with boisterous shouts.

"What's happening over there?" Meli asked.

"They're Outsiders," Ariden shouted over the din. "The number of city residents is capped; everyone you see here isn't allowed inside, except to watch the fighting tournaments."

Meli squinted at the brown-gray block in the distance. It looked more like a fortress than a city. "Why don't they just make it bigger?" she asked. "Then anyone could live there who wanted to."

"Caeridor was built long ago on a convoked platform over the sea. Most of the city has now hardened, and the outer walls are held sacred." Ariden covered his face as a line of chained caprans tromped past, kicking up dust with their hooves. "Or so they say. The real reason they do not expand the city is that those who run it maintain their status by keeping others out."

"I don't understand," Meli said. "Their status?"

Ariden coughed and spat. "The city administrators have access to things that others want—the best food, the best amusements, and the ships we're after. But such treasures would lose their worth if they let everyone access them. And so they have limited the extent of the city, forbidding anyone from convoking an expansion, while maintaining a system of power which rewards those who sponsor winning fighters in the arena."

The stage-watchers sent up a great cry behind them, but their shouts were already fading into the distance as Meli and Ariden walked among a group of Outsider tents, arranged in surprisingly orderly rows. Most of them had walls or flaps open, and beneath the canopies people of all descriptions talked and drank, arm wrestled, had sexual relations, or simply napped in the shade.

"But if these people aren't allowed to enjoy the city, why don't they build their own?" Meli asked. "Or go somewhere else?"

"This is their home. They consider themselves a part of Caeridor, even if the city does not share their view. Their demeanor and motives change over time—sometimes they work with the High Council, sometimes against them. Whatever they seek now is none of our concern."

Soon they approached close enough for the city walls to loom over them, and Meli saw that they were not walls at all, but the flat exteriors of buildings, pressed so tightly together that an insect could not have crawled between them. A bas-relief mural covered most of the outside, a great visual saga of drakenbirds fighting enemy armies. She followed Ariden to the right, avoiding the surrounding moat with its bottom filled with fog—it would rise higher during the wet season—heading toward a covered bridge, its sides shaped to resemble an enormous open beak.

In front of the bridge another crowd had gathered, though they seemed to be more concerned with loitering than with crossing. A trio of guards stood at the near side, hands resting on pikes, eying the Outsiders warily. Along the top of the walls, more sentries stood, shoulder-pads and chest-plates gleaming, no doubt watching for any attempts to convoke a crossing over the moat.

Ariden pushed his way onto the bridge and Meli followed him across, to where a lone guard stood before a small arched gate.

"Only one of you can enter." He struggled to speak against the burden of boredom. "No groups today."

"Stand aside," Ariden said. "We're not part of this rabble."

The guard let his pike drift sideways, so that it covered the archway diagonally. "Orders for today are no groups."

"So *two* is a group?" Ariden said with a hint of anger.

The guard shrugged. "When they include your type."

"My type?"

He grinned. "Troublemakers."

Ariden took a deep breath. "I am a former champion. No one is more deserving than I am to enter the city."

"That's fine." The guard looked him up and down. "But anyone can *say* they're a former champion, can't they?"

The two men stood for a while staring, breezy self-confidence against open hostility, until Meli pulled on Ariden's coat.

"Come on," she said. "There must be another gate. This isn't worth it."

Ariden regarded her briefly, then turned back to the guard. "Take a swing."

"What?"

"Throw a punch at me. As a test, to see if I am who I say."

The guard threw his head back and gave a hearty laugh, his armor jangling. He turned to the side and appeared to wipe a tear from his eye. Then his fist shot toward Ariden's head.

Meli didn't follow what happened in that split moment, but when next she looked, Ariden's head had moved slightly to the left, so that the guard's forearm was resting against his ear. Ariden had moved a step forward and his own arm was extended, his middle knuckle pressed slightly against the point of the bewildered guard's nose.

"When you bob your shoulder, you reveal your intentions," Ariden said as the guard stumbled back, touching his uninjured face. "And your strike needs to be straighter. You're wasting time moving it in an arc."

The guard stared at Ariden, his mouth open.

"Which club do you train at?" Ariden asked.

"The…the Populoso."

"Never heard of it. Is the Honorium still open?"

The guard shook his head. "No. Closed years ago."

"Ah. Well, ask around tomorrow for Ariden and you'll find where I'm training. Come to me there if you want your technique corrected. When is your next fight?"

"Six weeks."

"Plenty of time to make adjustments. That is, if we're allowed inside?" Ariden gestured toward the door.

The guard eyed them both one more time, checked back to the crowd on the other side of the bridge, then nodded and motioned them through.

"See?" Ariden said as they traversed the long tunnel through the wall. "No need to try another gate."

"Frankly, I'm amazed you restrained yourself."

"It's best to be on good behavior here. With so many fighters and ex-fighters with tempers, everyone is kept on a short leash. One false step, and your life could be forfeit."

They exited the tunnel onto a bustling thoroughfare, where pedestrians pushed past the tables of outdoor cafes and through crowds of gawkers watching street shows. Meli felt at once as though the buildings were closing in on her, so close together were their flat gray exteriors. Ariden turned and headed south, stepping around a muscular man using a broom to push a pile of dust.

Ariden noticed her staring. "All the guards and workers you see here are fighters who lost one too many times. By giving their labor to the city, they earn their way back into the rankings."

The man with the broom looked up at her. Meli hurried down the street. Even though she had no part in it, seeing the man in that strange position, giving up his time and effort solely for the benefit of others, made her feel ashamed. Such an arrangement would never be made in Sofidra—even the city watch were merely ordinary citizens who chose to serve in the case of raider attacks or other threats, because doing so appealed to them. Never would the Sofidrans degrade another person by having them perform menial labor, just to earn the right to do as they wished. And all of this, in service of such a senseless, useless activity as fighting—it was unfathomable.

They walked on, and Meli began to see the others around in a new light. When she overhead conversation in a cafe, it was the recounting of a spectacular knockout in the arena. A crowd had gathered at one corner to watch a muscular man posing as he shouted at them to attend his upcoming match. Everything here seemed to revolve around senseless violence, and everyone around her were purveyors and consumers of it. How could so many people celebrate the idea of hurting others?

"Our destination." Ariden stepped onto a wider street bordering a sheer brown wall that towered over the rest of the city. "Behold: the Fighting Arena of Caeridor."

"But you haven't arranged a fight," she said.

"The arena is the city's center, physically and politically. This is where the council meets, and where we'll need to make friends."

"You mean you're going to just stroll in and speak with the council? Will they allow it?"

"As long as we behave ourselves, yes. We are guests of the city for the day, but come nightfall, we shall be evicted unless we can convince someone to let us stay."

A long walk around the curving wall brought them to an arched entrance and a series of tunnels. Light streamed down from above, through horizontal bars that Meli realized were the bottoms of tiered benches. The arena complex seemed enormous, almost a city within the city. Here the shirtless and grizzled men she had come to recognize as fighters were more prevalent, and the confined spaces were rank with sweat. Ariden sometimes seemed sure of where he was leading her, only to fall into momentary confusion, stopping to get his bearings or directions from a passerby. They reached a long room where a half-dozen white circles were marked in the floor. Within most of the circles, two fighters circled or grappled, while their coaches or other compatriots looked on and shouted advice or exhortations.

Ariden pulled aside one of the onlookers to speak, while Meli watched one of the practice bouts. Two men, both bald and soaked with sweat, faced each other with fists high. The shorter man dove, grasping for the other's legs in a surprise attack, but the taller one stepped back and shrugged him away, then responded with a brutal strike directly to the shorter man's temple, sending his adversary sprawling to the dust-strewn floor, blood pouring from a freshly opened cut. Meli yelped and looked away.

"What?" Ariden and the man he was speaking to looked over. "What is it?"

"This place is awful." She pushed past him. "There must be another way."

Annoyed, Ariden waved to the man and started after her. "You couldn't ask for a better circumstance than this. A city obsessed with bare-handed fighting, and you with the best fighter in Aetheria at your disposal. You should be thanking the gods we're here."

"I'll thank them when we leave, on our way to rescuing Karis."

"In that case, we'll need a sponsor. This way." He headed for a musty staircase at the far side of the room.

They walked up four flights, coming out in the stands of the main arena. A great ring at the center lay empty, and the stands were populated with only a few layabouts enjoying midday drinks. Meli looked about, amazed at how many people the stands had been built to accommodate, and at how the building seemed to force one's attention to the relatively small white circle below.

They walked a quarter of the way around the arena, then up again into a series of windowed hallways built high into the outer wall. Along with a seemingly normal assortment of Caeridorian citizens, small groups of men and women in fancy dress congregated there, speaking in hushed tones and eating from small platters served by well-dressed specimens of former fighters. On the edge of hearing Meli detected negotiations taking place, bartering and begging and promising a fighter a bout with this, or the wager of some political post or servant on the outcome of that.

She followed as Ariden worked the hall, listening in where he could, studying the faces and shaking his head as if they all failed to stir his long-dormant memories. If he was expecting to be welcomed and hailed as a great champion from long ago, he was sorely disappointed, as the higher-ups of Caeridor's fight world seemed to think it best to ignore him. Ariden became more direct as they neared a complete circle of the building, tapping some of the negotiators to ask a question, only to be rebuffed with a shake of the head or a turned shoulder.

"Do we really need these people?" Meli whispered. "Surely there must be another way of becoming a fighter."

"I would need to apply to a club, work my way up the lower ladders. It might take years."

"Then we'll come back later. Perhaps another day."

Ariden huffed and shook his head. This is what we have to work with, his face said, and something in his eyes made her heart sink. She scanned the crowd again, looking for something, anything.

From within a tight pack of figures, a thin woman, her wide lips painted crimson, looked their way and smiled.

"Ariden," she said. "Is that you?"

Ariden turned and smiled back. The woman approached. She held a felid in her arms, which batted its large eyes each time she stroked it.

Ariden struggled for words, then finally managed her name. "Alalantia."

"Elaethim's mercy, I did not expect to see you." She laid a hand on his chest. Her fingers drifted upward, over his throat and chin, to rest on the top of his nose, which she gave a light tap. "How long has it been?"

"Too long." Ariden cocked his head as he grinned.

"Indeed. It seems like a million years, now. What fun we had together." She pressed close to him, touching his cheek with her hand and his thigh with her own. The felid growled between them.

Meli heard a crunching sound, and realized she was grinding her teeth. Perhaps Alalantia heard it too, for she turned and gave a nod.

"And who might this be?"

"Meli, meet Alalantia. When I...knew her...she was a junior member of the Caeridor High Council. Is that still the case, Ala?"

Alalantia chuckled and waved back her hair. She wore a swirling black gown, elegant and comfortable-looking, making Meli feel suddenly out of place in her dirty hiking gear. She had grown so used to her outfit in the preceding centemeran that she hadn't given a thought to changing it when they reached the city.

"I am still on the council, though no longer a junior. You'll find many things have changed since you were last here, Ariden."

"But some things have not. Great fighters are still rewarded, yes?"

"You've come for business, then. And you need my help? What reward do you seek?"

"Eventually, a skyship and a pilot," Ariden said. "But for now, I'd settle for a room inside the city."

"A ship? Why?"

"We're going north, as soon as possible. We have a score to settle there."

"We? You're planning on leaving so soon, with her?" Her big lips pressed into a pout. "Now why should I help you with that?"

"Well..." Ariden raised an eyebrow. "I didn't say I wouldn't come back."

"You wily old hornlizard." She smiled broadly and ran her fingers through his hair. "I'll find you a place to stay. A special favor for an old friend."

"And the ship?"

"You'll have to fight for that, I'm afraid. Let me ask around, make some arrangements. We'll meet tomorrow to discuss it. Unless, of course," she batted her eyelashes, "you would rather spend the night with me."

Ariden glanced at Meli, then grinned again. "I had better save my energy. At least until I know who I'm going to fight."

"I see." She stepped back and straightened herself, giving her felid a hard pet. "I'll fetch Pasierno. He can help with your accommodations. Stay right here." She excused herself with a kiss on his cheek and a sly nod at Meli, who stood frozen, her cheeks flushed.

Ariden watched her leave, then turned back to Meli. He started when he saw her color.

"What?" he said. "What is it?"

"Nothing." She turned her back and headed to the exit. "Why would it be anything?"

"Huh?"

"I'm getting some aer. Come find me when the room is ready. Assuming I'm welcome there."

"Why wouldn't you be?" he shouted to her back, a moment before his voice became lost in the groups of citizens in the narrow hall.

Meli woke to a knock on the thick partition she had convoked to divide their small apartment. It was day, and light streamed through the single window she had split in two, gray reflecting off the building across the alley, and stained brown from dust on the pane.

"Are you awake?" Ariden called. "Ala wanted to give us a tour of the city."

She shot up in bed and pulled the sheets close. She had let her traveling clothes crumble in the night, and the closeness of Ariden's voice had tricked her for a moment into thinking he could see.

"A moment," she said, struggling to convoke something new in her post-waking haze.

"I'll wait downstairs."

Meli did her best to copy what she had seen of Caeridor fashion, donning a high-necked green gown with a separate neck scarf, her hair pulled back and sprinkled with glittering jewels. When she arrived in the alley, Ariden wore the same long, dark cloak as ever. He nodded in greeting, looking less severe than usual, perhaps even mildly sheepish. He had left the apartment the previous evening and returned after she fell asleep—had he gone to see Alalantia?

"About Ala," he said, as if reading her mind. "I had completely forgotten her before I saw her in the meeting halls. Even during our conversation, I was making up half of it as I went along."

All right—she'd had enough of this silliness, from him and from herself. Whatever charade was happening would end now.

"What of it? My goal is to save Karis, that is all. Once that is done, you will claim your price and go on your way. Our deal still stands, yes?"

He grunted, his eyes traveling over her gown. "I suppose so."

"Then let's go on this tour, if you think it will help."

They returned to the arena, this time entering through the wide front archway, and headed directly to the stairs leading to the upper boxes.

"Ariden," Alalantia said when she saw them. "Meli. You are finely dressed today."

Meli bowed, and Alalantia led them outdoors, behind the parapets topping the outer walls, from which she could point out landmarks across the city, and make recommendations for places to eat, be entertained and be seen. Every so often they would pass a sentry standing atop the wall, looking outward, though what exactly they were meant to be guarding was lost on Meli. At least the men below who cleaned the streets were doing something useful—to make these ones stand here practically for show seemed the very definition of evil.

Alalantia's felid gave a low growl in her arms, as if the height made it nervous.

"Now, now, Xalix." She stroked its striped back and tail. "Hush, my little sweet."

"That's a very nice specimen," Meli said. "Did you convoke it yourself?"

Alalantia chuckled. "Oh, no. I ordered Xalix from the greatest animatist in Caeridor. The council keeps him here with as many bribes as we can manage. Making one so tame is quite a feat, you know.'"

"I know. I've practiced animatism most of my life." Meli smiled at Xalix and gave him a scratch behind the ears.

"Ah. In that case, you will like what I have to show you next. Up here is something very special." Alalantia waved them into a stout tower set into the rear of the arena, overlooking the sea. Meli climbed the circular staircase up to the roof, looked out from the doorway and gasped.

"Oh! You really have one!"

The drakenbird opened one bright yellow eye, hooted contentedly, then curled up and turned over, causing a slight rumble beneath their feet. It was dull orange, covered in a patchwork of scales and feathers, with a body the size of a small dwelling and a beak and claws which could have cleaved a man in two.

"We're lucky to have a nesting pair at the moment," Alalantia said. "I can't remember; did any live here when you were the champion, Ariden?"

"I don't think I ever bothered to check," Ariden replied.

They stayed a while, Meli watching the creature sleep from across the rooftop, while Ariden walked to the other side, looking out beyond the city to where the Outsiders had emerged from their tents.

"There are more beyond the walls than I remember," Ariden said. "They seem somewhat rowdy, as well."

"Yes." Alalantia stepped beside him. "They have something of a leader now, stirring them up. Elaethim only knows what they will demand next."

"Equality?"

"All citizens have equality, and they have the right to become citizens, if they earn a place in the arena. No, what they really want is to cause strife, because doing so amuses them. When I head the council, the Outsiders will be made to see that such dangerous behavior has no place in our society."

"You speak as if you are close to taking over," Ariden said. "How are your fighters doing?"

"Well enough. When you reach a certain level, there are battles to fight beyond the arena. It's taken me a very, very long time to work my way to this position; I am loath to predict I will reach the pinnacle soon." She returned to the stairs. "But I don't wish to bore you with politics. Let us see about fixing *your* problems first, eh?"

They headed to one of the spacious private boxes from which the upper echelons watched the fights, where several councilmembers and their guests were already waiting. They convoked a set of chairs at one end, Alalantia on one side of Ariden and Meli on the other, and watched as two fighters and one official walked into the arena and bowed to the sparse morning crowd.

Alalantia made a show of introducing them to each councilmember in turn, and each one made a requisite amount of small talk, the sum total of which stymied Meli's ability to keep any of it straight. She recognized Pasierno from the day before, and thanked him profusely for the honor of staying in a tiny room in a dirty alley.

As undignified as their lodgings were, however, at least now they were being treated well. Refreshments passed freely, and the interior of the box was decorated in tiny flowers and soft black carpet. It was gracious of Alalantia to choose perhaps the most exclusive location in all of Caeridor in which to speak with them. Perhaps Meli had misjudged her. Her lewdness toward Ariden had been bothersome, though Meli could not have said why, but she had displayed far less of it today. It was just such a shame that sitting in the clear-walled box meant there was no way to avoid watching the fights.

The fighters came up two by two, bowed to the audience, to the tower where the drakenbird roosted sight-unseen, and to each other. Then each fight would commence, continuing until either there was a winner or a gong sounded their time was up. To Meli's surprise, most fights ended relatively quickly—she would have thought that the rough-looking men could pound on each other for days at a time without one giving up. But often, the men would opt to wrestle after exchanging a few blows, scrambling in the dust until one broke another's leg or arm, or at least threatened to—Meli wasn't following the details. She certainly did not partake in the spyglasses that most of the others in the box used to view the fights—including Ariden, who watched the first few bouts with intense interest, sometimes shouting with excitement when someone pulled off what must have been a particularly good move.

"They have gotten better, I think," Ariden said. "At least for lower-tier fighters. But when I join the main ladder, this city will be turned upside-down."

"You are on your way," Alalantia put in. "Many of those in this room sponsor fighters who would make a good introductory match for you."

"How many fights would I need to barter for a ship?"

"It depends. You have an excellent storyline…a former champion from long ago, returned—"

"The greatest champion," Ariden corrected.

"Pardon me. Returned, to reclaim his title, climbing again from the bottom up. If you won say, ten fights in a row, you would have the wherewithal to ask any favor you wished."

Ariden glanced at Meli, then shook his head. "Ten is too many. I don't want to spend years wiping the floor with nobodies. Give me a big fight now."

"A fight that big will not be easy to arrange. Skyships are difficult to come by in Caeridor of late; the council believes having too many mekkanist citizens draws the attention of raiders."

"There must be some way," Ariden said. "Use your influence, Ala. For me." He rested his hand on hers. Meli breathed hard out her nose.

"Perhaps there is." Alalantia squeezed his hand tight and propped her chin on her other fist. "I do know of one opportunity, though it may not be exactly what you're looking for."

"Yes?"

"A fight against a champion. There was an incident, a street fight involving the prospective challenger, and now Lem has no opponent at the next Grand Events. I could put your name in as a last-moment replacement."

"Fantastic!" Ariden dropped Alalantia's hand and banged the arm of the chair. "Why would I not accept that?"

"Well, for one thing, the fight would not be in your division. And the terms would have to be rather poor as well."

"Fine," Ariden said. "I will take an opponent of any size."

"What do you mean, poor terms?" Meli asked.

"Lem's sponsor will demand a no-out clause, because of the late notice. That means once you agree to the contract, you must fight, or face a legal penalty."

"No matter what?" Meli said. "That sounds risky."

"And likewise," Alalantia continued, "there will be no official to stop the match. Both fighters will have the option to continue until death, if they wish."

"What?" Meli said.

Alalantia shook her head. "Now, now. It's unlikely such a circumstance would come to pass. We just need a bit of *oomph* to sell this match to the crowds."

"No." Meli leaned forward. "It's barbaric. We won't do it."

"We will," Ariden said. "We agree to the terms. But are you sure that winning will get us a skyship and a pilot?"

"A championship is a championship," Alalantia said. "If you win."

"Then I shall," Ariden said. "Will you be sponsoring me?"

"My roster is full, I'm afraid. I have someone else in mind, though. And rest assured I shall take a significant third-party interest in the match; I must claim some prize, after all. If you'll excuse me, I should locate Lem's sponsor as soon as possible. This opportunity may pass quickly."

As soon as she was out of earshot, Meli bent in close.

"I don't like this. A fight to the death? I thought such things were outlawed."

Ariden shook his head dismissively, as Alalantia had. "It's a formality, nothing more. Death matches are good sells for the crowd, but a dedicated fighter respects his opponent too much to kill without reason. And besides, Lem has never faced the likes of me. Do not trouble yourself over it."

"But why would they offer you this fight in the first place, if they didn't think you worthy before?"

"Because Ala will make it so. This is the way things are done in Caeridor, trust me. By seizing this chance, we have brought ourselves one step closer to Karis."

Meli sat back, still unconvinced. But she could think of no more objections which would satisfy Ariden, and so she waited, doing her best to ignore the violent spectacle taking place below her. Perhaps he was right—if they really could save so much time, then the undesirable terms were worth the risk. Karis's life could depend on it, after all.

Alalantia returned some time later with two men in tow, one squat with a thick mop of brown hair tinged with blond, whose wide shoes flapped on the ground as he walked, the other tall and thin, wearing the dark blue uniform of the arena officials.

"Ariden, this is Nikolatin. He is Lem's sponsor. I have also brought Darendin to act as a witness to the agreement."

"Excellent." Ariden stood and exchanged slaps to the chest with Nikolatin.

"Gentlemen," Darendin said. "On Elaesday, in two weeks and two days' time, the next Grand Events will take place. A match will be made between your fighters, with the rules to be as follows: no time limit, no weapons, free-form ringcraft, no official, no early withdrawal, and no penalty for continuing after submission. Do you both agree?"

Ariden and Nikolatin nodded and said, "Aye."

"Then by gods of this city and the drakenbirds which watch over us, I declare the match on, provided you lock your keys."

He opened his palms, and convoked in each a simple hook. Ariden took one and Nikolatin the other, and they linked the hooks together between them and pulled. The fragile solid aether bent, then cracked, and finally broke apart in a puff of dust.

"It is done," Darendin said. "Sailach smile upon you both. Your fighters will be placed under guard from now until the match, to prevent their early withdrawal."

He nodded toward the door. Two burly men with pikes strode in and took up positions on either side of Meli.

She looked back and forth and chuckled. "I think you have the wrong person."

"They do?" Nikolatin's eyebrows scrunched. "You mean you have another fighter to face Lemuria?"

"Another..." Ariden's eyes widened. "No. This is not right."

"What?" Meli asked. "What is it?"

Ariden wheeled to face Alalantia. "What are you trying to convoke? This is nonsense. I agreed to fight the champion. Me."

Alalantia crossed her arms, her eyes narrow. "You, or the fighter you sponsor, agreed to fight Lem, who as everyone knows is the current champion of the lightweight women's division."

Ariden's face went white. He stepped back as if caught in a gale. "Since when is there a *women's division?*"

"Wait," Meli said. "What are you talking about?"

"Hey!" Nikolatin shouted, pointing at Ariden. "We have an agreement, you dirty outlander. You can't back out now. Alalantia, what's going on?"

"Alalantia...tell them this is a mistake." Meli felt dizzy. All eyes in the private box were on her. "Ariden is the fighter, not me."

"Why, Ala?" Ariden said. "Why are you doing this?"

Alalantia stood with perfect composure, her mouth a thin line. Ariden waited in vain for an explanation, then shot her a look of utter contempt and turned to Darendin.

"What is your ruling? Is the fight on?"

Darendin nodded. "The match has been made, and sworn to the gods. If your fighter chooses not to compete, then she will face our justice."

The last words dripped off the man's tongue like syrup. Time had slowed down, and Meli's heartbeats felt long and deep in her chest. A fight? For her? She didn't know whether to break down in tears or laugh at the absurdity.

The force of Ariden grabbing her shoulder jolted her to awareness. "Let's go. We have work to do."

He pulled her along as he swept toward the exit, since she was hardly capable of propelling herself. At the doorway, he stopped and turned.

"You have challenged the wrong man, Ala. I'm going to beat you."

"If the two of us were fighting," she said, her voice dripping with disdain, "I'd say you were correct."

"This is a fight." His stare looked intense enough to shatter the windows. "Just one beyond the arena."

And with that, he took Meli in hand again and dragged her out.

25

"Focus, please!" Mentor Queslim yelled across the room, breaking Karis's focus. The fragile plate she had balanced on her thin spike fell, landing edge-up and rolling off her work table before she caught it in mid-aer.

"Nice one." Tementon smiled meekly beneath his green hood.

"At least I'm good for something," she said, re-balancing the plate.

He shrugged. "You're better than I was at this stage."

"That's hardly saying much!" Queslim came up behind them and slapped Tem on the back, causing him to flinch away. Queslim was stout and Tem slight, but the smaller man's reaction still seemed out of proportion to Queslim's strike. "Now, now, merely a jest, my boy. Karis, are you having trouble with the convocation?"

"A little," she admitted. "Maybe I'm too used to making accelerants. I don't quite see how the material is supposed to move while staying still."

Queslim rubbed his ample chin. "Accelerants are not difficult as esoteric convocations go, though containing them so they can do useful work can be. But the same principle of harnessing the motive forces of the aether is at work in agitism. What we must do is activate the accelerant properties of the material in question, while leaving it constrained in its solid form. Have you ever seen a transposist convocation before?"

"I've heard of them," Karis said. "Solids which become liquid, then change back."

"Correct; by invoking internal motion in the material, we cause it to deform. Agitism is the next step, using automatist principles to vibrate at a material's fundamental frequency. The frequency at which it will—" Laughter from the far end of the room pulled his attention away. "You there, I just told you to *focus!*"

He stomped off, his instruction to Karis forgotten. At the far end of the room, Paolem looked up from where he had been joking with a female apprentice named Ferici and frowned. The pair had chosen not to wear their green robes as Karis and Tementon had; not that they were strictly required to do so, of course. Perhaps Ferici felt the hood would disrupt her hair, which she had dyed blue and set up in spikes. Karis sighed and turned back to her table. She couldn't begrudge Paolem's behavior; after all, it wasn't as if he had ever voiced any desire to learn the ways of the automatists. Given that he was trapped here, it was a wonder he had changed completely from the sour-faced, obnoxious personality she had known on the ship to a rather jovial creature, currently disregarding the rather thorough chewing-out Queslim was heaping on him.

If only Karis had undergone such a transformation as well. Instead, she still found herself thinking of Meli often, slowly coming to accept that her friend had likely crumbled at the bottom of the sea, and it was Karis's own fault.

She wanted to move on, to keep her promise to herself, but the more she immersed herself in her work, the more she felt her ascent through the Automatia's ranks was proceeding at a frustratingly sluggish pace. Part of this, she sensed, was simply the way things were done—joining the school's inner circle and gaining access to its true secrets was supposed to take decades in the best case. But there was more: Again and again she had noticed herself being passed over in favor of the other apprentices, her considerable mekkanist talents ignored or taken for granted.

Why? She had suspicions, but little else. Jaela might be passing rumors about her to be spiteful, or Roi might be attempting to hold her back for reasons unknown. But she had also noticed the stares when no one thought she was looking, the whispers in the halls. The same ones she had heard all her life. *Smoothskin.*

Even here she could not escape them, despite the fact that many of the apprentices had arrived as outcasts, finding for the first time a group of people who thought and believed as they did. And yet, once arrived and assimilated, they wasted no time in excluding *her* for the crime of being different. An infuriating, though familiar feeling, and one that had already cleaved a great rift between her and her peers.

Well, most of her peers, anyway. There was always Tem. He was no substitute for Meli, of course, but he was good company in his own eccentric way.

"I'm ready to try again," she said to him. He didn't respond, distracted by something in the hall. "What is it?"

"Isn't that your prince there? With the administrators?"

Karis leaned over and saw Roi, Bressim and Corrindal striding down the hall. Roi's voice rose and fell the way it did when he was delivering the punch line to a story, and the two automatists broke into laughter before disappearing around a corner.

"Don't worry about him," she said. "Just get ready."

She leaned forward and narrowed her eyes, wishing she could follow her own advice. Since thir arrival, Roi had actually treated her rather well, which was infuriating in itself, since he acted as if most of their personal history had been nothing more than her imagination. But though she didn't fear him moving against her directly, it was clear he didn't want her knowing his business, and he was definitely up to something involving the Automatia's secret convocations. If he slipped up and the administrators became wise to him, what would become of her?

She closed her eyes, feeling the aer flow over the spike on the table. Tem had prepared the plate for her, loosened it so that it was slightly more flexible than normal. Automatism was a terribly subtle art—to give a portion of the aether an instruction like "move" might change it into an accelerant, but an automatist material had to deliver further instructions to itself, and only under certain conditions, so that an entire complex process could run independently without petering out or losing control. She focused her mind, laid her design, willed it to happen and opened her eyes.

A small, concentric ring of vibration moved from the outside of the plate to the inside, popping it upward when it reached the center. Tem gasped. The plate hung in the aer for a moment, then came down, smacked on the table and shattered onto the floor.

"Oh, mold!" Tem yelled.

"What do you mean?" Karis said. "That was great!"

"But you nearly smashed my foot."

"All right," Queslim said. "Enough for today, all of you. Go and rest your minds. I have my own work to do."

The apprentices began to file out, letting their plates and tables crumble behind them. By the time Karis was at the door, automatic sweepers were already combing the room, pushing the piles of dust down hidden chutes to the strait below.

"Come on," she said to Tem. "Let's go to the common hall."

The corridor outside shone in the mid-morning light from the wide aperture at the far end. Ahead, a whirring sound presaged one of the knee-high, box-like messenger drones gliding along the grooves in the floor. It halted just short of Karis's legs, waved its eye stalks, buzzed in annoyance, then backed up, twirled for a few moments to find a new track, and finally whirred away.

"It seemed a little upset," Karis said.

"It did." One of Tem's bushy red eyebrows rose beneath his hood. "Strange, since it has no feelings. Though I suppose someone might have been upgrading it."

"Is that the next goal, then? An automaton that can feel?"

"One of many, I'm sure." He walked on down the hall. "Time goes on and the designs get better, only for us to discover our goal is much further than we thought. We need more mekkanists like you, I think, to help us build bodies. Perhaps before you leave we'll have constructed the automaton man after all."

"Always with the automaton man." She shook her head and clucked her tongue.

"You don't think it a worthy goal?"

"Well, how come you never mention an automaton woman?"

"Eh? Well, I didn't mean…it wouldn't even really *be* a man."

"I'm joking." She smiled and gave him a playful shove onto the square lifting pad. They stood for several moments in awkward silence, waiting for it to move.

"I think this thing is broken."

He nodded. "We'd better take the long way."

"In seriousness," she said as they continued on toward the daylight, "I've never really understood the administrator's motivations. Yes, animals can be troublesome to deal with, but what good is a man or a woman who can't think?"

"They would think. They would be able to speak and solve problems just as we do, but without making mistakes. That is the foundation of the Automatia's philosophy—by disassembling thoughts down to their basic essences, we believe we can create a better world, a perfect world."

"But if you control their thoughts, then they're nothing more than slaves."

"Slaves are men with yokes and chains around their necks." Tem frowned, as if troubled by a memory. "But an automaton would not mind being controlled. Why would they, if that was their purpose in life?"

Tem reached the end of the hall and stepped out past the side of the building, where a convoked platform appeared below his feet to catch him before he fell. He spun on his heel and headed up a freshly growing staircase to the next floor.

"It's not life," she said, hurrying up after him. "If someone ever stops thinking of these mekkanikal men, they'll crumble like these stairs. So how could they be alive?"

"You're right." He stepped back inside, into a hallway filled with passing apprentices. "But no one has yet solved the problem of conferring self-awareness without also granting free will. Perhaps someday we will, though. How complicated can a man be? Like the automatons, we move, we talk, we crumble to the same dust. Just because we don't yet understand the convocation that makes us doesn't mean we should leave its working to the gods alone."

If only Meli could hear this. Karis sighed and dropped her shoulders.

"Is something wrong?"

"No. Never mind. Let's discuss something else, shall we?"

"As you wish," he said with a shrug.

They were well into the common room by then, and long tables lay on both sides of them, heaped with dishes and cups. Apprentices with a talent for savortism were in high demand, whisking from table to table with trays, competing to see who could proffer the most dishes to the diners.

"Look," Tem said. "It's Pheazal. Hey, Pheazal! May we sit with you?"

"What are you doing?" Karis said under her breath, but by then it was too late. Phaestal had seen them—and worse yet, Jaela was sitting next to him, already fixing Karis with a malignant stare. There was nothing she could do now, at least not without having to explain why she didn't get along with the "Azorkans." She shuffled along behind Tem, cursing the fact that the raiders seemed to show up everywhere inside the school, despite being outnumbered by the rest of the apprentices a hundred times over.

Tem slid up and bobbed his head at Phaestal. "And how does the day find my Azorkan friends?"

"Not too bad, actually," Phaestal said. "Mentor Kwylim said he'd take a look at some of my designs soon."

"My day just got a little worse," Jaela said, staring at Karis.

"Ah. Mentor Kwylin." Tem rolled his eyes. He convoked a combination bowl and ladle, then used it to scoop up some chunky, fragrant soup from a nearby tureen.

"What is it?" Phaestal asked.

"Well, you know about his work, don't you? He's attempting to convoke artificial bones to insert into an animal. Perhaps one day even into a human."

"That's horrible," Karis said, pouring herself a mug of chilled Bronbrigger. "If he put them into a person, it would be anathema."

"Not necessarily—anathematist convocations modify the body directly. If he convokes the parts beforehand, then inserts them after the fact...well, his work may still skirt the line too closely for some. But that's Kwylim for you—he's always been something of an iconoclast."

"A freak, in other words," Jaela said. "Seems they're everywhere around here."

Karis nearly choked on her drink. "What?"

"Hey, isn't that another one of your comrades?" Tem waved at Ferici and Paolem, walking two tables away. Paolem reared back in a bout of laughter as they passed, pulling Ferici in for a quick embrace before walking on.

"Seems like he's adjusted," Tem said. "Some don't take as well to life at the academy."

"He's taken to her, I guess," Phaestal said. "She's quite...unique."

"She's talented," Tem said. "I hear she's an excellent savortist, unlike whoever made this soup." He made a face and dumped his portion back in the tureen. "And how are you coming along, Pheazal? Do you envision yourself staying with us?"

"Oh, yeah. It's great here. I never realized before how much more there was to know. I've already started planning some big automation projects." Phaestal spread his arms wide, sinews stretching on his thin arms. "Karis, I want you to take a look at them."

"Me?"

"Sure. It's hard to get attention from the mentors and senior apprentices. You're the brightest of the newcomers by far."

Karis looked down, blushing.

"Careful," Jaela said. "You'll make her even more full of herself than she already is. If that's possible."

Karis's nostrils flared. "Now, you listen—"

"Ow!" Tem bounced in his chair, looking down. One of the messenger drones had rolled up and cracked him in the shin, and was following it up with a determined effort to crush his foot. "Get off me, you!"

The thing backed away and emitted a complex series of hoots and buzzes, then spun and zipped away as fast as it had come. Tem sat back down and stared after it, blinking.

"What was that about?" Karis asked.

"It has a message for me." Tem rubbed his neck, a worried look on his face. "One for my ears alone. Excuse me."

He pushed away and left, dropping his bowl on the ground behind him to be cleaned up by the sweepers. Karis looked back at Phaestal, fruitlessly seeking an explanation.

"Rather rude fellow," Jaela said, swirling her soup with a finger.

"You would know," Karis said.

"And you would know how to be a wretched little slime."

Karis stood and slammed her palms on the table, collapsing two pyramids of stacked cakes. "I've had enough. You're despicable—you deceived me, gained my trust only to destroy it, and now you have the nerve to treat me like I'm not even a person!" Her voice cracked as she said it, and she fought to hold back tears. "What have you been telling people about me? Hmm?"

Jaela stood as well, towering over her from opposite the table.

"I don't have to tell them anything. They see the way you act. *Oh, I'm Karis, look at me, I'm a smoothskin, I'm so unique and so smart.*"

That made Karis pause. "No. I don't—"

"You aren't supposed to be here, you know." Jaela ground her teeth, her fists shaking. "He said he was going to leave you behind. But somehow you always find a way to stick around. I know you want Roi for yourself. What did you say to him, anyway? How did you trick him into being so infatuated with you?"

Karis struggled for words. Roi infatuated? How to even begin explaining something so ridiculous?

"Well listen to me, you little rat." Jaela pointed at Karis's flat chest. "You can't have him, and if you try, I'll be there waiting."

She grasped a mug from the table and tossed it in Karis's face. Karis brought her hands up, but not in time to block the cold splash. She stood, soaking and dripping, as Jaela stomped away. The entire room was staring at her now, dead silent. The hair on Karis's neck rose. This was bad—they were too close to blowing their cover.

Phaestal sensed it too, sitting still as bedrock with his eyes wide.

"Phaestal?" Karis said, using every bit of self-control to keep her voice low.

"Yes?"

"Who convoked this drink?"

"Oh," he said. "I did. Sorry."

The liquid decomposed, turning to a yellow mud which Karis tried and failed to wipe off. Still flushed, she hurried out of the common room and back to the sleeping floor, ignoring the whispers of mentors and apprentices alike.

She stayed there in her room for the rest of the day, mulling over what had happened, wrestling with repeated waves of anger and embarrassment.

"I'm a smoothskin, I'm so unique and so smart," she mumbled.

That wasn't how she thought of herself. But like it or not, that was how Jaela saw her, and though Jaela was clearly an imbecile, who knew how many others agreed? It shouldn't have bothered her, but it did. In a place as small and tightly knit as the Automatia, the others' approval really did matter. But what chance did she have, if they judged her based on Jaela's opinion? It would have been almost comical, if her future at the school didn't hang in the balance.

She slept fitfully that night and did not rise at dawn, but stayed in her waking dreams, filled with fantastic images of lights in the sky and the tender caresses of unnamed hands. When she finally rose, her head felt clearer than it had the previous evening. Yes, Jaela had tossed a drink at her, had upset her, but it would do no good to dwell on it. Perhaps she *was* more driven than most people. She had learned in the long travels of her second life to be independent, to use determination and cunning in place of her small physical size, and she should be proud of that. She would succeed at the Automatia, and those who didn't like it could get poxed along with Jaela and the rest.

She made a new robe and attended what lessons remained in the day, attacking her automatist convocations with newfound intensity. Tem was nowhere to be found, though, and soon his absence bothered her enough that she put her projects aside and went searching. She visited each floor, but no one she asked had seen him that day. Then she remembered what had happened in the common room with the message, and began to worry.

The day dragged on, and she kept to herself. When the time came for the evening meal she slipped into the common room and took some sweettack away to avoid the raiders, feeling somewhat put aside and lonely. She stuffed one of the brown, chewy lumps in her mouth as she waited for the lift, and nearly choked when Tem walked by in front of her.

He looked even more harried than usual, with his hood back and rings under his eyes, running his fingers through messy hair. She hailed him and ran up.

"Where have you been? I looked all over."

He let out a deep breath. "Speaking with the administrators. Or should I say listening to them speak, and speak and speak...gods, I'm tired." He rubbed his eyes and collapsed into a corner, a pillow appearing behind him. "I'm only allowed a short break; they want me back in a few moments."

"What are they talking about? What's so important?"

"I can't say. They made me swear."

"Come on, Tem." She put her hands on her hips. "You can tell me."

He shook his head vigorously. "It's too huge, Karis. We're talking world-changingly huge. There's too much at stake this time."

Karis rolled her eyes. That was Tementon; he would probably be just as frightened if a stray gnat had flown inside the school. But still, whatever he was talking about sounded intriguing.

He rose to leave. "I've already said too much. The administrators would have my head if they found out what I've already told you."

"Hold on." She grabbed the green sash around his waist. "We have more to discuss."

"I'm sorry." He yanked himself away. "I'll make it up to you some other time, all right? I must go."

She watched him hurry away down the hall, thoroughly annoyed. *What was that all about?* Something about stakes, and a secret of some sort. But why would Tementon be privy to it? He was only an apprentice like her, even if he was more senior.

She paced a while, mulling the possibilities. So many questions, and not enough hard facts to draw inferences. But there was one thing she was sure of—she was in no mood to simply put the issue aside.

Administrators or no, she was going to find out what in the gods' names they were up to.

26

Ariden offered no words as they made their way down the stairs and out the side entrance of the arena. Meli followed him blindly, her mind too overwhelmed to do otherwise, until they stepped outside and she found her ability to speak.

"Where are we going? Can you wait?"

"Back to the room. And no. We have no time. You heard it yourself, the fight is in little more than two weeks."

"The fight!" She threw her hands in the aer and refused to walk further. "Just stop, please. We have to talk. I need this explained. I need something!"

He spun around and she saw that he was fuming, nostrils widening with each breath. "Fine." He motioned her into an alley. "You want an explanation? We've been double-crossed. Poxed sideways. Ala set a trap and I blundered into it."

"But why?"

"It doesn't matter. She has something to gain, politically. Perhaps she thought she might help us, then changed her mind at the last moment."

Meli held her forehead in a vain effort to stop the world from spinning. "How could you do this? I trusted you!"

"And I trusted her." He spat the words bitterly. "It was foolish of me, I do not deny it. I should not have let myself be distracted."

"Distracted? By her, you mean."

"No…" His face went sour. "Forget it. This is not the time for excuses. We should focus on what we can do."

"All right," Meli said. "Fine. We just need to reverse this somehow. There must be someone in charge, someone we can appeal to."

"No. The fight will go on. They'll make sure of it." He nodded toward the mouth of the alley, where the two guards who had followed them out of the arena stood, leaning on their pikes.

"This is insane. Preposterous. There's no way you can actually…wait—" She looked up and smiled. Of course, it was so simple. "You said that professionals don't kill each other in the ring, that they have too much respect."

"Yes?"

"Then I'll just lose immediately. Go into the arena and forfeit." And to think she had been so upset. Most of the fights she had seen had ended with one of the combatants giving up; she would simply arrive, raise her hand to signal defeat and be done with it.

"You'll do no such thing," Ariden said. "I don't run from a fight."

"What? Are you joking?"

His expression said he wasn't.

"You ran from the river monster!"

"That was different. A monster cannot think. What Ala did was the barest of betrayals. I'll die before I let her get away with it."

"Then die," she said. "But leave me out of it. I will take the non-violent solution."

"Putting aside that without a fight we would be cast out of the city, I'm not sure your gambit would work. Even if Lemuria accepted your forfeit, refusing to fight might cause the crowd to demand satisfaction—you could face justice for violating the agreement."

"What sort of justice?"

"That depends. But execution is not out of the question."

"This is barbaric," she whispered. "We have to leave. At night. Run away from here, find another city to get a ship from."

"Listen to me, Meli. If you wish to escape, I can get you out of the city. But there will be risks, and perhaps blood spilled. And there are no other large metropolises nearby; once we left, we would have to begin again our quest to find Karis, as though we had just departed the Inaali sanctuary."

She took a deep breath, letting the mixture of anger, fear and frustration stew inside her.

"Just remember, you do not have to decide today. Follow my lead, prepare yourself for Lem, and if you do not wish to fight when the time comes, then we can flee."

She spoke through clenched teeth. "How—can you *possibly*—expect me to fight her? What do you think I could actually *do*?"

"I don't know." He paced, kicking at a stray pile of dust in the corner. "If only we had more time to prepare. Twenty-two days! Twenty-two days to train someone who's never thrown a punch, against a champion."

"That's what I'm saying! It's impossible."

"Of course it is. But we're going to try anyway."

"Why?" Exasperated, she switched to pleading, her hands open. "Because you never back down from a fight? Well, I do. Tell me, please—what is the point of attempting something so futile?"

"Don't let yourself become overwhelmed. Think rationally. Lemuria is a human like you or me. She must be close to your weight, and you're muscled enough; she can't be much stronger than you. Every one of us is given a body on our appearance-day, and there's no way to change it. The only advantage she has is technique, and I can show you that, or the basics at least. And I can teach you strategy as well—that will be our strength."

"But I don't *want* to fight!"

"And that will be our weakness." Ariden looked down and shook his head. "Go back to the room and rest. Or do anything else you wish, but do not stay out too long. I will come and fetch you after I've made preparations."

He stomped off, leaving her with hundreds of questions and even more doubts. Hands clasped, she walked to the end of the alley where the two guards waited, looking bored. They shambled along after her as she made her way back to the room, probably wondering what a person like her was doing in such a circumstance. She wished she knew as well.

She lay down on her hastily convoked bedding, so that the simple white ceiling hung above her. Her head swam and she pressed on her closed eyes, trying to still her thoughts. It was all so absurd, the idea that hitting someone else with fists was an activity worth partaking in. Why would anyone live in a city which had grown to believe such a ridiculous lie? And why had she thought coming here would solve her problems?

Ariden. She had followed him, trusted that he knew how to negotiate this dark and violent world, and look what had happened. *Again.*

And yet, searching herself deeper, she felt a strange lack of ill will toward him. For all his fault and foibles, she had to admit that he was trying. And not just to serve himself, this time. The way he had spoken of Karis, it was as if he actually cared about her. About them both.

She turned over and curled up, uncomfortable with the thought of having two armed men right outside her door. She wanted nothing more than to run from the city and never look back, but what then?

She could not leave without abandoning Karis. The only choice was to let Lem injure her badly enough for the crowd to accept her forfeit, then stay and have Ariden win their ship like he was supposed to.

She imagined what it would be like to fight in the arena. She had been in physical danger before, from Vipretheon and from the river, but always she had emerged unscathed. Now Ariden was telling her to go and be beaten, hard fists smashing her flesh, breaking her bones. Anticipating the pain brought nausea welling in her throat, and she opened her eyes again to push the thoughts away.

Whatever Ariden had planned for her, she had to keep trying to impress the futility of his plan upon him, keep looking for another way to reach Karis.

She could only hope he would come to his senses in time.

"Well?" Ariden swung open the door to the musty gray room and stepped in, spreading his arms wide. "What do you think?"

Meli entered after him and sniffed. The training room was bare, lit by a small window in the ceiling, and covered with old dust. "It's somewhat...small."

He frowned. "I petitioned the council for a private training room, and this is what they gave us. It seemed unwise to risk word of our training sessions leaking out."

Footsteps in the hall heralded the appearance of a short, olive-skinned woman with black hair cut nearly to her scalp. Her body was wrapped in strips of brown leather, spiraling out to her extremities, with an especially thick cord woven across her knuckles. She acknowledged them both with a curt chest-slap.

"Ah, Zelgovsha," Ariden said. "Meli, meet your new sparring partner, Zelgovsha from Scharen."

"*Asti*," Zelgovsha said with a nod.

"To you as well," Meli said. "Where did you find her?"

"Remember our friend the gatekeeper? Zelgovsha here is a member of his club, and she's agreed to train with us for a while. Good luck for us—being able to spar with someone your own size will be invaluable."

Meli smiled at her politely, then leaned toward Ariden and whispered, "Do you really think I'll need a sparring partner today? I don't know what I'm doing."

"But you have not heard the best part: Zel here has trained with Lemuria. She knows everything—her strategies, her weaknesses. She has already told me Lemuria is nothing more than a wild brawler."

"*Nix,*" Zelgovsha said. "I say Lem tend to fight like brawler, to please crowds. But she no brawler at heart—if put in pressure, she fall back to old strategy: grab, hold down and beat till submission. Once Lem holds on ground, no one gets up."

"Oh, no," Meli said, holding her face in her hands.

"It's fine," Ariden said. "Either way, our basic strategy remains the same: work the lead and follow with a cross counter, stifle her takedown attempts, try for knees from the front headlock and use a wall to stand up if necessary."

"And what does any of that mean?" Meli asked.

He shook his head. "Never mind. Let's just start by convoking a fighter's uniform; you'll need to wear one in the arena, so you might as well get used to it now."

Meli looked down at the loose green tunic and brown shorts she had convoked that morning; she had been proud of her attempt to create something light and flexible. Then she stared at Zelgovsha in her outfit of interlaced strips. "What, *that?*"

"Yes," Ariden said. "What of it?"

"It's rather revealing, don't you think?"

"It's traditional." He shrugged. "I wore it." He caught her annoyed look and sighed. "Yes, I am sure it helps bring in the crowds as well. But right now we have more important things to worry about."

"I think what I'm wearing is good enough."

"Fine." He marched to the center of the room, removed his coat and convoked a black cushion on his left hand. He held it out for her, muscles flexing on his wide chest. "Now, let's see your lead."

"My what?"

"Your jab. Straight left punch. Stand with your hands to your chin, facing to the side. No, not that much to the side. All right, now, hit the pad with your left."

She reached out with her fist, but misjudged the distance and fell forward with an awkward step. Huffing, she straightened up again. He stood still, pad held in front of her until she tried again, this time smacking her knuckles on its surface.

"Ouch," she said. "It's hard."

He looked at the pad and rapped it with his other hand. "Seems fine. You barely touched it. Try again."

She did, giving it a good whack this time, wincing at the pain in her knuckles. He clucked his tongue and shook his head. What was the point of this? All he was doing was humiliating her.

"Straighter," he said. "And faster. Snap your hand out, turn it over, then bring it back just as fast to your cheekbone. Step forward when you punch, as well. Raise your shoulder, tuck your chin, rest your elbows on your ribs, and keep your right hand up at all times."

She placed her hands on her hips. "You're making this too complicated."

He tapped her lightly on the forehead with the pad. "Hands up."

She sighed and raised her fists again, then threw another punch, this time from further away. But again her step missed, and this time her arm extended too far, cracking painfully at the elbow. She cried out and turned away, holding her arm. In the corner, Zelgovsha snickered.

"Can we stop?" Meli said. "I'm not good at this."

"Of course you're not good. Yet. When you learn to measure the distance, you will avoid hurting your arm. Try again."

She tried, hitting the pad over and over until her knuckles were bright red and her shoulder sore. Ariden moved in and out and side to side, offering verbal correction with almost every strike, but otherwise made no move to introduce to vary the routine. The mind-numbing repetition began to dull her senses, and she found herself making the same mistakes over and over, or repeating variations on past errors, until the boredom and pain combined and she could no longer make sense of anything she was meant to do.

"Isn't there more to it than this?" she grumbled, stepping away, holding her throbbing arm.

"We have to establish your jab first. Without that, everything else is worthless."

"But I'm terrible. I've made no progress at all, and I can't lift my arm anymore."

"Take a break, then," he said. "Zel? Want a round?"

Meli went and collapsed into the corner in misery, while Zelgovsha, who had been watching the proceedings with an expression that drifted between amusement and concern, rose and worked combinations with Ariden. When she smacked the pads sweat flew off her in great bursts, settling on the ground as wet dust. Her movements seemed so natural, so capable and so strong. But that was to be expected from years of training—just as it had taken Meli years to become comfortable with vegetist and animatist convocations. How could Ariden possibly expect her to equal that accomplishment in mere days?

Ariden noticed her malignant stare after Zelgovsha's session ended. "What is the matter?"

"I think you're crazy," she said. "Do you really expect me to be able to do that?"

"No. But you'll do as well as you can, if you try."

"Zel not understanding," Zelgovsha said between deep breaths. "Why Meli take fight Meli does not want?"

Meli grumbled and turned away.

"It was a trick," Ariden said. "The match agreement was made between sponsors, with no names given. I was going to sponsor myself, but as the higher rank, Nikolatin has first choice of fighter, which means I have to choose someone from his division."

"But if no names are named, why not find another?" Zel asked.

"Wait," Meli said. "Is that right? You mean, someone else could fight in my stead?"

"Only a fighter who isn't on another sponsor's roster," Ariden said. "Which means no one. Our only options would be outside the walls."

"Then why not go outside? Among all those people, there must be one who wishes to take a chance against Lemuria."

Ariden shook his head. "If they could fight, they would be inside and not out. No matter what, our best asset in this fight is me, and my experience. And the best way to utilize that is to have a fighter who will follow instructions, and show up every single day. A stranger cannot be depended on to do that. Then again, I don't know if you can, either."

"What is that supposed to mean?" Meli said, upper lip curling. "I'm here for Karis. And because you claim this nonsense is the best way to reach her."

"You won't save Karis by sulking," he said.

"I'm trying!"

"Then will you keep trying? Even if it seems you are making no progress?"

She frowned and narrowed her eyes, but slowly nodded.

"Good," he said. "Then get up, and hit that lead again."

The second day came, with little result. Still she worked her jab, again and again, and always Ariden found her technique lacking. She convoked the traditional leather wraps around her knuckles to dull the pain, but they only delayed its onset, while chafing and reddening the skin of her palms.

At least Zelgovsha was not there that day to laugh at her, but that was her only solace during Ariden's crushing regimen. Why was he ignoring the truth? Why couldn't he see that she had made no progress, would continue to make no progress? As the day wore on, her motions ceased to have meaning or purpose. They were their own reality, the repetitive thrust of arm into pad the whole of her experience. And with each thrust, another defect: she had forgotten to step to the right afterward, she hadn't tucked her chin, she didn't hit hard enough— never, ever did she hit hard enough. He was blinded. Blinded to her lack of ability by his misplaced desire for revenge on Alalantia.

They took a short break, just long enough for the sweat to cake into dust and her breathing and heart rate to return to normal. No time for food or drink or even simple discourse. All day, any questions she had about the fight, the city, the rules, the only answer was jab, jab, jab. He called her back into the practice ring, but this time after standing up she hung back, petulant.

"Why am I always circling to the right?" she asked.

"We'll discuss it later," he said, tapping the pad.

She crossed her arms. "Now."

He grumbled. "Very well. Lemuria is right handed, which means her power hand will come from your left. By stepping to the right you are moving away from it. If you continually keep to the outside of her stance, she won't be able hurt you except with a left hook or kick."

"And what if she does throw a hook or a kick?"

"Then you'll move away, assuming she hasn't pressed you against a wall. We're going to work a back step jab soon, once we've mastered a basic one."

"And what if she does press me against a wall?"

"We'll come to that later. In the meantime, you must learn to make her fear your jab. Without that, she'll simply walk through you, and this discussion will have been moot. Now, shall we?"

Meli stood still. "How many fights has Lemuria had?"

"It doesn't matter."

"How. Many. Fights?"

Ariden sighed. "Her record is 24 and 3."

"So she's lost three times?"

"Yes, though not recently. She is on a sixteen fight win streak."

Meli huffed with exasperation and stomped to the far side of the room. Sixteen wins in a row. "This is pointless," she muttered. "She's unbeatable."

"My streak was one hundred thirty-seven," Ariden responded.

"Well, mine is zero!" Meli shouted into the corner.

She heard his footsteps in the dust, and then his voice came from just behind her, cold but collected. "I do not speak to brag. The point is that Lem is not *that* good. Yes, she is no pushover, but neither is she a living legend. A great champion needs great challengers to bring out their best, and she has trouble getting them because fewer women wish to fight."

"That's because women are smarter," Meli said, turning around.

"Why are you acting this way? Are you quitting on me, or not?"

She stuck a finger in his face. "You're the one who won't tell me what all these things mean. How can I possibly win if I don't even understand what I'm doing?"

"Don't discount yourself. Look at Zelgovsha—she probably knows ten different strategies to win a fight. But most of her moves she does wrong. Half the time I spent with her was used to un-learn what she has already learned. Once we are finished, you will know one strategy, but you will know it right. In the arena, that can be a powerful thing."

"I see what you're up to," she said. "The numbers, the misdirection. You're trying to trick me, make me believe I have a chance of winning."

Ariden raised an eyebrow, then held up the pad. "Is it working?"

She pushed him away with both hands, then delivered a jab so hard that the impact echoed throughout the tiny room.

27

Even though she had spent the better part of a year at the school, Karis had not realized until recently that there was another reason the Automatia was so clean, besides the sweeping automatons and its position over the cleansing liquid of the strait. The barrier itself—that great esoterica-enhanced dome which encircled the building—kept out the airborne dust. Even on a day which most Aetherians would describe as clear, free from choking yellow clouds or even a raging storm, the aer carried great amounts of the granular material, though it could only be seen deposited in a fine layer over every surface.

It was the plants, Meli had told her once. Aetherians were always concerned with their own leavings, spending great amounts of time sweeping out the piles of dust in their home from abandoned clothing and furniture, but the residue plants left as they grew and died over their vast tracts dwarfed what humans produced each day, like a mountain towering over an insect.

The barrier kept out the wind, too, which was more easily noticed, since the hallways of the Automatia, always open at both ends to let in the light, would have otherwise swept their occupants off their feet with channeled aer on blustery day. But inside, the Automatia more often than not was a busy place, filled with footsteps and chatter, and even after dark the endless whirring and clicking of the mekkanisms continued within its walls. It wasn't until Karis stepped outside that she understood just how different the aer within the barrier felt. It was still, calm, easy on the lungs like the aer high on the raider skyships had been, but without its biting chill. Outside the building her mind felt at ease, taking in the near silence, the slight rippling of the barrier's iridescence, and the gentle sway of trees on the mountains along the shores of the strait.

That is, her mind would have felt at ease any other time, if she hadn't been perched at a great height directly above the strait, her feet tangled in a net of rope, hanging upside-down.

Perhaps she should have taken more time to consider the situation before acting. But the mentors had already been speaking for over a day, and she hadn't known how much longer she would have to eavesdrop on them. Anyway, the more she thought about it, the more unfair the whole situation seemed. For two hundred years she had been an apprentice of some kind or another, learning patiently, never speaking out of turn. She was tired of waiting, tired of working within the system and being passed over. The time had come to step up and seize this opportunity.

Figuring out where the mentors were holding their meeting had been the easy part. Tem had gone to rejoin them on a lift heading up, which left only two floors above the level she had found him on. The one directly above she knew well, since it was home to several of the teaching areas she attended, but the top floor, where the mentors kept their private residences, was mostly a mystery. Still, she had seen parts of it, and based on deduction she felt confident that the meeting room in question took up its windward-south corner, in an area blocked off by one of the school's impassable sliding doors.

Of course, the room would still be open on the outside to let in the light, but convoking a stairway on the windward or south sides of the building as Tem had done the previous day was not an option. If the administrators knew what she was doing she would certainly be expelled, which meant she could not risk anyone noticing a large frame convoked adjacent to the forbidden area of the building. Instead, Karis walked, quickly but without appearing hurried, to the leeward docking bay on the lowest floor, just above the fog. Steps on the windward side might be noticed, but a thin ladder to the roof on the leeward side would not, provided she was lucky and climbed quickly.

That requirement was relatively easy to fulfill, as well; her small body conferred the advantage of climbing easily, provided she didn't let the height strike fear in her. And after so much time on the deck of a skyship, the mere sixty-foot drop to the strait below did not make for an undue distraction. After a few moments of hands gripping one rung after another, she emerged onto the gleaming, flat rooftop.

Stepping lightly, she went to the windward-south corner and convoked a smooth cone, then placed its large opening against the rooftop. She put her ear to the small end, but heard nothing. Perhaps the meeting was being held somewhere else after all, or maybe the ceiling below was too thick for sound to pass through. She crawled to the side of the rooftop and peered down, attempting to peek into the room below, but a six-foot span of wall lay between her and the opening. She could hear something there, though; a woman's voice, growing louder and fading as its owner paced toward and away from the window.

She sat back and took a deep breath. This was the point of no return; if she were caught on the roof, she might still be able to play it off as idle wandering. She should leave now, go back down the way she came and forget about this idea. Yes, she desperately wanted to know what was happening in that meeting, and had a strong feeling that it was important. But was it really worth the risk of them sending her away, dashing everything she had worked so hard to gain?

Hal, Dou and Parthen would have said no. So would Meli, most likely, along with most of Karis's mentors over the past century. But none of them were here.

What would Roi do? Take what he wanted, naturally, without hesitation or apology. How was it fair that he could do things she could not? That *he* had access to the administrator's ears? Which of them cared more about the future of the Automatia? Which of them was more deserving?

She bent over the side again, re-judging the distance. She could convoke a listening tube, but without the more advanced tricks some of the automatists knew for transferring sound, the end would have to be large to pick up noises in the room, and might be noticed from inside. No, she needed to see as well as hear, to know who was speaking and whether they were looking her way. That could be arranged with some mirrors and more complex inner-workings, but now she was risking running up against time. If she let herself fall into a mekkanist shrole-hole designing gadgets and solutions, then the meeting might be over before she knew it. Sometimes a direct approach was best. She would climb down, and use the listening and seeing devices the gods had given her.

She began convoking another fixed ladder, then hesitated; once crumbled, the dust from the heavy rungs could float inside the building, and a cavalcade of automatic sweeper drones would call attention to her. No, she needed something light which she could take back with her and drop into the strait on the other side.

A rope ladder, of course. She convoked a short one, anchored its ends to the rooftop, then rolled it over the side and continued convoking down until it reached a point just above the window. After convoking and wrapping one more fixed line around her waist for safety, she started down feet-first.

The silence returned to her as she climbed, that peaceful absence of wind. It was time to hang. Karis looped her feet under a rung, convoked a few extra ropes around her shins and, ignoring the sudden stroke of fear, fell backward.

She was facing the wrong way, but a convoked handhold on the side of the building and a quick spin corrected that. She had judged the distance well; only her forehead and short curls were exposed in the corner of the window.

"…and who says Fin can be trusted?"

Administrator Yilia was speaking, the back of her auburn hair facing Karis, which would have made her difficult to hear were her voice not so high and piercing. The other two administrators were present as well, along with mentors Orthanc and Kwylin, and last and very least Tem. He seemed to desire nothing more than to sink below the table, an imposing one colored deep green and divided into triangular sections convoked by each participant, with circular indentations on the outside edge, varying in size based on its maker's rotundness.

"She's a strange one, that girl." Mentor Orthanc's indentation was larger than all the rest, and his already indistinct words were muffled further by a bushy white beard, typical of a creasedskin. Karis barely knew the man, but had heard he was considered a master at convoking the coded puzzles embedded in most of the Automatia's mekkanisms. "But then, I suppose one would have to be, to accept such an assignment."

"Fin is perfectly loyal." Corrindal kept her eyes trained on Yilia as she spoke. "If the message came from her, then it is legitimate."

The two administrators stared at one another, Corrindal's face bordering on loathing. Orthanc cleared his throat and pulled his collar. Tem looked as if he were about to pass out.

Karis had never heard of this Fin before, but it was clear enough that she was one of the agents the Automatia had seeded across Aetheria. Their identities were always kept secret, and nothing was supposed to be spoken of them inside the halls, but the school was so rife with gossip that even she had heard of their existence fairly quickly. Apparently, it had been policy since at least the time of the Second Empire to send apprentices dissatisfied with the school's confining atmosphere to faraway cities, to rival centers of learning, or to live among any group which might pose a threat or possess interesting convocational knowledge. The only question was, why had this agent agitated the administrators so?

Orthanc broke the silence. "It is worth noting that the message was properly coded. No one but Fin could have sent it." He noticed what must have been a baleful look from Yilia and cleared his throat. "Of course, this does not preclude the possibility that the Inaali forced or tricked her somehow."

"It would be an effective way to draw us out." Kwylim slid a file back and forth over his nails. He seemed to pay the others little mind as he sat with one side of his mouth raised, lip trembling. His straight black hair and prickly manner reminded her of Ariden; now there was a man she would just as soon have forgotten.

Corrindal seethed with impatience. "What good would it do them to draw us into the Old Wise One's citadel?"

"They've laid a trap there." Kwylim blew on his fingers, a quick hissing puff. "Or perhaps *he* is the trap."

He? Who were they talking about? The Inaali sounded familiar, but she had never heard of an Old Wise One. Following the conversation was already hard enough, but Karis's head was swimming from hanging upside-down, and she could barely hear what they were saying. She relaxed her ankle, slipping further down the ladder and lowering her view into the window.

"A reckless trap that would be," Yilia said. "We've always had the wisdom to leave the Old Wise One alone, and I expect the Inaali would do so as well. Some dangers are best left undisturbed."

"I wouldn't put anything past the Inaali," Kwylim said.

"It matters little whether the Inaali are involved or not. The Old Wise One is too eccentric to be predictable." Yilia pointed at Corrindal. "I might go along with this venture of yours if he weren't involved, but not now."

Corrindal tapped her fingers and frowned at Bergan sitting beside her, still as a statue, the only administrator who had yet to speak. They numbered three so that there would never be a tie vote in disputes such as this, and it would be up to Corrindal to convince him of the correctness of her plan, whatever it was. After waiting in vain for him to respond, she stood up and paced—directly toward Karis.

"What do we know? Two forces—"

Karis ducked her head back and missed the next words as Corrindal approached. She bit her lip, listening to her heart thump in her ears, but Corrindal continued to speak uninterrupted, reaching the edge of the window and sweeping back the other way.

"—alone is dangerous, but together the consequences could be disastrous."

"With all due respect," Orthanc put in, "more likely they are not working together. The message said that the Inaali agents were planning to steal the Source."

"Or so they would have us believe," Kwylim said.

"If you are going to talk about what we know, then it would be wise to mention what we do not," Yilia said. "The latter far outweighs the former. Which of the convocations of legend does the Source represent? And what about this Daemon?"

Corrindal drummed her fingers on her gown. "We have not found out anything new about the Source since our last meeting."

"You're wasting our time, then," Yilia said. "We agreed that in the absence of new information, this decision was at a stalemate."

"Don't presume to tell me when I can and cannot call a meeting. You are the junior, here."

"That does not matter. I have a duty to stop you from destroying us all."

"Insolent," Corrindal hissed.

The room fell into silence. Orthanc cleared his throat again, but added no words. Kwylim grinned and convoked himself a drink. Tem gasped for breath, rolling his head back as if he lacked the strength to keep it upright. From his new position he noticed Karis peeking in the corner of the window and his eyes went wide.

"One of the four great convocations of legend." Bergan intoned in his deep, gravelly voice, bringing all eyes to him. "If we gain knowledge of it again, the power would be unimaginable."

Tem bit his lip, slipped his hand below the table and flicked his fingers at Karis. *Go away.*

Karis shook her head. *Nuh-uh.*

Yilia crossed her arms and frowned. "Even if it's true, that old geezer would die before he let the secret out."

"Do you really want to be the one who stood in the way of us finding it?" Corrindal asked. "After all these years, the dreams of the founders—"

"And what if the Inaali got hold of it?" Kwylim waved, spilling his drink in front of Orthanc. "Oh, sorry."

Orthanc waited for Kwylim to crumble the liquid, then swiped the dust away with the back of his hand.

"You're both changing the subject." Yilia said. "If we don't know exactly what the Source is, how can we say it won't pose a threat to *us* if we capture it? And you still haven't addressed the Daemon issue."

"Tem," Orthanc said.

"Ah!" Tem jumped out of his chair and landed with a rattle, snapping his focus away from Karis.

"Pay attention. What exactly is this Daemon? A god?"

"I…" He caught his breath and swallowed. "I don't know exactly. I was told the word means, 'one who lives within.'"

"Within what?"

"Anything. Everything. It could refer to a realm between ours and the gods', perhaps. Or a being who is a part of our world somehow, without physically manifesting inside it."

"See? He's not even making sense," Yilia said. "All we have are half-convoked riddles."

Orthanc smiled and patted Tem on the shoulder. "Just tell us what you can, Tem. Explain how you came to know of this being."

"Well, uh…" Tem stared at the table; perhaps doing so helped him imagine the room was empty. "It was many years ago, when I lived in Sidel. I met a man who said he had come from a remote area in the Aperandi mountains. He had a story to tell, one so chilling I've never forgotten it. In fact, until you all called me here, I had always hoped he had made it up to scare me.

"He said that he and his companions had gone to investigate an area they called the Drop's Touch. It was a crater, present since the beginning of time, but of late, strange happenings had been reported there. When he arrived, he found the Lost Jungle growing inside."

"The Lost Jungle?"

"That was what he called it. He said there was a presence inside the crater—not a god, but something…else. A being beyond anything he could comprehend. I'm not sure what he meant exactly; I didn't pry further because he seemed half-mad. He told horrible tales about how all his friends had been killed inside the Jungle. But he also said that before he escaped, he touched minds with the entity. It spoke to him through his thoughts, and he saw a glimpse of its plans. He said the thing had a name. It called itself 'The Daemon.'"

"Why would this *thing* share its plans with a stranger?" Yilia asked.

"Because...he said something about it having two minds. There was another entity inside the Daemon. Less powerful. It tried to warn them, to save them, but then..."

"And the plans?" Orthanc said. "What were the Daemon's plans?"

Tem licked his pale lips. "He said that once the Daemon made real contact with the aether, it would be able to control it. All of it. And then...who knows? Its desires were not human. Perhaps it would sweep everything clean, start over before it remade the world to its liking."

Mutters of consternation filled the room.

Yilia groaned. "Dramatics. Instead of the ravings of a madman, look at the facts we have: two people, on a journey to reach a very old and very sour hermit in the mountains. Let's not get carried away with ourselves."

"But remember that the Inaali are obsessed with dispersal," Kwylim said. "This 'clean sweep' sounds just like a scheme they would convoke. It would not surprise me at all to learn that they were in league with this Daemon."

Karis furrowed her brow. That was right; the Inaali were that disperser cult somewhere on the Leeward Coast. In her mind's eye, ragged cracks in a tan wall replaced the clean lines of the Automatia. She shook away the memory and frowned. How evil the Inaali must be to promote such a practice. Corrindal was right—whatever this Source was, it needed to be kept from them.

"I still say we're looking at this the wrong way," Kwylim said. "We should kill these agents before they reach their goal. Then we don't have to worry about the Source being disturbed."

"I've considered that," Corrindal said. "But it won't work. Fin said they chose to travel overland instead of by sea, on a longer route. What reason could they have to do that, other than to evade detection?"

"If Fin had simply followed them and done the job herself..."

"It was her choice not to take the risk; we don't know what odds she would have faced against them. In any case, we'll never find them out in the wilds. Taking the Source from the Old Wise One ourselves, before the Inaali arrive, remains our best plan."

Yilia sighed. "The drawbacks of which we have been over, numerous times."

Corrindal paced a circle around the table, while the others—save Bergan—followed her with their eyes. "I have conferenced with Orthanc and some of the other mentors in our time apart. I am confident that we have the contingencies planned for." She paused, making sure she had their attention before delivering her final stroke. "Roi and his crew will not be able to make use of the ship, beyond what we will set them to do."

Karis nearly yelped, slapping her hand over her mouth. Roi? They were going to send Roi to this place? Tem looked up at her again, horrified at the squeak she had made, but the others had taken no notice.

"There must be someone else who can go," Kwylim said. "Even if the other apprentices are not fit, mentors have left the school before, in times of dire need."

Corrindal shook her head and resumed pacing. "We don't know how much time we have left; the mentors cannot train for this mission and build the ship at the same time. And even if they could, in some ways Roi is a superior choice to any mentor."

"You must be joking."

"I am not. Who better for a mission like this than a—" Corrindal glanced at Tem. "Well, anyway, I don't want to dredge that issue up again. The plan has been made. The ship will only work for its intended purpose, to bring Roi and his followers to the Old Wise One's fortress, then return them here with the Source." She faced the window, looking out into the strait, and gave a smirk only Karis could see. "Roi has already agreed."

Karis had been steadily withdrawing as Corrindal approached, staying out of her line of sight. But as the administrator stepped closer, Karis's foot caught in the ladder. Her heart skipped a beat and she kicked, but the foot remained trapped. Could she crumble the rungs without dropping herself into the fog? Corrindal stepped closer again, then again.

"You spoke with him?!" Yilia yelled.

Corrindal stopped walking and turned.

"I had an opportunity to persuade him. It wasn't easy to get him to go along, but now it is done."

"You broke our pact. We agreed, no word of this outside the room."

Karis curled up so she could see her foot, then worked it from between the ropes. Too close, there. When she let herself back down to the window again, Bergan was speaking for the second and final time.

"…but if indeed Roi already knows, then our path is set. Simply remaining here is no longer an option."

"You can't do this," Yilia said. "Don't let her get away with it!"

More shouting ensued. Karis climbed away. She had heard enough, taken enough risks, and the news about Roi had put her head in such a spin that hanging from the outside of the building seemed even less of a wise choice. She pulled the ladder onto the roof after her and hurried off to leeward.

So Roi was leaving, then, going on a raid for this mysterious convocation. Whether Yilia managed to delay the mission or not, Karis knew it would happen sooner or later; if Roi had set his mind to going, he would ensure that. And what did that mean for her? If Roi left and took the raiders with him, she would be free of them, possibly forever. Whether or not they succeeded in taking this Source, that was good news, wasn't it?

She climbed back into the docking bay, then dropped her rope ladder into the fog and let the fixed one crumble. A bit of dust wafted inside, and a passing automaton swiveled and hurried to it, brushes whirring. Karis stepped over the automaton and stood still, making sure no human had taken notice of her.

Hearing nothing, she took the nearest lift to the sleeping quarters. There she lay down in bed, her eyes open, turning this way and that. Getting rid of Roi and the others would be good, but was it really enough? Something else was pulling her. The Inaali, the Automatia, Roi…all of them were attracted to the Source. What was it? Exactly what power did it promise its wielder?

She sighed. She felt far too fidgety to sleep, but she didn't want to visit the common room either, so she got up and began pacing the halls. She took the lift up one level to where she could walk among the empty classrooms, her eyes on her feet, mumbling her thoughts. A motion at the end of the hall caught her attention. Her heart skipped a beat when she realized Corrindal was coming toward her.

Karis's unease lasted only a moment; the tall woman had her eyes fixed on a distant point, looking over Karis's head as most people did. As they passed one another, Karis nodded and said, "Good evening, my lady." Corrindal gave her a small nod back, and they continued on their separate ways.

Karis was almost at the far corner when a voice came from behind.

"A moment, if you please?"

Karis froze and bit her lip, then put on a smile before she turned. "Yes?"

Corrindal approached and smiled back kindly. "You're Karis, aren't you?"

Karis nodded.

"You've been with us for over a centemeran now. How are you getting along?"

"Oh, wonderfully," Karis said. "Everyone here has made me feel very welcome."

"Good. Sorry if I disturbed you; I just like to check in on our new apprentices now and then. Do come to me if you have any problems, will you?"

Karis nodded.

"Excellent. Well, I'm sure you're busy; go on, get along."

Karis made a little bow and turned to leave.

Once again, Corrindal's voice fell on her back, this time harsh and cold.

"Karis?"

She froze.

"Did you really think I wouldn't see you hanging outside that window?"

Karis shut her eyes. *Mold.* She turned and stammered, a thousand insipid excuses running through her mind, but all she managed was, "I...I..."

"You're the girl who spends all her time with Tementon, aren't you? I suppose that's how you discovered the meeting?"

Karis looked at her feet. She wouldn't say anything to get Tem into further trouble.

"So what am I to do now?" Corrindal continued. "You're one of Roi's crew, aren't you?"

"No," Karis said, indignant. "No, I'm not."

"I see. Well, if you're not with him, then I suppose I might as well get rid of you."

Corrindal turned and walked away. No, it couldn't end like this, not so quickly. There had to be something she could do.

"Wait!" The words came out before Karis had fully formed the thought. "Make Roi take me with him. I'll be your safeguard."

Corrindal stopped and raised an eyebrow. "My safeguard?"

"You said the ship you're giving him will only work for its intended purpose, yes? Which means you'll have some sort of control over it. But what if the control fails somehow? If I'm on board, I can keep an eye on Roi, make sure he does what he's supposed to do and brings the Source back here."

"A worthy task. But you're only an apprentice—why should I choose you for it?"

"Because Roi is used to working with me. He wouldn't be here now if it weren't for me."

"And how do I know you tell the truth? What if your loyalty lies with him, and not with us?"

"He and his crew betrayed me; I nearly died because of them. Please, you must believe; ask anyone who was in the common hall yesterday how I really feel about them. This is my home now. I swear, I only want to help the Automatia, to bring back whatever it is you seek, for the greater glory of us all."

Corrindal narrowed her eyes, her hands folded by her waist. Karis sensed putting her on the spot like this did not work in her own favor. But the hall behind her was empty of interlopers, and Corrindal could keep Karis waiting as long as she liked. Long moments passed before she grinned.

"You're a little one, Karis. You think that means no one notices you, and sometimes you're right. You like to worm around, get into business you have no right to see. I suspect it's gotten you into trouble in the past, as well.

"Personally, I'm still inclined to expel you. You're a dangerous sort, clever and persistent, with a disarming appearance. But those same qualities could benefit the Automatia, if I put you to work for us."

"Then you'll send me with Roi?"

"Perhaps I will. But it will be your last chance. You had better hope that Roi is among those who have underestimated you. Because if you do not return with the Source, you shouldn't bother coming back at all."

Her gown swished as she walked away, shoes clacking on the smooth floor.

28

O n the fifth day, Ariden had Meli throw a right hand for the first
time.

The results were as disastrous as before: a slow, sloppy
movement which wouldn't have hit a Behemoth taking a long nap.
Ariden took some time to walk her through the proper way to turn her
hips, then returned to jabs again, only occasionally requesting she
throw the right. The jab was still too slow, he said, and not liable to tag
a fighter of Lemuria's caliber. Still, he began to set up more complex
scenarios, throwing mock punches himself, overreaching in an attempt
to show her the best time to use her right.

"The idea is to stifle her with the jabs, get her angry and moving
forward. If she is coming in to meet it, the right hand could be a
knockout blow." He set up the pads again and Meli threw a left,
ducked out of the way of his counter, then came forward with a right.
Ariden's hand darted out and smacked her on the side of the head.

She lost her balance and ended up on one knee, looking up at
him angrily. "Don't do that!"

"Do not drop your left while you punch, or you'll get worse from
Lem."

They lined up and started again, Ariden's hand at the ready to
strike her if she forgot to keep her guard up. After a few tries, he
stepped back and crossed his arms.

"Strike the pads, not the space in front of them," he said. "What's
happening? Why won't you engage?"

"Because I'm afraid you'll hit me!"

"Why?"

"Because it hurt," she said, annoyed at the obviousness of the
statement.

He tossed the pads off to the side of the room, then convoked a
chair in the corner and sat down. "This is a problem," he said. "You
will not be able to progress unless I convince you that pain does not
matter."

"Well, it matters to me."

"Does it? You felt pain a moment ago, did you not? Now, it's gone."

"Don't get philosophical on me. That's not relevant. It hurt me in that moment."

He straightened up and crossed his arms. "Pain is a sensation, and like all sensations it comes and goes. What lingers is our emotions. Tell me, do you fear pain?"

"Of course I do."

"I'm not so sure. You may dislike it in the moment, but to fear it means it would control your actions. I have seen you take a great many actions—escaping the Sofidran watch, journeying across sea and land, defending yourself in battle. These are not the deeds of a woman who fears pain."

"What are you getting at?"

"The pain is not the issue. You choose to see it as one because of your hesitance to fight. So where does that hesitance come from?"

"It doesn't need to come from anywhere. Fighting is ridiculous."

"Why?"

She threw up her hands. "Why should I explain to you why hurting people is wrong?"

"Then you wish to help people, not hurt them?"

"I'm here to help Karis," she said. "That's the only reason."

"But your good will extends to all people. When you feel a strike, you imagine yourself inflicting such pain on others, don't you?"

Meli scowled, but nodded.

"And you know that in order to help Karis, you will have to hurt Lemuria. Not just physically, but hurt her pride, take away her championship, her victory, the thing she holds most dear. And so you cannot in good conscience defeat Lemuria in order to get what you want. Do you see?"

"I suppose."

"But consider this: Lemuria does not desire to fight an empty shell, a string-less puppet who will not offer her a fight. No true warrior does; we treat such engagements as a waste of time. What she wants most is to be challenged, for you to enter that arena and give her everything you have. To give her less would not be to hand her victory, because that is not the sort of victory she wants. It would only be cheating her, along with yourself."

He rose, preferring to let her mull over the thought than demand a response, and continued the training.

They boxed through the day, and then the next, and the next after that. Always the same routine: rise at dawn and walk together to the training room, guards in tow, with time for only a few words before their practice began. The endless repetition of the pad work was enough to make her doubt her sanity. When she wasn't training, she felt exhausted and disheartened, as much from the feeling of constant failure as from any blows Ariden sent her way. If she was going to end up beaten to a bloody mess, she would have at least liked to enjoy herself just a little beforehand; splurge on some food, some entertainment, even some simple conversation.

To that end, she tried to speak with Zelgovsha occasionally, but the Scharenian woman would often pretend not to hear her questions, perhaps out of embarrassment at not understanding her. That left only Ariden to talk to, and so she set about trying to bring back the man she had seen glimpses of in the latter part of their journey through the wilderness. She found the best results by focusing on her training, which caused him to relax and consequently open up with stories from his early days in Caeridor.

"When I started at the Honorium," he said during an evening session, "Korkeski, the lead trainer, would not have me."

"Why not?" she asked, hopping away from an incoming elbow strike.

"I was only a lower-tier fighter then, and he said I was unproven. Though truth be told, it may have been because he thought me irritating."

"Hard to believe." Meli lined up for a punch, but ended up too close to throw it, and so she pushed Ariden away as she had been told.

"Good," he said. "Don't let her steal your distance."

"You were saying? How did you get into the Honorium?"

He looked up briefly, dredging long-lost memories. "I returned again and again to ask for admittance. Finally, Korkeski agreed to train me if I first cleaned out their refuse room. They had been throwing broken pads and dummies in there for years, and the space was filled with dust piles eight feet high. I told him I would be happy to—if he would let me wrestle one of his larger students first, to test whether he lived up to their reputation."

He ducked as if coming in for a takedown on her legs, and she shot her hips out behind her, sprawling down on her stomach. The motion knocked the wind out of her, and she took her time rising again.

Ariden stood by as she got up, then looked her up and down as if taking the measure of her. Apparently satisfied, he backed up and held up the pad again.

"So what happened?" Meli asked.

"Korkeski denied my request, and told me to get shoveling immediately. But I had injured the pride of his fighter, I believe his name was Opun or something similar. He demanded a match for satisfaction. After a short struggle, I managed to throw him head-first into the open door to the refuse room, so that only his ankles emerged from the dust pile. 'Opun has volunteered to clean up for me,' I said, and then proceeded with my training."

Meli rubbed her forehead. "Oh, Ariden."

He flashed that rare smile, then advanced again. "Let us proceed as well. Talk will not win the match against Lemuria."

There came a day which passed like the wind, when she and Ariden felt completely in tune, their movements a harmonious dance. He held her gaze steady, prompting her with his voice, and she responded, never breaking eye contact, her mind blank, following him as he followed her. When they finally took a break, Meli felt as close to exhilarated as she had in a long while. Fighting, hurting others, that was disgusting, but what they had just accomplished together was a thing of beauty.

She turned to Ariden to try and express as much, to let him know the effect he had had on her, but all the words seemed empty, almost silly. He had trained with plenty of fighters before, real fighters; perhaps the feeling that something special had happened was just her imagination running away with her.

They began training again, and this time she avoided his eyes and focused on the pads.

"I heard the guards talking about the Outsiders," she said in time, filling the silence. "There are rumors of growing unrest outside the walls."

"They will do what they do," he replied. "It is no concern of ours. The audience in the arena will be mostly Outsiders as well, but you should not let them distract you from the fight, especially during the ringcraft."

"…which you still have not explained."

Ariden rolled his eyes. "Very well. You will step into the arena and hear a gong," he said between strikes on the pad. "From that moment until the second gong sounds, you can convoke whatever you wish outside the ring, though nothing small enough to carry."

"What happens if I perform a convocation after the second gong?"

"Disqualification, which, for the rules of this bout, might result in execution."

She looked away and sighed. At least Ariden did not coat hard truths in sweetness.

"We will begin practicing our ringcraft soon," he continued, holding up the left pad. "But Zelgovsha assures me that Lemuria's strategy is quite predictable. She favors trapping her opponents in a tight corner, so she can prevent them from evading her punches."

"I can't stop her from making a wall," Meli said, feinting a jab and then following through with a real one. "Unless I build a ramp to go over it."

"That would mean running away. I would prefer to meet her head on. But a wall can help us as well. If Lemuria decides to take you to the ground, you can push your back on a flat surface to return to your feet." He paused to absorb a volley of punches. "Just remember, try to convoke wide, flat surfaces. Flat is good for you, corners are good for her. You do not want to be trapped."

"Does anyone ever try to convoke something in secret?" she asked. "Like a weight in their fist?"

"Of course. All the time."

He struck out with his left hand. She slid slightly to the right, letting the pad slide past her ear, then stabbed back with a jab.

"Would Lemuria do it?"

"If she feels it is worth the risk, then she will."

Another slip, another jab. Ariden held out the pad for a right hand and she swiveled and struck. Her knuckles bounced off the pad and came back to her temple just in time to block the shot he had aimed there.

"Then should I do it?"

"Should you cheat? No."

"How moral of you. Don't you think I'll be at a rather large disadvantage if she cheats and I don't?"

"Surely," Ariden said. "But if you cheat, you will get caught. If she does it, it means she knows how to get away with it. That's why our best strategy is to avoid getting hit."

He punctuated his words with a punch that grazed her forehead.

"Don't lean backward to evade. Tuck your chin." He nodded at Zelgovsha as she entered and tossed the pads away. "You are improving, you know."

"I can throw two punches," Meli said. "And not even very well."

"The walls of Caeridor were not convoked in a week. It's time for wrestling."

He instructed Meli to convoke a soft, flat wall to practice against, then positioned her flat on her back with Zelgovsha squatting over her ankles.

"Our rule for groundwork is very simple," he said. "Get away from it. Lemuria's specialty is striking on the ground, not to mention the danger from chokes and joint locks. Therefore, you will resist her takedown whenever possible, and if she does drag you down, pull yourself to a wall and use it to stand up as soon as possible."

He gave the signal to begin, and Zelgovsha flattened out and grasped her legs. Meli kicked and tried to squirm away, but Zel held tight like a stranglesnake, clambering up her body until she was able to wrap her arms around Meli's neck. Zel squeezed and Meli's vision became spotted and then faded completely. When she came to, she was lying on her back in the dust, Zel and Ariden standing over her.

"Again," Ariden said. "Try harder this time."

Again they went, and again the same result, except that this time Meli's arm was nearly broken before she lifted her other hand in submission. Many more trials followed. The light from the window above changed from bright white to gray, and still Meli had failed to disengage herself and rise to her feet a single time.

"Not like that." Ariden pointed to Zel's right shoulder. "Put your hand here. Keep your arm straight."

"I don't get it," Meli said through clenched teeth. "Anywhere I push, she stays on top of me."

Ariden paced, struggling to maintain his composure. In nine days of training he had yet to lose patience, but now he was reaching his limit. "Like I keep saying, sit up, then hips away."

"I don't see what you're telling me to do," she said. "It doesn't make sense to me."

"Look!" He sat on the floor. "You try and hold me down. Do what Zel has been doing."

She shuffled over to where he rested on his elbows, chest muscles flared and abdominals flexed. "Grab here?" she asked, holding his legs.

"Yes. Now lean toward me. Watch." He placed his forearm on her collarbone, gently, put his other palm on the ground and levered himself away. "Do you see?"

Her pulse throbbed beneath his touch. She nodded and sat back.

"Now you try," he said.

She sat back and took his place on the floor, while he knelt in front of her. They kept the motions slow at first, feeling each other out as she worked through the technique. Then he began to press his weight harder, changing directions, lithe as a snake and implacable as an armadon. She worked faster, scooting her hindquarters through the dust. Her hand slipped and he fell forward. They lay there a moment, chest to chest, staring into one another's eyes, his moist breath filling her nostrils.

As quickly as he had fallen he stood up to full height, bringing his face as far from hers as possible.

"That should be enough to get you started." He turned away and went to fetch his coat. "Continue to practice with Zelgovsha until the light fades."

"Where you going?" Zelgovsha asked, cracking her knuckles.

"To take a walk." He pulled on his coat and strode out.

Meli slept uneasily that night, trying to put her thoughts of the day's events aside. There was too much happening, too much at stake to dwell on such things. The halfway point of her training was coming up fast, and Ariden knew it as well as she did. Perhaps that was why he was losing patience; he was driven by his goal of achieving victory over Alalantia, and he saw his chances crumbling when she failed to perform as well as she should have.

The only thing to do was to refocus herself, to train better tomorrow. She went back over her recent mistakes, trying to cement Ariden's corrections in her mind before their morning session. She saw herself dancing before him again, slipping left then hopping right, while Ariden followed her, sweat dripping off his bare chest, his shoulders high and tight, framing that square face where dark hair passed in front of his eyes, so brown they were nearly black…

Meli opened her eyes and sighed in frustration. Sleep. She had to rest or the next day's training would be a misery. She thought back over her flower convocations, reminding herself of the different methods of producing colors for the thousandth time. She tossed and turned and then time slipped into dream and she was standing on the edge of a precipice.

Farundei, the fabled edge of the world, where all dust was taken by the wind. Great clouds billowed around her, obscuring the horizon, pouring past her legs and over the cliff-side, down into a brownish-yellow maelstrom which periodically flashed white light. The sight was too much to behold, and she averted her eyes only to discover that in her arms, swaddled from head to toe in white cloth, was her child.

She cried out in joy. It had been so long since she had seen him. Tears filled her eyes and she pulled him up close, whispering and taking in his delicious scent. She felt the bundle wriggle and then a high, sweet voice sounded.

"Mother."

That word—she knew what it meant without having to be told. She smiled. "You can talk?"

"Mother, be careful…"

Something was different this time. Her child's face was obscured. She began to unfold the blankets. As she did, the clouds parted and the ground gave a slight quake, as if by digging through the cloth she was upsetting the natural order of things.

"Mother*rrr*…" the bundle said again, its voice deepening. "*It found me.*"

She continued to undo the swaddle, but each layer twisted upon itself, revealing more and more folds of cloth. Panic rose in her throat as she worked.

"*I couldn't stop it.*" Deeper again, the voice vibrated in her bones. "*Stop. IT.*"

With each pull the ground shook more, until the wind whipped around her and the cliffs crumbled, the bedrock becoming dust, defying all natural law. She gritted her teeth and blocked it out, focusing on her child, pulling aside the last cloth to reveal his face.

She could not breathe. The face was wrong—not human, but two black eyes set above a flat nose coming down to a sharp point. The child-thing smiled, a picture of calm in the surrounding chaos.

"*MOTHER.*" A bolt of fear went through her. She had heard that voice before. During her vision at the Inaali Sanctuary.

What are you? she asked without words.

"*THE DAEMON.*"

She shot up in bed with a loud gasp, tossing aside her sweat-soaked sheets. Her breaths came hard and fast as she looked about the room to confirm that it was real. Behind her, the first gray strand of daylight shone through the window.

On the other side of the partition, Ariden moaned and rolled in bed. "What's wrong?" he mumbled. She heard him stretch and yawn. "Time to train."

He went downstairs while she stayed in bed, her thoughts a blur. She had seen her child, actually seen him, and held him in her arms again. All her old joy and desire and sadness came rushing back, and for a time she sat with her knees pressed to her chest, rocking herself gently, letting the feelings wash over her. But there was something new as well. That face was wrong, not the same as before. And the voice from her vision had returned, saying things she didn't understand. But did any of that have meaning, or was it merely her mind playing tricks?

Light brightened the window; Ariden would be expecting her at training. She wanted to take the day off, but deep down she knew it would do no good to sit in her room, and Ariden would never accept her excuse, anyway. And so, with her heart heavy and her mind elsewhere, she made the trek back to the arena.

They passed the morning with their usual routine, shadowboxing followed by pad work. Meli gave each strike her all, trying to avoid Ariden asking questions about why she was feeling off. But despite her distraction provoking more than a few scowls, she could not stop herself from thinking of the dream. The fact that it had come now must have meant something, but what? And how was she to interpret the appearance of that voice? Just an echo, her mind inserting her own past experiences at random? The idea did little to comfort her.

Annoyed, Ariden put her to work on a new task: convoking a large cushion shaped like a kneeling woman and then hunching over it.

"Yesterday we drilled what to do if Lemuria drags you to the ground," he explained. "But if she fails, it may be that she ends up crouched in front of you. If this happens, I want you to grasp around her arm and neck like so, and deliver as many knee strikes to the head as you can manage."

"All right." She grasped the dummy and struck down with her knees until the caps were red and her thighs sore.

"Do not just throw the same knee again and again," Ariden said, watching from the corner. "Take your time and work slowly to improve your power."

Meli huffed. Couldn't anything just be easy? "What exactly am I trying to do?"

"Your strength comes from here." He thumped his torso. "All your muscles connect to your center. If you want to throw a powerful strike, your entire body must work in concert."

She tried again, and he nodded.

"Better. But not all at once. There is a proper timing for each part of the body. Let the movement flow through you like a wave, building speed."

He observed a while longer, then left to fetch Zelgovsha for their afternoon sparring session. Meli closed her eyes and focused on her movement, flowing like the whipping tail of a scorpion. She snapped her abdomen forward as she loosed a strike, and it landed with a satisfying smack, producing a small divot in the dummy's head. She tried again, this time with the other leg. The divot grew larger.

She sat back on her haunches and breathed, feeling a small sense of peace for the first time since her dream had returned. It was as if there was a potential hidden inside her, coordination and timing she had always assumed she lacked. Given a year or two to train properly, she might have actually turned out to be good at this.

She stood and convoked a cloth, then wiped down her leather wraps. Ariden would return soon, and then sparring would begin; perhaps it was better to end the knee training on a high note.

She quit the training room and wandered the halls of the arena, guards clanking behind her. Other fighters passed her on their way to their own training sessions, some wearing identical uniforms. She met their eyes when they looked, and did not flinch away. Even if she wasn't truly their equal, at least she could carry herself as if she was.

She climbed up a stairway, walking past the locked room where Ariden had told her they kept the hunks of bedrock used to set the balance for the various weight classes. Once there had been no divisions, he said, and the only fighters were the biggest of the men, and those brash enough to challenge them. But as the sport had grown to encompass the entirety of the city's politics, allowances had to be made to allow more fighters to participate.

Because having more fights was *so* important. Right.

In truth, she had come to see a certain beauty in the whole enterprise, like a small shining light tucked into the depths of a malodorous pit. She almost understood now what drove Ariden and others like him to excel. But she would still never seek out violence for its own sake. After her match with Lemuria, whatever the result, the punches she had thrown would be her last.

She climbed higher, out into the open aer at the top of the arena wall. If she went much further, she would risk not returning before Ariden. He might feign anger, then, but beneath it would be a certain…disappointment. She didn't know whether he would admit it, but a part of him seemed to truly enjoy being her instructor. Incredible, in a way—she would never have imagined that the coarse, irritating brute she had found hanging in her pet tree could let himself enjoy anything.

But in fact, he had turned out to be a gifted teacher. He never bullied her, never spoke down to her or treated her unfairly. Would he ever return to this city after they had parted ways, and continue to help other fighters, ones more worthy of receiving his knowledge? Or would his drive to find the Scarred Man consume him until his death?

She climbed up a circular stair to the top of a tower, directly opposite the large one where the drakenbirds roosted, though an angled parapet blocked her view of them. Apparently, the great, majestic beasts enjoyed their privacy. It made her wonder who had convoked the first of their kind, and what they were like. Had it been someone from Caeridor? Or had the animals become associated with the city by some other means?

She was looking out over the rooftops, contemplating, when a black bird in the distance caught her attention. The creature swooped overhead, then stopped in mid-air, slowly dropping straight down until it landed in front of her with a great roar of propeller wash.

"Elsa!"

"*Meli! Meli sosogood to see oh Meli missing is finding Karis Meli is missing!*"

"Oh, Elsa!" Meli's eyes welled. She pressed her face into Elsa's body and stroked her feathers. "I can't believe you're here, my darling."

"*Found you on arena circling for days insect found call message Meli.*"

"Yes, all right. Slow down, please. You got my message?"

"Yes yes. Message coming in bug to see meet fly and come to Caeridor. Long flight, confustication all over, many askings and tellings."

Meli patted Elsa's head, trying to catch her breath. If she didn't get hold of herself then the excitable bird never would calm down, and it was nearly impossible to understand her otherwise. "Just tell me slowly what happened."

"Going to raider skyship and flying, very high so high can't reach, but found current and also and Karis."

"You found Karis? Where is she?!"

"Elsa following, all the fly follow up into raider ship. Finding Karis but raider watch, watch always watch until battle."

"A battle? There was a battle?"

Elsa bobbed her head. *"Verrrrrry big large. Big ships, all around and up. Elsa on bottom of ship, watching for Karis return, then ka-ka-room-room-room, all dusting."*

Meli felt her heart sink in her chest. "Dusting…the ship fell apart? The one with Karis on it?"

"Yes, ex-ship-ploded all over. Elsa run dodge run and search search through sea. Days and days avoiding raiders and looking all over."

"You…what do you mean…you searched for days…"

"Search and search. But not finding. Sorry Meli, but is failure. Karis is gone goo, splat in sea or on ship. All gone for good."

Elsa pulled her neck in sheepishly, then hid her face beneath her wing, cooing softly. Meli stared for a moment, her mouth open. Her legs went weak and her head swooned. Then, to the sound of Elsa's *squark*, her eyes rolled back and she collapsed, unconscious.

29

Karis rolled her dolly away from the ship, sat up and stretched. The underside of the craft the automatists had designed for them was as impressive as the rest of it. It had turned out about the same size as the ship they had arrived in, just large enough for Roi and seven crew, but it was sleeker, all silver with graceful curves, and much, much faster. And within its mekkanisms, embedded at the lowest level of its materials, lay Orthanc's codes, preventing any attempts to examine or copy its workings. Orthanc would remain at the Automatia, of course, his portly creasedskin body not made for adventuring, but the method by which automatist convocations relayed instructions would allow his codes to survive without him, provided the ship they were embedded in remained in existence.

"There's still time to call it off, you know."

Tem sat behind her, his feet on a stool, forming bubbles of viscous fluid and tossing them in the aer. Some of them popped near the top of their arcs, while others bounced off the floor a few times before meeting their end.

"I'd rather leave today," Karis said. "But Roi is holding out for that weapons system he was promised." She pointed up at two apertures mounted over the primary wings.

"I applaud your initiative, Karis. But I still don't like it."

"You've told me. Many times."

He grumbled and let loose a torrent of tiny bubbles. "I just don't understand why you're so eager to plunge headfirst into danger. Who knows what the Old Wise One is capable of?"

"You worry too much." Which was true, though in this instance he was right. "I'll be back before you know it—and I'll bring the Source with me."

"You mean you'll all be back?"

"Yes. Of course. Roi and me and all the others."

Tem let out an unsatisfied breath and continued his game, and Karis resumed inspecting the exterior of the ship. She didn't like pretending to be enthusiastic about this little trip, but in the absence of a better explanation she saw no other choice. Perhaps it helped that her act was based on a half-truth. There was a part of her that wanted to go, the part that had suggested the idea to Corrindal in the first place, that wanted to be the first to see the Source, to claim that glory and place in history with the rest of the Automatia. But that didn't mean the idea of actually doing it terrified her any less.

Tem gave her only a few moments' peace. "It's a strange relationship you and the Azorkans have. I wish I could say I understood it."

"What's to understand? They helped bring me here, so I'm helping them."

"Indeed. But your relationship with them has been so...tumultuous."

"What of it?" A hint of annoyance crept into her voice. "Does that mean I'm not allowed to help them?"

Tem sighed. "I don't mean to upset you. I only wish I knew what you were thinking. First you act like you'd rather have the Saentis between you and the Azorkans, and now you cannot wait to go on a dangerous mission with them. And then there's the Azorkans themselves...strange folks, you will pardon me for saying. They put me in mind of an acquaintance from long ago."

Uh oh. "Who's that?"

"A man I met once, not from Azorkas, but from another city far to leeward...Despernzi perhaps, or somewhere nearby. He was a nice man, a frequent traveler, and prone to telling long stories of his adventures, though to be honest I've forgotten most of them. There was only one thing that stands out to me: his accent. I've been repeating it back to myself over and over these last days, to refresh my memory...he had a high lilt on his 'u' and tended to skip over syllables, I believe. The point is, he spoke nothing like the way your off-and-on friends speak."

"Well, you said yourself he wasn't from Azorkas."

"True, and yet one would not expect such a discontinuity for a neighboring region. If I didn't know better, I would almost say they sound more like a thinly disguised accent from along the north-windward—"

"All right!" Karis stood, her hands on her hips. "Enough already."

"Hmm?" Tem batted his eyelashes.

"You're right. They don't have Azorkas accents. Because they're not from Azorkas. And Roi's not a prince, either." She took a deep breath. "He's a raider captain."

Tem shot to his feet as if he were a marionette on strings. "Are you serious? *You're* a raider?"

"No, not me. I'm not one of them; I just helped them get inside the school."

That didn't come out right at all. Tem breathed heavy and fast, his eyes wide. When he failed to slow down, Karis took a step forward in an effort to catch him if he fell.

When he saw her coming, he sped away toward the exit. "I must go. I must tell the administrators."

"No!" Without thinking, she convoked a small block anchored to the floor, just in front of his feet. A direct hit; his big toe stubbed into it and he tripped, flying forward and smacking the ground face-first with a wail.

"I'm so sorry," she said, rushing over. He continued to cry out as she pulled his head onto her lap.

"I'm bleeding! I'm bleeding!" He convoked a cloth and brought it to his mouth, then showed her the splotch of red from his tongue, already drying into brown dust.

"Calm down," she said. "Just be calm."

"I have to go! They're sending a raider after the Source! He'll steal it to use for himself!"

"There's no point in you telling them. They already know Roi's a raider."

He stared up into her eyes, confusion crowding out his pain. "They do?"

"Yes. They're not stupid, after all; they had the same suspicions you did. But once they found out the truth, they thought they could use Roi to suit their purposes."

"But if they know, why did you trip me?"

"Because I don't want word leaking out that I told you." She stroked his head as she spoke. "I need Roi to trust me, so that his crew can help me retrieve that convocation. But I'm not going to let them make off with it. I'll bring it back here, so we can learn its secrets. It's not going to be easy, but I do want to try. I've dreamed of finding something like it for two hundred years."

Tem shook his head, mussing his hair through her fingers. "But what about Roi? He'll come after you."

"Then the Automatia can deal with him when I return."

"But he could escape, and bring more raiders back with him. An entire army. They know where we are, now. The gate will be useless."

"Will you stop worrying? The mentors will take care of it. They're the ones who are letting Roi stay here, and they're the ones who are letting him go. They must have some sort of plan to deal with him."

She helped set him on his feet, then patted the remainder of the blood-dust from his robe.

"After I go, you can tell anyone you like about Roi," Karis said. "Try to make them understand what I'm doing for this school."

"I should lie down." Tem clutched his forehead. "I wish you'd stay, Karis. I have a bad feeling about this."

"I'll be back soon."

He nodded, trying to convince himself she told the truth. "You will." He pulled her close and kissed her on the cheek. "Be careful, all right?"

She pushed him away playfully. "You crafty snake."

"Just a parting gift." He bowed. "I'll be back tomorrow to see you off."

She watched him go, then returned to the ship to finish her work. Her heart was still pounding from the excitement of revealing Roi's secret. It felt good though, to remove that weight from her shoulders. Now she could turn all her attention to the Old Wise One; hopefully Tem would be rallying the Automatia to support her when she returned.

Footsteps echoed in from the hall. Karis called, "Did you come back to shower me with more affection?"

"Of course!" replied Roi's voice.

"You." She rose.

"Me. So, how's the ship? Ready for our grand adventure?"

"It'll get us there." She turned back to her work, doing her best to act casual. It wasn't as if he could know what she had just spoken to Tem about.

"You know, you certainly have been shy lately. I cannot imagine why you asked Corrindal if you could come on this venture, instead of approaching me directly. I would have told you exactly what I told her—pleased to have you aboard."

She gave him a half smile. "Well, I didn't want you to have all the fun."

"Ah, so we have discovered your raider soul after all."

She chuckled and turned back to the ship.

"All right, enough of that nonsense." His words made her snap to attention. "I know what both of you are after. You're not here to help me, you want that convocation for yourself."

Her heart gave a thump, but she ignored it, facing him with her chin high.

"I've come to offer you a deal," he said. "We can both have what we want. The automatists may be skilled in preventing the copying of their mekkanisms, but I don't expect the same of this Old Wise One. So, once we find the Source, you can have a copy to bring back here and impress your cowardly friends, while I go off and put mine to a real purpose."

Karis narrowed her eyes. On its surface, the deal sounded good—he would simply hand over what she wanted, then go and leave her alone. But what was the other side?

"A real purpose? You mean fighting your war?"

"*My* war? I'm the one trying to end it. It's not as if I'm the cause of all the strife in the world. Believe me, the residents of Aetheria would be glad to kill each other with or without my involvement."

Karis chuckled again, ruefully this time. "You know, someone once told me everything in life is a fight. I suppose you'd agree with that."

Roi did not answer, but instead walked to the far side of the room, where soft light streamed in from apertures near the ceiling. He stared at them discontentedly, then made a series of gestures with his hands. The puzzle pieces that made up the wall in front of him slid apart, until he stood in front of a wide-open threshold, staring at the blurred image of the cliffs.

"Do you ever think about distance?" He spoke toward the view.

"What?"

"How large the world is. How much room! And yet Aetherians never seem to have enough. All the wars we've had, all the suffering— why? Why don't those with disagreements just go somewhere else?"

"Some would say it's in our nature," Karis said. "Just look at the arena of Caeridor, or the animal fighting pits of Porlanim. Perhaps a sickness runs through this world, older than the plagues, which causes us to long to kill each other."

"Some would say that. But would you?"

She paused for a moment, lost in thought, then shook her head. "When I first appeared, the Third Empire was in its death throes. The entire north of the Leeward Continent had no rule of law. Killers ran amok, destroying everything they could for their own pleasure. The ordinary people fled, or hid, and hardly anyone with power stood up and tried to make things better.

"But then a strange thing happened. Over time, the madmen were cast out. The people returned to their ruined villages and reconvoked, and made new laws and new societies. It was as if the Third Empire's collapse was only a cut—a deep cut, painful, but one that only needed time to heal."

He nodded. "So people are fundamentally good, hmm? And yet, as you say, they stood by for so long, watching the suffering. How can we explain such a paradox?

"The answer is quite simple. It is not that humans want to be at war, or at peace. Rather, most people want to do as they're told. Yes, I can feel your skepticism from here, but you're too much of a free spirit to understand. Most people need to follow someone, more than they need anything else—food, sex, even aer. The First Emperor discovered that fact in the course of his travels, and the Second Emperor took advantage of it to seize power for himself.

"Which brings me to your question: is life a fight? I would say it is, but not in the sort of dirty, silly hand-to-hand and sword-to-sword fashion most people think about. Rather, it's a fight for control. To see who can influence the most people, to see who can influence history. A war for any other purpose is just loosely organized stupidity."

"I don't understand," Karis said. "You said you were going to war with the Reviled for killing your mentor."

Roi snorted. "Please. You think I give a pox about Tiresius? The old man got what was coming to him. Yes, he had valuable skills to teach, but in the end he was more useful in death than in life. No, no—what I have in mind is much grander than a simple vendetta."

"What do you see yourself as, then? A king?"

"An emperor."

She let out a laugh before she realized he was serious.

"And what's so funny about that?" For the first time in their conversation, a hint of anger crept into his voice. "All the First Emperor needed was purpose, conviction and time. Why should I be different? Both of us came from nothing, both of us had a dream."

"You're not the First Emperor," she said snidely. "You're more like the Third, I think. Delusional, seeking power to fuel his own depravity."

Roi stood there for a moment, facing the strait, frozen like a statue. Had she gone too far that time?

The even tone of his reply seemed to indicate she had not. "Delusional? What do you know about delusions? Try being locked underground in a six-foot box for years, and then see what your mind shows you. Trust me when I say there is no greater authority than me on the difference between delusion and reality."

"How did you do it?" she couldn't help but ask. "What were you doing in the darkness all that time?"

"Making plans. At first I thought only of those who stole my freedom to move, to see, to make my own future. I imagined what I would do to them when I emerged. But as the years went by, I had to go bigger, grander, until no ordinary life could contain my ambitions. Really, I'm not sure your question is fair. I've yet to meet anyone capable of understanding what I lost, or what I will need to accomplish to make myself whole. And yet, people like you still have the nerve to *laugh* at me."

He spun and flashed her a big smile. "You're right, though. I'm nothing like the First Emperor. He was a fool, whose only real impact on the world was to usher in his own defeat."

"What are you talking about? He was one of the greatest Aetherians who ever lived—thanks to him we have skyships, the calendar, architectural wonders—"

"A *fool*." He spat the word out. "He oversaw the creation of skyships, then watched as others used them to overthrow him. You and your friends love inventions for the sake of inventing, as if being remembered for adding flanges to some gods-forsaken valve is worth a celebration. What good are inventions unless they are used to effect change? By the measure of changing lives, the Third Emperor was far more successful than the First."

Karis's skin prickled at hearing the Third Emperor praised as such. She had always held a special place of loathing in her heart for him; after all, it was his rages, paranoia, and ruthlessness that had led to his own "empire" crumbling mere weeks after its founding. After his death, his legion of madmen had dispersed, seeding destruction wherever they went, leading to the conditions surrounding her own appearance.

"And is that how your empire would be run?" she asked, her gaze on the floor. "Would the Fourth be the same as the Third?"

"Not the same." Roi took a deep breath, composing himself. "I am my own man after all. As I said, I had time to make many plans. Some you would like. Others—well, we can't please everyone. All I can tell you is that no one is prepared for what the stories will say of my works. No one.

"Remember this, Karis. There is no use in composing a beautiful melody which few will hear. Measure your impact on the world by the volume of your song, not the sweetness of its tune." He turned to leave, then called over his shoulder, "The magnitude! Not the tenor."

And then he was gone.

Slowly, the hairs on Karis's neck settled. *Well, that was certainly unexpected.* Feeling confined, she walked to the open wall and convoked a long, cantilevered beam over the fog. At the end of the platform she placed a seat, and there she sat in thought.

It wasn't like Roi to reveal himself like that. No doubt she had touched something in him, made him say more than he meant to. But what about his proposed deal? Try as she might, she still couldn't see much of a downside. So Roi would run off to form his empire, or more likely die trying. It wasn't her job to protect the citizens of Aetheria from his plans. And what could she do about it, anyway? Despite her hastily made promise to Corrindal, she doubted she could control Roi and seven of his loyal allies. What kind of power could a smoothskin have over a full-sized man?

That question, and its answer, she had pondered before.

Her last night with Sylas's commune.

She was lying in the dark on the packed dust, the other members of the troupe sleeping around her. Her eyes were wide open, staring upward, but the empty black sky did little better than her eyelids at keeping out the visions of people melting on the road.

She had been punished already, but the soreness was mostly gone. She had seen others take beatings like that before, and had always wondered if she would be able to stand one. It had not been so hard, though—when the pain had gotten really intense she had gone blank until it was over, as if she had left her body and become someone else.

None of that mattered, now.

She rolled herself up and sat, waiting for anyone else to stir. No motion except the gentle rise and fall of breathing, and clothes flapping in the breeze. Her pulse thudding, she rose and set off across the desert, back in the direction they had come. They had walked four or five miles since their encounter with Yan and the other townspeople, and she could not imagine what Sylas would do to her if she did not return before dawn. But still, she had to go, had to find out what was there.

The sky was still ink-black when she came upon the sharp spike of bedrock Yan had been impaled upon. Karis could not remember the act, only the screams of agony as the commune walked away from her. But now the area was silent, empty, no trace remaining of Sylas's burning liquid or other signs of struggle. In the dim light, she could make out traces of material which could have been dried blood, and a small pile of dust which might have once been cloth, but there was no way to be sure either of them came from Yan.

Karis knelt, sick to her stomach, thinking of Yan's kindness and her own helplessness. She didn't know yet whether Yan had dispersed on the rock, or if someone from the town had come and cut her down. Karis could not bear the thought of facing them to find out. Guilt smothered her like fog on the sea, her rage flowing freely beneath. She hated Sylas, hated his commune and hated herself most of all for letting this happen.

"Yan. I'll do it. I'll make this right."

Her anger carried her on fleet feet back to the camp, where she stepped lightly among the sleeping bodies. Sylas lay somewhere to her right, nestled in among his "luckier" followers, but she let her black-clouded mind carry her to where Vikter's hulking mass was sprawled out, his mouth open, snoring.

Teeth bared, breath wheezing, she held up her palm and formed the dagger.

It was a poor copy of the one Yan had shown her, stunted and bent, but the point was sharp enough, of that she was sure.

As if in a dream, her hand moved beneath his chin. She grasped the stiletto in both palms to keep it from shaking.

Shove it upward. Shove it upward as hard as you can, he won't bother you anymore.

She pressed the point to Vikter's neck. He let out a small grumble of sleepy irritation.

She couldn't do it. In Ba-ael's name, she wanted to, but her hand wouldn't move. *You're betraying her. Betraying Yan's memory.* But it just wasn't right. This was a male way of thinking. Stick something into something else, and everything would get better. Except it didn't. All it caused was more pain. She didn't want it anymore. No more death. No more suffering.

She let the dagger crumble, crushing it in her hand and letting the dust fly away slowly on the wind, then she rose and took off in a run, disappearing like a shadow into the night.

Karis opened her eyes over the Kalsten Strait. The feelings of the memory lingered on in her, sadness, pain, but also pride. Yes, there was horror and tragedy, but in the end she had left. She had never questioned the choice she made that night, even after she found out Yan had died, even after spending twenty years in the wilderness, never learning Sylas's fate. At least Yan's wish had come true: She had escaped Sylas, and his influence over her life was no more.

Wasn't it?

How was it now, so many years later, that she found herself again in the company of a powerful, ruthless man? Just a twist of fate? How many times could she have left Roi like she left that night, except that the time wasn't right, the search for the Automatia was more important, she had to find out more about the Old Wise One—had her own thoughts been betraying her all this time?

No. She had to trust in her judgment. She had left Sylas hundreds of years ago—what did that have to do with today? She walked back to the hangar and stared at the sleek black ship, lingering over the mysterious weapon ports on its wings. The codes inside the ship's control systems were one of the Automatia's protections against Roi's plans. She was the other. And when the time came, she would make the decision that was best for herself and the school, in that order.

At least, she hoped she could.

30

"Gods, have you ever seen such mountains?"
Mylon sat with his nose upturned against the porthole. Beyond it, the endless peaks of the Aperandis rose to staggering heights, their tips spikes of black bedrock.

"Of course I have, you ignorant sod." Isky called from the cot he shared with Dikta across the aisle. The interior of the ship was cleanly designed but cramped, hemmed in by mekkanism-hiding bulkheads. The raiders could barely lay claim to a horizontal space to call their own.

"Why does the Old Wise One want to live way up here, eh?" Mylon asked. "The view?"

"He wants to be alone, obviously," Dikta said. "Sod."

"Stop calling me that!"

Karis sighed and shifted her back against the cabin wall. The miles had slipped below them day by day, until they found themselves in this alien landscape, with peaks so high that the fierce winds whipping between them would have blown away their previous ship. The crew was irritable, nervous. Even Roi, usually at his best around the others, had been sitting with his arms folded all day, his face pensive. Doubtless the same questions plagued him which ran through Karis's mind daily. Who was the Old Wise One? What sort of power had he cultivated in his long solitude, and how would he use it? He liked being alone, that was all they knew—exactly the sort of person one should be wary of dropping in on unannounced.

"I've got another one." Phaestal came up from behind and handed her a palm-sized box made of interlocking pieces: an automatist puzzle block. She pressed a few of the shapes, popping them out of place, then turned the box over and examined it from another angle. After several more adjustments, she flipped a piece and the entire box fell apart.

"That's it?" Phaestal pouted. "It only took you a few moments."

"It takes practice to make a good one." She handed him back the pieces. "Don't feel too bad."

"I worked on that all day."

He headed away, eyes already locked on the pieces, planning another try. Despite his awkward nature, Phaestal did possess a certain naive charm. It wasn't saying much, but he might be the only raider Karis would miss if she managed to return to the Automatia.

And then there were those she wouldn't miss. She watched as Jaela approached Roi and draped her arms around his shoulders. He didn't look up at her, didn't even move except to whisper some words that Karis couldn't hear. Jaela frowned and stiffened, then headed to the back of the ship without so much as a glance in Karis's direction.

Maybe Karis was being too hard on her. The more she had thought about their blowout in the common room, the more her view had begun to change. Jaela was petty and vindictive, surely, but now Karis could see just how pathetic she was, how much Roi controlled her with the force of his carefully crafted persona.

"Everyone, meet in the main corridor," Roi called.

One by one, the raiders stopped their chores or roused themselves from stupor. Roi stood closest to the front of the ship, arms crossed and eyes narrowed. Something was wrong. The others sensed it too, shifting their weight uneasily while waiting for him to speak.

"We'll find the fortress soon," Roi said. "We don't know exactly how much further, but it's only a matter of time."

The others looked back and forth, probably wondering why Roi had bothered to tell them this.

"Before we do, I have something to say. Something I've been putting off a long time." He let his eyes drift over the assembled crowd. "One of you is a traitor."

The raiders grumbled and whispered, their disbelief mixed with wariness.

"A traitor how?" Mylon said.

"For how long?" Cindlan added.

"For quite a while." Roi stepped into the center of the tight circle. "But before we left was the last straw. The traitor revealed who we are to the automatists. I cannot stress the seriousness of this offense enough—all our lives were put in jeopardy. All of us."

Karis's throat clenched. How? How had he found out what she said to Tementon? The room seemed to darken as blood pumped into her head.

Roi snarled, "If I hadn't been able to smooth things over, we could have all been killed because of *you!*"

He pointed at an accusing finger at Paolem.

"I never!" Paolem shouted. The entire group was staring at him, and he snapped his head around to meet his accuser's gazes. No one noticed Karis's sigh of relief.

"You did," Roi said. "You told Ferici not only about us, but about our plans. You spilled everything, and for what? Because she plied you with that junk you're so obsessed with."

"I don't have to—"

"Shut up. You know, I had friends who took Vipp back when I was running the streets in Vaetan. What fun they had. Until they took a bit too much one day when I needed them to watch my back. I paid dearly for their mistakes, Paolem."

"This is poxing ridiculous. I never said anything." Paolem showed them his back and headed toward the aft side of the cabin, only to meet a pair of walls closing in on him from either side. "Hey!" He yelled to the others. "Don't let him do this! Mylon! Phaestal!"

The crew stayed quiet. The aer grew thick with tension. Sweat tingled on Karis's arms and back.

"I told you what would happen if you didn't get off that stuff." Roi approached, and hard material formed around Paolem's ankles, climbing upward until his legs were trapped in a solid cylinder. "But you just needed it that badly, didn't you?"

"No, it's not—"

"Enough. I can't have you as a liability anymore, Pao. You're off the crew."

He grabbed Paolem by the chin, shook his head, then spun and headed back toward the pilot's room.

"What?" Paolem said. "You're just going to leave me out here? To walk out of the mountains by myself?"

Roi stopped, then slowly turned around, his face expressionless. "Of course not."

Roi closed his eyes. The cabin lapsed into silence, save for Paolem's hurried breathing and the quiet hissing of the wind. Karis barely noticed the small motion out the porthole near the center of the ship. Above the wings, the hollow tubes had raised into firing position and turned inward, aiming directly at them.

Directly at Paolem.

He followed their stares outside, glanced briefly at his trapped ankles, then at Roi. "No!"

A *click* sounded from outside, and then the ship filled with a low, steady rumbling, gaining in volume. The hull began to shake, at first wobbling, then cracking. Karis grabbed a handhold and sank against the wall. She recognized this convocation—the same agitism she had practiced on the plate with Tem. Only larger.

It all happened at once: a thin area of the walls blew apart in a plume of dust, shearing off the entire back of the ship, sending Paolem and his encasement flying backward over the suddenly bright mountain landscape.

One moment he was hanging there, a look of disbelief on his face, and the next he was a speck, tumbling end over end toward the moss-covered rocks below. Karis turned away, pressing herself into the aerframe to keep from being sucked out. Gradually the deafening noise of the wind decreased as someone patched up the hole where the agitist weapon had shaken the ship apart.

When she looked again the aft bulkhead was a ragged joint of material spiraling inward from the walls. Most of the raiders had taken up similar positions to hers and were slowly uncoiling. No one spoke, though Karis saw Mylon and Phaestal share uneasy glances.

"Well," Roi said. "I guess we know that thing works."

He faced the rest of the crew, inviting a challenge, but none came.

"Phaestal, coordinate replacing all the parts of the ship that Paolem convoked. We'll need a new tail as well. And make it a good one.

"We may be leaving in a hurry."

The Old Wise One's tower would have appeared an imposing giant, were it not for its station among the even more gigantic peaks of the Aperandis. They had found it in a grassy plain between two ridges, sitting on a natural pedestal of bedrock. That the building was the one they sought was beyond question; its construction was clearly the work of an eccentric hermit. A bulging, oblong ovoid hundreds of feet tall, its facade was composed of interlocking diamond and hexagonal panels, black with purple edges and layered over one another like scales, forming layers of curves that spiraled down from a relatively small dome near the tip.

If nothing else, Karis thought, it was not the sort of place one just strolled into without a plan.

Which of course was exactly what they meant to do.

The raider ship had spent most of the afternoon hovering just beyond the nearest peak, waiting for any response from the strange building. None came, the only movement the occasional small bird taking off from its roost near the top. Roi paced the ship, keeping one eye on the tower, until Karis wondered if he was planning to approach it while there was still daylight.

"Found it." Phaestal dropped his head through a hole in the ceiling and held out a gray box with cables extending at all angles.

"Give it here," Roi said. He held it up to the porthole to see in the light.

"What is it?" Karis asked.

"A little surprise from our automatist friends. Or at least they intended it to be."

"Is this the safeguard Corrindal spoke of?"

Roi shook his head. "The safeguard is embedded in the coding that runs through the hull. Unless it's disabled, it will cause the ship to fall apart in less than a week. The administrators were nice enough to warn me about that—but I suspected if we traced the lines running away from the code, we'd find something else interesting."

"It's a spy device." Phaestal dropped back into the cabin. "It transmits messages about what we're doing through the aether."

"How can that be?" Karis asked. Unless the messages themselves were alive somehow, they wouldn't be able to exist so far from their convoker.

"I heard a little about them back at the school; they work the same way a normal automatist convocation does, but there's a trick to make the communication self-sustaining. And as long as the message is only sent in one direction, it doesn't have to loop back on itself and become self-aware."

"But you said the self-destruct could be disabled—if they can't monitor us, then they'll probably let the ship crumble."

"Better to walk the edge on our own accord, than stay safe on a leash." Roi dropped the box and smashed it under his boot, then ground the pieces with his heel. "Are there any more, Phaestal?"

Phaestal shrugged. "Probably not."

"Then we're ready. Join Mylon in the pilot's room. We're going in."

"Where?" Phaestal asked. "The only things I see in the tower that look like entrances are some holes midway up. I suppose we could convoke a dock."

"Yes, fine. Just take us down there."

Phaestal did as told, the ship whirred and the aer rushed. As they descended, the tower loomed over them like an executioner.

"Make sure you keep the engines running," Roi said.

"Weapons?" Dikta asked. He pulled up his "Azorkan" shirt to reveal his well-muscled frame.

"No, no weapons. And stay in these ridiculous outfits for now. No raider gear."

"Really?" Karis said as Roi moved past her to the exit. "What are you planning on doing in there? How will we get the Source?"

He gave a breezy smile. "We'll turn on the charm offensive."

"You think it will be that easy to talk the Source out of him?"

"Nothing seems easy until it's been done," Roi said, showing her his back.

Karis stepped down the gangway and made for the shelter of the tower, turning her face from the wind. Just before she entered, she looked up again at its full dizzying height, and the intricate layers of its construction. Then she stepped into an arched tunnel, reaching out and feeling the polygonal tiles up close for the first time. They were smooth and slightly flexible, not made of any material she had ever seen, and not the least bit worn.

The group shuffled forward, staying together, and soon the light from the opening behind them faded, plunging them into blackness.

"I don't think whoever built this meant for people to walk in it," Cindlan said. "What's that sound?"

Karis heard it as well; in addition to the howl of the wind past the doorway, a bass grinding was coming from all around them. If she stood still, she could feel the vibration in the soles of her boots.

"This way," Roi said. "The passage turns here. Feels like it's leading upward."

Karis moved with the others into a circular tunnel heading up at a sharp angle; she guessed that they were in one of the spiral bulges that ran along the outside of the building. With her small stature she could climb easily while the others had to duck and scrape their heads, so she took the lead. The tiled material that made up both the tunnel's inside and its outside had its own peculiar smell, not pleasant but not terrible either. The aer tasted clean, not clogged with dust, and the inside of the tunnel was so smooth that climbing up the incline would have been impossible if not for her convoking footholds on the overlaps between the tiles.

"It just goes on and on," she said into the darkness, a hint of anxiety creeping into her voice.

"It must reach the top sometime," Roi called behind her.

"What if it doesn't?" Mylon said. "What if the Old Wise One is using some kind of trick to make it into a circle?"

"What are you on about now?" Roi said.

"Maybe that's the ancient convocation. He's joined the two ends of the tunnel so it just goes upward forever."

"That's impossible, idiot," Dikta said.

"*You're* the idiot!"

"Quiet!" Roi yelled.

They fell silent. Something was coming down from ahead of them. Something heavy and loud. The aer pressure built on Karis's skin as the giant mass rumbled toward them. She flattened herself against the tunnel wall. "Roi…"

"Run!" someone called. "Head back down!"

"No," Roi said. "Twins, punch a hole here. Now!"

She heard grunts and shoulders smacking the wall, followed by the clank of swords. The noise ahead was a roar now, so loud her ears threatened to burst. A hand grasped her wrist, and then she was tumbling through the wall, rolling backward onto a hard floor. She hit her head and saw lights behind her eyes, green tracers in the darkness. The roaring noise crescendoed in front of her, then decreased, as whatever had been rolling toward them headed past and down.

"Did everyone make it?" Phaestal asked, letting go of her wrist.

Before they could answer, a new sound sprang up all around them, subtle and pervasive, shifting, hissing. The tower was changing shape. A flare of light came down through a crack in the wall high above, then another. Tiles turned, rotating behind one another to open a row of windows. The floor squealed. Karis hopped to her feet, still woozy, and watched as the center of the cavernous room rose upward and turned, forming a circular staircase as it went.

As quickly as it had begun, the process halted and the tower was at rest.

"What's that?" Jaela asked, pointing at the columned staircase.

"Looks like an invitation," Roi said.

"You mean we have to go up?" Cindlan said.

"It would be rude to decline, wouldn't it?"

One by one, they stepped onto the stair, Roi taking the lead. Karis swallowed. Who knew what they would find up there? The turning of the stairs hid her destination until she was directly below it; then she saw they were exiting through a hole in the high ceiling which led to another room, nearly as large as the one they were leaving. She held her breath and walked through to join the others.

The raiders huddled in a tight group, facing a wide dais at the far end of the room. At its center, a figure stood with its back turned, hooded in a brown robe. The figure was short, and made shorter by stooping over to examine a low pedestal. Light shone down from a hole in the ceiling far above, coloring the top of the robe a grayish yellow.

Roi cleared his throat. "Greetings. My name is Roilan, and these are my associates. We came to see a man known as the Old Wise One. Are you he?"

The figure rose, turned around, and lowered its hood. Karis gasped. He was a smoothskin. But not just any smoothskin—his features were far more exaggerated than anyone she had ever seen. He was shorter than she was, with shining, downy hair that fell flat around his head, the same length all around. His eyes were large, with long lashes and dark rings around his irises which seemed to draw her toward them. But the grotesqueness of the rest of his face would just as easily keep her away, especially his upper teeth, which jutted out over a too-small chin. Karis shrank back, using her small size to blend into the crowd, away from his gaze.

"Have you come to kill me?" the Old Wise One said. His voice was so high pitched it neared a screech.

"No, no," Roi said. "Of course not. We wish to be your guests."

"Who sent you?" His tiny nostrils flared.

"No one. No one sent us," Roi stammered. "We're…students. We sought you out, so that we could learn more about the history of—"

"You're a liar! You came here to destroy me. Look at this mob of ruffians and villains you've brought with you."

"Good Sir!" Roi motioned to the others. "These are my friends. All of them devoted to their studies, showing great honor and courage in helping me locate you."

"Shut up. Anagoraxis sent you, did he not? That sleaze. He will never rest until I'm *dead*."

"Ana…goraxis?"

"Of course, Anagoraxis! The Second Emperor!"

He raised his finger as he spoke, as if propelling the words upward. They echoed off the high ceiling for a few moments before the room fell silent again.

"Ah," Roi said. "Well, Sir, as it happens…the Second Emperor died. Three hundred years ago."

The Old Wise One blinked. "He did?"

Roi looked at the others for confirmation. "Yes."

"Oh." The Old Wise One took a moment to mull that over. "Well, who are *you* then?"

"Like I said, we were hoping to…become…" Roi trailed off as the Old Wise One stepped off his dais and came toward them, hands clasped behind his back, studying him intently. "…become your pupils. To study your—"

"I do not take pupils." The high-pitched words scuttled quickly out of his mouth. "And if I did, they would be promising scholars, worthy of instruction. Not some rabble like you."

"But we've come so far. Perhaps we could stay a short while? Just being in your presence would be an honor. Your fame is—"

The Old Wise One suddenly turned and strode up to Roi, staring at him from below. "Honor?! Do you know who I am?"

Roi leaned back slightly. "Uh, you're the Old Wise One? The ancient, learned scholar—"

The Old Wise One stepped back and laughed, then doubled over and laughed harder, jumping up and down with glee. The display went on and on, and the raiders began to move back and spread out in their unease.

"So you want to stay here, eh?" The Old Wise One said, gradually recovering. "As my *guests*." One more chuckle. "I have not had a guest for eight hundred years. I have quite forgotten what having one would be like…bothersome, I would imagine."

"But Sir—"

"Say nothing more. You've amused me enough, but leave now and I shall…" His gaze passed over them as he spoke. When he came to Karis's face, he gasped and straightened himself. "Oh! You've brought me something. Why didn't you say so before?"

He approached. The others backed away, leaving Karis standing alone, her mouth slightly agape. The Old Wise One took her hand and kissed it, tiny red lips to brown skin. "My dear, you set my heart aglow! You are utterly beautiful."

Karis glanced left and right. The others all stared at her, offering no hints as to how to respond. "I, uh…thank you," she managed.

"I have changed my mind!" The Old Wise One's robe swished as he swept away from her. "You are welcome to stay here—" He opened his arms wide. "—and behold the wonders of my palace! You already have first-hand experience with my Transpirmarbralum, yes?"

"You mean the tunnel?" Roi stepped to the front again.

"Indeed. I felt you break the wall. When you've been convoking as long as I have, you know, you learn to sense any changes to your creations, as if they are a part of yourself."

"I apologize," Roi said. "We didn't mean to damage it. Something came toward us."

"That would have been a marbrum." The Old Wise One gestured behind him, and the scales composing the wall slid open, revealing a row of enormous spheres. They were perfectly smooth and reflective, and looked to be the same width and height as the tunnel the raiders had been crawling in. "Do not worry yourself about the damage; I make changes to the apparatus often. I'm performing experiments, you see, investigating the nature of the force that holds us to the ground."

"How interesting. Sir."

"Sir? How formal…you really don't have any idea who I am, do you?"

"I…how would you like to be addressed?"

The Old Wise One chuckled. "When you live such a long time, you collect many names. Long ago I was called Raendal. And after that, The Old Wise One and after that, Chitarus the Despised. But I believe you may be most familiar with another name of mine." He paused and grinned, bits of spittle clinging to his lips. "The Plague Bringer."

The raiders' mouths fell open, color draining from their faces.

"Cursed be his…" Mylon mumbled, then swallowed the remainder.

The Old Wise One let out a laugh, followed by an excited yell. "Ah! The looks on your faces! Oh, it's priceless!" He held his sides and chuckled. "How I wish I had told someone that years ago."

"Wait," Karis said. "You're serious? You really are the Plague Bringer?"

He grinned and nodded.

"But they killed you. Over three thousand years ago."

He winked. "But my beauty, life goes on. Life goes on. I will explain it all to you, if you like."

He snapped his fingers and the room shifted, panels turning and sliding. The raiders rocked to and fro, trying to keep their footing. Moments later the changes ceased, and a new door had appeared to their left.

"Come." The Old Wise One waved them toward it. "Do not be afraid. You are quite safe here. I do not convoke plagues anymore, nor did I ever do so on purpose. They were an experiment, you see, one which got out of hand, back before anyone knew what animatism was."

His voice faded slightly as he headed down the hall. "Of course, there were still plants and animals about in those days—don't believe anyone who says otherwise. But no one knows who convoked them, and anyway there wasn't nearly the menagerie you find now. You've seen the infestation of flowers below the palace, haven't you?"

"Infestation?" Roi said.

"Oh yes, I hate the things. They spew dust all over the valley. Even at this altitude I can't avoid them anymore."

Karis trailed along behind, keeping her distance from the Old Wise One, or the Plague Bringer, or whatever it was they should be calling him. The others hung back as well, gawking at the shifting walls of the tower, leaving Roi with the burden of conversing with the most reviled figure in Aetherian history.

"In truth, the era just before the plagues was not so different from today. The time of the true ancients was already well in the past. Many cities had been constructed and destroyed. Knowledge came and went, was discovered and forgotten, until I and some like-minded contemporaries founded the first of the philosophical schools, devoted to systematizing the study of new convocations."

They entered a long, curving hall with rooms to either side; Karis had the impression it been constructed moments before they entered.

"At the time, I had been searching for a rumored ancient convocation for creating bedrock. Believe it or not, that's how it all started! In searching for the property of the rock which allowed it to exist without being held in the mind, I eventually discovered animatism. My first creations were small, too small to be seen with the eye, and since I lacked proper animatism skills they tended to die soon after they were made. The solution I found was meant to be a temporary measure: having the miniscule creatures reproduce themselves at an enormous rate. Of course, I didn't see the problem with that little gambit until it was too late."

He chuckled, and the sound gave her a chill. The odd little man's laugh was strange enough, but what exactly did he find so funny? How many people had died as a result of his "little gambit"? Millions? Tens of millions?

The Philosophic age—it was too long ago to comprehend. How could he have lived so many years, and how long had he spent in such severe isolation?

The Old Wise One paused and pointed at a door. "See here, I've made some rooms for you all. I've come to favor these panels as a method to reduce dust—only the joints between them need to be re-convoked each time they're shifted. I've put little chutes in the back walls there, so if you could take care not to let the stuff loose inside my home…"

The raiders spread out, peeking warily inside the rooms. The Old Wise One continued down the hall, expounding on to anyone who would listen.

"I was lauded for my achievements, you know. Heaped with praise and honors. It was not until later that some of the little beasties acquired a taste for flesh. Then everyone was quick to point their fingers at me as the one who started it all. As if they had not been copying my methods for thirty years! That was around when things got a bit out of hand with the so-called 'Plague Wars.' Instead of anyone simply asking for my help, I was forced to go into hiding, never revealing my true identity…"

A hand gripped Karis's shoulder and pulled her backward into an alcove. She started to yell, but another hand covered her mouth, and a moment later Roi stood in front of her, his finger to his lips. Dikta released his hold on her face, giving her a severe look to remind her that it could be replaced.

"What are you doing?" she hissed.

"He likes you," Roi replied.

She pushed away from Dikta and looked around the corner, where the Old Wise One was walking on ahead, gesticulating with his back turned.

"I noticed that."

"You're the one who has to do it, Karis. The rest of us might as well be decorations, now."

"Do what?"

"Use your influence over him to find the Source."

She shuddered. "I'd rather not have anything to do with him."

Roi nodded to Dikta, who grasped her lapels and lifted her up, tightening his grip on her neck until she began to gag.

"Get him alone," Roi said. "Make him let his guard down. Find out what the Source is. And Karis—" He leaned close, eyes burning into her, and spoke through his teeth. "Don't pox it up."

Dikta dropped her. She stumbled, then leaned against the wall for support. After one last deathly stare, Roi returned to the others, the larger man following behind.

31

Meli had blacked out the half-window on her side of the apartment, so that darkness surrounded her. Elsa dozed at the foot of the bed, keeping her company while for two days and two nights, Meli had cried all the tears she could cry. Now she simply stared into nothing, her mind as blank as her vision.

A knock on the partition. "Meli?" Ariden's voice called. "How long will you stay in there?"

Meli rolled over. "Leave me alone."

"I understand you've lost a friend. I've lost many."

"She wasn't *a* friend. She was my *only* friend." Meli felt her composure breaking and went silent. Sweet, selfless Karis, the only one who had cared enough to risk everything in search of Meli's dream. "It's my fault she's dead."

"We're running out of time. You must train."

"For what? Your honor? I don't care. Find someone else to take my place."

She waited for his retort, but after a period of silence he marched from his side of the room and slammed the door. Good. She wanted no part of any it. The killing, the fighting, it was all the same. Stupid, so utterly stupid.

She closed her eyes and tried to sleep, but remained wide awake. How far along was the day, anyway? She released her mental hold on the black paint covering the window. To her surprise, bright light streamed through, highlighting Elsa's feathers. It must have been nearly midday already. Meli sat upright and stretched her aching joints.

"Come, Elsa." She made for the door. "Karis is gone, and I'm going to have the piss beaten out of me soon. Might as well have free run of the city, first."

As Meli entered the main boulevard with her guards, Elsa flapped down from the window. "Do not speak in front of the crowds, darling. If these barbarians find out what you are, they are liable to enter you in some sort of bird-fighting division."

They walked and flew down a wide, curving avenue framed with worn buildings, while the city geared up for the evening's post-fight entertainment. All around people scurried like insects, gawked and pointed at Elsa, or parked themselves at tables, draped over sofas like lumps of moss while they drank and chatted. They seemed happy, carefree. In her early days in Sofidra Meli would have liked nothing more than to join such festivities, to meet new people and see new sights. But now they all seemed to amount to nothing, just pointless jabbering and empty spectacle.

She stopped at a food stand and took her pick of the delicacies, while the other patrons nodded and backed away, giving her the deference due to a fighter. But the cakes tasted bitter, and she soon grew bored and wandered away. Further ahead a line of barkers, some doing spins or flips on each other's arms, shouted for a comedy show beginning soon. *Comedy.* She turned her shoulder and walked on.

She lost herself in the stones of the street, squares cemented with lines of dust, convoked so long ago that they had hardened. When she looked up again, she had followed the circular avenue most of the way around the city. To her right, a street cut through like a spoke to the wide front entrance of the arena, while ahead the path led back to her boarding room. No, she didn't wish to return there, yet. Something in her wanted to stay in motion, to keep her mind working. She sighed and headed down the crossing.

She had done something like this once before, that morning after she first dreamed of her child. Walked and walked, because she knew she had some puzzle in her mind that she had to unravel. But the answer then had been one of joy, the beautiful realization that she would convoke her seedling. Why was she walking now, when her present held only sorrow, and her future held only the fear of facing Lemuria?

No, not only Lemuria. There was also the dream. That voice. Would she have to face it again if she wanted to hold her child? And she did want him, needed and missed him more than ever, thanks to the dream's return. Was that why her mind had brought him back? Had she sensed somehow that Karis was gone, and that she would need to see her seedling again to go on?

She walked up to the arena entrance, and so used was she to going inside that she almost continued forward without thinking. She stood and stared into the depths of the entrance tunnel, where streamers of light shone down through the benches overhead. Something about the gloom and the rank smell struck her as bittersweet, almost nostalgic. Ridiculous. Could it be she actually missed spending her days in that cramped, dingy room?

"Meli." Ariden stood in the street behind her. "You've come to train?"

She shook her head and looked down. "I told you to leave me alone. Why would you pester me about fighting at a time like this?"

"I wasn't the one who brought you to this spot."

She bristled. "I wandered over by mistake. A force of habit."

"Was it? Or is there a part of you that wants this?"

No. She never wanted it. It was forced upon her. "You're trying to trick me. All of this is your fault. You want me do this for *you*, because of your rivalry with Alalantia." Her raised voice echoed in the tunnel.

He said nothing, just stood and let the rage drain from her, bit by bit. Eventually she spoke again, in an even tone.

"You're thinking of our deal, aren't you? Well, it's off. I'm releasing you from your obligation. Once I feel well enough, I'll make you the creatures you asked for and you can be on your way."

He considered that for a while. "Fine. But not yet; first we see this through."

"I can't, Ariden. I have too much on my mind." She imagined mountains sliding beneath her in the dark tunnel. Even with Karis gone, she could still use that ship…but did she really want to? "Everything is too complicated. There's you, Alalantia, Lemuria, the Inaali…"

"Forget it. Forget it all."

She spun to face him. "Why?"

"Because it doesn't matter what's at stake. What matters is the fight. The struggle is its own reward."

"That's easy for you to say. Someone who loves violence, who revels in it."

"Violence is change. For giver and receiver. Two contestants in the arena; win or lose, both come out different people than when they entered."

"Creation is change, too."

He shrugged. "I do not deny it. In a way they are mirrors of one another. You and I may differ in approach, but we both struggle. You, to create what will someday crumble to dust. I, to crumble the weak, so that something stronger may rise in its place."

She shook her head. Some role model for her decision making—a man trapped in an eternal quest to kill someone. "Tell me, why are you so dedicated to ensuring I subject myself to something I hate?"

"Because you hate it. Because I've seen the change in you, and how much more you're capable of. Though people cannot grow like plants, we can mature in other ways—but only if we force ourselves out of places of comfort."

"And that's all? You're doing all this just because you want me to grow?"

He rolled his eyes. "Very well, my pride is also a significant factor. Satisfied? You're pledged to fight, and we've done a good amount of work already. If we don't try, then there's no way we can win."

"You think I can win?"

"It is possible."

She approached and looked up into his eyes. She knew the look that would be there when he hid something, but now she saw only earnestness. He really did believe in her, as foolish as that made him.

"If I say yes, you'll take it easy on me today?"

"Not at all."

"Ariden! Give me *something*."

He scoffed, then looked at his right hand. No sooner had a circular black pad appeared there than he swung it in an arc at her head. She ducked out of the way and the pad came around, colliding with his opposite fist, his knuckles sinking in.

He turned it to face her, showing the deep imprint. "See? Much softer."

"Let's go," she said, and the two of them walked into the arena, as Elsa took off and soared up above.

Meli sat in the fighters' waiting room, adjusting her leather wraps for the thousandth time. She had been entertaining a daydream that the officials would find something wrong with them and disqualify her, and no amount of fiddling could quiet her mind. Of course, it wouldn't have been that easy to escape her fate—after all, this was the Grand Events. The council needed her to perform, and nothing short of a plague would be accepted as a sufficient excuse not to.

On the other side of the wall, the crowd roared, then quieted. Some commotion came from the hallway, and then Ariden stepped through the door.

"They are almost ready for you."

"They're not ready for me," she said with mock confidence, clenching her fist.

"Good. Walk out with your head high."

An official appeared in the doorway and motioned them forward. It was time.

She gave Elsa a final pet, then walked the hall in silence, Ariden at her shoulder, until they came to the gate with light spilling through its bars, blinding her with white. The circle beyond was empty, the crowd quiet as they waited for the next match to begin. Her match. She tugged at the wrap on her arm and ran her fingers over her tightly braided hair. Was this really happening?

Ariden spoke behind her ear. "Think back to your training, especially the sparring sessions with Zelgovsha. Keep a calm mind and do not become overwhelmed."

"All right."

"And remember, if you get her in trouble, do not let up for a moment. You must have a killer instinct—if an opportunity comes for victory, then take it." He gave her shoulder a squeeze. "I will be watching you from the box above. Fight well."

"…Meli of Sofidra, fighting for the cause of Ariden!" The announcer called.

The gate opened. Meli took a deep breath and stepped out. Her body was moving on its own now like an automatist contraption, her legs taking her to the edge of the white ring. The center of the arena was small, much smaller than it had appeared from the stands; the opposite side of the ring was practically a few steps away, and the outer wall not much further beyond. The stands loomed high above, filled to capacity. Such an incredible number of people, of all shapes, sizes and colors. She could even see the guards on the distant city walls, facing inward to view the bout. Though most of the crowd was quiet, some were actually cheering for her. She looked up at their faces, people she had never met who took it upon themselves to root for this unproven stranger. She wished she could tell them how much it meant to her.

A worker swept dust from the previous bout around her as she waited, her mouth dry and temples throbbing. Why hadn't they announced Lemuria's entrance yet? She had spent two weeks hoping the fight would never begin, and now she only wanted an end to this delay.

The announcer stepped to the center of the circle, speaking-trumpet in hand.

"Citizens and visitors! It is my great pleasure to call upon this *Champion* of our city." He paused to allow for cheers. "A fighter triumphant in sixteen matches, twelve by knockout, with eight further victories to her name. Great fortune has she brought to her sponsor Nikolatin of Caeridor, and great pleasure has she brought those blessed enough to watch her these many occasions. I give to you now, Lemuria of—"

The rest of his words were lost as Lemuria entered the arena and the crowd jumped to its feet, hollering, chanting and singing. Lemuria seemed to not hear any of it as she made her way to her side of the circle. Meli studied her carefully, trying to see her for what she was, ignoring the intimidating nature of their circumstances. What she saw was a mean woman, limbs wiry, hair shaved save for two spiked strips down either side. Lemuria kicked at the dust and cracked her knuckles. She saw Meli and glared, baring her teeth, and the look sent a lump into Meli's throat.

The champion was not made to wait. Within moments of her taking her place, the first gong sounded—ringcraft. Meli closed her eyes, connecting with the aer in the arena, cursing herself for not using the time when Lemuria had been entering to prepare. The breeze changed behind her—Lemuria's convocation rising. She turned to see two walls coming together into a sharp corner, just as Ariden had said. *Flat is good for you, corners are good for her.* Meli convoked her own wall in the angled space, filling it with whatever hard material she could make most quickly, panicked at the thought of falling behind.

But she didn't. In moments the corner was filled and flush, and Meli directed her own convocations to several others that Lemuria was raising. She filled those as well, forming them into a smooth semicircle. Lemuria looked left and right, fists clenched, face strained. Meli's heart skipped a beat—she was better at convocation than Lemuria. Far better. She bit her lip, trying not to let the temporary victory overtake her. She had a plan for what to do in such a circumstance, but it would be a risk. Nevertheless, she stopped reacting to Lemuria's moves and instead began to convoke her own obstacles, head-height square blocks of smooth green material spread outside the circle.

Lemuria watched her with narrowed eyes, puzzled at the strange formations. Giving up on trying to trap Meli in the inner ring, she shifted tactics, convoking irregular bumps and ridges on the arena floor. Ariden had warned Meli this might happen—the bumps would make it harder to keep her footing, which meant it would be easier to take the fight to the ground. Meli focused and covered as many as she could with high walls to push off from, made of her specially-prepared material, until the space surrounding the ring resembled a field of ancient monoliths.

The gong sounded again. The crowd, which had been boisterously watching the ringcraft, grew silent as its tinny sound faded, waiting to see the fighters' reactions. Meli surveyed the arena without looking, aware of the positions of the convocations she was maintaining. She had done well. Perhaps too well. Lemuria stared balefully, eyebrows slanted, and when the gong finally went silent she stepped off her line with destructive intent.

Meli had imagined this moment countless times. All Lemuria had to do was rush her at full speed, and she was done for. All the subtle motions of her training would never be able to stand against such an onslaught. But instead the champion took the center of the ring and began to circle, keeping her distance. So perhaps all of Ariden's measures of secrecy had not been wasted. Meli was a mystery, someone who had appeared out of nowhere and was judged worthy of a championship match. Fighting was a game of inches, he had said, and an unknown variable in a match could as dangerous as any strike or submission hold.

Meli glued her knuckles to her cheekbones and advanced, standing just out of what she hoped was Lemuria's punching range. Lemuria danced from side to side, shoulders bobbing, elusive and innocuous. Meli sensed the danger only just before the first flurry.

Three punches, the first one just in front of her nose and the next two hitting her face, so fast she didn't understand which direction they had come from. The taste of blood bloomed on her tongue. Meli jumped back, keeping her hands high and her head away from those furious hands. *Keep your chin down*, Ariden yelled in her mind, but she was already leaning back, off balance.

She had to get further away. Two quick shuffles brought her out of the small white ring, into the field of uneven, raised flooring. Lemuria smiled and came forward. Straight forward; if Meli squinted, she could almost picture Ariden doing the same, pads held high. Meli dropped into her stance and focused on Lemuria's fists. Ariden was right, she realized, about the pain. It was just a feeling on her face, a temporary buzzing of the nerves. What had she been so afraid of?

Lemuria threw her next strike and this time Meli read it, turning right and popping a jab in return. Meli felt the *thunk* of her leather wrap on Lemuria's skull and gasped. She had done it. Not much to be excited about, but her quick blow had made Lemuria hop back. The crowd let out a collective "oooh." Lemuria seemed to hear it and jumped forward in irritation, trying to maintain her momentum. It was exactly the wrong thing to do. Meli slipped and thrust, and Lemuria ate another jab, this time to the nose.

More punches came in, looping hooks and overhands. Zelgovsha had thrown them often in sparring, but never at this speed. Meli dodged one and parried another, connected with a jab and then missed a poorly timed right. Lemuria fired off a right hook, and Meli, losing focus, caught it above the eyebrow. The crowd shouted as if it were a knockout blow, but Meli barely felt it. When Lemuria hopped back to observe her reaction, Meli wiped the blood from her eye and cracked her in the mouth with an advancing jab.

Lemuria shook her head and backed off until she was in the center of the ring. She snarled and pumped her fists, circling, re-evaluating her strategy. Meli walked to the white perimeter and waited. Lemuria hopped forward, watched Meli's fists warily, then thought better and backed off again.

The crowd grew restless, annoyed at the lack of aggression, and a smattering of boos crossed the arena. The sounds clearly bothered Lemuria, who hunched her shoulders and stomped her front foot. Meli avoided the bait, holding her place back at the edge of the ring. The jab counter had worked for her so far, and she had no ego to be swayed by fickle spectators.

Lemuria hopped forward and Meli readied another slip, but this time her opponent feinted a kick before coming in with an overhand right. It was a wide, slow punch, and Meli was already moving away from it, but Lemuria seemed to have expected it to miss. She continued her forward motion behind her fist, and before Meli realized what was happening, Lem was diving for her legs.

Too late, no time to sprawl. Lem's arms wrapped her waist and they flew backward, then hit the ground in a heap. Meli looked down at the champion wrapped around her legs, and in a blink Lemuria popped up to throw a punch at her midsection. It landed like a battering ram on her guts. Meli sat up and pressed her hand on Lem's face, scooting away. Lemuria scrambled, slipping in the dust as Meli's back reached a nearby wall. Sitting down and entangling their legs together, Lemuria seized one ankle with both hands and twisted.

Meli gritted her teeth. Two distinct pops came from her foot, followed by a wave of pain. Behind her, the wall was light green and slightly pliable—one of her own. She kicked Lemuria's hands off her throbbing ankle with her other leg, then leaned on the wall, using the support to push herself up. Lemuria, seeing that she wouldn't be able to stop Meli from rising, gave up her hold and jumped to her feet. The crowd roared. Lemuria threw a left hand, but she was off-balance and it was slow, looping. Meli saw it coming, slipped, and delivered a hard right to her face.

If the crowd had been loud before, Meli's strike turned them deafening. Lem staggered, one eye closed, then growled and came forward again, slamming her upper body into Meli's. They grappled, chest to chest, breath in face, sweat slipping over arms and hands. Lemuria worked the legs, first with a knee, then a stomp to Meli's feet. Gods, she was strong; similar their builds may have been, but Lemuria pressed herself forward at better angles, controlling, suffocating. Meli shouted and shucked her shoulder forward to gain room for a short punch, and in the tangle of arms a finger went into her eye. She screamed and stepped away, back against the wall. Lemuria knelt, then lunged forward to slam into her.

If they had been against a corner, Meli might have been trapped, but as it was she moved to the right and Lemuria slid by, impacting the wall with her side—or at least what used to be a wall.

When Lemuria hit the green object at speed, it collapsed into liquid, splashing around Meli's legs. A simple trick, courtesy of the Inaali, but it had the desired effect. The crowd gasped. Lemuria fell to her hands and knees, sputtering, unable to process what had just occurred.

If she fails, it may be she ends up crouched in front of you. If this happens, I want you to grasp around her arm and neck like so, and deliver as many knee strikes to the head as you can manage.

Meli dropped, hugging Lemuria around the neck and armpit, chest to back, and raised her knee for a strike. It came down in a glancing blow, but Meli was already winding up for another. This time Lem reached up and hugged her leg, preventing her from drawing it back, but in doing so she lost her base, causing her head to tip forward into the ground. Meli shook her loose, then struck again. Not hard enough. She had done it so well in practice, but in the tumult of battle her blows felt like a lover's playful swat on a pillow.

She had to hurt Lem, had to want to do it. A killer instinct, Ariden had called it. She needed something, some reason to follow through.

I need to win this.

No, she didn't. It was pointless, meaningless.

I need that ship. I need to find the Daemon. She's trying to stop me. She's trying to take away my child.

Rage coalesced in her gut. She threw another knee, still not hard enough. All those years since her dream, all that work, all that longing. She had to hold him again, or her life would be over. All that stood between her and him was this fight, this woman below her. She wanted that ship, and Lemuria was trying to stop her from getting it.

No one stands between me and him!

Another knee, and this time Lemuria's head rocked to the side with an audible crack. The crowd grew louder, their gasps mixed with cheers. More of them were coming to her side.

Lemuria wiggled in desperation and pulled apart Meli's hands with her own. Meli squeezed harder, but Lemuria slid out through the sweat, then rolled onto her back. Meli rose to her feet, standing over the prone champion.

She stayed in place a moment, unsure; Ariden had never told her what to do from this position. Lem looked slightly dazed, her legs and arms raised protectively, expecting a strike. Showing weakness. Ariden had told her to always press her advantage, go on the attack. She came forward, one step, then two, standing between Lemuria's legs.

Lemuria reached forward and grabbed Meli's right ankle in one hand, placing her own foot behind Meli's left ankle and kicking the other into her waist. Suddenly their positions reversed—Meli fell on her back, limbs flailing, while Lemuria came up on top of her.

Before Meli could think of pushing her away, the champion latched on and encircled her body, then put all her weight on Meli's chest. Meli panicked and turned on her side, but Lemuria shifted and moved up behind her shoulders, wrapping her legs high under Meli's armpits.

The first punch hit her on the temple, sending a flash of light across Meli's vision. Two more followed, the pain intense and sickening, rattling across her skull. Meli rocked and wriggled, trying to shift her face away, but Lemuria's legs only squeezed tighter around her shoulders and neck.

Another punch, this one to the mouth. Blood oozed over her tongue. She closed her eyes and covered her head but the blows kept coming and coming. She had lost count of their number, could no longer feel their full impact. Meli waved her arm, signaling surrender, but more punches came down on her unprotected face.

Why? Why was Lemuria doing this? Meli couldn't move, had no chance of escaping. The fight was over. The sounds of the crowd faded as the world turned black. A jolt of pain brought her back to consciousness, then her vision faded again.

Ariden arrived in the council's private box to find it decked it out in plush seating and shaggy carpet, with banners and bunting of blue and gold, and pots in the corners for long stalks of matching flowers. Nearest to him, a large couch with unoccupied seats looked especially comfortable, with extra pillows and savortists standing nearby to deliver refreshments.

Ariden went to the other side of the room and convoked a simple stool to sit alone, resting his chin on his fist, watching Meli as she waited for Lemuria to arrive. Nikolatin was standing nearby with his friends, but if he had noticed Ariden's entrance, he seemed disinclined to speak. That was good. The last thing Ariden wanted was for someone to come and distract him from—

A cool breeze presaged the convocation of a soft, high-backed chair to his right.

"Ariden." Alalantia sat down.

"Ala." He grunted. "Looking forward to seeing the results of your handiwork?"

"I did say I had a significant third-party interest, did I not?"

Ariden frowned and turned back to the picture window. In the ring below the announcer finished his speech, and Lemuria entered to great fanfare.

"If only I had known what you meant. So tell me, what do you gain if Meli loses?"

She chuckled. "It would not be helpful to bet against Meli. The odds are terrible. What I stand to gain is *you*. The last time you were here, I was not in a position to sponsor such a great fighter. Now I am."

"An interesting recruitment method—do you always double-cross people before asking them to fight for you? Besides, I thought your roster was full."

"A space can open, if need be. But that would be a waste of effort, if you were planning to rush off with your lady-friend on whatever errand she's convinced you to undertake. So, to keep you here, it was necessary to be rid of her. I figured a good, solid beating would suffice."

"Perhaps. Or perhaps the thrill of fighting will appeal to her. If she manages to put on a good show, she may wish to try again."

Their conversation paused for the opening gong, the private box quieting so the councilmembers could observe the ringcraft. Alalantia lowered her voice and said, "Ariden, you're not really angry at me for winning, are you? Don't take my actions as an insult. I did what I did because the man I knew years ago respected a good contest, won or lost. Have you changed?"

"Not as such. But you haven't won yet, either."

"She's no fighter, Ariden. That was quite obvious from the start. But you have no cause for regret. I am sure you did your best with her. And now you will be free. Free to join me in ruling this city. Whatever you were to gain from helping her, I can offer you as well. Together, there is nothing we cannot accomplish. Together in purpose—" She laid a hand on his shoulder. "—and in deed."

He hunched forward, shaking off her touch and getting a better look as Meli filled the corners around her. "All the same, I would prefer to watch the fight."

She straightened and sniffed. "I suppose there is a small chance it will be worth watching. The Outsiders at least seem to have taken an interest in your story. I have never seen such a crowded stadium for a women's match."

Murmurs in the box grew as the ringcraft continued, with Meli easily outpacing Lemuria's efforts. That was no surprise to Ariden—he had seen how quickly Meli could convoke under stress. Still, there was little reason for Nikolatin or Alalantia to be nervous. Superior ringcraft was an advantage, to be sure, but only skill and spirit could win a fight.

"It must pain you to be stuck up here, sitting helpless, while someone else fights in your stead," Alalantia said.

"It is a new feeling. How do you deal with it?"

"I've always somewhat enjoyed it. Then again, you may recall I liked being tied up, as well."

Ariden glanced at her, and for a moment he saw her back then, lithe body sliding over silk sheets. His loins stirred despite himself. Whatever her lack of scruples, Alalantia was an attractive woman, there was no doubt of that.

The gong sounded again, and the familiar surge of quiet anticipation went through the crowd. Meli took her stance, but remained at the side of the circle. With her back to him, Ariden couldn't see her eyes, couldn't see how much fear lay in them.

"Poxing guards need to mind their business," Alalantia said, stealing his concentration. "I will have a word with them later."

A look confirmed the guards on the city walls had gathered on the high towers and were taking in the action, watching the arena instead of the plain outside the city. He seemed to recall that it had been the same in his day, a fringe benefit of an otherwise boring post.

The crowd gave a shout. Meli was falling back, away from a flurry, and for a moment it seemed as if the fight would be over quickly. But the gods of combat would not be so easily predicted, and Meli found her feet and stuck a solid jab between Lemuria's eyes. Ariden's throat unclenched as the crowd roared again.

Alalantia was quiet for once as Meli stuck to the game plan, jabbing and circling, dodging and countering. Xalix the felid growled softly on Alalantia's lap. Lem fell back, evaluating her options. This would be a decisive moment—would she continue to try and brawl to please the crowd, or fall back to her best strategy, as Zelgovsha had said she would? To Ariden's horror, she did just that, shooting in and taking Meli down with an impact that made half the stadium grunt in sympathy.

Xalix purred.

"It is over now." Alalantia said. "Too soon for an entertaining match, I am afraid."

Ariden bit his lip. Meli was making a heroic effort to reach a wall and rise, but as soon as she regained her footing Lem was all over her again, bullying from the clinch. Ariden stared into his lap, contemplating the taste of defeat, when the crowd both inside and outside the box let out a collective gasp.

Lemuria was on her hands and knees, face down in a puddle of green slime. Ariden jumped to his feet as Meli dove in for the kill. "Sly girl!" he shouted, smiling at Nikolatin and Alalantia in turn.

It took a few knees, but Meli found her range and began raining down hard blows, while the champion still struggled to make sense of the situation. Then Lemuria rolled away and Meli stood up. The crowd roared and Ariden clenched his fists.

"Back up," he said. "Let her come to you."

Meli dropped her hands, hesitated, then took a step forward.

"No! Stop!" He pounded on the thick window.

The inevitable occurred. Lem tripped her and came on top, and this time Meli had no space to maneuver. Ariden hunched his shoulders and sat, his wind gone.

Alalantia stroked Xalix. "A better show than I thought. Good fight, Ariden."

Below, Lem had locked in a solid high mount, and was laying in with a series of brutal punches and elbows. Ariden half-expected the official to step in at any moment before he remembered there was none.

"What is she doing?" he said. "Meli is done." Even from his distance he could see her drifting in and out of consciousness with each blow, lifting her head and dropping it slackly into the dust. If her brain took too many, became damaged enough...

Ariden gripped his seat and leaned forward. "She's going to die if this keeps up." He stared at Alalantia accusingly. "Did you arrange this?"

"I did not. Lem has always been prone to rages. I suppose she did not enjoy nearly being made a fool of."

The blows continued. The crowd quieted, some looking away, and Meli's cries of pain filled the arena. On the far side of the window, Elsa flew down, hysterical, shrieking and scratching her claws on the smooth surface.

Ariden stood. In his right hand he was surprised to find the hilt of the Scythe.

Alalantia noticed it as well. "What are you doing?"

Ariden's only answer was to look down at the hilt, then back to the action below.

"Do not even think of interfering," Alalantia growled. "The sentence would be death. I will not be able to save you."

For a moment he deflated, then a long moan of anguish came from below. Ariden turned and raised his weapon.

"You're being foolish," Alalantia said. "You don't want her. She's not like you, Ariden. She's not a fighter."

"You're right," Ariden said. "She's not." He pointed the hilt at the window and loosed the blade.

The aer in the box turned frigid, then rushed outward as a cloud of window fragments-cum-dust exploded into the arena. Ariden leaped through it, shielding his eyes with his coat sleeve, and reached out so Elsa could catch his hand. A moment of freefall, then they made contact. Together, they drifted down over the heads of the mystified crowd.

Once over the arena center, he let go of Elsa, fell onto the ground and rolled, coming to rest just beyond the inner ring. Two long strides and a kick to the shoulder sent Lemuria tumbling away from Meli. Lemuria scrabbled up, looked at Ariden in confusion, then realized what had happened and rushed him in a fury. Ariden raised the point of the Scythe in front of her face. Lemuria bared her teeth, but backed away, her eyes fixed on the blade.

Beside him, Meli groaned and stirred. So he had not been too late—thank the gods, he had not been too late. She rolled over and attempted to rise to her hands and knees, then collapsed face-first in the dust.

The crowd was on its feet by then, calling out blasphemy and defiler. On the far side of the pit the fighters' gate opened, and an array of armed guards poured through it, after his blood.

32

The guards fanned out to surround them, stepping around the dust piles where Meli had convoked her walls. Elsa took to the aer, safe since the men didn't carry crossbows, only pikes, short swords, shields and flails, all of them now directed at Ariden. He stepped back, keeping his eye on them, and hooked his arm under Meli's shoulder to lift her upright.

"What happened?" she mumbled. "Did I win?"

"Not quite. And on top of that, I've gone and done something rash."

Meli shook her head and tested her balance. Then she saw the guards. "We're dead."

"Not yet. More are coming behind. Can you put up a wall?"

She closed her bruised and swollen eyes, and a gray wall grew upward behind them. The guards in front shouted and rushed in to attack. Ariden readied the Scythe.

The lead guard came in well ahead of the others, but he lacked the physical prowess to match his bravery. His speed came from a short, wiry frame, and his inexperience with a sword showed when he lifted his too-small weapon well over his head. Ariden came down low and struck hard enough to put him out of the battle without an arm.

The next two guards were real threats, men from the largest weight division who carried it all in muscle, one with a pike and the other a lengthy blade. Ariden slipped inside the pike's reach, chopped it off at the handle and sliced its bearer across the thighs with one stroke. He twisted away from the sword-wielder's strike, catching a gash across his chest, and fell into the man he had just wounded, causing him to scream out in pain. The swordsman squared up and came forward again, but his foot slipped in blood, and he stumbled just long enough for Ariden to lay a good chop into his collarbone.

Clutching his burning chest, Ariden swung about to face the others. Three from the left, and more further back on the right, newly arrived from elsewhere in the arena. He stepped back until his shoulder blades hit Meli's wall—not a traditionally valued position for armed combat, but better than being surrounded, and its concave shape meant his enemies would have to bunch together in front.

He readied his sword again, and a small, straight blade smashed through the wall inches from his head.

"A little thicker, please!"

"Sorry!"

A meaty fist had come through with the blade. Ariden considered chopping it off at the wrist, but Meli had already convoked more material around the hole, binding the man in. No sense wasting time; more would be climbing over the top soon, not to mention the growing crowd of guards in front, now hanging back warily, eyes on the Scythe.

Absurdly, Ariden felt relief that their situation wasn't worse; if the entire audience had decided to rush them, they would have been gone by now. But it seemed the majority of those in the stands—Outsiders, they must have been—were holding back the ones who wanted to jump in. His lucky day.

One of the guards got bold and thrust her pike into the walled alcove. Ariden side-stepped, pointed the Scythe at the woman's sternum and extended it to a thin point. It pierced through the back side of her ribcage, then snapped when she collapsed.

"If they keep falling for tricks like that, we'll be drowned in dust soon," he said, eying the rest.

"Stop," Meli said, swooning from the effort of her convocation. "Don't kill them."

"What?"

"If we're going to die anyway, I don't want their blood on my hands."

"Very well." He grabbed her wrist. "Make a hole and we'll run."

He pulled her into the side of the semicircular wall, which crumbled at her command. They raced for the nearest gate. The guards came after and Meli put obstacles in their paths.

"Some are flanking!" Ariden yelled. Two high walls appeared on either side of them, forming a narrow alley. An incredible feat of convocation, but by the time they reached the gate, guards were already scrambling over top. Ariden reached the end of their passage and came up short; someone had laid a hard block across the archway.

"Brace yourself." Ariden lifted the Scythe and focused, holding back the blade until the last possible moment, pushing the sword with every iota of his being, far more than he needed to break the block.

The blade shot out with a bang that burst his eardrums and knocked Meli flat, then the blistering cold traveled as a second wave through the makeshift alley. The walls fell, guards hollered, and a cloud of dust mixed with aether-snow blew over everything.

Ariden took a moment to survey their former pursuers scattered in disarray, then let the broken blade fall and helped Meli back up.

"This way."

The dust cleared under the arch, and another five guards appeared in the hole behind the shattered barrier.

"Oh, mold."

Ariden spun around. Beyond the radius of the Scythe's blast of cold, tens more guards approached, with Alalantia and two other councilmembers in the center.

Slowly, their pursuers congregated around again, picking up and dusting off fallen comrades, muttering anger and revenge. Alalantia pushed to the front, her eyes wide, her nostrils flaring.

"You have a choice," she said. "Die now, or submit to justice, and be executed with what honor you have left."

Ariden took a long look at Meli, who had fallen again, shaking from pain or fear.

"All right," he said. "We give up."

"The sword," Alalantia said. "Crumble it."

He did. The handle was so cold he could barely hold it, anyway.

Guards came up behind and bound their arms behind them in blobs of tacky goo. One of them approached Ariden in front, the one whose thighs he had sliced before tumbling into him. The man sneered, then struck Ariden in the face. Ariden's legs went weak, but he righted himself and raised his chin, curving his throbbing cheek into a grin.

"Stop that," Alalantia said. "Prepare a blade, instead. I'm sorry, Ariden. I wish...well, no use for wishes, now. I'll do my best to get it over with quickly." She motioned to the others. "Bring the officials. We will have the trial here, and the execution."

The crowd shuffled about, making way for those carrying out Alalantia's orders, convoking parts for the guillotine or making raised stands to get a good view of the upcoming trial. Meli sat on her knees, head lowered, shoulders rising and falling. Ariden swiveled his head, looking for an escape. There was none. A hundred guards surrounding him, hands bound, no Scythe, and the officials would arrive in moments to deliver a verdict. No, there was nothing, no way out this time.

A horn sounded in the distance. Everyone in the stadium looked through the great archway up to the city wall. Some sort of platform had been convoked on top of it, and the guards there were yelling, running, pointing at something beyond. A great roar emanated from the crowd, echoed by a distant rumble, and then hundreds of Outsiders and caprans streamed up over the wall, screaming and bleating a battle cry.

"Ten gods!" Alalantia screamed. "What are they doing?"

The Outsiders took over the section of the wall in moments, tossing the guards into the moat outside, then began sliding down ramps into the city, their animals tumbling after them. The Outsiders in the crowd headed for the exits, screaming their excitement, some convoking bags of powder and confetti to add to the confusion.

"Get people up there!" Alalantia shouted and pointed, but in the rush of the stadium crowd the guards were too disorganized to respond. "What are they doing? You, what are *you* doing? Get away from me!" She disappeared into a gang of Outsiders running across the arena center, tooting hand-held horns.

Ariden glanced at Meli; the look on her face confirmed he wasn't hallucinating. Obviously the Outsiders had planned this in advance, chosen the Grand Events as a good time to cause as much disruption to the city as possible. But despite the pandemonium, the guard who had bound their hands remained beside them. One of them saw Ariden looking about and smacked him. "Don't even think about it."

A buzzing sound came from overhead. "Think about what?" Ariden asked. "This?"

Elsa swooped down, screaming and harrying the guard with her claws. Ariden hopped back, waiting for an opening, and when he saw the back of the man's head exposed he spun in reverse and laid the guard out with a strike from his heel.

Ariden pulled his crumbling bonds apart, then turned to face the other guard, who assumed a look of terror and backpedaled away.

"Come on!" Meli shouted, hobbling off after Elsa into the tunnel.

"*No, no, must upward! Outside not,*" Elsa said, flapping and buzzing furiously. Ariden took one look down the hall, where Outsiders were streaming by in a blur of motion, then turned and followed Elsa and Meli up a stairwell.

The scene upon their exit was no less chaotic, as the crowd flooded in from the stands, convoking slides from the scaffold-like walls down to the street level. Ariden pushed against the flow of people, jostling to maintain his view of Elsa and Meli, until he crossed into another stairwell and ran up again.

The next floor had no direct route from the stands. They paused at the threshold to watch a group of guards run past them through the otherwise empty hall. "Where to?" Ariden said, just loud enough to be heard over the din of the crowd below.

"*Far stairway, there,*" Elsa whispered, craning her neck.

"Where in the gods is she taking us?"

"I don't know," Meli said, her back to the wall. She made a run for the stair, then let out a yelp as a tall, black-haired guard turned the corner at the end the hall.

"You!" he shouted. "Hey, the blasphemers are here! Erlin! Makol!"

"Better go," Ariden said. Without waiting for agreement, he made for the next stairway, pausing at the landing to heft the collapsing Meli onto his shoulder. They climbed in such haste, he didn't realize where they were until they exploded out into the daylight.

The drakenbird stood, its massive chest facing the riot-filled streets below, its head turned toward the door. It let out a worried hoot when it saw Ariden, but relaxed when Elsa flapped past him.

"*She helps escape. Name is Frarifrafra. Speaking earlier friends, made now helps.*"

The drakenbird sat back on its haunches. The skin of its stomach parted, opening to a pink cavity in its belly. Yelling and clattering came from the stairs behind them.

"Who are we to refuse?"Ariden said.

He bundled Meli into the opening, then climbed through and collapsed into the squishy interior. Guards shouted on the roof. The drakenbird shifted, rocking his equilibrium, then it leapt, arcing downward at a stomach churning angle before spreading its wings and lifting skyward.

Ariden sat up and looked out a small porthole the drakenbird had opened for them, covered with a flap of clear skin. Streets passed by below, filled with Outsiders smashing food stalls and running from sword-wielding guards, followed by a quick flash of moat and then the wide brown plain.

"Ships," Meli mumbled. "They'll send ships. To kill us."

Ariden formed a new Scythe hilt, keeping his eye on the receding city. The square of aether-stone shrank to a thumbnail, then a dot, and finally vanished beyond the horizon without anything arising from it.

"We're safe." He let the half-finished sword crumble.

Meli tried to sit up, then let out a scream and dropped to the floor. Ariden came and pulled her close, cradling her head in his chest as she cried.

"You'll be fine."

"The pain..."

"It will heal."

"Ariden...oh, it hurts."

"Shhhh."

"Gods, it didn't hurt like this before. In the fight. Did you see me? Agh, my jaw feels strange."

"Your teeth are growing back." He hugged her tight. "You did it, Meli."

She looked up, big eyes glistening. "You did it. You saved me."

"We wouldn't have escaped without you." He cupped the back of her head, his fingers interlacing with the loose braids.

"Ariden."

They held each other's eyes for an endless moment. He leaned forward, their lips met, and they were one.

33

The balcony on which Karis sat was made of the same hard-yet-soft material as the rest of the tower, as was the table before her. She stared at the design inlaid on its surface, purple lines intersecting on a field of black and red. She much preferred the view there to what was sitting across from her.

"I hope your companions are enjoying their stay as much as you are."

"Oh, yes. I'm sure they are." Karis did her best to smile, though whether the Old Wise One's statement was meant in earnest she couldn't tell. Even if her act was good enough to convince him he didn't make her skin crawl, Roi and the others had done even less to hide their growing unease before they had retired early to their rooms.

Days had passed since they arrived, and still they were no closer to finding the Source. Or rather, she was no closer. The Old Wise One had relegated the raiders to a daily regimen of "study" which seemed to Karis like busywork: convoking small geometric shapes which fit together into larger sculptures, spherical pendulums which could be suspended next to each other and clacked back and forth, and so on. Only Karis had the honor of spending most of her time with the Old Wise One himself, taking in the view ("filthy flowers spoil everything"), observing his incomprehensible experiments, and most of all listening to him lecture. So, so many lectures.

Unfortunately, it had become quickly apparent that they weren't going to stumble across the Source at random in one of the winding, ever-shifting hallways. The only way to the ancient convocation was through the Old Wise One himself, as Roi had repeated to her several times.

"You must make progress today, Karis." Roi had approached her earlier that day during a rare moment of the Old Wise One's distraction, while he was upbraiding several of the crew for failing to convoke their shapes to his standards. "No more fooling about."

"I'm not fooling about. I just don't know what to say to him. I can't come right out and ask him where the Source is, can I?"

Roi jerked his head toward the high-pitched voice on the other side of the main chamber. "Keep it down. And it's clear he doesn't care what you say to him. Only what you do to him."

"You're suggesting that if I fuck him, he'll give me what I want?"

"Couldn't hurt."

She suppressed a gag. "There's another way. I just need more time."

"We're out of time. Produce results soon, or I'll have to take—" He glanced at Isky and Dikta. "—alternate measures." He hurried away as the Old Wise One noticed them talking and glared in their direction.

Couldn't hurt—easy for him to say. Roi was making a difficult task practically impossible. And for what? They still had half a week or more before the ship fell apart. And even if they didn't have the time, the idea of attacking or threatening the Old Wise One made her profoundly uneasy. No, she would have to do this herself, just not the way Roi wanted.

The problem was, she didn't much like talking to the Old Wise One either, or being in the same room with him. Even now, sitting across from him during their meal on the balcony, there was something about the way he stared through her, the constant shifting of the walls and floors, and that high-pitched cackle which made her want to jump out of her seat and bolt to the ship.

And then of course there was *that*. The plagues. The subject hung between them always, unspoken but no less disturbing for it. Even stories of anathematists gave her shivers; she had never thought she would meet one in person. But an anathematist that actually created plagues? *The* Plague Bringer? He was the *original* anathematist!

"Do you like the pudding?" The Old Wise One pointed to the off-white glob on the tip of her finger.

Looking down, Karis realized she had been absent-mindedly swirling it in her bowl. She put the glob in her mouth. "It's delicious." It actually was, too. The Old Wise One had convoked one of every type of foodstuff Karis could have imagined for dinner, as well as a few she hadn't. Regardless of what else she thought of him, she had to admit he knew his savortism.

"I call it Raendal's Delight. Usually, of course, dishes are named after their inventors, but I've forgotten who invented it, so I renamed it after myself."

Karis nodded politely and took a big bite, her full mouth giving her an excuse not to talk to him more. She shouldn't have been doing that, though. This was a good chance to find the Source, and here she was, distancing herself from the man who possessed it. She had to at least make him think she desired him, to lull him into complacency.

She reached for a plate of brown cakes and the dish slid away from her hand, riding on a section of the tabletop.

The Old Wise One grinned. "Did you want that?" Without warning the table folded itself in half, and his seat moved along with it, until he was next to her.

"The light is fading." He handed her the plate. "Romantic, isn't it?"

His fingertips lingered as she accepted the plate, brushing the side of her hand. It took all of her self-control not to slap it away. She needed a change of subject.

"You know," she said. "It's rare I get to speak with another smoothskin."

"Smoothskins? Is that what they call us, now?"

"Uh…yes. I've noticed the ones I've met all tended to have unusually good memories. Tell me, do you remember your earliest days?"

He smiled and waved his hand dismissively. "I am sure my memory is better than most. But after three thousand years? I do not recall most of the names and faces from back then. Why should I waste my precious thought on unimportant matters?"

"Of course you shouldn't." She nodded, sensing an opening. "There must be other things which occupy your mind. Like convocations—do you remember the ones you learned thousands of years ago?"

"Certainly I do. I always keep in practice. " He puffed out his meager chest.

"Then you must know some that are truly ancient—perhaps ones that everyone else has forgotten?"

He drew back and narrowed his eyes. Not good—she had tipped him off to what she was after.

But his face drew into a smile. "The trouble with the ancients was that they knew both too much, and too little. For example, I remember a time when the prevailing theory of ethics was that each person learned them from experience, and from the standards of their community …"

Oh gods, not another lecture on philosophy.

"…completely ignoring all of the evidence we have of people appearing with ethical values already in place! Of course, there are arguments to be made for variations as people age, but I swear, take a roomful of learned philosophers and try to explain that to them, and you might as well have been speaking Phranengian—"

"That's all well, but—"

"—thank the gods they're all dead—eh?"

"What do you mean, 'too much and too little'? In terms of convocations?"

"Oh." He flashed that suspicious look again, then adopted a milder stare, folding his hands in front of him. "Well, it is true the ancients knew of convocations barely dreamed of today. But they had no systems, you see? They made great discoveries, but never followed them to see how they fit into a picture of the whole. For example, do you recall me saying I once searched for a method of convoking bedrock?"

She nodded.

"Well, that was pure nonsense, as it turns out! As silly as the notion of turning dust back to working aether."

"I see," she said, with slight disappointment.

"Yes, yes," he went on, taking no notice of her. "Once I refocused the philosophical schools on systemization, it became quite clear that bedrock is a fundamentally different substance from all aether-derived material. The idea that the ancients could create bedrock at will was nothing more than a false result of the initial studies of the ancient ruins. We had assumed them to be the work of our classical-age forebears, and never considered that they might be much older than that."

He looked up, saw her frowning and echoed her expression. "My beauty…does this subject bore you? It has been many centuries since I spent significant time researching new convocations, but I have hardly been tarrying. On the contrary, I have learned much in the studies of music and motion. And anatomy—did you know that inside your body are at least seven distinct organs which appear to have no purpose whatsoever?"

"No." Unease crept up her spine. How exactly had he found *that* out?

"Yes, yes, I have always taken fascination in the study of why the gods made us as they did. Take food, for example." He lifted a morsel from his plate. "Such a complex system of taste and smell we have, and for moving the remnants of what we eat through our bodies. But why? If one forgoes eating for a lengthy period of time, no ill effects are observed. So why did the gods bother fashioning us so?"

"I had a friend who wondered something similar," Karis said with a hint of melancholy. "She didn't accept that the gods wished us to live a life of pleasure. She thought something wasn't right with the world, that perhaps the gods had made a mistake."

He chuckled. "A mistake? Oh, the theories of simpletons and amateur philosophers will never stop amusing me." He gazed off into the distance, missing her deep frown, and twirled his finger in his cup. "Still, pleasure itself can be paradoxical, that much is true. After all, what could be more pleasurable than sex, and yet we do not see mankind engaging in sexual intercourse on a constant basis, do we?"

She took a drink, hiding her eye roll behind her cup.

"Of course, orgiastic cultures do spring up from time to time, but the historians always report them dying out after a short while. And who can blame them? After thirty or forty years of non-stop copulation, I imagine people tend to get a bit bored, hmm?

"If I may be so bold, my dear, I have found there's something lacking in the pursuit of pure pleasure. An emptiness. If anything, it interferes with other important activities. For example, I have definitively concluded that my research proceeds optimally when I masturbate no more than twice a day."

She choked, and liquid shot through her nose and onto her lap. The Old Wise One jumped up and grabbed her shoulders as she coughed the rest out.

"My beauty! Are you all right?"

"Fine," she sputtered. "I'm fine." She shooed him back to his chair and cleared her throat. "It's just that I'm...in awe. Of your insight."

He smiled widely. Could he really be so susceptible to flattery? And why hadn't she thought of that earlier?

She cleared her throat. "It's so rare for me to be in the presence of knowledge that eclipses my own."

The Old Wise One sat back in his seat. A single curly hair grew out of his chin, and he pulled at it as he stared at her.

"Tell me, my beauty: In all your years of learning, what is the key insight you have gained about our world?"

His demeanor had changed somehow. He wasn't flirting anymore—no, this was more like a test. She looked down at the table and said, "I believe that there is more to this world than what we experience."

"Certainly," he said in a bored tone. "There is the realm of the gods, to be sure."

"No, not just the gods. I mean aspects of this world. Things that are within us; within everything. We take the aether for granted; every day it passes under and into our noses, and yet the aer itself is exploding with possibilities. Vast energies…mysteries waiting to be unlocked." She became flustered, searching for words. "I cannot explain it well enough."

She looked up, expecting his derision, but he was smiling from ear to ear.

"Yes, yes. My beauty, perhaps you do have the capacity to understand."

She did her best to ignore how insulting that sounded. "Understand what?"

"Let me show you something." He held out his hand. Karis held still, and so he reached and took hers in it. "Come, do not be shy. I guarantee you have not seen this before."

He cupped his two hands on opposite sides of hers, then closed his eyes, falling deep into concentration. Nothing happened, and she began to wonder if all of this was a trick to enable him to touch her.

Then she felt it.

She gasped and snapped back. "What was that?" She rubbed one hand in the other—the strange sensation was already fading.

"I call it, 'warmth.'"

Her heart beat faster. "Show me more. Please. How did you do it?"

"In time, my dear." His face brimmed with delight. "You do have a long stay ahead of you, do you not?"

She swallowed. "I suppose." The evening light had almost faded, throwing shadows over his glaring eyes. Something pulled within her, telling her to leave the tower as soon as possible. She ignored it. "It's getting late now. We'll have to go to bed."

"Oh, really?" His eyelashes fluttered.

"Yes. I mean, in my room. Alone. That's where I'll be in bed."

He grunted, cleared his throat and straightened up. "Of course, my lovely. If you are tired, then please take your leave."

Karis pushed away from the table and headed toward the high-ceilinged main chamber, the same one in which the Old Wise One had first received them. A black and purple door spiraled shut in front of her with a loud thud.

"Please." The Old Wise One stood behind her and tapped her shoulder. "We'll walk down this way, instead. I want you to…see the windward side at dusk."

She looked back at the door again. That was odd behavior, but then what wasn't, coming from him? She followed him down a stairway formed by panels flipped up from the side of the building. The Old Wise One moved carefully as they came about into the wind, his thin shoulders bobbing with each step. Her gaze drifted from him to the sky, a solid sheet of near-black as the remains of the light left it.

Another day lost. What was she going to do? Even if he didn't know her true intentions, he seemed to understand that by hiding his secrets he could keep her interest longer. If only she wasn't under so much pressure from Roi. And as much as the Old Wise One made her nervous, she knew how volatile Roi could be when he felt threatened. Just look what had happened to Paolem.

Here she was, alone, caught between these two very different but very dangerous men. And yet—was that the answer? Could she use one against the other?

She might not have been able to pry the Source from the Old Wise One yet, but she did have a measure of control over him. With a little push, could he buy her the time she needed?

The Old Wise One turned and entered the dark hallway where he had placed their guest rooms. He walked hunched over, still sulking from her rejection. "Here we are." He motioned toward her door, gave a slight bow and waited for her to enter. Instead, she sidled up to him.

"There's something I want," she whispered.

He cocked his head, eyes wide.

"But I can tell only you," she continued. "None of my companions can know."

"Of course, my lovely. Your secret is safe."

"Are you sure? No one can hear us now?"

"Quite. I have them locked in. The walls are quite thick."

She leaned in. "Roi is giving me trouble."

"Trouble? How so?"

"He wants to take me away from this place. He feels he has learned all he can here."

"Certainly *he* has. But I would not let him run off with you, my sweet."

She racked her brain, trying to come up with a convincing lie which wouldn't get anyone killed. "I don't think he would take me by force. But his insistence is distracting. I wish you could find something to keep him busy. Something to keep him out of the way."

"Out of the way…"

Clenching her fist, eyes screwed tight, she leaned down and flicked the tip of her tongue on his ear.

The Old Wise One shot up straight so fast he nearly smashed her nose, then proceeded to do a poor job of acting nonchalant, clearing his throat and readjusting his robe. A sick feeling of self-loathing welled in her gut.

"I see," he said. "In fact, I believe I have a convocation that might be suitable."

"A convocation?"

"I will make your problem disappear, Karis." He looked up at her, and his eyes gleamed despite the darkness. "Like dust on the breeze. You shall see results soon, I promise."

"Wait. What—"

He jumped up and planted a kiss on her lips. She yelped and hopped back, wiping her mouth with the back of her hand.

The Old Wise One smiled wickedly, then dashed back down the hall, making a celebratory hooting noise as he went.

34

Meli sat up and stretched, then looked about the cabin and smiled. How nice to wake with a body that felt new again. She couldn't say as much for her head, but the dull pain behind her eyes could have been the result of a night of so little sleep as much as anything else.

Ariden lay beside her, nude except for the bedspread, breathing softly. She ran her fingers through his hair, then reached down and gently pinched his nipple. His eyes shot open, searching for an adversary. When he saw her, he grinned and pulled her down for a kiss.

"You are not being fair," he said. "A man needs his rest."

"I merely wish for you to enjoy the day, not sleep through it."

"Who said I would not enjoy sleeping through it?" He cupped her breast and kissed her again, and they shared a quiet embrace.

"What shall we do, then?" she asked, after he had shoved his face in the pillow again.

"Take a walk," he said into the cloth. "You can explain the workings of plants while we take some food and drink in the next glade. Perhaps if we feel adventurous we can explore further— avoiding rivers, of course."

She sat and let him doze on a while longer, staring out at the white sky beyond the window.

"Ariden," she said. "What will we do after today?"

"Ask me tomorrow."

"You know what I mean. We can't stay here forever."

He turned over and sighed the sigh of a contented man presented with a serious topic of discussion. "I suppose our next destination should be the Automatia. We had a deal, didn't we?"

She chuckled, though it wasn't funny. "I am not opposed to the Automatia in theory. But to go there without Karis seems...wrong somehow. I have to think on it more."

"Then by all means, stay here a while and think. The world can manage its battles without us."

"A strange sentiment to hear, from the world's greatest fighter."

He snarled playfully at her sarcasm. "I have been a fighter most of my life, because I was good at it. But that does not mean I was meant to do it. A talent and a purpose are not the same thing."

"And what of everything in life being a fight?"

He began to turn back over, slowly, then at the last moment tugged her on top of him, their faces nearly touching.

"Do we fight when we make love?"

"No."

"Then I was wrong. Perhaps not *everything* is a fight." He let her roll away, put his hands behind his head and sighed again. "For many years I searched for a way to fill the hole in my heart, to gain satisfaction through another's death. But in my desperation, I forgot the reason why I had succumbed so easily to the enchantment. My true purpose is love, Meli, not fighting. Thank you for reminding me of that."

"You're welcome." She smiled and kissed him. "I'm going to see what the day has brought."

"Wait," he said. "I will accompany you."

"Take your time." The aer tickled her bare skin when she stepped out of bed, and she convoked a white gown to cover herself, soft and comfortable with tufts of fur around the collar. Past the door, a wide glade stretched out before her, nestled deep in the foothills of the Aperandis, its purple and green flowers stunning in the morning light. A wild place, untouched by human convocation, far beyond the reach of their enemies in Caeridor. That made two cities now in which she was a wanted criminal. It almost would have been amusing, had not the regret of losing Sofidra stung her still.

Regrets. This journey had brought her and Ariden together, that was true, but she had lost so much in return. Karis was gone, and with her Meli's desire to visit the Automatia. To enter the school without her friend would have simply felt wrong; the Automatia had been Karis's dream first, after all. And Meli had her own, more troubling dreams to contend with. She rubbed her hand over her flat belly and sighed.

Ariden arrived dressed in his coat, and the two of them headed toward the copse of trees where Fra the drakenbird was roosting. Elsa, perched on one of the outer branches, saw them coming and flapped excitedly.

"*She is talking last night and saying leaving soon if can come.*"

"Fra? She wants to leave?"

The drakenbird moved its head behind the trees, peering at them from the camouflage. It gave a grunting bark.

"*Yes, leave soon. All go with but seeing offspring and partner in Caeridor, is timing go back.*"

"Offspring? She has offspring?" Meli felt a twang pass through her belly again and frowned.

"*Yesyes. Away too long is she.*"

"Will the city punish her for helping us?"

Elsa relayed the question in hoots and whistles, and the Drakenbird responded with a low grumble.

"*Is not punish. Drakenbird held sacred by city. She doing whatever is wanting, and wanting to help. She drops whereever wish to go.*"

Meli and Ariden at each other, as if reading each other's thoughts. Meli sighed. Another few days in the cabin would have been so sweet. "It seems we will have to make plans a bit sooner than we thought."

He nodded, his expression flat, and headed across the meadow. "Tell her we will have a destination soon," he called.

Meli followed after him. "Where are you going?"

"On our walk."

He took her hand and led her away from the cabin and the trees, toward a shallow pass between two hills. Ariden stayed silent, and Meli did as well. Something was bothering him, and she suspected she knew what, but the time didn't seem right to voice it. So instead they shuffled through the high grass, listening to distant bird calls and insect chitters, until they came to a low rise overlooking a sheer mountainside.

"We can't go much further," she said. "The cabin will crumble."

"We don't need it anymore, remember?"

They went on, over increasingly rocky ground, until the base of the mountain loomed above them. To continue further would turn the walk into a trek, so they found a clean spot of bedrock and sat to watch flutterflies alight on the meadow.

"Meli," Ariden said, turning toward her. "I saw you minding your belly."

She looked down. "What of it?"

"You told me of it in your dream, the connection with your little one. You desire him still."

"Of course I do."

"And you desire to go to Raendal, to see what truth your vision held. I don't know why you refuse to speak of it."

"Because of you," she said. "You never trusted the Inaali, were always wary of Raendal. Just now, you told me we should go to the Automatia—"

"Meli—"

"You made a joke about our deal. But it wasn't a joke, was it? You haven't given up on finding the Scarred Man, have you? You wish to kill him now more than ever."

Ariden hunched forward and stared off into the mountains, choosing his words carefully. "You're angry."

"I'm not angry. Just…disappointed. All that talk about re-finding your purpose—I thought I would be enough to take your mind from her."

"It doesn't work that way." He shook his head vigorously. "No matter how much I care for you, the Scarred Man is like an itch I cannot scratch. I can ignore it for so long, but sooner or later it comes back, and it will not be denied."

She took a deep breath, attempting to moderate her tone, to sound less spiteful. Even if she didn't understand him, she could try to feel sympathy. But she would not pretend that she condoned his actions.

"I will not help you kill this man. That is final. To be honest, ever since I heard your story, I thought it likely that he was already dead."

"Very possible," Ariden said. "But that would be the worst fate of all. Unless I can find proof of his crumbling, I would be doomed to wander forever."

"Then we'll find another way. Locate an anathematist, force them to use their powers to make you whole."

He snorted. "Not an easy task. Even if any still exist, they wouldn't make their whereabouts known."

"I thought you liked a challenge."

He snorted again, this time turning to a chuckle. "Very well. You drive a hard bargain, but I'm willing to try. We'll wander together from city to city, seeking an anathematist who somehow manages to practice their art while remaining alive." He paused, then his tone turned harder. "But first, we'll pay this Raendal a visit."

She looked up, surprised. "But the danger—you were the one who warned me."

"Even so, this opportunity may not come again soon. The drakenbird can fly as well as any ship, and we sit now below the same mountain range you saw at the Sanctuary. You can find Raendal's location, yes?"

She closed her eyes. "'Give the Source to the Daemon which dwells there, and he will grant your wish.'" She shook her head. "It's not so simple. A part of me does not want to go. The Daemon has a secret, Ariden. I could feel it. And when I uncover that secret, I won't like what I find."

"And yet you must uncover it."

"Yes."

"Then we will leave straight away."

The words came with a rueful finality; Ariden liked his conversations short and to the point. But Meli would not have it. "I've been watching you as well, you know."

"Oh?"

"I've seen how you hurry after me when I threaten to stray out of sight. How you question my whereabouts."

Silence.

"You're scared. You fear losing me, like you lost her. How could I ask you in good conscience to take me to that tower? Who knows what—"

He pulled her close, beholding her as if he wished her face to make an indelible mark on his memory.

"Meli, listen well. It is true that losing you now would destroy me. But I know what your dream means to you. If I let you leave this chance behind for my sake, you would never truly forgive me.

"Sometimes the path before us is not the easy one, but we must accept life's trials as they come. The gods have chosen to set one more task before us before we may be on our way. I am willing to face it. For you."

They kissed, deep and long, bodies close enough to feel his heart beating on her chest. Then they rose and walked back to the glade hand in hand, past the crumbled cabin, to where the drakenbird waited in the trees.

And with each step, Meli felt a dull thudding in the back of her skull, the echo of a memory.

The Daemon, and the secret of her dream, both intertwined.

Both lying ahead.

35

The man knelt with his head in the stockade, eyes glassy, emotionless. If he heard his executioner approach or understood the spoken list of his crimes, his face did not show it. Only when the axe rose did his gaze lift, then come back down, focusing on the shallow bowl where his head would soon rest. The axe fell and his head came off cleanly. It hit the bowl with a clank, then cracked into three pieces, each of which turned a pale brownish-gray and began to flake.

"Very good!" Mylon shouted. "Well done!"

Karis huffed from her seat in the open-aer auditorium near the base of the Old Wise One's tower. The puppet play was somewhere in its fifth act, and she had lost much of the plot somewhere in the third, though it appeared the meticulously crafted execution scene was blessedly meant to represent some sort of climax.

On stage, the Old Wise One appeared from behind a yellow curtain and bowed. Mylon and Cindlan clapped enthusiastically, the others less so. The amphitheater was too large for the audience, twelve rows of semi-circular seating, set off from the main tower on a nearby bluff, and connected to it by a pair of thin walkways that swayed in the rising and falling wind. The gusts made the Old Wise One hard to hear, even after he held up his hands for silence and raised his shrill voice to a shout.

"Thank you, ladies and gentleman, thank you. And now, to conclude this evening's performance, we have one final musical interlude. Enjoy!"

He bowed again and stepped back, hiding behind a set of automated horns rising from a trap door. Their fanfare drowned out the other instruments, an assortment of strings and drums hobbling around downstage on awkward mekkanikal legs.

A few moments later the Old Wise One appeared from a side entrance and entered the stands. To Karis's surprise he chose not to sit next to her, but instead approached Mylon and Cindlan, who seemed eager to discuss the show. Karis could only guess at their words, thanks to the dueling cacophony of the wind, which howled against the baffles surrounding them, and the instruments, which were hideously out of tune. She would have covered her ears and hidden her head had the Old Wise One not been so close, or would even have convoked a set of earplugs if she dared.

"You would think after thousands of years he would have figured out how to make them sound a little better."

She hadn't noticed Roi sitting down just above her.

"Maybe that's the point," she said. "After so long, maybe one gets bored of music that sounds the way it's supposed to."

"We'll have to see." Roi grunted. "If you take any longer to find the Source, we'll all end up as old as him."

She frowned and looked away. "Does that mean you're willing to wait?"

"Not at all. In fact, I believe the time may have come for those alternate measures I spoke of."

"And what exactly are those? You really think confronting the Old Wise One with force would turn out well for us?"

"Perhaps not. But we have the ship. The agitist cannons. We could blast this whole place to dust if we wanted to, and sift through the ruins for the Source. It would be a shame, but your incompetence may force my hand."

She snarled, "You speak to me of incompetence? You told me you were going to be the Fourth Emperor. Just look at you, out here in the middle of the Aperandis, trapped listening to the worst puppet symphony of all time."

The horn section blew an ear-splitting *blatt* to punctuate her words.

Anger pulled his face tight. "The automatists seemed to think controlling the Source would be world-changing."

She scoffed. "You know, you're supposed to be such a great leader, the one who sees the strings, who controls it all. But ever since I've known you, all you have done is lose more and more of your crew, become more and more isolated, sink lower and lower. And now here I am, your best chance, the one you have your hopes pinned on—and you still don't trust me. You know I want the Source as well, so why don't you stop interfering and let me work?"

Roi pursed his lips, searching for an answer as the pace of the "music" increased.

"Sweetness! Come sit with me." Jaela called from several benches away. "What are you doing over there with her?"

He waved at her, a smile on his face, then turned back to Karis with the same severe expression as before. "We'll continue this conversation soon," he said, and left.

Karis sat back and exhaled. She didn't know quite where that had come from, but it felt good. Perhaps she didn't need the Old Wise One's help after all to push Roi around. And she certainly didn't want the tower destroyed yet, not after feeling the sensation the Old Wise One had made on her hand, and his promise to let her see more.

Phaestal interrupted her thoughts by shuffling into the seat next to her. "I heard what you two were talking about," he mumbled, still facing the stage. "You should keep your voices down. He might be listening."

Karis looked quickly at the Old Wise One, but the little man had risen from his seat and was waving his arms in time with the crescendo of his performance.

"Do you think you can get it?" Phaestal said. "The Source?"

"I said I'll get it, and I will."

"And then you'll return with it to the Automatia?"

He glanced at her and she nodded.

"You know," Phaestal said, "the first memories I have are of being aboard a raider ship. I appeared near the shore not long after a battle, the others told me. I wandered into the raiders at port, and they took me in, gave me food and shelter, taught me how to repair engines. You don't understand how it is. They're much more than just a band of fighters to me. They're a commune. They're my life."

"Why are you telling me this?"

He took a deep breath. "The crew has made a decision, and I thought you should know about it. We're abandoning this place. Leaving without the Source, without Roi if necessary."

"What? No."

"It's what's best for us. I love Roi, he's my captain, but his obsession's gone too far. Remember Paolem…"

"Of course I remember. But does Roi know about this?"

Phaestal shrugged guiltily. "I think he suspects."

That would explain much of Roi's recent behavior. Karis was still struggling to put it all together when Phaestal spoke again.

"This is hard for me, Karis. I know I'm betraying Roi, betraying everything I've lived for. But I can't do this anymore. I want to stay at the Automatia. I'll take you back there with me, and the rest of the crew will go on their way."

"Listen, Phaestal. You can't leave yet. I'm closer than you know to getting the Source."

"We don't *care* about the Source."

"Please! It's important." She tapped her knee, searching for a persuasive argument. "Think of your duty. You're a raider, you can't just leave a mission unfinished. You're really going to leave Roi here, stranded in these mountains with no escape?"

He lifted his face, his eyes narrowed. "All right. I'll think about it. For a little while."

With a final sweeping flourish of the Old Wise One's hands, the play ended. The wind had died down, and the auditorium was deathly silent. The Old Wise One turned and bowed again, and the raiders responded with a smattering of applause.

"Is that it?" Isky asked. "We can go?"

The others answered his question by getting up and filing out.

"We'll have a full discussion of the performance this evening of course, after we have eaten and rested!" The Old Wise One called to their backs. "I wish to hear in-depth critical feedback from each of you."

Karis, who had been seated near the left side of the stage, reached the narrow causeway suspended between the auditorium and the tower first.

"Karis!" The Old Wise One called. "Might I see you over here for a moment? Alone."

Karis looked over her shoulder, still gripping the handrail. There was something strange about the Old Wise One's expression—wide-eyed and slowly nodding. The little beast was up to something. Roi, directly behind her in line, noticed it too, looking back and forth between them confusedly.

The Old Wise One smiled wide and gestured for her to come. Fingernails pressed to her palms, she strode toward him. Roi studied her suspiciously, and his hand snaked out and caught her as she passed by him on the right. He held here there for a moment, staring eye to eye, saying nothing.

"What's wrong?" She pulled away. "He wants to see me."

Roi's eyes flicked to the Old Wise One, then back to her. He slowly nodded. She walked away, ignoring the others, keeping Roi in the corner of her eye as he began to cross the bridge. Behind him, the other raiders filed after, one by one. The Old Wise One stared at them in silence. Dead silence, everywhere.

The wind was gone.

He wanted Roi to cross the bridge without her. But what would he do? He couldn't be planning to simply crumble the bridge; the drop straight down to the top of the bluff below wasn't that far, it wouldn't cause more than minor injuries.

I will make your problem disappear, Karis. Like dust on the breeze.

He was controlling the wind somehow. The gusts suddenly dying off were his doing, as would be their sudden return. Could that really be his plan? She had heard legends of such convocations before, but did the Old Wise One possess enough power to blow the raiders clear off the bluff, down hundreds of feet to the valley below?

Of course he did. He wanted to be rid of all of them. They knew he was the Plague Bringer. He would never feel safe if he allowed them to leave.

But then, that meant he would never allow her to leave, either.

"Stop!" she yelled. "Don't cross."

Everyone was staring at her now, the raiders confused, Roi baleful, the Old Wise One flustered.

Before she could speak again, the Old Wise One's expression turned to a frown. He looked up to the top of the tower.

"Something's wrong," he said. "No. No!"

"What?" Roi called, stepping toward them. "What is it?"

The Old Wise One tugged at his hair, his eyes wide with fury. "How could I have been so stupid? This was all a trick. You did this!"

"Did *what?*" Roi yelled.

"It's gone!" The Old Wise One screamed, his high-pitched wail echoing off the baffles. "Someone's taken it!"

36

The drakenbird coasted on outstretched wings over the tower resting on its pedestal. The sky had only begun to turn gray, but the structure below seemed to hold a foretelling of night within its purple and black hues. Ariden turned away from the porthole to check Meli's face. Her expression told him they had found what she sought.

"I don't remember exactly what the building in my vision looked like," she said. "But something about that place calls to me."

"And you have no idea what could be inside?"

She shook her head, then stared at the tower again. Whatever was calling her, Meli clearly did not think well of it. "There is something else down at the base. A structure away from the main tower. It's open to the aer, but the walls are too high to see inside. Perhaps we should land there."

Perhaps. But perhaps not. "Elsa, is it possible to land on top of the tower?"

Elsa hooted a translation to the pink flesh of the drakenbird. An answer came, muffled to a rumble.

"Yes, can land. Top good roosting."

"On top?" Meli said. "I don't know the protocol, but it seems like it might send the wrong message."

Ariden paced and considered, then spoke. "The top would be best. Perhaps coming down on the roof would be impolite, but propriety may be the least of our host's concerns. All things considered it would be better to have the drop on him."

"Raendal," Meli said. "The Inaali said he was just an old hermit."

"If I believed that, I'd probably accept an invitation from Caeridor for a banquet in our honor." Ariden studied the ground a few more moments, then signaled to Meli.

"Elsa," she said. "It's time."

They held on to the walls as the drakenbird swooped around, judging the high winds before landing. A great flapping slowed their descent, then the gentle bump of claws on the tower roof heralded their arrival.

"Find the Source," Meli repeated from her vision. "Let's hope we can be quick about it."

A portal opened in the drakenbird's side. Ariden stepped out, clutching his coat against the cold, and knelt on the circular roof. The interlocking plates sloped gently downward toward the edge, and he convoked small footholds to keep the wind from blowing him off. "This material is unknown to me. Best not to take lightly the one who could convoke it. Could the tower itself be the Source?"

"No." Meli ran her fingers over the surface. "It's an interesting arrangement of the aether, but ultimately ordinary. There's no esoterica here."

She crawled to the leeward side and peered down. "I can see the other structure, now. It's some sort of the theater, with people inside. So Raendal does not live alone, after all."

"If you can see them, they can see you."

"I don't think they've spotted us. Elsa, tell Fra to make sure she stays near the center of the roof. And keep her wings folded. I suppose we'll have to climb down the windward side to remain hidden."

"In this gale?" Ariden hugged his flapping coat close.

"I thought you were my brave fighter," she said with a hint of mockery.

"And I thought you were the brains of this venture." He winked, then knocked on the hard, yet springy, surface below his feet. "There may be a better way inside. This feels hollow. Look how the plates slide together."

He convoked a strong hook and slid it between two of the plates, then hauled it toward him, grunting and straining. The drakenbird hooted with unease behind him.

"It will move," he puffed, and convoked two new footholds to lean back on and pull with his legs straightened. His knees shook and his shoulders ached, but the panel slid at last, creating an opening the shape of a quartered circle.

He tossed his tool away and peered with Meli into the opening. A cavernous room lay below, taking up almost the entirety of the tower's upper story.

"A stair, if you would," Ariden said.

Meli nodded, and in a few moments a web of piping spiraled downward, terraced with triangular steps. Ariden went first, Scythe in hand. By the time he reached the floor, his eyes had adjusted to the relative dimness. The walls about them were ornate, covered with columns and buttresses, and composed of the same black and purple sheets as the roof. On the floor, a pedestal sat on a dais, lit from above. Ariden kept it in focus as he descended. Something about it stirred his mind, but he could not name exactly what.

They stepped lightly across the floor, concealing their footsteps. Meli cast her gaze about the interlocked walls. In the distance, a faint wailing could be heard over the wind, like the horns blown by the Outsiders during their riot.

"There's no other way in," Ariden said. "A strange way to fashion a room."

"These panels must be able to slide at Raendal's command," Meli said. "If so, he could create as many doors as he wished."

"How nice for him." Ariden tucked the Scythe away and headed for the pedestal. "Why does this seem out of place?"

He leaned over and studied it closely. Across the top were strange markings, symbols he could not understand, but aside from that it appeared to be an ordinary hunk of aether-stone.

"There is something about it..." Meli took a moment to examine the pedestal as well, then stood back and shook her head. "I don't know. We'll explore elsewhere, first. Perhaps we can revisit it on our way back."

Frowning, Ariden went to pull one of the wall panels aside. It slid apart more easily than the roof, though it still took a measure of effort. Beyond it lay a dark, seemingly empty corridor. He replaced the wall and slowly worked his way around the perimeter of the tower, searching carefully. But for what?

"So empty," Ariden said. "Not even a chair to rest in."

"Not even a grain of dust." Meli ran her hand over the smooth wall. "Perhaps this upper chamber is unused. We should head downward."

Ariden chose a suitable spot on the floor and sank a hook in again. Below, yawning darkness welcomed them.

"I fear we'll find nothing down there, either. This place is a bare monument. If we wish to find the secret of Raendal's tower, we may have to confront Raendal himself."

Meli nodded. "We'll go back up top, then make plans to approach the people outside." Her eyes drifted from the hole he had made, back in the direction of her staircase. She started. "The floor. Ariden, look at the floor."

He followed her gaze back to the base of the pedestal, but noticed nothing amiss. "What are you—"

He saw it, then. Two spots of light on the floor. Two light sources shining down, one from the opening he had made in the tiles letting in the pale evening glow, and another, embedded in the ceiling itself, shining directly onto the pedestal, yellow and bright. Directly above it, the roof they had stood on had been solid. Opaque.

"How...?" she said. "Is there a mirror hidden up there?"

"We'd best find out."

They climbed the stair again until they reached the top of the room, then Meli convoked a platform to bring them above the pedestal, supported on the floor by high stilts. Light poured forth from the ceiling there, so bright that Ariden had to force himself to look away as he approached. It was...different, somehow. No contraption of lens or mirror could produce that glare.

The Source. It had to be.

Meli reached her hand into its glow, as if the yellow light were a liquid she could drink. She pulled her hand away quickly. "It feels strange." Her voice was full of wonder. She pressed her palm into Ariden's cheek. The feeling sent a shiver through him, though it was not at all cold. It was as if cold had an opposite, as if her touch could dispel the chills of wind or wave.

"This is dangerous," Ariden said. "The only time I have seen anything like this was during our encounter with Vipretheon. Do you remember what that bolt of light did to the ship?"

"You mean this is a weapon?"

"Whatever it is, it should not just be sitting here for the taking. This is too easy."

Meli frowned and passed her fingers through the light again, then rubbed her hands together. "Can we pull it out?"

"If we take it away from Raendal, it will crumble."

"Not necessarily. Targael thought the Source might be old enough to have hardened. I'd rather study it on the roof; it feels safer there, closer to Fra if we need to leave."

Ariden examined the light. The object it emanated from was not composed of the black tiles, but was embedded in a separate spherical casing. Seeing no obvious way to slide it free, he pulled out the Scythe. "Stand back."

Despite the tiles' strange material, they yielded easily enough to cuts from the sword. Ariden reached in and yanked the sphere free from behind, cursing as the heavy case slammed down on the catwalk. Echoes reverberated through the room. The sphere was composed of some dense material, cool to the touch. Ariden convoked a simple handle attached to the side opposite its lit opening.

"It might be easier to roll it," Meli said. "You get behind and I'll guide—"

A vibration rattled up Ariden's boots and into his body. "Meli. The tower—"

His words were lost as the vibrations widened into shaking, followed by a roar from below. The catwalk listed, and Ariden caught Meli by the wrist to keep her upright.

"I knew it was too easy," he said.

The supports of the catwalk came unmoored, and they tumbled down. A dizzying roll, then pain erupted through Ariden's neck and spine as he hit the floor. The Source landed beside him with a crack, then bounced away, flashing light about as it spun.

"Meli?!"

"I'm all right." She dragged herself up.

The room shifted, the panels rotating over one another, forming slopes and protrusions. Sharp protrusions.

The building was trying to kill them.

Ariden sprang up, cutting off the ends of the panels before they could organize around him. The Scythe's fresh blade sliced easily, but there was too much happening around him; he could no longer trust the walls to shield him, or the floor to hold him up. Meli was having much the same problem, stumbling over shifting tiles as she made her way to where the Source lay. Ariden cut down a section of the floor that was rearing to attack her, and yelled to get her attention.

"Over here! Into the hole!" He pointed with the Scythe toward the piece of floor he had opened earlier. At least, he assumed it was the same area; they might as well have been standing in a completely new room by then.

"We have to get to the roof," she yelled.

"We'll never climb in this."

A razor-thin section of the ceiling flew through the air, aimed at his neck. Ariden held up the Scythe in its path, cutting it neatly in two. Meli was a few steps away by then, kicking the Source ahead of her. Ariden crumbled his blade, glanced nervously at the black pit below the opening, and hopped down feet first.

Thankfully, the passage was sloped at an angle and curved, as if it wound around the perimeter of the tower, and he slid down easily on his rear end. He heard Meli coming down above him, and the tunnel flickered with yellow light from the Source, the flashes coming at regular intervals as the sphere rolled. Light—he was actually seeing light inside a closed tunnel. His amazement at the sheer novelty was cut short when the walls began to fall apart around him.

It began as a rumble, deeper and more pronounced than the one that had presaged the tiles coming alive. A great crack sounded that nearly bounced him up to the low ceiling; then, framed in a flash of light, he saw a great chasm ahead where the floor of the tunnel should have been.

Ariden pressed his hands and feet to the sides of the tunnel, coming to a halt just before the abyss. The Source bounced over his leg; he reached out just in time to grab the handle. It swung down over the hole, and if it had been just a bit heavier it would have pulled him over with it. Light washed over the empty space below, but the bottom lay beyond its reach.

Meli coasted into him a moment later, almost sending him over again. With her help Ariden came upright and set down the Source. The building was still shaking, the rumble growing louder. A piece of the ceiling came down and struck him on the head.

"Cut through!" Meli yelled.

He already had the Scythe in hand. A burst of cold, and the wall on the outside of the building exploded. Fresh aer and evening light rushed in. Ariden stepped through, hanging by one hand and leaning outward to get a better view. Dust and debris blew below them. The building looked as if it might tip at any moment.

Above, an orange shadow moved against the gray sky. The drakenbird had already taken flight. Meli turned the Source over, pointing the light in the beast's direction. A moment later, it folded its great wings to arc down toward them.

"We're only getting one chance at this." Ariden clasped her hand. The drakenbird seemed to move slowly against the great backdrop of the valley. Ariden knelt and tensed, feeling Meli do the same. The drakenbird swooped, wings spreading, claws extended, the opening on its belly as wide as she could make it.

They jumped.

37

W ho stole it?" Roi rushed off the bridge toward them. Any pretense that they didn't know what "it" referred to was gone.

"You know!" The Old Wise One pointed, his face bright red. "They are working with you! That is why you came, to take what is mine!"

The amphitheater came alive, seats clacking, panels folding outward to jut from walls. Karis stumbled and dropped to one knee.

"Isky! Dikta! Go up and stop them," Roi commanded. "Phaestal, get the ship!"

"No. You will not escape." The Old Wise One's nostrils flared, and the bridge behind them folded and broke in two. The floor under Roi's feet shifted, opening a hole beneath him. He leaped and rolled to avoid being swallowed.

The raiders scattered, seeking safe hiding places, but there was nowhere to run. Jaela crouched with Cindlan among the clacking seats. A blade appeared in Isky's hand, but he was forced to scramble by a moving wave of what had been the floor. In the center of it all, the Old Wise One stood, silky hair blowing in the breeze, arms raised and shaking as he pitted the building against them.

"Wait," Karis said. "It's not us! We didn't do it."

She tugged on his robe and he flung his arm at her, elbow connecting to her mouth with surprising force. She sprawled away and he turned, teeth bared, then saw her and gasped.

"My beauty! I'm sorry! Please forgive me!"

He offered her his hand. She shuffled away. Out of sight, someone screamed.

"Stop," she said. "Don't kill them."

"Please, darling. Come." He stepped closer. Beyond him, she saw Dikta sprawl unconscious across the stage, smashed from behind by a horn on legs. "You can be mine forever. We will live together in happiness, once I rid us of these thieves."

"Get away from me!"

More yells, driving wind, smacking and clatter. The Old Wise One smiled, his eyes open wide, and deep in their pits an otherworldly glow formed.

A short sword protruded from his abdomen. He looked down, mouth open, and another blade emerged between his lips. He froze into a statue, then exploded into a plume of dust, propelled by the bottom of Isky's boot.

The clacking stopped. Isky dropped his swords, shook his leg clean and went to comfort the still-stunned Dikta. Dust settled in the still aer, and the only noise remaining was from raiders groaning.

"Thank you." Roi raised himself from inside a pile of floor tiles. "Now, let's—"

A rumbling began, coming from all around them but especially in the direction of the tower. To Karis's right a panel fell from the wall, followed by several more. The raiders knelt, hanging on to whatever was nearby as the amphitheater shook.

Roi looked about in panic at tower. A large chunk was already falling from it. "The ship, Phaestal. Can you bring it?"

"I don't know." Phaestal grimaced with eyes closed. "It's far. I can't find a path."

Karis sprang to her feet and ran up beside him. The ship had been designed to be flown by thought as well as touch, but doing so was by no means easy, even in the best of circumstances. She closed her eyes and felt through the aether. Surrounding the tower was only chaos, dust blowing. The dock where the ship lay at anchor seemed a million miles away.

"Look!" Someone shouted. She opened her eyes in time to catch a glimpse of a winged creature flying near the tower. Two figures leapt from a hole in its side, landing within the creature's belly before it soared off again. The thieves? No time to think of them—if she didn't fetch the raiders' own ship the falling debris would crush her. Karis gritted her teeth, searching, thoughts swimming through eddies in the aer, ignoring the sounds of destruction and the panicked yells. A vein throbbed in her temple, her head ached, but she pushed through, commanding the aether, forcing her will further. She found the ship.

She grabbed Phaestal by the arm, too focused to speak, hoping he would understand what she had done. She needed him to let the dock and mooring crumble as she gave the command to rev up the engines. That was the easy part, but starting the engines alone would only make the ship fly off and crash. She needed to steer it somehow, bring it closer to them.

"Phaestal." The word was a knife-blade through her concentration. "How do I...control..."

"The stick," he said. "There's an autopilot attached to it. You have to give it commands...do you remember your lessons?"

I paid more attention than you. She searched the ship for something that would listen to her. Automatist structures felt different, not like solid, unyielding material, but poised on an edge, ready to flip one way or another with a slight nudge. But she might as well have been locating a dust speck in the storm. She leaned forward, pressing outward, extending her presence over the entire ship until her mind stretched beyond its limits, then she felt the tiny switch and told it her wish.

Come.

She fell back, her body useless, and her head slammed on the floor. The world spun as she sat up. Two copies of each raider scrambled about, convoking furiously to try and stop the amphitheater from collapsing. She heard a yell as the top half of the tower tipped, broke off with a tremendous crack and fell.

It dropped in slow motion, panels falling off, arcing ever-so-gracefully to the pedestal of bedrock.

The dust cloud knocked her back to the floor again, striking like a battering ram. She coughed and sputtered, a million pin-pricks erupting all over her skin.

"Come on." Phaestal grabbed her by the arm. She couldn't move herself, so he lifted her. Tears blocked her vision. She rubbed more dust into her eye with the back of her hand, then rubbed it out with her palm and saw the ship. The others were already running inside. Phaestal pulled and she followed.

"Follow that bird," Roi said as the raiders slid into their ready positions. "They've taken the Source for us. Our work is almost done." He jumped into the co-pilot's seat and slammed the lifter.

"Let's make sure they're well rewarded."

38

How quickly events changed. One moment Ariden was watching the tower crumble beneath them, and in the next it was gone, out of sight over the mountainous horizon. Behind him, Meli sat hunched, knees to chin, still recovering from their daring leap into the bird's open belly, staring at the light as if hypnotized.

Her guess had been correct—the Source must have been far older than the tower itself for the artifact to have remained in existence. But what event had caused the tower to fall? And how did the Source work? A strange form of dust emanated from small holes in the back of the casing, finer than usual, tickling the fingers if touched but otherwise inert. Beyond that, Meli had decided not to investigate how the light operated. "I'd rather take it to the Lost Jungle intact," she had said. "I want nothing more to do with the thing."

They had left the sphere on the floor until the drakenbird had complained of what Elsa called the *"fizzy feeling in belly,"* and so now it hung from the ceiling, swinging slightly with each beat of the creature's wings, flooding the interior with brightness even as night reached its blackest depths outside.

"Elsa," Meli said, breaking the silence. "Please thank Fra for her help. Especially for flying us to the Lost Jungle. We are in her debt in a way that can never be repaid."

Elsa looked up and squawked a conversation. *"She saying knowing of Lost Jungle before, large valley in Great Peaks. Strange doings there, sooner years coming and growing. She worrying about Ariden and Meli Meli Meli."*

"She's worried about us?"

"Frarifrafra saying people too small and little little like bugs. Snuggle in tight and keeps little people safety."

Ariden returned to watching the dark mountains pass by below. Something caught his eye on the horizon, a gray shimmer flaring and fading within the span of a moment. Ariden pulled back, touching his fingers to the window of skin, watching the light play off it. Had the shimmer been a trick of the eye? With a cargo like theirs, no potential threat could be ignored.

"Meli," Ariden said. "Can you cover the Source?"

"Why?" she asked, catching the sharpness of his tone.

"We do not know what's lurking out there. Elsa, can we fly any faster?"

A series of hoots followed, each less hopeful than the last. *"Southward flight and crossing wind, wings spread full. No fast says she."*

Meli set to work convoking a cover for the light, which to their consternation proved a difficult task. The otherworldly glow shone through all but the heaviest materials, and even when obscured would soon melt through its container unless it was constantly tended to. Meli sat back after a long period of work, head down, and Ariden knelt to rub her sagging shoulders. She tilted her neck, and cheek to hand, they weathered the night's darkness and uncertainty together.

Sometime later, he heard her whisper, perhaps in sleep.

"The Daemon's secret…"

Dawn broke and Ariden lolled his head, blinking at the gray daylight filtered through pink drakenbird flesh. The Source was shining through again, with Meli asleep beneath it. Leaving her to rest, Ariden staggered to the porthole. He rubbed his eyes and looked out, stumbled back, then looked again to make sure he was right.

"Wake up!" he yelled. "There's a ship!"

There it hung, at first no more than a black pinprick on the horizon—but in the time it took Meli and Elsa to rise, it had grown a pair of sleek, fixed wings.

"Elsa, tell Fra to land now," Ariden said. "If they want to fight, we'll take them on solid ground."

"Not is landing in deep mountains, too danger."

"Danger? A fight in mid-aer isn't dangerous?"

"Fight not fight not, Lost Jungle close. Can speed, home return for with dropping off."

"What in the gods' names are you talking about?!"

"Fra is afraid." Meli's eyes were glued to the porthole. "But she thinks she can make it to the Lost Jungle and be off before the ship reaches us."

"Then tell her she had better find some way to speed up."

The drakenbird complied, folding its wings and diving to gain momentum. The Source came loose from the ceiling, bounced and rolled. Ariden and Meli held onto each other. Dust particles blurred past the window as Frarifrafra leveled off and accelerated straight ahead, slicing through the aer like a crossbow bolt.

The ship had stayed even with them. As they watched, it grew like a flower unfolding as it came up from behind.

"It can't be," Meli said. "The speed."

"They know we've seen them. Elsa, tell her to drop further into the mountai—"

The shot came with a *thrum* and knocked him off his feet, stealing the breath from his lungs. What was that weapon? The drakenbird screamed and banked downward. A glance at the window revealed a wall of bedrock coming up to meet them. Ariden closed his eyes, feeling a pulling in his gut. Fra was executing a mid-aer roll. He stayed low, waiting for the force holding him to the wall to abate.

"*Wing almost cut!*" Elsa screamed. "*Weapon comes, sound at wing kapow.*"

"It was a warning shot," Ariden said. "Tell her to open the door. Let me out."

"Let you out?" Meli shouted.

He pulled the Scythe. "I'll be more use out there."

"No!"

Their argument was broken when Fra swooped again, executing a hard turn between towering peaks. The approaching ship's engines roared and quieted as it banked through behind them. Another *thrum*, and the rock wall in front of them exploded, sending fragments sailing toward the porthole. Ariden ducked, only to find himself rolling onto his hindquarters as the drakenbird twisted away.

No good—they would lose too much altitude this way, with no way to maneuver through the narrow gaps between the peaks. The drakenbird changed course, flying low in the space between a ridge, the tops of the trees scraping its belly so that Ariden felt them in his feet. He heard more shots from the ship, but felt no accompanying shock. What were they aiming at?

A sudden jolt answered his question. A chunk of bedrock fell into the drakenbird's path and it flexed its body, knocking Ariden and Meli across the cavity. More *thrums* came and more boulders fell. The drakenbird shimmied violently. Ariden made a grab for Meli, but couldn't stop himself or her from slamming into the interior walls.

Fra roared, and with a whip-crack of her wings took off high into the aer again. It was a bold, dangerous move, one that left her back exposed to the approaching ship, but it caught their attackers by surprise. The enemy sailed past, unable to stop or maneuver in the narrow canyon, and the drakenbird slipped up and over the ridge toward another set of peaks.

Ariden jumped to the porthole again. "There!" he shouted, pointing to a nearby fold in the rock face. "Hide there before they see us."

Elsa relayed the command, and the drakenbird alighted on the wall with several great flaps, then made a few bone-jarring hops until it was enveloped in the vertical outcropping.

Inside, the dust settled. Meli held onto the drakenbird's flesh, holding her breath, every muscle tensed. Ariden closed his eyes, listening. The engines of the gleaming ship roared over the ridge, whirring toward them. Closer. Closer. Stopped. The ship was hovering, waiting. Fra growled softly.

"Meli," Ariden whispered. "The light."

The Source sat below them, at the base of the drakenbird's tail, its light spilling up and illuminating the interior. Within moments, Meli had covered it again, leaving them in the morning shadows of the mountain.

"Let me out." Ariden tapped on the wall. "Now."

"Don't…"

He quieted her with a stare. "We're not waiting for them to leave; we're readying an ambush. If I catch them unaware, I will end this in an instant." A portal opened behind him, and a sudden chill entered the cavity. Ariden pulled Meli close, burying his fingers in her hair. "I will return."

A kiss, over too soon, and then he turned and jumped out. A hand on the drakenbird's scruffy feathers allowed him to swing up and over. He crouched on the great creature's back, Scythe at the ready.

He waited, staring at the space between the cloven rock, aware of every mote of dust rushing by in the wind. The hairs on the back of his neck stood up, and his limbs shook from the cold. He counted heartbeats. One, two, three, four. The rumble came.

Thrum.

A distant crackle of falling rock followed. Then another, closer, with an aftershock Ariden felt in the roots of his teeth. The ship knew where they were. Whatever their weapon was, it had enough power to destroy the entire ridge. Fra twisted her long neck and made eye contact with him. Somewhere in those flat pupils surrounded by yellow irises, he saw that she understood as well.

"Go," he whispered. "Do what you must, and I will do what I can."

The gun *thrummed* again and Fra detached, falling head first into the valley below. A brief glimpse of a distant rock wall crumbling, then Ariden's head swam as Fra broke off her dive. They coasted up and over the next peak and the ship's engines whirred again. Wind buffeted, slamming Ariden's face and chest. Then they crested the ridge and he saw it.

The Lost Jungle. It wore its name well. A sprawl of twisting plants, dark green and black, their tendrils extending up the walls of a circular bowl the size of the largest cities. He twisted to view their pursuers in the same moment their weapon fired. Fra fell away, and then he was flying alone.

He reached down through the aer, stretching his body to make contact with the drakenbird. Her screams were piercing even over the wind. Her tail and one leg were gone, a mess of gore and bone and dust-caked feathers. Ariden caught hold, squeezed his fingers tight and felt his shoulder pop as she fell from the sky. His blood rushed and somewhere in his vision fading to black he saw a hole open in Fra's body and Meli's arm come through.

"Come on!" She pulled his wrist and he dragged himself forward with his other arm. Fra's wings were outstretched but the jungle was coming up fast.

"Meli, get down and hold on."

"Shut up and get in here!"

"I love—"

The tips of the plants went through him like sword points, and then the impact sent him into oblivion.

39

Karis scanned the periphery of the tangled mass of plants, but saw no trace of where the drakenbird had crashed. The great creature would be dead now, of course, its dust scattered by the impact, but she had expected some sort of disturbance where its body had cut through the jungle. Instead, the plants seemed to have swallowed it up, their thick, thorn-covered tendrils writhing inward to fill the damage. Examined closely through the dusty haze, a few among them were moving still.

"It's gone," she said, her voice tinged in sadness. She had never seen a drakenbird before, and from the brief glimpses she had caught as they gave chase it had seemed as magnificent a creature as the legends held.

Roi paced the cabin, hands behind his back, neck veins pulsing. "The Source is in there somewhere. That doddering old fogey built it to last. Phaestal, bring us down on the far side of the crater."

"There's nowhere to land," Phaestal said. "I've never seen plants like this. What is this place?"

"The Lost Jungle," Karis said. "I heard Tem speak of it."

Isky spoke up for the crew gathered in the back of the ship. "What's going on, Roi? What are those automatists up to?"

"I don't think they knew, either," Karis said. "Tem said the Daemon controls this place. I never heard of such a thing before. Perhaps it's a new name for an old god."

"You want us to take on a god?"

"I want that convocation," Roi said. "Whatever the god does is his own concern."

They flew in a slow circle, coming in low to view the mass of brambles up close. Different sorts predominated in different areas of the bowl, but no place was free from at least seven or eight of the greenish-black species intertwined together. Different plants, not at war, but acting as if controlled by one mind. What was their purpose?

"There." Roi pointed to a patch of lighter green, a gathering of one of the few plants with flimsy leaves for covering rather than unyielding thorns. "Drop us through."

"Weapons this time?" Dikta asked.

"Many," Roi said. "And that means everyone. Whoever was in that drakenbird may still be alive. If you see the Source, make sure no one keeps it from you."

As the others convoked their short swords and axes, Karis ignored the instruction to arm herself, watching the leaves and branches brushing the far side of the porthole. Roi shot her a brief glare, but did not raise the subject again. For the past day they had all been so caught up in the chase that there had been no time to raise old arguments. Now, she found herself wondering again what he was thinking about her.

The ship dropped further and further, until it was clear that the true depth of the plant life inside of the bowl was much greater than they had supposed. By the time they stepped out of the ship hovering above the jungle floor, only thin strands of light filtered down to dapple on the leaves and vines. Karis sniffed at the musty aer and felt a pressure in her temples, as if the thickness of it refused to be confined to her nose and throat.

"They were flying roughly on this line when they went down," Roi said, heading south toward the center of the jungle. The others followed, and Karis fell in behind them. In the distance they heard swishes and cracks. A skitter came from somewhere close, and Karis stopped short to listen. But the raiders moved ahead of her, and she was forced to hurry to avoid being left alone.

They traveled on through ever-thicker tangles of stalks. Phaestal walked directly ahead of her, bumping his tall head on the foliage. In front of him was Jaela, muscles working in her skin-tight raider suit, then Cindlan, wheezing as he pushed his frail body forward. Mylon stayed close to Roi, who was flanked by the twins, as always. In front of them, a row of vines blocked an easy path, and Isky raised his sword to cut them. Roi stayed him with a wave.

"Just duck."

Karis hunched past with the others and closed her eyes. The strain in her head was growing. At first it had been a slight tug, then an increasingly maddening itch in the space between her eyeballs. As they moved further and further toward the center of the jungle, the pressure became so intense that she had trouble walking in a straight line. The others felt it too, Cindlan rubbing his gray brow, Jaela blinking away a sudden burst of pain. Karis heard noises again, this time a deep, rhythmic pounding, lulling her, enticing, pulling her forward…

WHY.

The voice was everywhere and nowhere, out in the trees and pouring through her body. It did not speak words, only ideas. A concept embedded in her mind, formed into a question.

WHY HAVE YOU COME.

I seek the Source. It hurt to think the words. The raiders ahead of her had stopped walking. Phaestal rubbed the back of his head, while Roi stared into the darkness and blinked.

YOU COME WITH THEM, BUT YOU ARE NOT ONE OF THEM.

That's right. I'm not one of them.

BUT YOU COME LIKE THEM, TO TAKE THE SOURCE FROM ME.

No! The presence intruding in her mind was angry.

I SEE YOUR INTENTION. BUT YOU MAY PROVE USEFUL. COME. COME AND BE WITH ME.

Ahead, the jungle shifted, the plants rolling into a circular tunnel, ending in total darkness.

"Stop," Roi said, convoking a low wall to bar the way. "Don't follow the path."

"What is this?" Mylon said, his voice trembling. "I don't understand."

"I feel it too," Cindlan said.

"I heard something," Phaestal said. "A voice. It wants us to leave."

"No!" Roi bared his teeth. "Don't listen—"

"Dikta!" Isky whirled around, his sword at the ready. "Where did Dikta go? Dikta!"

The others muttered and cast their gazes about. In the back of Karis' mind, the drumbeat began anew, louder this time, more insistent.

"We need to find him." Isky's eyes filled with tears. "Dikta! Where the *pox* is he?"

"Calm down, damn you!" Roi grabbed his shoulders.

"Don't you—*gurlk!*"

Roi let go and backed away, staring wide-eyed at the vine around Isky's neck. Two more vines followed, encircling his legs and arms, growing thorns which left great bloody rents everywhere they squeezed.

And that was all Karis saw, because then she was running.

She heard the others scramble away, then screams, but could not tell who was who. The entire jungle had come alive, and each species of plant was its own deadly trap, strangling, slicing, laying down beds of spikes as small as a toe or as large as a torso. Karis vaulted through a thicket, wiped blood from her scratched cheeks, and caught a glimpse of a plant shaped like a giant maw with glistening red teeth, with Mylon's body mangled inside it. Too out of breath to scream, she closed her eyes and darted away, using her small stature to bob and weave through the interlocking maze.

From behind a trunk, a hand reached out and grabbed her.

"Karis!"

Phaestal. His face was marred with a brown stripe of crumbled blood.

"Run away from the center, Karis," he yelled. "That way. He's weaker there."

He pushed her and she stumbled. "Wait. Phaestal, don't—"

The tree he was standing beside came alive and grasped him with its branches. Phaestal screamed, then disappeared into the darkness.

"Phaestal!" She stumbled back, her vision a blur, and darted off toward the edge of the jungle.

She didn't know how long she had run before her legs settled into a stumble, and how long after that she had wandered in a daze. She only became aware of the fading day when she realized the branches above her were thinning, but no more light was passing through their cover. Then the jungle ended, and she stepped onto a field of crumbled rocks faced by a smooth black wall.

The edge of the crater. She hobbled further up the slope, slipping on the scree, until she came to an area too difficult to climb without convoking stairs. There she turned and sat, her head in her hands. She should have been more upset after what she had just seen, but something held her feelings back, as if her mind was afraid to let them in. It seemed unfair. Didn't Phaestal deserve her tears? And what was she going to do now? The ship would be gone, crumbled by dying raiders and smashed by the plants.

She opened her eyes and looked out over the darkening jungle. All was still again, save for clouds of dust overhead. To her left, behind a boulder, a pale yellow light shone.

A pale yellow light.

Karis staggered to her feet. It couldn't be. She approached warily, remembering what Roi had said about the crash survivors. Behind the hunk of rock a sphere lay on its side, half-buried in a shallow cone of fine dust. She wiped it off and turned it over.

It was beautiful. So achingly beautiful. Like being on the lake again.

She stared down at it, letting the light soak directly into her eyes, marveling at the blue afterimages it left. She ran her hand over it and felt the warmth the Old Wise One had shown her before, but stronger this time, so strong that if she held her skin to it for more than a moment it would burn through her flesh.

She needed to see more. She needed to get inside.

Her exhaustion forgotten, she convoked a small drill, even improvising an accelerant chamber so she wouldn't have to turn it by hand. She set the sphere below it and pressed down. The *squee* of the bit cutting into the hard material filled the area below the high bedrock wall. A few more holes, and the back of the sphere gave way. She reached her hand inside.

It burned, sizzling on her skin. She bit her lip and cursed the pain—intense, like she was being torn apart on the smallest of scales. Blisters formed on her palm, then burst and wrinkled as they healed. Karis took a deep breath and held it. If she was going to understand this power, she knew what had to be done.

She made a fist, stuffed it deep into the sphere, and let out a hoarse cry. The *pain*. She closed her eyes tight and gritted her teeth. She could feel the inner workings, sense what was happening, but the pain was so intense it blocked out all other thought.

She opened her eyes and fell back, breathing heavily. Her hand was a black, bubbled mess, but her mind was locked on what the sphere had told her.

The aether was not one substance as she had always thought, and not one mind. It was many particles, countlessly many small units bouncing into one another, speaking and passing along her commands. And one of those commands was to split apart. When each particle split, it gave off just a tiny bit of light, which in turn was picked up as a signal by the others...

Renewed stinging in her hand interrupted her thoughts. For a few moments it had gone numb, but now as the burns began to heal the pain roared back. Karis rolled over and curled up, holding her arm out in front of her, guttural moans escaping her clenched teeth as the agony came and went in waves.

After a seeming eternity of the pain intensifying and receding, she looked at her arm again. Ridges of scar tissue marred the flesh from her wrist to her knuckles. She sat up, trying to get a better view in the light. Footsteps on gravel sounded in front of her, and a figure stepped out from among the rocks.

Karis shot up immediately, clutching her arm above the elbow. The figure walked as if in a trance, long hair swaying back and forth, entering the Source's circle of light.

Karis's mouth fell open when the recognition struck.

40

Meli stumbled through the stones, wheezing, her head still pounding from the crash. How long had she been unconscious, and how long had she wandered? It didn't matter. Nothing mattered now. Fra was gone, reduced to a pile of orange-tinged dust. Elsa, her beautiful, sweet Elsa, smashed to pieces, had breathed her last. And Ariden, her love. It was too much, too horrible to contemplate. She had destroyed them all for a pointless hope. A hope for a child, yes, but now, with the Source gone, even that was lost.

How simple it had seemed when they had left the glade; go and retrieve the Source, find out for certain whether that path led to a dead end like so many others. She had almost wished then that they would not find the tower, or that it would not hold what they sought, so that they could turn their backs on the vision forever. Then the chase had happened, and there hadn't been time to say all the things she wanted to say. The light, Ariden, Elsa, all gone, and her world along with them.

She looked up. A glimmer shown just beyond a distant ring of boulders. Pale yellow. Could it be? She looked up at the sky, faded now from bright white to pale gray. Yes, nothing else could shine like that. She stumbled on, her mind still reeling, but bent now on a purpose.

Meli rounded the final boulder and came upon a small woman kneeling, dark features tinged yellow in the light. The woman looked up.

Meli gasped. "Karis?!"

Karis rose, her body trembling, her jaw shaking too much to form words. Then she rushed forward and threw her arms around Meli's waist.

"Meli!" Tears streamed down Karis's face staining Meli's coat. "Oh, Meli, Meli!"

Meli held her as if for dear life. "Karis...by Elaethim, what are you doing here?"

"I could ask the same of you." Karis pulled back and flashed that big, toothy smile. It was her, it was really her. She wiped her eyes as tears of joy flowed freely. "Meli, you're *here*. I thought I'd never see you again."

They embraced again, Karis's small head rubbing against Meli's chin, just like it had in days gone by. Meli was suddenly reminded of Ariden's strong arms, his body so tall. Her face twisted and tears fell again, punctuated by aching sobs.

Karis lifted her head. "What's wrong?"

"Ariden's gone," Meli croaked. She tried to explain more, but broke into a choked wail.

Karis backed away several steps. "Ariden? He was with you?"

The confusion on her face changed to searching, and then her eyes widened as she understood. She frowned. "You...you and him..."

"What? What is it?" Meli shook her head. Why was Karis acting this way—retreating from her in her time of need? At once a rift seemed to have opened between them, as if they were separated by the Saentis rather than a few feet of dust and crumbled rock.

And then, Meli knew.

"You," she said. "You were in that ship. *You* killed them."

Karis stiffened, and her face changed from anger to sorrow. "Meli. I'm sorry. I didn't know. Please, you have to—" She came forward, arms wide.

Meli shoved her back. "Get away from me!"

"Meli, no!"

Karis began to cry then. Meli turned away, fury rising in her throat. She couldn't look at Karis anymore, couldn't think about her. The light was still there. Her child was the important thing. She moved to pick up the Source.

"What are you doing?" Karis said.

"I have to take it inside the jungle."

Meli knelt and began to convoke a pair of new handles for the casing. After some moments, Karis spoke again.

"You can't do that."

"I can't?"

"Listen to me. There's something in there. It wants the Source. It's dangerous."

"I know."

"Meli, stop. It's a mistake. You're being used."

Meli ignored her, grabbing the Source on both sides and preparing to heft it. Karis stepped in and pulled her by the shoulder.

"Stop!"

"You stop!" Meli screamed. "I've sacrificed everything to come here, because of you!"

She pivoted and struck on instinct, connecting a right cross that reverberated up her arm and sent Karis sprawling down the slope. Her small body came to rest and lay still, eyes rolled up into her head.

Meli looked down at her own fist and cried out in horror.

"I'm sorry!"

She lifted the Source and headed away, scrabbling down the slope with her heavy load, focused on the edge of the jungle. Her child, that was all that mattered. Through her view clogged with tears, it almost seemed as if the plants were parting to make a path for her. She stepped inside and lost herself in the darkness.

41

Karis sat up and groaned. What in burst boils? She had been arguing with Meli, had moved in front of her, then there was a flash, and the next thing she knew she was lying on the ground, her head pounding.

She opened her eyes, and through the moving black splotches she caught a glimpse of Meli hurrying toward the tree line.

"No!"

She lurched to her feet, but the plants had already coalesced around Meli's form. A few hesitant steps to test her balance, and then Karis raced forward, heading toward the growth.

She reached the edge of the jungle and paused, remembering how easily the plants had torn apart the raiders. How had she escaped? Was it simply luck, or had the Daemon let her go? No time to think about that now; if Meli was inside, she had to find her.

Karis entered and ran through the undergrowth, watching for the species of vines she had seen strangling and slicing the others. The burned skin on her arm itched, and she balled her fist to stretch it. If only she had known that Meli was inside the drakenbird. But what difference did that make? She had no more right to kill a stranger than she did her closest friend. She hadn't been the one piloting the ship or shooting the weapon, but she should have done something, said something. Had her desire to get the Source blinded her so? Or was it something about Roi's presence that made her ignore her most heartfelt principles? Stupid, stupid. Now she was paying the price, and Meli was in danger because of her. Again.

She stopped to catch her breath and get her bearings. No good; she could be anywhere, now. The closer she drew to the center, the darker the jungle became, and the easier it was to lose her way.

The light—that would do it. She might not have the Source, but she had felt the convocation, she knew how it worked. She stopped and held out her ruined palm, focusing on the aer moving above it. *Break apart*, she told it, and it complied, sending a shower of yellow sparks into the breeze. The sight took Karis's breath away, but she tempered her excitement, focusing on the task at hand. She needed more than a trickle of light; she needed to be able to see, to find Meli and stop her.

She tried to convoke more this time, extending a faint yellow glow from her hand that cast shadows behind the leaves. But no matter how much light she made appear, the breeze kept blowing the particles away. The Old Wise One had found a way to bind the convocation to something solid and keep it self-sustaining, but Meli had taken the sphere before Karis could figure out how he had done it. She tried binding her convocation to the surface of the leaves and to a stone at her feet, but her attempts fizzled. The aether was blocking her somehow; she needed some sort of special material, one which would not only pass on her commands, but amplify them.

A snap came from the trees behind her. She spun, throwing a burst of light in that direction. Nothing. Just fluttering leaves and curving thorns. Still, better to keep moving. She headed again toward what she believed was the center of the crater, illuminating the space in front of her in fits and flashes, until she heard the snapping sound again.

That one was real. Something was following her. She quickened her pace gradually, to avoid letting on that she knew. The noise shifted to her right, moving with her, stamping over branches and shrubs. Karis broke into a full sprint. She jumped over a low-hanging vine and entered a clearing. No sound behind her; her lead was increasing.

A wire cut into her leg and she tumbled forward, head over heels.

She landed on her behind, dazed, a strip of pain running over her lower shin—a tripwire, convoked between the trees.

Roi stepped into the clearing. Karis's heart skipped a beat, then another when Dikta came up beside him.

"Ah, Karis," Roi said. "Funny meeting you here."

His voice had a strange tone. Menacing.

"Stay back."

"Did you hear that?" Roi said to Dikta. The tall man's eyes were puffy, the dusty remnants of tears staining his cheeks. He clutched his sword so tightly his arm shook. "You know, she wanted me to go away yesterday, too. To the bottom a cliff."

"What?"

"Please, don't deny it. We both know you conspired with that old man to get rid of me."

"I didn't. It was—"

"Oh, you did." He smiled wide. "Little, innocent Karis. Always with the bad luck—of all the people in Aetheria you could have chosen to try and kill, you had to pick me."

She turned to run. Dikta kicked the back of her knee, sending her sprawling with a shriek of pain.

"Karis, Karis. Has anyone ever told you, you have a tendency to play the victim?" At Roi's command, Dikta rolled her over by kicking her in the ribs. Fear coursed through her, pumping in every vein. "When they tell the story of the Fourth Empire, how do you think they'll judge you? All you've done since the day I met you is take my kindness and spit on it. You plotted against me on my own ship, at the Automatia and again at the tower."

He pointed, and Dikta pulled her to her feet by the front of her shirt, then lifted her off the ground. Up close, she saw the focused rage in Roi's eyes. "You know, I could have forgiven your earlier treachery. All's fair in the game, isn't it? But trying to have me murdered, that I just won't stand for."

Dikta held a dagger in his right hand, pressed to her neck. Pain, then drops of blood fell onto her shirt. The shirt Dikta was holding. She released the aether and the cloth turned to dust between his fingers. Karis dropped onto her feet and dashed away.

"Karis!" Roi's strides crashed through the trees behind her. "I'm going to cut out your heart, Karis! I'm going to tear out that lying throat and stuff it up—*ooph!*"

She stopped. Roi lay on the ground, rubbing his head, looking up at the wide chest he had just bounced off.

"Hello," Ariden said, resting his sword handle on his shoulder. "I believe you have a debt to pay me."

Roi snarled and shuffled away. With an ear-splitting scream, Dikta jumped out of the jungle, his blade aimed at Ariden's head. Ariden hopped away, barely avoiding being cut in two lengthwise. Dikta recovered his footing and stepped back, and the two men circled each other warily.

Gritting his teeth, Dikta readied another strike. Ariden raised his hilt, pointing the end directly at Dikta, then loosed the blade. Karis felt a familiar shock of cold as the line of steel shot outward, but Dikta dodged, and its tip *thunked* harmlessly against a tree trunk. Staying in motion, Dikta came in for a low swing. Ariden let his blade crumble, flashed out a new, smaller one, and parried Dikta's attack in one motion.

"I remember you," Ariden said. "Didn't you have a friend with you last time?"

Dikta went red, his whole body shaking, breath coming between his teeth in wheezing gasps. With an animal cry he leaped in, slashing and thrusting with all his strength. Ariden moved away, parrying instead of blocking, not meeting force with force.

Something was wrong. Ariden was falling behind. Karis hadn't noticed the deep gash on his scalp, the limp in his right leg. His movements were sluggish, pained; he hadn't recovered from the crash. With one final roar, Dikta cut a deep gash in Ariden's side, shredding his coat with the sound of blade scraping bone. Ariden dropped his sword and staggered back against a tree. Dikta stood before him, raised his own sword with both arms over his head, then brought it down.

Ariden moved his head to the side just enough for the blade to embed itself deep in the trunk. The two of them stared at one another for a long moment, and then Ariden stamped his foot. He had changed the shape of his fallen sword's blade, turning it into an upward curve, and when his foot came down the hilt popped up, spinning, into his hand.

Dikta dropped his sword and turned to run, just in time for his head to fly away from his shoulders.

Ariden watched the head fall, bounce, and break apart. He took a deep breath, saw Karis and nodded in recognition. Then a look of profound illness crossed his face, and he stumbled back into the tree, clutching his side.

Karis was about to approach when Roi stepped in. Ariden saw him too and made to get up, but too slowly; a blob of black goo appeared, binding his wrist to the tree. Roi convoked another blob, then another, until the material covered Ariden's limbs and most of his torso.

"About that debt." Roi walked around the broken statue of dust that was Dikta's remains. "I'll have to repay you in the form of a lesson."

Karis tensed, pulse thudding in her temples. Roi held out his hand. A curved short sword appeared in it.

"The lesson is very simple." Roi smiled as Ariden struggled to free an arm. "It's one I'm demonstrating acutely right now, in fact: control is always superior to brute strength. Take the world's greatest fighters, the swiftest ships, the strongest weapons—what are they without someone to guide them, to unite them in a common purpose?"

Roi pulled back on Ariden's hair, exposing his neck.

"Stop!" Karis yelled.

"Shut up," Roi said. "I'm sorry, good fellow, that we didn't meet sooner. With your strength and my guidance, we could have gone far together."

Karis felt her body in motion, the metal forming in her palm, cold on the scarred skin. Three long strides brought her close. Roi's arm swung back for the killing blow.

The stiletto sank deep into the flesh of his shoulder, behind the collarbone. Roi squealed and staggered back, yanking it from her hand, stinging her palm. He grasped at the handle to no avail, his voice lost, eyes wide.

Ariden stood, shaking off his crumbling bonds, and projected a blade through Roi's abdomen and out his back.

Karis staggered and fell, breathless. The world spun around her, and she closed her eyes, rubbing her palms against them. Slowly, her heart went from a hammer-like pounding to a mere hard, steady thump.

"Short one," Ariden said from above her. "Need a hand?"

She nodded and let him pull her up to her feet, then grasped his arm to stay upright.

"I keep telling you," he said, "I had him right where I wanted him."

She actually chuckled at that, though it came out more as a cough. Not far away, Roi lay curled in a pool of blood, whimpering softly.

"Shall I end him?" Ariden asked.

"No," Karis said after a deep breath. "There's no need. He's lost everything. His ships. His followers. Leave him to whatever misery he has left."

Roi groaned. Karis breathed again, lifting her chin high, feeling suddenly full of life. She could have killed him, if she had to. But if she was unable to show him mercy, that would have been just another form of his control. And his kind didn't control her, not anymore, not ever.

Ariden grumbled. "I knew it was wise to ask. Meli would have denied me as well."

"Meli!" Karis spun. "We have to find her. She went toward the center of the jungle. Toward the Daemon."

"This way," Ariden said.

He led her through the trees, his ragged, dark coat blending into the shadows. Karis's own shirt was still half-gone from when she had escaped Dikta's grip, but she wasn't going to stop and mend it now.

"Meli told me you were dead," she said to Ariden's back.

He shrugged. "One pile of dust looks much like another."

He walked with long, purposeful strides, so that she had to jog to keep up. The near-death encounter with Roi hadn't shaken him in the slightest. A steadfast man. She knew then that her hunch was right, that Meli really had fallen in love with him.

Karis stopped walking, overcome with resentment. Meli and Ariden…it still didn't seem possible. She had *hated* him. And yet he had accomplished what Karis had aspired to in her most blissful dreams. It was a bitter morsel to swallow, but for now there was nothing for it; she had a feeling she would need him when they found where Meli had gone.

"Do you hear it?" Ariden asked from ahead.

She swallowed. The drumbeats in her head had returned. "Yes."

"It's growing stronger the closer we are to the center." He raised his sword. "Come on."

The trees loomed over them, branches like hands waiting to snatch.

"The plants in this area, they attack people," Karis said. "Be on guard."

He nodded, slimming his blade but leaving it perched on his shoulder as they advanced. They walked quietly, gazes darting, listening for a sign of attack. The dim light from above faded further, and the pressure inside Karis's mind grew stronger.

"We're getting close." Karis rubbed her eyes. The brain-crushing feeling made it difficult to see, trapping her in a haze, as if the world were a lucid dream from which she could not wake. The pounding intensified as they reached the edge of a clearing. Beyond the line of trees, a pale yellow light flashed.

They stepped into the clearing, which had a floor of vines growing outward, straight like spokes of a wheel. At the center, a row of shrubs formed a backdrop for an altar made of branches. Meli stood in front of it with her back to them, cradling the Source.

"Meli," Ariden said.

Vacant-eyed, she turned away as if they weren't there. She lifted the light skyward like an offering, then placed it onto the altar.

"Wait!" Karis yelled.

The altar changed shape into a bowl, folding the light source into itself. Karis ran forward, but before she had made it two steps the clearing began to change shape. The vines grew, slithering over one another, taking her footing.

Between each of the plants, light burst forth.

Blinding, brilliant light, pure white. It spread from around the plants to inside them, until every surface emitted a glow. The motion continued, the vines forming walls and then expanding, writhing in distinct motions which nonetheless seemed unified in purpose. A strong wind kicked up, knocking Karis into Ariden. She pressed her hands to ears as the wind intensified, growing to a maelstrom of pressure and dust and light. The plant-room was enormous now, its walls arching toward the night sky, but bright as day, each leaf and thorn and tendril illuminated in their reds and purples and greens.

And then the Daemon stepped forth.

42

He had the form of a man, made of intertwined plants extruded from the walls, and, as he stepped forward, from the floor. He stood a head shorter than Ariden, but held himself straight and proud. His features were striking despite being formed of branch and leaf, wide cheekbones set in a perfect triangle above a pointed chin, with long, waving hair of grass. When he opened his flower-petal eyes, light burst forth from his pupils.

"Oh," Meli whispered. "He's beautiful."

When the Daemon walked, no muscle flexed, no limb swung. The plants grew in front and shrank behind him, forming a new foot and leg exactly in time to catch his weight. He moved to the center of the chamber with graceful strides, then smiled at Meli.

"Hello, mother."

Ariden hefted his sword, the point drifting. "Why did you bring us here, god?"

"I am no god." The Daemon's voice was deeper than a distant rumble, and when he spoke Karis could feel the edge of the words penetrating her mind. "The ones you call gods were beings from a nearby plane, who came here in pursuit of power or amusement before they were banished forever. I come from a place beyond where they dwell. I live in the in-between, an entity of the fabric of the aether."

"You called me mother." Meli spoke slowly, entranced. "The word from my dream."

The Daemon looked down, his eyes spotlighting the floor. He took several long, flowing strides toward Meli, then knelt and kissed her hand. "Dear mother. I am the one whom you saw in your slumber. I am your child."

Meli shook her head and stepped back. "What?"

"I will tell you a story, Meli. One you will not like to hear, but it must be said. A story of a new mother, pure of heart, who loved her child as fiercely as any mother has. But fate was not kind to her, and though she did her best to save him, she was forced to watch him slowly fade in her arms.

"It is an old tale, repeated far too often throughout history. But this mother was special. Of all those who have lived and died, she was one of the few who passed on. She gained entrance to a new life, a new world. This one."

Meli's hands were shaking, tears streaming from her face. "I…"

"You. And me. And them. All who live in this world once died in another. But when you returned, your pain came with you, buried deep in lost memory. That shared pain was a link, allowing your child to cross the door between realms and find you. Do you remember me, mother? Do you remember my name?"

She reached out and touched his cheek, rubbing the red hairs growing from the vines. "Ma…Mateus. Oh, Mateus."

"Mother. I missed you ever so much."

Her face reacted to the memory, twisting under pain of matchless depth and intensity.

"My little Mateus. I let you go." Tears streamed down her cheeks. Her lip trembled. "I'm sorry. I love you. I'm so sorry."

"No, mother." He touched her hair with his leaf-fingers. "You have long been working to bring me to this world, though you were not aware."

"The plants," Karis looked up and around the chamber, thinking back to Meli's studio. "He used the plants."

The Daemon nodded. "And the animals. Just as your bodies are formed from a network of small particles, so is my existence formed from fragments of thought, spread among the self-aware minds of Aetheria. Some years ago, the time came when I was able to bend those minds to my will."

"The birds over the sea," Ariden said. "You were controlling them."

The Daemon nodded again.

"And the Outsiders at Caeridor. You helped us escape?"

"By living as they did, so close to their animals, they opened their minds to my influence. Much as the Inaali did by their mediations."

"But you still needed the Source," Karis said. "The last piece, to complete your transformation."

"Not the last piece."

The Daemon strode away again, his motions hypnotic. He stopped in the center of the chamber and a new altar grew by his side, this one flatter, rectangular.

The perfect size for a human body.

"This is your purpose, Meli. You lost me, once. Now you can make me anew. It was your memories that carried me here, but I need your essence to make me whole. Join me. Bring me to life once more."

Meli stepped forward, body shaking.

"Wait," Karis said. "Meli—what will happen?"

Meli looked over at her and Ariden, dazed, her eyes pinpoints from staring at the luminescent Daemon. For a moment she seemed to recognize them, and surprise washed over her face. Then, determination.

She lay down on the table.

Stop. Karis tried to form the word, but her lips wouldn't move. The pressure squeezed inside her head. The Daemon waved his hands over Meli's eyes and they closed. His own eyes fluttered and the glow in the chamber changed. A deep rumble came from below and around them. The light drew inward, focusing itself on the Daemon's body. Karis tried to walk but failed. Her feet remained anchored to the floor. To her left, she saw Ariden straining to move, the sword crumbling in his hands.

"What…" The words barely escaped her lips. "…are you…doing…"

The Daemon stared at her, his eyes glowing.

"Your mind is open to me, Karis. I know what you truly desire." He placed an image in her thoughts, of the lights in the sky above the lake, of wanting to be that power. "You are here because I offered you the chance to serve me. Help me to fulfill my purpose, and you will gain all the knowledge you wish and more."

"You…you're not Mateus."

"I am. And I am not. The story I told was true; Mateus lived, and died. But *I*, the Daemon, existed long before, as a being whose form you cannot comprehend. Mateus longed to rejoin his mother in her new life, but a mind so young could not be reborn in the aether. When I found him, I saw in their link an opportunity to breach the door of this world. And so I joined the two of us together.

"Even now, the part of me that is Mateus resists. He fears what I will do here. The world of Aetheria is power incarnate. You have only seen the barest hint of the aether's energy in your travels. But most of all, he fears what will happen to Meli. Because for me to be reborn, she must give up her own life."

"No…" Ariden growled.

His voice drifted into an abyss. Karis's mind shrank away, the pounding overwhelming her, the world growing remote. Then all was black.

A glimmer appeared in the darkness. The light spread, arching over her vision. She floated, bodiless, in a field of white, surrounded by dreamstuff. Then her feet touched down, and she was standing on a flat surface. The white was still everywhere, and she was alone in a featureless, borderless world.

"Hello?" she said.

Her sight wavered, and before her stood a tiny human form, much smaller than the Old Wise One, with tawny skin and full lips like Meli's, and brown eyes sparkling with intelligence.

"Mateus." Somehow she knew it was him. "Where am I?"

"The in-between." His voice was high and soft. "The realm of the mind." He spun his head, looking with alarm at something she could not see. "The Daemon's realm."

He held out his hand, beckoning her to take it and follow. She reached, but as she leaned forward the distance between them grew, and Mateus shrank to a speck as the ground beneath her parted. She fell, tumbling end over end. The whiteness flashed to gray, then brown.

She landed hard on a plain of reddish dust. The particles covered her arms, chest and face, and she coughed as she rose. A shadow loomed over her, and she looked up in alarm.

"Karis. Good to see you again."

Karis shuddered. "No. Not you."

Yan showed her calm, sad smile. "I was hoping you could help me. We could make beautiful music together."

Karis got to her feet and looked around. It was all there, the yard of Yan's home, the small tree with its hanging chimes. Karis backed away, shaking her head. "Please. You have to go. They'll kill you. They'll—"

"You can't run from this," Yan said.

Karis turned and slipped. The road was mud, bubbling and frothy. The scene around her had shifted. Daylight gave way to night, and now she was kneeling before a great rock, watching Vikter march up to it with a body slung over his shoulder. Yan's body.

"No! Please! Don't hurt her!"

She closed her eyes and lunged forward, arms outstretched. The rock wasn't there. Something soft struck her face. She had fallen onto...a bed?

Her bed. Her house. In Ventituras.

"Oh. Oh, gods, not them." She wanted to see them again so badly, and yet… "I can't lose them again."

A crack ran up the wall before her. She wouldn't go this time. She wouldn't watch it happen. Karis grasped the sheets, pulling them over her eyes, but they turned to dust in her fingers.

The wall split, fell apart, and on the other side the three of them sat. Halela, Lepri and Parthenia, glassy stares locked on her, postures frozen as they were in death.

"Everything dies," Parthenia said.

Tears streamed down Karis's face. "Don't go."

"Everyone you loved has perished."

Parthenia's face began to crumble, and Karis screamed. She turned and jumped through the opposite wall, arms covering her head, legs drawn up so that she rolled through the cloud of dust and out onto a rocky plain.

She lay there for some time, catching her breath, trying to keep the images of Yan and her commune out of her mind. It was evening and she was wearing her usual clothes, her shirt still un-ripped. Her arm itched, and she stared down at the pattern of burn scars, freshly marked. Next to her, the Source sat in its chamber, glowing brightly.

She was sitting again at the edge of the jungle. But it wasn't real. It couldn't be.

A noise came from behind her, a person tripping on the rocks.

Meli.

Karis stood, trying to think of a way to explain. "Meli. We're not here. It's the Daemon—"

Tears stained Meli's face. She walked toward Karis with purpose, hatred burning on her face.

"You were in that ship. *You* killed them."

Karis tried to speak, but the memory overcame her and she let out a crying gasp. What could she say? It was true. She had done it.

"Meli, I'm sorry. You have to understand."

Meli bared her teeth, her breath a hiss, her fists balled.

"Meli, please!"

Meli shook her head. "I'm gone, and there is nothing left for you."

She drew back her fist and struck. Karis fell backward, her head struck the ground and the world went black.

No, not black. Night. The empty, dark night sky. She was lying on her back, bobbing gently on the waves. Slowly, she rose. Her arm was no longer scarred, her head no longer in pain. She cast her gaze about and saw the surface of the Meventi lake stretching out to every horizon, and the line of rafts leading back to where she'd come from.

She knew where to look, ahead and above. That was where the lights would be. They grew from the sky, shimmering in brilliant colors, writhing in great arcs, reaching toward her.

"You saw it back then." The Daemon's voice came from everywhere and nowhere. "The potential of the aether."

Karis blinked back tears at the beauty. "What are they? The lights—they're like the Source?"

"Yes. The aether's energy, given visible form."

"By who?" She understood the danger of such questions, how the Daemon was seducing her with its knowledge. But she had to know. "Who convoked them?"

"No one. Such self-sustaining processes appear due to the confluence of many beings creating according to their whims. That is the purpose of Aetheria—to harness the collective intelligence of many minds, to form something new, unique, something its creators could not conceive of themselves."

"Its creators?"

"Beings like myself, of vast power and resources. It was they who banished the Gods from your world, and who protect it still. In a place beyond what you can fathom, they wait for the result of their labors."

"What result? What are they trying to make?"

Above her, the lights brightened. "What, indeed? Why create countless particles of aether? Why build engines which drive the wind that blows the spent dust around the world to be recharged and released again? Why collect the minds of beings without their knowledge from places so far away, and set them loose here, ages upon ages after their first deaths?

"Only one thing could be worth so much effort: a weapon."

"No." Karis shook her head. The lights writhed more quickly. "I don't believe it."

"Why? All beings have forces arrayed against them. The creators wished to dominate their enemies. You are a small part of a process lasting untold millennia, a process that ends when they gain the power to destroy as they see fit."

"No!" Her hands shook as she shouted up at the lights. "I know the truth. I've felt it my whole life. We're here to discover things. To find what lies beneath reality. That's what the creators want: Answers to the questions which haunt us all."

The lights slowed and faded. For a time the aer above the fog-covered lake was silent. Then a low quake began, a steady beat like…chuckling?

"The two goals are one and the same." The Daemon sounded pleased. "Discovery and destruction, creation and annihilation, always they coincide. The answers you seek are here, Karis. Help me use this world as I see fit. Once we end the reign of those who govern Aetheria, everything they covet will be ours to take."

A wide stair appeared before her. Glowing, crystalline, it led up into the heart of the multicolored tendrils of light.

"How?" She took a step forward. "How will we do it?"

"I will show you how to control the entirety of the aether. We will wipe away everything, start anew with its power at our command."

"E—everything?" She looked back, where the towers of Ventituras would be beyond the horizon.

"Do not hesitate, Karis. Think back on what I have shown you. The pursuit of love has brought you only pain. All along, you had a true path. Combing the world, seeking knowledge, dreaming of something greater. And here is your dream for the taking. Step forward, embrace it—"

"Wait."

Karis looked down, startled. Something was tugging her ankle. A tiny hand, rising from the lake. She turned and dropped to one knee.

"No," the Daemon said.

"Come inside, please?" a high voice whispered. "Just for a little while."

The arm slipped below the surface. Karis leaned closer, but below was only gray fog.

"STOP." The lights flared more fiercely than ever before.

"I want to show you something," the high voice said, fading.

Karis looked back at the sky. The Daemon's anger radiated hot like the Source.

But it didn't get to tell her what to do.

Closing her eyes, she leaned and fell head first into the cold waves.

Karis was nowhere. Nothing. She could see, but had no form, no body to control. At first there was only a blur, a great multitude of locations passing beside her, and then the world slowed, and she settled onto a grassy field.

It was like no field she had ever seen. The grass was short and green, and all around were unfamiliar objects: tall black cylinders with clear tops, pathways snaking between rows of strange flowers.

And the sky. Bright, light blue, with an intense glow at its apex. It took her breath away.

Mateus was there. He stood in the center of the field looking confused, worried. How could a person so small exist? His tiny eyes scanned the scene, and he looked ready to cry until they found what he was searching for.

Meli. She stood near a flower bed, beautiful as ever, wearing strange clothes with her hair tied back.

"Mateus, I told you not to run off!"

She held her arms open and Mateus ran toward her, pure joy written on his face. Meli smiled too, and when they embraced Karis felt a new kind of warmth, on the inside this time, but no less intense for it.

Meli and Mateus seemed to hang there, him in her arms, while the scene around them shifted. Mateus was different. He had grown slightly, his limbs longer, but those limbs were frail, his skin pallid.

They were inside, now. White walls. Bright lights. A bed with tucked blue sheets, perfectly square. Everything was straight here, right angles and sharp corners. Except for Mateus and Meli. Gently, Meli placed him in the bed and leaned over, touching his face. Whispering sweet songs, prayers.

"You're going to be all right, Mateus."

"It hurts."

"Shh. My love."

He moaned, a sound all the more terrible with his small voice, and she pulled him close. Karis felt warm again. This was Mateus's memory, and he was letting her experience their love.

And their sadness. Meli was lying about him being all right. Even at his age, he knew. But he was tired, and sick and in pain. He pressed his face to her chest and the darkness closed in. Beeps and screeches came from some mekkanism behind her, and Meli cried out. Karis felt what Mateus did, calm, exhaustion, letting go.

Emptiness.

They stood again in the field of endless white, Karis and Mateus facing each other. But they weren't alone. There was a presence nearby, dark, cool, angry. Pressuring inward.

"What happened next?" Karis said. "Where did you go?"

"I don't know." Mateus shook his tiny head. "A long time passed, maybe. I couldn't tell. I didn't think I was anywhere, didn't know I was lost. Until *it* found me."

The darkness pressed in harder, staining the surroundings gray.

"Why did you show me these things?"

"So you would know who we were. I love my mother. I know she wants to help me. But I don't need her help anymore."

It seemed a strange statement, coming from a creature so small and fragile. But Karis sensed a hidden strength behind Mateus's words.

"My mother is the one who needs help now." As Mateus spoke, cracks appeared in the whiteness, and the Daemon began to seep through. "Don't listen to it, Karis. It promised me things too, but my mother is more important. You've known people like that, haven't you? Loved people that way?"

Karis nodded.

"There's still time. Help her. Save this world, and my mother. Please."

And then he was gone, and the Daemon rushed in and flooded over her, blinding her like a torrent of ink. Its presence whirled about, surrounding her with pressure, forcing her down...

No! She struggled, fighting the gloom. With no body to act with, she writhed against the mental coils, tearing her way upward. The Daemon was strong, but this was her mind. She ripped and clawed and found a gasp, then a breath, and through them her path back to reality.

She opened her eyes.

Across the chamber of vines, the Daemon fixed her with a wary, luminescent glare.

Karis rose slowly. A strange peace came over her. She knew now what she had to do.

"Leave this place," she said. "You're not going to hurt any more people."

The Daemon snarled.

Karis closed her eyes and felt the Source's convocation grow within her, prickling over every pore and sizzling every hair. She had always been taught that convoking inside herself was wrong, disgusting. But those were just words; she needed action. Light burst forth from her eyes, and when she looked at Ariden, he stood transfixed in the twin lamps of her gaze.

"Ariden." The words flowed easily, now. "Treasure your time with her."

He nodded. "I will."

Then, to the Daemon, "My dream is not yours to give."

She let go. The messages of light moved faster than aer, and she let them permeate every particle in her body. *Break apart.* The pain shattered her. She tried to scream, but no sound could express it, and soon she had no body to make sound. She drifted upward, free from material bonds, a creature of light.

Floating, she turned her attention to the Daemon.

It stared up, passive, waiting for her to act. She obliged it: a ray of searing white, focused on its chest. In an instant its plant-body was ash. The chamber grew darker, and a hush fell as its remains settled.

Laughter.

The sound came from all over, reverberating through the high walls as they sparkled and flashed. The Daemon was out there, watching her, readying its counter-attack. She floated up, the effort of keeping together her aethereal body stealing her focus. She had to get higher, away from Meli and Ariden, before the blast came.

The aer around her turned purple, the wind whirled, and the Daemon appeared: burning red eyes, in a halo of white that outshone a thousand midday skies.

She struck first, sending out a bolt of energy, the aether ripping in its wake. But the Daemon split apart, dividing its essence into millions of tiny points, surrounding her in a sea of purple. The points flashed, lighting the sky with power and sending her reeling toward the ground.

She spun, her body and mind wracked with pain, threatening to black out. She gathered herself, every iota of her being dedicated to holding her light-body together, and stopped in mid-aer. The Daemon hovered over her, arms crossed, awaiting her next move.

She flew up, faster than thought, letting the wind pull her in a spiral. She seeded explosions and flashes in all directions and all colors of the spectrum, from below red to the harshest violet. She could see it all, process every particle, but the Daemon was always one step ahead, crisscrossing the aerial battlefield, flitting between her attacks.

Then it was floating just in front of her, hairs away, and its rage tore her open. She sailed backward, her light sputtering, and the

Daemon attacked her from behind. The force of its blow felt like being struck with all the bedrock in the world.

She slammed down through the trees, sending a cloud of dust high into the night sky. *The pain.* Every joint, length of skin, hair, nail and tooth made of light hurt. She could sense the Daemon above her still, gathering his energy. How could it be so strong? They both drew on the same power—the aether. She could sense the energy all around her, practically limitless, but she couldn't call upon it, couldn't order enough of it to strike at once.

The aer lit up, the dust drifting skyward as the Daemon readied its attack. Then the area around her vaporized.

She flitted away just in time, skipping low over the ground, tearing through the plants just ahead of the shockwave. She landed hundreds of feet distant, barely out of range of the smoking crater. Her strength had left her; she wouldn't be able to move like that again. In a moment the Daemon would find her, and then she would be gone, her particles spread from Vaelam to Azorastas and beyond.

Spread...

That was what the Daemon had done, spread itself through the aer, covering the entire crater with its essence before re-forming. But if she did the same, could she ever find herself again?

Above, the Daemon appeared through the dust haze, red eyes scanning the ground. She would die anyway, whether she acted or not. She only had one chance. Digging deep, gathering whatever strength she had left, Karis flew skyward, counting on surprise to buy her crucial moments. The Daemon saw her and turned. The aer crackled before his strike.

Karis screamed.

She screamed in her light-voice, yelled out all her suffering, from the day of her appearance right through the burning torture which wracked her body that moment. She screamed for Meli, for Tem, for Phaestal and for Hal and Dou and Parthen and Yan, for all she had learned and would never learn, and for the love that made it worthwhile. And instead of aer, she pushed her essence out, flooding the space between them with light, draining herself into the aether.

She reached out to every particle, and with her last tiny bit of existence, focused them on a single point at the center.

Burn.

There was a flash.

Ariden found himself able to move soon after Karis ascended. He staggered for a moment, his head still pounding, but found his legs and made it to the altar.

"Come, darling." He hefted Meli on his shoulder. "It's time we left."

Lights flashing above, he raced as fast as he could manage with her legs dangling over his chest. He reached the edge of the chamber, stuck a hand through the interlocking vines and pulled. The poxing things held fast, so he convoked a pry-bar and winched them open. The flashing overhead intensified. *Don't think about it, just go*—he wedged open a hole, squeezed through and headed into the jungle.

He ran long and hard, working every muscle to its limit, saving nothing. Behind him, the sounds of battle raged, but he focused on keeping the noises to his back, staying on a straight line. He had long stopped feeling his legs when Meli stirred and mumbled.

"I...can...walk..."

He set her down and pulled her along by her hand, lifting her occasionally over thick brambles. A tremendous explosion sounded behind them. Meli stopped to look back, and Ariden nearly broke her arm pulling her away.

"Come on!"

They raced ahead, and moments later the second burst came. This time he sensed its magnitude even before the pressure swept over them. He grabbed Meli and dove, hugging her under his body. The force propelled them in mid-aer, and the trees bent and snapped back.

A long silence followed, except for muffled breaths. Ariden raised his head, gasping, and shook off the half-foot of dust covering him.

"Meli?"

"I'm alive," she whispered.

He pulled her up. The battle had ended; no more light flashes, no distant pounding of explosions. Around them, plants began to shrivel and crumble.

They walked on, taking their time, nursing their aching limbs. Meli wept. She cried for Karis, but though Ariden mourned her as well, he knew she had chosen her own path. And she cried for her Mateus, but Ariden could not hope to understand the depth of that grief. All he could do was hold her, and hope that by learning the truth, she had moved forward, advanced to the entrance of a long tunnel with a small light waiting at its end.

The time came when they left the remains of the jungle and met the slope of the crater, but they did not stop, did not look back. Climbing carefully in the darkness, they made their way up the sheer rock wall, step by convoked step, until at last they ascended onto the flat lip at the summit.

Only then did they look. Hand in hand, cheek to shoulder, they stared out for the first time to stars twinkling in the night sky.

さ♡⊚♡そ

And so
the tale of my rebirth ends.

My new life
shorter than my first
arrived at nightfall
to die before dawn.

But mourn not.

For though I have faded
I am not gone.

Oh no
not at all.

Not

AT

ALL

Acknowledgements

It took more than four years for AETHERIA'S DAEMON to reach this stage of completion, during which so many people helped that I preemptively beg forgiveness for any I leave out below.

First and foremost I thank my wife Margaret, to whom this book is dedicated. She was the one who listened to my half-coherent ramblings about immortal characters who create objects with their thoughts, and helped flesh it out into an actual narrative framework. Not to mention her usual role as my alpha reader, beta reader, and various other levels of readers which are nameless because most books don't go through as many drafts as this one did. Also not to mention she came up with the idea for the cover after I failed for years to think of anything decent. Love you, Hun.

Big thanks are due to my editor Debra Doyle, and others who read and critiqued, especially Andrea Phillips (www.deusexmachinatio.com), Martin Hodo, Ian Everett, David B. Coe (www.davidbcoe.com) and Christopher Ruz (www.ruzkin.com). Also thanks very much to M. Todd Gallowglas (mtoddgallowglas.com) for advice and support (#GallowglasArmy).

Thanks to Susan Ostrov Weisser for her endless encouragement and final proof reading, Bill Scalia for input on Meli's big fight scene, and David Meltzer for all the high-quality IRC.

Finally, thank you for reading this book.

-W.W. 1/27/2017